WATERFRONT WEDDINGS

TWO-IN-ONE COLLECTION

Annalisa Daughety
Cara C. Putman

BARBOUR
PUBLISHING

A Wedding to Remember in Charleston, South Carolina

by Annalisa Daughety

Dedication

This book is dedicated with love to my grandmother, Ermyl McFadden Pearle. You taught me to roller skate when I was four and you've been teaching me things ever since. Thank you for answering endless questions about gardening and cooking, saving articles that you think I might want to read, and always having time to talk. Knowing that you are praying for me gives me the courage to face any situation. If there ever was a woman who embodied Proverbs 31, it is you. Thanks, Grandma, for being an example of the kind of godly woman I strive to be. I love you.

Acknowledgments

Thanks to all who helped me as I wrote *A Wedding to Remember in Charleston*. Freda Pearle Mixson and Carol Pearle Bates—thank you for your wonderful Southern hospitality and for answering my many questions about life in Charleston. I so enjoyed spending time with the two of you during my visit to South Carolina. Vicky Daughety, Sandy Gaskin, Jan Reynolds, and Lynda Sampson—thanks for reading along as I wrote and for your honest feedback. Megan Reynolds and Kelly Shifflett—thanks for checking on me frequently as I was faced with back-to-back deadlines. I am blessed to have such an amazing support group of people who encourage me and pray for me as I write. Thanks to the team at Barbour Publishing and to my agent, Sandra Bishop, for the support and encouragement.

He heals the brokenhearted and binds up their wounds.
PSALM 147:3

Chapter 1

Summer Nelson blinked against the bright sunlight that filtered through oak trees older than time, their branches heavy with Spanish moss. She squinted at a tall figure in the distance, solemnly looking down at an ancient headstone. A figure she recognized, even though it had been at least fifteen years since she'd last seen him.

Summer had grown up hearing tales of the many ghosts that inhabited Charleston. She'd scoffed at the idea of homes haunted by long-dead Confederate soldiers, and she'd certainly never given any thought to attending one of the Ghosts of Charleston walks that took place in the historic city almost every night.

But on that random afternoon in late May, she encountered a ghost of her own. Except that Jefferson Boudreaux was the worst kind of ghost. The flesh-and-bone kind that served as a direct link to a past long forgotten. Or at least a past mostly forgotten, except for those sleepless nights of late when she couldn't stop herself from wondering if she'd chosen the right path.

Summer and Jefferson had been the "it" couple of their tightly knit circle since their days in cotillion. Everyone had always expected the two of them to marry and settle into a life of Charleston society. Jefferson would follow in his daddy's footsteps and run for office, and she would host garden parties and raise their perfect children.

Yes, that was the path everyone—particularly Summer's parents—had expected her to take. And Summer herself had been on board with that plan—for the most part.

Right up until the lazy July afternoon when she met Luke Nelson. Sweet Luke, who mowed the yard of her family's enormous South of Broad home—the same home her great-great-granddaddy had somehow persuaded the Yankees to leave alone all those many years ago.

She watched the man in the cemetery for another long moment, not daring to move a muscle. She'd grown so still and cold, she couldn't tell where the stone bench ended and her body began. "Jefferson," she finally whispered, her voice tinged with uncertainty. Maybe the man was a look-alike tourist who just happened to be standing at the Boudreaux family plot. Because the alternative wasn't something she wanted to face.

But as soon as the name escaped her lips, the tall man turned toward her, and his tanned face broke into a smile.

And with a few long strides, Jefferson Boudreaux walked right back into her life.

Luke Nelson chewed on the end of his pencil, a habit he'd had since his school days when yellow number 2 pencils were harbingers of standardized tests. Most of the kids feared taking tests, but Luke lived for those days. He'd always been a good test taker. Inevitably when the scores came back each year, his were the highest in the class. His teachers expected great things from him, but his daddy had sneered at Luke's academic aspirations. "No son of mine is going to spend his

days in some stuffy office like he's better than the rest of us,"
Daddy would say, usually with whiskey on his breath.

Luke had never aspired to follow in his father's footsteps,
never been one of those little boys who idolized their dads.
Roy Nelson had always been hardest on his oldest son.
While Luke's sister and baby brother might have been able
to avoid Roy's wrath, Luke hadn't been so lucky.

But the past was the past, and he certainly didn't want
to spend time dwelling on it now. He tossed the pencil onto
the table and leaned back in his chair. Why was he having
so much trouble with this song? The tune had been in his
head for weeks, but getting the lyrics right was causing him
all kinds of problems.

He stood and paced the length of the living room, decorated with furniture that had been in Summer's family
for generations. When they'd first moved into the spacious
South of Broad home after they'd gotten married, he'd been
a nervous wreck. "What if I spill something?" he'd asked.

Summer had just laughed. "This isn't a museum. It's our
home." She'd tipped her glass of sweet tea so a little dribbled
onto the tiled kitchen floor. "See?"

Sometimes it was hard for him to believe they'd been
husband and wife for nearly seven years. And yet their
anniversary was coming up in a few weeks. He had the
perfect gift in mind, too. He might not be the world's best
husband, but he'd been able to make Summer happy. At
least most of the time.

The opening strains of a George Strait song pulled him
from his walk down memory lane. He grabbed his phone
from the table and punched the button. "Yeah?"

"How do you feel about shooting some pool tonight?"
Justin Sanders asked.

Luke exhaled loudly. He didn't want to let down his closest friend and the drummer in his band, but he'd already been out two nights this week and they were playing a gig on Friday evening. Summer hadn't said anything about all his time away from home, but she'd sure given him the cold shoulder this morning. "I don't know."

"Come on, man. Jimmy and Will have permission from their wives for a boys' night out. Don't leave us in a lurch."

He looked at the silver clock on the end table next to the couch. It was already after six. Summer must be working late again. Last night she hadn't gotten home till nearly ten. So maybe she wouldn't care if he made plans. "Yeah, okay. I'll be at your place in half an hour."

"Summer Rutledge." Jefferson Boudreaux grinned down at her. "I don't believe it."

"It's actually Summer Nelson now." She shaded her eyes with her hand. "But I think you know that."

"Things can change." He winked. "Mind if I sit down, Mrs. Nelson?" he asked, his green eyes twinkling.

Summer regarded him for a long moment. "Sure." For a second, she wondered how she looked. Had she aged a lot in the years since they'd seen each other? Just that morning she'd plucked out a gray hair. Granted, she'd looked hard to find it. But today had been the first time she ever wished she were blond instead of brunette, just so the gray hairs wouldn't be as obvious when they really started sprouting.

Jefferson sat down on the bench next to her. "I figured I'd run into you at some point, but the cemetery isn't exactly what I expected." He motioned around the secluded grounds.

She didn't meet his eyes. "It's so peaceful. And you know how I've always loved the old cemeteries around here." Most of the numerous churches in downtown Charleston had a cemetery on their property, some with graves that dated back to the 1600s.

Jefferson gestured at the ancient headstone in front of them. "No one you know then?"

Summer bit her bottom lip. She'd found this grave about six months ago and felt drawn to it. So much so that she'd begun to visit at least weekly, sometimes bringing flowers. "Nope." She patted the edge of the stone bench. "I just like this spot because there's a place to sit."

Jefferson was silent for a long moment. "So how are you? I guess it's been. . ." He trailed off and glanced at her, his eyebrows raised in question.

"Fifteen years," she finished for him. "Graduation night." She and Jefferson hadn't exactly remained friends after she'd dumped him for Luke. The breakup had split their circle of friends in two. But on the night of their high school graduation, they'd all posed together for one last picture, mostly at the prompting of a group of overbearing mothers wielding cameras.

He nodded. "That's right." Jefferson flashed her a gleaming smile. "I think Mom still has a framed picture of all of us from right after the ceremony." He shook his head. "It took her a long time to accept the fact that you and I were no more."

Summer let out a breath. "Yeah. But I'm sure she's over it by now." She glanced at him. Time had certainly been kind to Jefferson. If anything, he was even better looking now than when they'd been eighteen. His shoulders were broader and encased in what looked like a very expensive suit. The hint of crinkles around his eyes when he smiled and a tiny bit of silver mixed in with his dark hair gave him a distinguished look. The difference in the way men and women aged was totally unfair.

Jefferson chuckled. "Clearly you underestimate your power. Every girl I've ever introduced her to has tried and failed to live up to the memory of you."

Her face flamed. "Whatever." She shifted uncomfortably on the stone bench.

"I hear your business is doing well. Mitch keeps me posted on the latest with everyone here."

Summer's younger brother, Mitch, had been one of Jefferson's best friends. "I don't see him very often." She hated saying the words aloud. She and Mitch had been close once. But they'd drifted apart after she left home for college. These days they only saw one another on major holidays, and that was only because their grandmother insisted she show up. And since Gram had always been so good to her, Summer obliged.

Jefferson nodded. "That's what I hear."

Obviously her brother still had as big a mouth as ever. "This is my busiest season," she said, as if that were the reason behind her behavior.

"And how's Luke?" Jefferson's green eyes bored into hers.

"He's great." The less said about Luke, the better. "We're very happy." She hoped her voice didn't give her away. The last person on earth who needed to know that things in her life might be less than perfect was Jefferson. Not only would he probably take personal satisfaction in that knowledge, but he also wouldn't think twice about sharing it with her family.

His eyes searched her face. "I heard about Luke's brother. I'm so sorry. I remember how close they were."

She nodded. "It's been a trying year, but we're making it."

"I'm glad to hear it." He cast one more gaze at the headstone in front of their bench. "Wow. Sad story here, huh? Only a day old." He shook his head and stood to trace his fingers over the cherub that sat on top of the stone.

Summer rose and grabbed her bag from beneath the bench. She suddenly wanted nothing more than to be away from the cemetery and away from Jefferson. "It was nice to see you again. I hope you have a great visit." She turned to go.

"Oh, it's not just a visit," he said quietly.

She turned slowly to look at him.

"I'm back for good."

Chapter 2

Ashley Watson sat on a park bench at the Battery, her face turned upward and warmed by the diminishing sun. When she first moved to Charleston, she called the spot White Point Gardens, like the guidebooks said. But now that she was a local, she knew to refer to it as the Battery. A seagull squawked from its perch on the wooden rail that ran the length of the promenade.

Anytime she regretted packing up and moving hundreds of miles to Charleston, all she had to do was come to the Battery. A few minutes of watching the boats and breathing in the salty sea air, and Ashley knew she'd made the right decision. She'd always heard that the ocean had healing properties. Although after three years of coastal living, her heart was still bruised. Maybe not broken anymore but definitely not whole.

"Thanks for meeting me," a familiar voice called.

Ashley looked up to see Summer leading her huge dog, Milo, down the sidewalk. Or maybe Milo was leading Summer. It was hard to tell. "Hey," she said, rising from the bench. She bent down and scratched Milo behind the ears. "Is it possible that he's even bigger than he was the last time I saw him? And that was only last week."

Summer chuckled. "That's one reason we came out for a walk today. Poor Milo has paid the price of our crazy lives." She knelt down and nuzzled the big chocolate Lab. "He's become a bit lazy and has packed on some extra weight."

Ashley watched her friend adjust the harness around

Milo's big midsection. Summer and Luke had rescued Milo from the side of the road when he was a puppy. He'd become like their child. Summer even brought him to work sometimes. "Where are we headed?"

Summer stood and looked out over the water. "I don't care. Let's see where the road takes us."

Ashley raised her eyebrows. Summer had never been one to see where the road took her. Everything she did was planned, usually down to the minute. Something was on her mind, and Ashley had a good idea of what it might be. "Sounds good."

They headed toward South Bay Street. It wasn't even June, and already tourists were out in droves, most of them trying to soak up the remaining sunshine before they'd head to Hyman's Seafood or Slightly North of Broad for dinner.

"Thanks for all your work lately," Summer said after they walked in silence for a few minutes. "I know I've dumped a lot on you, especially with these last couple of weddings."

Ashley smiled. "No problem." She loved working with Summer as an event planner at Summer Weddings. She'd started out answering phones a little over a year ago, but as business had picked up, she'd taken on more responsibility. "I know you've had a lot on your plate over the past few months." Ashley hadn't complained about the added responsibilities, mainly because Summer was her friend. But it had been kind of a burden to carry most of the workload alone. In fact, the long hours she'd been keeping almost made her thankful she was single. There was no way her hectic schedule would allow for a meaningful relationship. Although having a date every now and then might be nice.

"Still though, you've stepped in and kept things going

when I could barely get out of bed." Summer shook her head. "I want you to know that it hasn't gone unnoticed."

"I appreciate that." Ashley wondered if this was a good time to approach Summer about her idea of growing the business. Of course, part of the growth she hoped for included becoming a partner and not just an employee. But Summer seemed distracted today, plus she didn't want the request to put a strain on their friendship.

"Mind if we sit for a minute?" Summer motioned toward a bench.

"You and Milo lead the way," Ashley agreed.

They sat in silence for a moment, watching people walk past. Finally, Summer cleared her throat. "Luke's out with the guys again tonight."

So that's what this was about. Luke. "*Again*, you say?" Ashley asked.

Summer didn't talk about her relationship with Luke very much anymore. In fact, some days she didn't mention his name at all. Ashley had been worried they might be headed for trouble but wasn't sure how to broach the topic.

Summer tucked a wayward strand of dark hair behind her ear. "Yeah. Monday night his band played at some little dive bar. Then Tuesday was bowling night. Last night I had that event at the art museum, so I didn't get home until late. And tonight when I got home, he'd left me a note that he was playing pool with the guys." She met Ashley's eyes. "It's like we see each other less and less."

Ashley was in no way qualified to dispense relationship advice. But she considered Summer one of her closest friends. And Luke had always been quick to help her out, especially when she'd moved from an apartment into a house. He'd rounded up his buddies, and they'd moved her stuff in less than a day. "Can you talk to him? Maybe try to carve out time this weekend to go on a date or something? Or cook a nice dinner and have an evening in?"

Summer sighed. "That would all be nice. Except that Luke has some big gig on Friday night. It's the opening of the outdoor deck at some little restaurant on Folly Beach. I think he's hoping it might turn into a regular thing."

"Saturday then?"

"We've been summoned to my parents' house on Saturday for a family barbecue." She rolled her eyes. "Believe me, I don't want to go. Luke doesn't even know about it yet, and I know he's not going to be happy." She absently stroked Milo's head. "But Gram called me on my way home from work and asked me to come." She smiled. "Okay, she *told* me to come, but she said it nicely."

Ashley grinned. Summer's grandmother was the epitome of a Southern belle. Sweet as the tea they serve at Jestine's Kitchen, but not someone to be crossed. She thought for a second. "Tell you what. I don't have anything to do on Friday." Her stomach lurched for a second at the thought of being out on the social scene. She mostly kept to herself. But lately she'd started to worry that she was becoming a sad, lonely old lady. All she needed were a couple of cats and a flowered muumuu and her face could practically be on the Old Maid card. "So what if we surprise Luke? How long has it been since you've seen him play?"

Summer chewed on her bottom lip. "It's been ages. Seriously. He wouldn't know what to think if I showed up to see him." Her face suddenly brightened. "But that's a good idea." She glanced at Ashley. "You sure you don't mind coming with me?"

Ashley forced a smile. "I'd love to." She needed something

to get her out of her comfort zone. "Besides, I've never heard his band play. It will be fun."

Luke pulled his truck into the driveway next to their historic home. Even though he'd lived there for years, sometimes he felt like he didn't belong. Their house on Legare Street was even on the yearly home and garden tour put on by the Charleston Historic Foundation. It was a far cry from the neighborhood where he'd grown up.

The outside light came on as he rolled to a stop. For a second, he thought it meant Summer was waiting up, but then he remembered the motion sensor they'd had installed a few months ago. There was a time when she'd sleep on the couch until he got home because she said she couldn't stand to be in their king-sized bed without him. But those days were long gone.

He quietly let himself in. The alarm wasn't set, and Milo didn't meet him at the door. That meant Summer was letting the big dog sleep in their bed. Again.

He punched the code and armed the alarm before he went upstairs. Summer forgot to set the alarm more often than not these days. In the old days, he would've teased her for being scatterbrained, but not anymore.

Luke avoided the creaky spot on the next to last step as he reached the top of the stairs. If she was asleep, he didn't want to wake her. He knew how much trouble she had getting to sleep. A glow coming from their bedroom told him that she'd at least left the lamp on so he didn't have to walk in total darkness.

He tiptoed into the master bathroom and closed the door before he flipped on the light. He'd grab a quick shower and save himself a little time in the morning. He worked as a park ranger at Fort Sumter, and his shift started promptly at eight. He'd been late a couple of mornings recently and didn't want his boss to think he was making a habit of it. It might not be his dream job, but he enjoyed it.

Luke opened the linen closet door to grab a towel and noticed the overflowing clothes hamper. He'd asked Summer this morning if she'd be doing laundry tonight and she'd said yes, but clearly that hadn't happened. And he'd worn his last clean ranger uniform today. *How hard is it to remember to do a load of laundry?*

He dug through the hamper and came up with three uniforms. Looked like he was in for an even later night than he'd anticipated. It would easily be after midnight by the time they were dry. He quickly brushed his teeth then grabbed the dirty uniforms. Stepping out into the bedroom, he saw Milo's head raise from *his* pillow. *Some watchdog.*

He walked over to his side of the bed and tugged his pillow from beneath the large dog. It was amazing. On his dog bed, Milo slept curled up in a surprisingly tiny ball considering his size. But whenever he had permission to get in his and Summer's bed, the dog insisted on taking up as much space as his large frame would allow.

He tucked the pillow beneath his arm. He'd sleep downstairs in the guest room tonight. He paused at the door and glanced back inside the bedroom. Summer hadn't stirred through all of the commotion. Either she was sleeping soundly or she had nothing to say to him.

Luke headed to the laundry room downstairs, stifling a yawn.

Tomorrow was going to be a long day.

Chapter 3

Summer waited until she heard Luke's foot hit the squeaky spot on the stairs before she sat up. As soon as he had gone into the bathroom, she remembered his work uniforms needed to be washed. She might be the worst wife ever, but she'd sooner walk across hot coals than admit to him that she'd forgotten. He probably thought she'd done it out of spite over his impromptu boys' night out, and she'd let him think so. Served him right.

She leaned back against the plush pillows and put a hand on Milo. She'd read somewhere that stroking a dog's fur helped to calm people when they were under a lot of stress. She'd certainly put that theory to the test over the past few months. Her stomach knotted as she thought about Saturday's barbecue. It had been weeks since she'd seen her family. And she knew it would be a fight to convince Luke to go with her.

She rolled over and burrowed further underneath the covers. Sometimes she wished she could stay there forever.

The next morning, she grabbed her pink robe and padded downstairs. Milo trailed along behind her, stretching and yawning as he went. "Hey," she said, stepping into the kitchen.

Luke stood at the counter, slapping turkey onto a slice of bread. He covered it with the heel of the loaf and shook his head. "We're out of bread."

"Good morning to you, too." She grabbed her favorite mug from the cabinet and filled it with coffee. Luke's sweet gesture wasn't lost on her. He didn't drink coffee, so the

fresh pot had been made just for her. But she didn't mention
his kindness. It made her feel too bad. She couldn't even
remember to get bread for his sandwich, yet he'd made her
coffee.

"Mornin'." Luke slid his sandwich into a ziplock bag. He
leveled his brown eyes on her.

Those brown eyes might have been the reason she fell in
love with him in the first place. Summer could still remember
the day they met. She'd been sitting in the hammock in the
backyard, reading *Pride and Prejudice* and wondering if she'd
ever meet a man like Mr. Darcy. She hadn't realized anyone
was watching her until he cleared his throat. She looked up
to see Luke standing there, a sheepish grin on his handsome
face. "Hey," he drawled softly. "I didn't mean to scare you."

She quickly closed the book. Her friends made fun of her
for reading too much, especially when they caught her with
her nose buried in the classics. "You didn't."

"I'm Luke. Luke Nelson." A shadow crossed his
tanned face. "I'm helping my uncle this summer. He owns
a landscaping company." He motioned toward the push
mower. "Hope it doesn't disturb your reading." He smiled.
"That's a great book."

At that moment, Summer looked into Luke's chocolate
brown eyes and felt her heart skip a beat.

They were seventeen at that first meeting. At thirty-four
it was hard for her to fathom that she'd known Luke for half
of her life. And there had been lots of times over the years
when Luke's slow smile and beautiful eyes had made her
heart skip beats. But that happened less and less these days.
Sometimes it seemed like she barely knew him anymore.

"I'm sorry I forgot the bread." She took a sip of coffee

and watched him grab a bag of Doritos from the pantry. "I'll go to the store on my way home today so you'll have lunch tomorrow."

He put his sandwich and the chips into his lunch bag. "Don't bother. I'm not working this weekend, so I won't need any." He shrugged. "Until Monday, at least."

"Oh. Right. I guess I'd forgotten today is Friday." *What was wrong with her?*

Luke looked at her for a long moment. "Are you feeling okay? Maybe you should go back to bed. I'm sure Ashley can handle things."

She tensed. "I'm fine. This week has gone by fast, that's all." She noticed the way his hand held on to the counter. It had been forever since they'd held hands. Too long. She stepped toward him, her fingers suddenly itching to touch him.

Luke turned away before she reached him. He opened the refrigerator and pulled out a can of soda. "Don't forget that I'm playing tonight after work. I'll probably go straight there." He motioned at his duffel bag by the door. "I'll change at Justin's. I'm picking him up on the way."

She smiled to herself. He would be so surprised to see her show up. Maybe this would be the first step at getting them back on track. She missed the way things used to be. "Okay. Be careful." She watched as he grabbed his phone and keys then knelt to scratch Milo behind the ears.

Luke stood. "Thanks. Hope you have a good day." He slung his bag over his shoulder. "I'll be in late tonight. Don't wait up."

"Hang on." She walked to the doorway and faced him. "Tomorrow we're supposed to go to a barbecue at my parents' house."

He furrowed his brow. "Why are you just now telling

me this?"

She pushed a strand of hair from her face. "Gram didn't call me until yesterday. I haven't gotten to talk to you until now." She reached out and touched his arm, but he shrugged her away.

"Did you tell her we'd come?"

She narrowed her eyes. "Of course. Both of us—so don't think you're getting out of it."

He inhaled deeply and blew out his breath. "Great. Fine. Whatever." He glanced at his watch. "I'm not happy about it, but I'll go." He walked out without giving her another look.

Summer stared at the closed door for a long moment and clutched her coffee mug. There was a time when Luke never would've left without kissing her good-bye. A time when she would've made sure the last words they said to one another were "I love you" and not anything cross. They'd always vowed to have a different marriage than the ones their parents had. But sometimes it seemed like they were two strangers who happened to share a home.

And Summer could pinpoint exactly when the change had happened.

The problem was, unless she could pull a Marty McFly and go back in time, she had no idea what to do about it.

Justin Sanders loved Fridays. Especially every other Friday. But not for the same reason most guys his age did. Sure, he liked to have a good time on the weekend, but every other Friday was special.

He pulled into the driveway at Samantha's townhouse and wondered if she remembered that he was coming today. Two weeks ago, she'd forgotten about his visit and had taken Colton to day care already.

Justin jumped out of the SUV and walked to the door. It swung open before he could knock.

"I'm so glad you're here," Samantha said. Her bleached blond hair was pulled into a messy bun, and she had dark circles under her eyes. "The baby was up every hour, and then as soon as I got to sleep, Colton woke me up." She managed a smile. "He was so excited that today was his day with you, he couldn't sleep."

Justin's heart warmed. "I'm glad. I'm planning to take him fishing if that's okay with you." He'd bought Colton a Snoopy fishing rod at Walmart the other day. It was identical to the one he'd had when he was a little boy.

"Whatever. That's great." Samantha ushered him inside the tiny townhouse.

"Justy!" Colton exclaimed. The little boy ran toward Justin and grabbed him around the leg.

Justin scooped him up into his arms. "I missed you, little man."

Colton threw his arms around Justin's neck. "I missed you, too."

A cry came from down the hallway. "The baby's awake." Samantha sighed. "Have him back by three, 'kay? He's staying with my mama the rest of the weekend, and I need to get him over there before supper."

"Sure." Although if it were up to Justin, he'd keep Colton forever.

Luke wiped a trickle of sweat from his forehead and slapped his ranger hat back on his head. It wasn't officially summer, but it was as hot as an oven outside. He hated to think of how it would feel in July.

"Excuse me," a woman said from behind him.

He turned and flashed her a polite smile. "Can I help you?"

She held up a cell phone. "Would you mind taking our picture?" She motioned toward a man holding a little girl who couldn't have been more than two. "It's our first vacation as a family," she explained.

He took the phone. "Sure."

The family stood beneath a large flag pole. "Get as much of the fort and the water as you can," the woman called.

Luke grinned. Every tourist wanted the same picture in nearly the same spot. He was such an old pro at this by now he could practically work for Olan Mills. He counted to three and snapped the picture.

"Thanks," the woman said.

Luke handed her the phone. He watched the couple fawn over the little girl. The woman pulled out a bottle of sunblock and rubbed it on the girl's face. The child squealed and wrinkled her nose.

He couldn't help but smile. Part of him wanted to tell the parents to relish those moments. He knew all too well that those happy times could quickly be replaced by sad ones. Life really was a vapor.

"Hey, Luke," his supervisor called from the entrance to the bookstore. "You got a minute?"

He nodded. "Yes sir." He walked toward the older ranger. He'd worked at Fort Sumter for three years now and still had a hard time figuring out if Walter Young liked him or not. Mr. Young was a man of few words, not unlike Luke's daddy.

"With it being the end of the school year, we've got several school groups scheduled for the next couple of weeks," Mr. Young said. "You always have a good rapport with the kids, so I want you to take care of them."

Luke nodded. "Yes sir." Relief washed over him. Every time he was summoned by Mr. Young, he was always afraid he'd messed up somehow. "I'd be glad to."

"You can check the schedule inside. I think there will be six different groups coming. Just do a basic introduction and answer their questions."

Luke knew the drill. "Will do."

Mr. Young turned and went back inside without another word.

Luke sighed. It wasn't even lunchtime yet. This day was dragging on forever. He'd like to chalk it up to the fact that he was looking forward to playing with his band later. But he knew that the main reason the day wasn't going well was because of the way he'd left things with Summer. He didn't know what to say to her anymore.

He watched another couple laughing and walking hand in hand. He wasn't sure if he and Summer would ever get back to that point. And deep down, after everything they'd faced, he wasn't even sure it was possible.

His cell phone vibrated. He pulled the phone from its holster and glanced at the screen.

Rose.

Luke shoved the phone back in the holster. His sister had

left two voice mails in the last week, but he hadn't listened to either of them yet. As long as he didn't know what she wanted, he wouldn't feel any obligation toward her.

"Can you tell me how many cannons were here during the battle?" A man asked, startling Luke.

"Sure." Luke went into his canned speech, thankful for the distraction.

Chapter 4

Ashley clicked SEND on an e-mail. From the amount of inquiries they'd had lately from people wanting to hold their weddings in Charleston, it looked like they were in for a busy year. *All the more reason for me to be a real business partner.* She glanced at the clock. Summer must be running late.

Again.

She wished there were someone to share her concerns with. But as far as she knew, Summer didn't have much of a relationship with her family. She'd heard her mention a couple of friends, but even they didn't seem that close. In the years she'd known Summer, it had always been obvious that Luke was her best friend.

And Ashley was pretty sure he was part of the problem in the first place, so talking to him wouldn't help.

Lord, help me figure out how to help her.

The door swung open and Summer walked inside, Milo padding along beside her. She unhooked his leash, and the dog went straight to his familiar spot in front of the large window.

"Sorry I'm late," Summer said. "I didn't sleep well, and then this morning I felt like I was moving in slow motion."

"No problem." Ashley rose from her desk and knelt down to scratch Milo behind the ear. She watched as Summer thumbed through papers on her desk. Despite her lack of sleep, Summer still managed to look put together. Ashley had always been intimidated by women like that. Women who just seemed to know what went well together and how to pull off accessories without looking like they were trying too hard. Or maybe it was the fact that money wasn't an issue for Summer—Ashley didn't know. She only knew that for Summer, looking classy seemed effortless. The tailored pink jacket and slim-cut black pants showed off her trim figure. Ashley knew there were some days that Summer didn't even stop to eat lunch, and if the weight loss she'd experienced in recent months was any indicator, maybe that was true for supper, too.

"Anything big going on?" Summer asked.

Ashley sat down at the computer. "There was a message on the machine for you." She glanced up at Summer. "It was Rose Drummond. She wanted you to call her back." Ashley shook her head. "She must be a new client, because she's not on our list."

Summer drew her brows together. "Rose is Luke's sister." She shook her head. "I haven't talked to her in a long time." She looked at Ashley. "Anything else?"

Ashley nodded. "I just e-mailed an info packet to a couple from Georgia. They're looking at a destination wedding sometime in August or September and wanted to talk about available dates."

"August or September?" Summer shook her head. "That's not very far off. Why don't people plan in advance these days?"

Ashley didn't mind quick turnarounds, but if it were up to Summer, every couple would spend at least a year planning for their big day. "You know how it is. They're so excited they just can't wait that long." She chuckled at the grimace on Summer's face. "Surely you remember that feeling."

Summer tucked a strand of dark hair behind her ear.

"Not really. I mean, I knew I was going to marry Luke by the time he brought me home on our first real date." She gave a tiny smile. "But we didn't actually get married for several years after that."

Ashley furrowed her brow. She'd never heard the story of Summer and Luke's engagement and wedding. "Why did you wait so long?"

Summer sighed. "I had to finish college. It was part of the agreement with my parents. They would pay for everything, but I had to live in the dorm and all that." She grimaced. "Honestly, I think if it had been anyone but Luke, they would've relented."

"They didn't care for him?"

"It was complicated. I guess you could say that Luke wasn't exactly who they had in mind for me. Adjusting to the idea of him was difficult for them." She chewed on her lip. "And at that time, his only dream was to be in the music industry. So waiting to get married worked out. He went to Nashville for a few years."

"Wow. I had no idea." Ashley had assumed Luke's band was just a hobby. She'd never imagined that he'd actually pursued music.

"It didn't pan out. So he came back and started going to school at night. He worked odd jobs during the day." Summer shrugged. "We got married as soon as I finished my master's."

"I'll bet your wedding was beautiful." Summer's parents would've undoubtedly spared no expense for their oldest daughter's wedding.

Summer laughed. "If you think city hall is beautiful, then yes."

"*You* didn't have a traditional Charleston wedding?"

Ashley couldn't hide her shock. Her own wedding back home in Alabama had been full of all the bells and whistles. She'd felt like a princess as she'd floated down the aisle on her daddy's arm. Except that she'd turned out to be a princess without a happily ever after. So maybe a city hall wedding wasn't such a bad idea.

"Nope. Too much trouble. Luke's family was kind of scattered, and mine wasn't very supportive. Except for Gram. She'd been a fan of Luke's from the beginning. But I didn't even tell her."

Ashley sat, stunned. "Were they mad?"

"Let's just say we had some tense holidays after that. But everyone came around." She tapped her fingers on the desk. "Enough about that though. I'm meeting with Sarah Gentry at noon to go over the details for her flowers. We need to let the florist know soon."

Back to business. Summer had been that way since they'd met. It was almost as if she were two people. As soon as she let down her guard and let Ashley in on anything personal, she'd raise the walls back up and flip into business mode. "Okay." Ashley nodded. "And don't forget that I'm getting some quotes for a new web design. I have the components ready, but now I need to find a designer who can put it all together." She grinned. "I can't wait until the site is ready to launch." Ashley took a great deal of pride in the web project. She'd handled it almost single-handedly.

"Awesome. Thanks for your work on that." Summer looked up from her computer screen. "And I don't remember if I mentioned that Luke has a friend who is a web designer. You don't have to use him, but at least add him to the list of people to get a quote from." She leaned back in her chair. "I can't wait to see how the new site impacts business. I think it will make things so much easier, particularly for people from out of state." At least half of their business came from couples who came to Charleston for a destination wedding.

Ashley nodded. Once the site was live, clients would be able to log on and choose from a variety of options to build their own dream wedding. The whole thing would be interactive, so they'd be able to read reviews of venues, watch videos of potential bands, and even see a variety of cakes to choose from. It would be so helpful for brides who wanted a destination wedding in Charleston but were unable to visit ahead of time. "I'm really excited about it." Now would be the perfect time to talk about a promotion. But as usual, the words caught in Ashley's throat.

Would she ever find the courage to speak up for herself? History and a failed marriage said no.

But Ashley would keep trying to build her confidence. Until then, she'd just keep quiet.

Summer added a few tasks to the to-do list in her planner. Some people preferred to keep track of things on their iPhones or BlackBerries. But she liked the feel of a paper planner. She liked to write down lists and check things off. Planning her days, weeks, and months gave her such satisfaction. Luke accused her of being a control freak. Even when they traveled, she always had a map printed out with the route highlighted. And if he ever tried to go off that highlighted path, as he often did, it filled her with tension.

The unknown scared Summer. Change was not her friend.

And time passed so quickly, sometimes she found herself paralyzed with fear that she wouldn't get to accomplish all she planned. Because when it came right down to it, life was short.

She flipped to the monthly calendar where she'd carefully recorded all of her business meetings and civic obligations. If there was a committee, she was on it. She glanced at today's block. The client meeting at noon and then Luke's band tonight at eight were the only things penciled in. "Are you still able to go with me to Folly Beach?" she asked.

Ashley glanced up from her computer. "Sure. I'm looking forward to it." She sighed. "My social life isn't exactly on fire these days."

Summer considered Ashley to be a pretty good friend. But she'd never pried into her personal life. She figured if there were things Ashley wanted to share, she would. She'd hate for anyone to think she was nosy. But she was a little curious. She knew Ashley had been married, but that was about it. "I thought you weren't interested in dating."

Ashley shrugged. "It's not like I'm out perusing the grocery stores or coffee shops for available men. But if I happened to meet a nice one, I wouldn't complain." She shook her head. "You have no idea how hard it is to meet someone once you're a certain age."

Summer rolled her eyes. "You aren't old."

Ashley stood and came over to lean against Summer's filing cabinet. "Okay, fine. Thirty-six might not be over the hill, but I also know I'm not a spring chicken anymore." She giggled as Summer made a face. "What? At least I'm a realist."

Summer twirled her pen between her fingers. "I'm only

two years younger, and I'd bet money that everyone who sees us together thinks you're younger." She gave Ashley the once-over. "You dress a lot cuter than I do."

Ashley laughed. "Translation: sometimes I dress too young for my age." She smoothed her green sundress that was almost the same color as her eyes. "I should probably send half of my wardrobe to my cousin's daughter in Birmingham. And she's sixteen."

"Whatever. You look amazing." With her long, dark blond hair and porcelain skin, Ashley could easily pass for someone in her late twenties.

"Thanks." Ashley looked pleased. "Speaking of clothes, what are you wearing tonight?"

Summer glanced down at her outfit. "This, I guess." She thumbed the jacket collar. "I thought I could take the jacket off and wear the cream-colored shell that's underneath."

Ashley raised her eyebrows and took in Summer's outfit. "Oh. Don't you think that's kind of . . ." She trailed off.

"Uptight?" Summer finished for her. Even when she was a teenager, she'd never been one to follow trends. Her sister, Chloe, had accused her of dressing like Gram on more than one occasion, never meaning it as a compliment. Summer's wardrobe was stylish, but in a classic, refined way. Not trendy and current like Chloe's or Ashley's.

"Actually I was thinking it's kind of businessy. You look more like you're ready for a boardroom than a beachfront restaurant with outdoor seating and a band."

Summer nodded. "I guess." She leaned back in her seat. "Except that my closet is full of stuff like this. I do have a couple of sundresses that I bought last year." She sighed. "I hate shopping. You know that."

Ashley laughed. "Oh, I know. Which is kind of a mystery to me. I adore it."

"Believe me, if you had my mother and sister, you would've grown to hate it, too. It's like their national pastime."

Summer did most of her clothes shopping online now. In fact, she hardly went to the store at all except for groceries. And considering that she'd forgotten to get bread on the last run, maybe she should start doing that online, too. Surely there was some kind of grocery delivery system.

"I was actually going to hit a couple of stores on my lunch break. We could go before your meeting. It'll be fun." Ashley raised her eyebrows in question.

Summer groaned. She'd rather get her teeth cleaned. "I don't want to be late to meet a client."

Ashley chuckled. "Okay, it's not like I'm driving across the country. I'm just going to walk over to King Street."

Summer Weddings was a couple of blocks away from King Street, one of the main shopping districts in downtown Charleston. There were stores for every budget, from discount shops to Louis Vuitton and everything in between. "How about if I give you some cash and you pick me up a new top?" Summer reached for her purse. "Or is that too much of a copout?"

"Hey, it's a start." Ashley shook her head. "You own a pair of dark jeans, right? And strappy heels?"

Summer nodded. "I sure do."

"Okay, I can work with that. Just think of me as your stylist for the night."

"But nothing too flashy. Or revealing." Summer narrowed her eyes. "And no spaghetti straps. Or anything with animal print."

"Is that all?" Ashley smirked.

"Also nothing that looks like something a Kardashian would wear." She smiled. "Other than that, feel free to choose whatever you think is best. But I still have veto power if it doesn't look right on me, so save the receipt."

Ashley laughed all the way to her desk.

Summer turned her attention to the notebook in front of her, filled with possibilities for flower arrangements and bouquets. She tried to keep her mind on the task at hand, but she couldn't help but feel a little excited. Luke had practically been looking through her for months. Maybe tonight if she wore a new outfit, he'd finally focus on her again.

Chapter 5

Justin carefully placed his guitar case in the back of Luke's truck. He'd had such a great day with Colton. Granted, they'd only caught one fish. But those moments were precious. Days like this made him wish he were actually Colton's biological father. At least then he'd have some rights. As it stood, he knew that Samantha could up and move at any moment and he might never see the child again.

"You ready?" Luke asked.

"Yeah. Ready as I'll ever be."

Luke chuckled. "You still have stage fright after all these years?"

Justin nodded. "Little bit." He loved to play, loved to write songs. But actually being on stage in front of people freaked him out. A lot. The other guys made fun of him for it, but Luke never did.

"Look at the bright side," Luke said once they were in the truck and on the way. "At least we don't play for free anymore." He flipped on his turn signal. "I figure that this way even if we're out of tune or if crazy Jimmy falls off the stage again, we'll still make a buck."

"Like you need it," Justin said with a chuckle. "Wish I could find me a girl with old money. Life sure would be a lot easier."

Luke tightened his grip on the steering wheel. "It's not like that, and you know it."

Justin glanced at Luke from the corner of his eye. Maybe he'd been out of line. But he'd been over to their house. Not just anyone could afford to live South of Broad. The taxes alone on those houses were more than most people made in a year. "Sorry. I meant. . ." He sighed. "Just that times are tough."

"Fair enough." Luke relaxed his white-knuckled grip on the wheel. "But for the record, being the poor man in a rich family isn't all it's cracked up to be."

Justin could see where that might be true. But he'd be willing to give it a shot if it meant he could finally buy a house instead of renting and maybe pay off his student loans. "Y'all going anywhere for vacation this year?"

Luke merged onto the James Island Connector. "I wish. It's the busiest time of the year for Summer. I keep telling her that Ashley can handle things for a week or two, but she doesn't seem to be open to that possibility."

Justin knew they'd been through a lot this year. "I'll bet y'all could use a vacation though."

Luke sighed. "Couldn't we all?"

Justin had been friends with Luke long enough to know that he didn't open up very well. No matter the situation, he never showed much emotion. Even at his little brother's funeral last summer, Luke hadn't even flinched. Justin couldn't understand how anyone could stay so strong. Or why anyone would think they had to, for that matter. "I got to hang out with Colton today," he said, feeling a subject change was in order.

"How old is he now? Two? Three?" Luke asked.

"Two and a half," Justin said. "We went fishing. I got him one of those little Snoopy poles." He chuckled. "Of course, he was more interested in playing with the worms than actually fishing. And he was so dirty when I took him home I was afraid Samantha was going to kill me. She actually made me hose him off outside before she'd let him in the house."

"I'll bet." Luke slowed down as they got closer to Folly Beach and the traffic began to thicken. "How's that going?"

Justin sighed. "I know it's weird. It's not like Colton belongs to me. And Samantha and I barely even dated." He shrugged. "But that little boy needs me."

"I'm sure you're right. But be careful." Luke glanced over at him once he'd parked the truck in front of the restaurant. "The more attached you get, the harder it's going to be if Samantha ever moves. Or if she gets married to someone who might not appreciate some other dude hanging around playing daddy to Colton." Luke climbed out of the truck and shut the door, his words lingering behind him.

Justin knew there was truth to what Luke had said. And he also knew that his friend didn't want to see him get hurt.

Even so, the words stung.

Luke would never admit it to Justin, but he still got jittery before going on stage, too. Those years when he'd lived in Nashville, guys like him were a dime a dozen. If he were too nervous to go on, there was always someone waiting in the wings more than willing to take his place.

That was probably one reason why he'd failed. Because honestly, singing lead vocals wasn't his real dream. He'd much rather be behind the scenes, writing the music and lyrics. But somehow that didn't sound nearly as manly as being the lead singer. He'd grown up listening to Chris LeDoux and George Strait. Even his daddy had listened to them and been impressed. No one ever cared about the guy who wrote the song.

"Mr. Nelson?" An older man walked toward him. "I'm Charlie Hamilton."

"Nice to meet you in person," Luke said, shaking the man's outstretched hand.

Charlie smiled kindly. "We enjoyed your demo tape very much. The cover songs sound great, and of course, you're welcome to mix in some original music as well."

That was one reason Luke was so excited about the possibility of this particular gig. A lot of places just wanted a cover band. But the Sand and Suds would allow them to play original songs, too. "Thanks so much for the opportunity. We'll do our best to keep everyone happy."

Charlie chuckled. "Now son, you know that's not possible. It's one of the great lessons in life. You'll never please them all." He pounded Luke on the back. "But if you're taking requests, I'm kind of partial to Kenny Rogers."

Luke nodded. "I'll keep that in mind." He followed Charlie to the stage area where Justin was setting up.

"I'll let you boys get settled. We advertised the music starting at eight, so you've got plenty of time. Just let me know if you need anything." The older man walked back inside the restaurant.

"I just got a text from Jimmy. They're almost here."

Jimmy Baxter played lead guitar, and his brother Will played keyboard and sang backup. They were good guys, always laughing and joking around. By day, Jimmy was an accountant and Will worked as an insurance adjustor. They joked that they only played music for the groupies, but in reality both were happily married with two kids apiece.

"Great. You want to grab something to eat? We've still got an hour."

Justin nodded. "Nothing too heavy though." He patted his stomach. "If I get sick in the middle of the set, they'll never hire us for the summer."

Luke chuckled. "True."

They sat down at a table near the stage.

Within a minute, a cute waitress set glasses of water on the table. "What can I get you boys?"

"Just an appetizer platter," Luke said.

Justin smiled at the college-age girl. "We're in the band."

"Well, in that case, I'll have it right out," the waitress said with a wink.

Luke punched Justin in the arm. "We're in the band," he mimicked, laughing.

"Dude. I'm so single it's not even funny. I figure if being in the band gets a girl to notice me, I'd better take advantage."

"Whatever works." Luke shrugged.

"I don't get it. It seems like every time I meet a girl, she ends up dumping me for some jerk." He grimaced. "My brother says I'm too nice."

Luke shook his head. "You just haven't met the right one yet." He certainly wasn't equipped to dispense relationship advice. He used to think he and Summer had a bulletproof relationship. But lately he wasn't so sure. She'd always been a little tightly wound. But now it was like everything put her on edge. And sometimes he heard himself saying things that sounded just like the stuff his dad used to say. Like this morning when he'd given her a hard time about forgetting the bread.

"I guess you're right." Justin let out a sigh. "There's a new girl at church I'm thinking of asking out. She just moved here from somewhere up north. She's pretty cute." He grinned. "Even with that Yankee accent."

Luke tensed. He definitely didn't want to discuss church. He hadn't set foot in a church building since the Sunday before Bobby's accident. Summer had finally given up on asking him to go with her, but he knew it bothered her. "That's nice." He saw the waitress come through the restaurant door. "Looks like our food is here."

"Enjoy," the waitress said, placing a heaping platter on the table. "And let me know if you need anything, okay?" She glanced pointedly at Justin before she walked off.

"Looks good, huh?" Justin asked, reaching for a loaded potato skin.

"You're talking about the food, not the waitress, right?" Luke chuckled.

Before Justin could answer, two women stopped at their table. The taller of the two fluffed her red hair, a broad smile on her face. "Luke?" she asked.

He nodded, trying to place her face. Every now and then he ran into a tourist who recognized him from a Fort Sumter tour. "Yes."

She slid into the seat next to him, motioning for her friend to sit in the other empty chair. "I'm Jimmy and Will's cousin, Sherry." She reached over and plucked a french fry from the appetizer platter and popped it into her mouth. "This is my friend Maggie." She jerked her chin toward the other woman who was busy batting her fake eyelashes at Justin.

"Hey," Maggie drawled. "We heard y'all play a few weeks ago at that little place on East Bay Street." She leaned closer to Justin. "Y'all should get on one of those reality talent shows or something."

Luke cleared his throat and met Justin's eyes across the table. "Nice to meet you ladies," he said. "Jimmy and Will should be here soon."

"Actually I came to see you," Sherry said. "I heard that you might need my services." She winked. "Jimmy was telling me that you're considering a pretty big purchase for your wife's anniversary gift." She let out a tinkling laugh. "And it just so happens that I can help."

Luke nodded. "Great. Do you have a card or something?" He jerked his chin toward the stage. "It's almost time for us to go on, but I'd love to discuss it sometime next week."

Sherry's full lips turned upward in a smile. "Oh, it would be my pleasure." She reached into her leopard print handbag and pulled out a card with her photo plastered on the front. "Here you go, hon. Call me anytime. I'd be glad to help." She reached over and grasped his forearm. "And if you think about it, could you play some Brad Paisley?" She clutched his arm tighter. "He's my favorite."

Justin tossed his napkin on the table. "Oh, he would *love* to play some Brad Paisley." He smirked in Luke's direction. "Don't you ladies think he looks like Brad?"

Luke's resemblance to Brad Paisley was a running joke with the band. Every time they performed one of his songs, the women in the audience went crazy.

"Oh, he does. We noticed that right off, didn't we, Maggie?"

Maggie nodded, still mesmerized by Justin. "Sure did."

Luke caught Justin's amused expression. "That might be so, but did you ladies know that you're in the presence of one of Charleston's most eligible bachelors?"

The scowl on Justin's face said it all. *If you're going to dish it out, you have to be able to take it.* Luke leaned back and watched the women fawn over his friend.

Chapter 6

"A re you sure I look okay?" Summer asked. She adjusted the red drape-neck top for the tenth time. It was way more flamboyant than her normal style, but she had to admit it flattered her figure.

"You look amazing." Ashley giggled. "I seriously thought that guy in the parking lot was going to get whiplash when we walked past him."

"Whatever. He was totally looking at you." Summer glanced at her friend. Ashley had chosen a turquoise tank top paired with dark denim capri pants and wedge heels. Her chunky coral bracelet and necklace completed the look. Summer never would've paired the colors together, but on Ashley they worked.

"Does Luke know we're coming?" Ashley asked as they walked inside the restaurant.

Summer shook her head. "Nope. He's going to be so surprised." She smiled at the hostess. "We'd like seats out on the patio."

The girl nodded. "Great choice. We actually have a band about to start."

Summer grinned at Ashley. "Perfect."

They followed the hostess through the restaurant and out another door that led to the outdoor seating area.

"Here you go." The hostess pointed at a table for two that offered a view of the stage and the water. "Your waitress will be with you in a moment."

As Summer sank into her seat, she scanned the deck for

Luke. Her eyes landed on a table near the stage. She watched as a woman with hair that was a very unnatural shade of red grabbed Luke's arm and laughed.

"I don't believe it," she whispered. "Look at that. She's all over him."

Ashley followed her gaze. "Man. That's some outfit." She laughed. "And most of the time I'm hard to shock."

Summer swallowed hard. "Do you see how he's laughing with her?" Luke hadn't laughed that way at home in months.

"Hey." Ashley reached over and patted her on the arm. "Don't read into things. Luke is the lead singer for a band. Those are probably just fans."

Even so, Summer's stomach tightened. She watched as the table broke out into another round of laughter. This wasn't how she'd wanted the night to go. She'd hoped to sneak into the crowd once the band started playing and see the pleased expression on Luke's face when he saw her. But now she wished she hadn't come at all. "I think we should leave."

Ashley waved away a smiling waitress. "Give us a minute," she said to the girl. She turned back to Summer. "Don't be silly. Go over there now and surprise him. You'll see that it isn't a big deal."

Summer sighed. "Come with me." She jerked her head toward the table where Luke sat. "I want to introduce you to Justin anyway. When Luke and his buddies helped you move into your house, Justin was out of town." She stood slowly, keeping her eyes on Luke.

As they made their way to the table, she wished again that she'd stayed home with Milo. She could be watching a movie or going for a run. Or even back at the office answering some e-mails. But no. She was trying to get her husband's attention away from some groupie.

Justin saw them first. "Summer." He jumped up, a smile on his face. Justin was by far the best of all of Luke's friends. She'd seen time and again how tenderhearted he was.

Luke looked up, his eyes wide. "I didn't expect to see you here." The expression on his face seemed more shocked than pleased.

She cut her eyes at the redhead and then back at him. "No, I guess you didn't." She turned her attention back to Justin. "This is Ashley," she said, putting an arm around her friend's waist. "I don't think you guys have met." She turned to Ashley. "Justin is a webmaster by day but a drummer by night," she explained. "He might be a good candidate to redesign our website."

Justin nodded in Ashley's direction. "Nice to meet you."

The redheaded woman stood and held out her hand to Summer. "Hi, I'm Sherry. Jimmy and Will's cousin."

As if that explained everything. "Nice to meet you." She glanced down at Luke who hadn't made a move to get up. He looked uncomfortable. *Serves you right.*

"I guess Maggie and I had better go find a table," Sherry trilled. "We want one with a good view of the stage." She motioned for Maggie to get up then focused her attention back on Luke. "Don't forget what we talked about. And I'll be expecting some Brad Paisley before your set is over." She giggled.

Once the two women were gone, Luke stood. "I can't get over you being here. You never come see me play anymore." He smiled, suddenly looking more like his old self than he had in a long time.

Summer cocked her head. "Ashley's never heard you guys

play. She didn't want to come alone." She watched as his face fell and she choked back the truth—that she'd wanted to surprise him. Instead she gestured in the direction Sherry and Maggie had gone. "Friends of yours?"

Luke furrowed his brow. "Nope. Just met them a few minutes ago."

Summer glanced over to see Ashley and Justin sitting at the table, making small talk. "We'll be right back, okay?"

Ashley looked up and nodded.

Summer motioned for Luke to follow her back to her table.

"It's like old times having you here. Remember when you used to come hear me play every weekend?"

She kept her face neutral. "Yeah. I remember."

He reached across the table and took her hand.

She instinctively jerked it away. "You looked awfully cozy with that—that. . .Sherry person."

Luke regarded her with wide eyes. "She's Jimmy and Will's cousin, just like she said. I've never seen her before in my life." He shrugged. "Sorry if I didn't send her and her friend away when they sat down. I didn't realize that speaking to fans was off-limits."

Summer realized how ridiculous she was acting. "Sorry. I wanted to surprise you, and then when I saw you sitting with those women and laughing like old friends. . ." She trailed off. "Sorry I overreacted. It was stupid of me." She reached across the table for his hand but was too late.

Luke stood. "Don't worry about it." He jerked his chin toward the stage. "Jimmy and Will are here. And it looks like Mr. Hamilton is ready to introduce the band. I've got to go." He nodded at her. "Hope you and Ashley enjoy the show."

She watched as he walked off and couldn't help but wonder if the sick feeling in her stomach was from her marriage slipping away.

Luke put his old cowboy hat on top of his head and stepped up on stage.

The crowd applauded, and someone in the back let out a wolf whistle.

He grabbed the microphone and peered out at the crowd. "Thanks to the Sand and Suds for the warm welcome and a special thanks to you guys for coming out to support us." He glanced back at Justin and nodded.

Justin tapped his drumsticks together for a four count, and the band started up on cue. Whenever they played at the beach, they always opened with a Jimmy Buffet song. Tonight they'd decided on "Cheeseburger in Paradise."

Luke noticed that Summer and Ashley had moved to a table closer to the stage. Even if she was only here to accompany Ashley, he was still glad she'd made the effort. And she looked really great tonight, too. He'd seen a couple of guys give her the once-over, and it had made him want to smack them.

He couldn't help but remember the first time she'd heard him play. They were seventeen, and she'd snuck out of her house and met him down at the Battery. They'd sat in the bandstand, and he played his newest song for her.

"It's called 'Summer Girl.'"

"You actually wrote me a song?" She'd tackled him, and his guitar had fallen to the ground with a thud. But Summer in his

arms was much better than a guitar, even one he'd saved up six months to buy.

"It's not finished yet though." He'd laughed as she covered his face with kisses.

"That's okay. Just play me whatever you've got."

He strummed the chords and began to sing, loving the way her eyes never left his.

"I love it," she said when he stopped playing. "When will it be finished?"

He'd grinned. "I'm not sure how it ends yet."

Luke held on to the microphone and sang the last line of "Cheeseburger in Paradise," loving the way the audience joined in. His eyes found Summer's as the crowd applauded. All these years and he'd never finished "Summer Girl" for her. Did she even remember it?

The problem was that just like on that balmy August night when they were seventeen, he still wasn't sure how their song would end.

Chapter 7

"They're really good," Ashley remarked after she'd heard several songs. "Luke has an awesome voice."

Summer nodded. "He's very talented." She turned back to look at the stage. "But his real strength is in his songwriting. He's written several that are catchy enough to be hits."

"Has he ever tried to send them to any record labels?"

Summer shook her head. "It's been years. I think he's resigned himself to playing with a band locally." She shrugged. "It seems to fill the need he has to make music."

"Either way, they sound great." Ashley leaned forward as the band started another song. "So Justin seems nice."

Summer looked at her with an eyebrow raised. "Yes. He's a real sweetheart."

"I set up a meeting with him for next week. It sounds like he'd be easy to work with on the web project." And easy on the eyes, too, but Ashley didn't mention that to Summer. He could be married or engaged for all she knew. Which would further solidify her theory that all the good ones were taken.

"Great. I hope that works out." Summer smiled. "But if you think someone else would do a better job, don't feel like we have to go with his company just because he's Luke's friend."

Ashley appreciated the confidence Summer had in her to make the decision. "Thanks." She turned her attention toward the stage. Luke was doing a perfect rendition of a George Strait song. "I can't imagine having the confidence to get up on stage like that."

"He used to break out in hives before he went on. I think being in Nashville broke him of that problem. He told me once that he realized that there was always someone younger and more talented out there. The difference was that he wanted it more." Summer shrugged. "But songwriting is where his heart is. He's an amazing singer, but he has such a way with words."

The last strains of the song ended, and the crowd broke into loud applause.

"Now we're gonna slow it down a little bit and do an original song." Luke grinned from the stage. "This one's going out to all of the lovebirds out there. It doesn't have all the bells and whistles as some of the others we've done tonight, but I think you'll like it." He began to strum on the guitar, and soon his rich voice filled the air.

"Wow. Just him and his guitar," Ashley said. "Have you heard this one before?" When Summer didn't answer, Ashley glanced at her friend.

Tears streamed down Summer's face, and she didn't even bother to wipe them away. She kept her eyes on Luke, never blinking.

Ashley sat back in her seat and averted her eyes. It seemed almost voyeuristic to watch such a personal moment. She had no idea what was going on inside Summer's head, but she could see the emotion pour out. And one thing she knew for sure about Summer, those emotions didn't come out easily or often.

Summer looked around as if suddenly aware that she was in a public place. She pushed back her chair. "I'll be right back," she whispered.

Ashley half rose to go after her but sat back down. Some

things you had to face alone, and she had a feeling whatever Summer was dealing with was one of them. She turned her attention back to the band.

Luke sang the closing lines of the song, and the crowd cheered. "We're going to take a little break now," he said. "And if you're interested in purchasing one of our CDs, see Jimmy during the break." He motioned toward the keyboard player.

Jimmy waved and pointed at a table near the stage.

Ashley watched as Luke shook hands with a few people from the audience who'd crowded around him. Mostly women, but at least the redhead from before wasn't one of them.

A few minutes later, Luke made his way to her table. "I saw Summer rush out. Did she get a phone call or something?" he asked, concern etched on his handsome face.

Ashley shook her head. It wasn't her place to tell him that Summer had been crying. "I think she went to the restroom."

"Oh." Luke rubbed his jaw where the faintest hint of a five o'clock shadow was beginning to show.

"I'm sure she'll be back soon though."

Justin walked up to the table. "You enjoying the show?" he asked. With his sun-kissed blond hair and tanned skin, he looked like he spent his days surfing rather than working on websites.

"Y'all are so talented." She smiled.

"Thanks." He turned to Luke and gestured toward the stage. "There are a few people who want autographed CDs. I told Jimmy I'd come get you."

Luke nodded. "Sure." He looked back at Ashley. "Will you remind Summer to set the alarm when she gets home?"

"Of course."

Justin gave her one last glance. "Looking forward to our lunch meeting next week."

Before she could respond, he and Luke headed toward the CD table.

As she watched them go, she couldn't help but wish it were already Tuesday. But at least she had time to prepare. Their meeting might call for a new outfit. Maybe a cute skirt. Definitely some new shoes.

With that happy thought, she set off to find Summer.

Justin sat in the passenger seat of Luke's truck. He was way past ready to get home and into bed. The crowd had stayed pretty thick until nearly midnight, and by the end they were a little rowdier than he'd have liked.

He peered out the window. Luke and the restaurant manager stood talking outside the entrance. Maybe he should've caught a ride with Jimmy and Will.

"Sorry about that. The old man is a talker," Luke said once he'd climbed inside the truck. "The good news is that the job is ours if we want it." He turned the truck toward Charleston.

"That's great." The prospect of every weekend being tied up with a performance wasn't as appealing to Justin as it was to Luke. But the extra money would be nice.

"They liked our original stuff, don't you think?" Luke asked.

"Seemed to." Justin looked over at Luke's profile and wondered again why he hadn't tried harder to work in the music industry. He, Jimmy, and Will were in it for fun. Luke was the real talent. "You know that contest I was telling you about? The songwriter showcase?"

Luke nodded. "Yeah."

"The entry deadline is coming up soon. All you have to do is send in a demo." He'd been trying to get Luke to submit an entry for weeks. "And the final round judges are some big names. People who might actually record your songs if they like your style."

Luke shrugged. "Nah. I wouldn't even know which one to submit." He slowed the truck down as they came to a red light. "I do have a couple of unfinished songs though. I've been thinking about finishing them."

"You should do it, man. I think the deadline is at the beginning of July."

Luke sighed. "I'll think about it."

"So it was great to see Summer tonight." Justin had always liked Summer a lot. She'd gone out of her way to make him feel welcome every time he'd been over to their house. Once when his hot water heater had gone out at his apartment, she'd even insisted he stay in one of their guest bedrooms.

"Yeah. I'm glad to see her get out a little bit. If she's not working, she's off at some committee meeting or something." He shook his head. "Usually she just wants to stay home and watch some chick flick on TV."

"And I'm glad to finally meet Ashley." Justin had heard about Summer's coworker, but somehow they always missed meeting one another.

"Ashley's great. She's been a real lifesaver. You know how bad things were there for a while. . ." Luke trailed off. "And Ashley stepped up and ran the company on the days when Summer couldn't handle it all." Luke pulled into an empty space in front of Justin's apartment. "You know, I didn't think about it earlier, but I don't think she's dating anyone." He raised his eyebrows at Justin. "I'm not positive, but I can find out."

Justin had wondered about her status. "Cool." He opened the door. "Thanks for the ride. See you next week." He hopped out of the truck. Once he was on the sidewalk, he motioned for Luke to roll down the window. "If you guys want to go with me to church on Sunday, I think we're having potluck."

Luke's jaw tensed. "I think I'll pass." Without so much as a wave, he backed out of the space.

Justin pulled his keys out and unlocked the door. He knew it made Luke mad when he invited him to Sunday services.

That didn't mean he was going to quit asking. He'd just pray about it a little bit harder.

Chapter 8

Luke hated get-togethers with Summer's family. He always felt like such a nobody around them. Granted, her grandmother had always been good to him. Even the house they lived in had been a gift from her, something that hadn't set too well with her other grandchildren. She'd said it was her prerogative and they'd all have to get over it.

He pulled on a faded pair of jeans and an old brown T-shirt he found hanging in the guest bedroom closet where his casual clothes had been relegated to. This might pass muster on stage, but he had a feeling Summer would hit the roof when she saw it. "Too bad," he muttered. "I'm not going to pretend to be somebody I'm not." He looked in the bathroom mirror and raked his fingers through his hair. Not bad.

"You ready?" he called up the stairs to Summer. He hadn't seen her yet this morning. He'd gotten in so late last night that he'd slept in the downstairs guestroom. Summer usually stumbled downstairs first thing for coffee, but one glance in the kitchen told him that the pot he'd made for her hadn't been touched. She must've slept in.

He checked his watch. If they didn't leave within the next fifteen minutes, they were going to be late. He sighed. "Summer?" he called.

No response.

A sudden panic gripped him, causing his stomach to lurch. He hadn't gone upstairs last night to check on her. The alarm was on when he got home though. And her car was in the driveway. But still. That didn't mean she was home.

Luke took the stairs two at a time, bile rising in his throat. His beating heart pounded against his chest as he threw open their bedroom door.

She was curled up on her side, sound asleep. She held Luke's pillow tightly to her chest.

Milo sat on the floor, staring at her. He cast woeful "I need to go outside" eyes at Luke.

"Summer." Luke said her name sharper than he intended. But during those moments between the kitchen and the bedroom, he'd been so scared something had happened to her. Robbery gone wrong, kidnapping, brain aneurysm—and those were only a few of the scenarios that had played out in his mind. Now, seeing her blissfully unaware filled him with anger. "Summer, wake up." He grabbed her shoulder and shook it.

Milo let out a low growl.

Summer jerked upright. "What? What is it?" She peered at him through sleepy eyes. "What time is it?" She glanced frantically at the clock. "I can't believe I overslept." She jumped up and threw the pillow on the bed. "Why didn't you wake me up?" she asked, glaring. "You know we can't be late." She stomped to her closet. "I don't even have time to shower."

Luke ushered Milo out the door then turned to face his wife. "Simmer down. If we're a few minutes late, it won't be the end of the world."

She scowled. "My whole family will be there, and you know they're always looking for a reason to criticize me." She flung a pair of gray pants on the bed. "I can't believe this."

Luke watched her flip through the vast assortment of

tops in the walk-in closet. It had always amused him how she arranged her clothes by color. "You could wear that red top you wore last night." He winked. "It looked nice."

Summer looked at him with wide eyes. "I'm surprised you noticed it."

He shrugged. "Most of the stuff you wear isn't as bright as that. I liked the red."

She yanked a light blue top from a hanger. "Yeah, well it wasn't my style, so it's no wonder you liked it." She stood on her tiptoes and grabbed a shoe box. "Ashley picked it out."

Only he could give a compliment and still manage to say the wrong thing. "I'd better go let Milo out." He paused at the door. "Do you want me to pour you a cup of coffee into a travel mug?"

Her expression softened. "That would be great, thanks."

Luke headed downstairs to tend to Milo. The upside to her oversleeping was that she hadn't had a chance to criticize his choice of clothing.

He figured she wouldn't notice until they were in the car. And by then it would be too late.

As soon as Luke was gone, Summer sank onto the bed. What an awful way to start the day. A day that would probably contain plenty of trouble all its own without the added stress of running late and fighting with Luke.

And why couldn't she have just been nice when he tried to compliment her on the way she'd looked last night? It was no wonder he'd slept downstairs.

Again.

She hurriedly ran a brush through her medium-length hair, thankful she'd started wearing it wavy. A few drops of texturizing cream, and it looked like it had yesterday when it was freshly washed.

She put on the outfit she'd picked out and grabbed her makeup bag. Thanks to the Saturday beach traffic, it would take at least thirty minutes to get to her parents' house on Isle of Palms. She'd have to do her makeup in the car.

"You ready?" she asked once she made it down the stairs.

Luke glanced up from his favorite spot on the couch. "No." He clicked off the TV and tossed the remote on the couch. "But I guess there's no way out of it."

Summer grabbed the travel mug of coffee that Luke had prepared and knelt to kiss Milo good-bye. "Be a good boy. I'll take you for a long walk when we get back."

Milo yawned and jumped up on the couch. He rested his head on the couch arm and watched her with sad eyes.

"That dog is spoiled rotten." Luke chuckled as they headed out the door. He opened the passenger door on her SUV and motioned for her to get inside.

She brushed past him and climbed in. "He's not too spoiled. He just likes to relax."

Luke glanced at her as he got behind the wheel. "Whatever you say." He started the SUV and slowly backed out of the driveway. "The new crepe myrtle looks good, don't you think?"

Even though his days of working for his uncle's landscaping company were over, Luke insisted on taking care of their yard himself. "It's beautiful." One thing that always cheered her up was their home and garden.

The stucco-over-brick home had been in her family for generations, built right after the American Revolution. Summer's grandmother had lived in the home while Summer was growing up, and her best memories had been made in the lush garden or sitting out on the second-floor piazza listening to stories of Gram's childhood.

Gram's decision to give the home—along with a generous trust for its care—to Summer and Luke as a wedding gift had caused quite a stir in the Rutledge family. Summer's siblings, Mitch and Chloe, had been furious. Her parents hadn't cared too much—until Gram's announcement that she would be moving to a home near theirs on Isle of Palms.

"We have the prettiest house on Legare Street," Summer observed as they drove down the historic street. "And the most gorgeous flowers, too." Most of the homes, including theirs, were in the traditional single style so common in Charleston. What looked like the front door from the sidewalk actually opened to a porch where a second door served as the home's true entrance.

Luke chuckled. "Our neighbors probably think the same thing about their homes." He stopped at the intersection of Legare and Tradd and waited for a throng of tourists to pass before turning left.

She leaned her head against the seat, trying to shake the bad mood she'd woken up with. "You guys sounded great last night." She glanced over at Luke. His profile was perfect. No wonder that redhead had been fawning over him.

"Thanks." He turned onto South Bay Street. "The weekly gig is ours if we want it. The manager liked our style and said he'd heard a lot of compliments."

Summer chewed on her bottom lip. A weekly show was

a big commitment. Over the years, she'd gotten used to Luke's band playing shows every few weeks. But weekly seemed like a big step. "What did you tell him?"

Luke merged onto Highway 17. "I told him I'd talk to the guys. Justin is on board, but I have to check with Jimmy and Will. I figure they might need to run it past their wives."

Summer inhaled sharply. Normally she loved the sights from the Arthur Ravenel Bridge that connected Charleston to Mt. Pleasant, but not today. "So Jimmy and Will's wives get a say, but you weren't going to ask me what I thought?" Her voice came out shrill and sounded way too much like her mother for her liking.

Luke wrinkled his nose. "I didn't think you'd mind. You know how much this means to me."

"Yeah." She closed her eyes. "But sometimes you don't think about what things mean to me."

"So what are you saying? You want me to turn it down?"

Summer flipped through her bag to find her sunglasses. She could feel hot tears welling up in her eyes, and she didn't want to give Luke the satisfaction of seeing her cry. "Of course not." She pulled on the oversized glasses. "But it would've been nice to have been consulted. To feel like my opinion matters." She paused. "For once."

Luke groaned. "You have got to be kidding." He reached over to take her hand, but she pulled it away.

"No, I'm not kidding." She looked out at the water and for a moment wished she were out there in it, swimming toward a deserted island. "It's like I don't count anymore." Her chest was so tight, she wondered if this was what a heart attack felt like. "We never make decisions together. It seems like we live totally separate lives." Despite the pain, she felt a sense of relief at having the statement out in the open. Except that now it hung between them like a haze.

"I can't believe you're doing this just as we're getting to your parents' house," Luke said angrily. "Don't you think you could've saved this conversation for a better time?"

She shook her head. "There isn't a better time. When is the last time you and I talked about anything bigger than who was going to walk Milo or who forgot to take out the trash?"

He slowed down as they got into traffic. "We're both busy, that's all."

She felt his eyes on her but refused to look at him. "We've been busy since we met. But this space between us hasn't always been here." Her voice was barely above a whisper. Saying it out loud was almost as painful as keeping it inside.

And now that the floodgates had opened and the truth was out, she knew they would have to deal with it.

Except that she wasn't sure if either of them was up for that right now.

Chapter 9

Luke silently followed Summer up the steps that led to a huge wraparound porch decorated with white wicker furniture. He'd been to her parents' home plenty of times over the years, but still marveled at what it must've been like to grow up with the beach practically in the backyard.

Every time he came here, he couldn't help but be reminded of the difference in how he and Summer had been raised. His daddy was a shrimper, weathered by the sun and wind. He'd raised his kids with an iron fist, especially after Luke's mama had died. Summer's family, on the other hand, had lived lives full of luxury. Her parents both came from money, and the thought of worrying that there might not be enough food on the table was a foreign concept.

But Summer wasn't snobby like he'd expected. The first day he'd met her in the backyard of the home they now shared, she'd peppered him with questions about the flowers and plants. She'd even invited him to sit with her on the piazza and have a glass of lemonade. His uncle had been furious with him until Summer's grandmother offered them a contract to care for the yard the rest of the year.

Luke met Summer's eyes as they reached the top step. "Truce?" he asked. "At least until we get back in the car?"

She managed a tiny smile and nodded. "I need you to be on my team while we're here."

"I'm always on your team."

The door swung open, and Vivian Rutledge stood before them. "Summer, Luke. . .come in." Vivian greeted both of them with a kiss on the cheek. Her flowery perfume stung Luke's nose, and he resisted the urge to cough.

"Thanks for having us," he said to Vivian.

His mother-in-law gave him a broad smile. "Everyone else is already here. They're out back by the pool." She raised an eyebrow in Summer's direction. "I was beginning to think y'all weren't going to make it."

Luke stepped in. "It was my fault. I had a late night last night." He grinned, hoping he still had some charm left. "But we're sure looking forward to some delicious barbecue."

Summer caught his eye. "Thanks," she mouthed silently.

He nodded. "No problem," he mouthed back with a wink. He put an arm around her waist and led her to the french doors that opened into the backyard. He wished he could pull her to him and hug her tightly and tell her how worried he'd been that morning. But this wasn't the time or the place, and besides, she'd been so cold toward him lately that he wasn't sure if his affection would be welcome.

"There you are." Gram greeted them with a smile. She hugged Summer and then Luke. "I guess I'm going to have to start dropping by your office if I want to know how my oldest granddaughter is doing."

Summer hung her head. "I'm sorry I haven't been out to see you lately." She shrugged. "We've been super busy."

Gram raised one drawn-on eyebrow. "Sweetie, when you are too busy for the people you love, you are too busy." She looped her arm through Luke's. "And how is my favorite grandson-in-law?"

He chuckled. "You might not want to say that too loud, considering I'm not your only grandson-in-law."

Gram shot him a mischievous look. "When you've lived

as long as I have, you can do as you please." She patted his arm. "Someday you'll know what I mean." She winked.

Summer walked over to them carrying two glasses of sweet tea. "Here you go." She handed one to Luke. "The food looks wonderful."

Luke looked over at the spread of food. "Impressive." He glanced at Gram. "Catered?"

She laughed. "Of course." She shook her head. "I wanted to do the cooking, but Vivian wouldn't hear of it."

"Well, it looks good, but I know your cookin' would taste better," he said with a smile.

Gram's wrinkled face lit up. "Thanks." She motioned toward a table next to the pool. "I'm going to go have a seat. But once you've filled your plates, come sit with me."

Summer nodded. "We will." She turned to Luke. "Guess we should go say hello to Daddy and Mitch."

Luke looked around the expansive backyard. "There sure are a lot of people here. I thought this was just going to be a small family gathering."

"I have no idea what's going on." She motioned toward where her father stood with a group of men. "There they are. Come on."

Luke clutched his sweet tea and followed behind her.

"Hi, Daddy," Summer greeted her father.

Thomas Rutledge bent down to kiss his oldest child on the cheek. "Hey, baby." He nodded in Luke's direction. "Luke."

Luke nodded and shook his father-in-law's outstretched hand. "Thanks for having us, Mr. Rutledge."

"Well, well." Mitch Rutledge stepped from behind his father. "I haven't seen you two in a while."

Summer smiled at her brother. "We've been busy."

"Busy?" Mitch shook his head. "That sounds like a flimsy excuse to me." He pounded Luke on the back. "After y'all skipped out on Christmas with the family, we were all beginning to think we'd done something to offend." He smirked. "I figured it was something Chloe had done, but she denied it."

Luke locked eyes with Summer. Except for Gram, her family had no idea why they hadn't made it to Christmas. "We both were a little under the weather," he explained. It wasn't a lie, exactly. The events before Christmas had made both of them physically ill, but not with an actual sickness.

"Summer *Nelson*. I haven't seen you in fifteen years, and now I see you twice in one week," a deep voice said from behind them.

Luke turned to see a tall, familiar-looking man with his eyes on Summer.

"Hi, Jefferson," she said softly.

Luke fought to keep his face neutral. Jefferson Boudreaux had been Summer's first love. His family and Summer's family had been friends for generations. There were even pictures of Jefferson and Summer playing together as babies. The guy might be rich and good-looking, but as far as Luke was concerned, he was a pompous jerk. "Hi there, Jeff." He knew the nickname would get under Jefferson's skin.

A shadow crossed Jefferson's face. "Luke." He held out a hand. "So good to see you again."

Luke reluctantly shook hands. Back when they were teenagers, Jefferson had done all he could to make Luke look stupid in front of Summer. He'd mocked his clothes, made fun of his vehicle—even accused him of stealing a watch one time. "Good to see you, too." He almost choked on the words. "Hope you enjoy your visit."

Jefferson smirked. "Didn't Summer tell you?" He raised his eyebrows in Summer's direction. "I'm back for good. I'm house hunting now." He pounded Luke on the back. "Maybe we'll wind up neighbors."

Luke would rather walk over hot coals than have Jefferson as a neighbor. "Great." He considered it a minor miracle that he was able to keep from punching that smirk right off Jefferson's face. He turned to Summer. "Babe, let's go get something to eat. I'm starved." He put an arm around Summer's waist and guided her toward the food.

As soon as they were out of earshot, he leaned down to Summer. "Why didn't you tell me that Jefferson was moving back?" he hissed. "And when did you see him?"

She wrinkled her brow. "I ran into him Thursday." She sighed. "And I haven't had many conversations with you since then to tell you." She reached for a plate. "Besides, it's not a big deal."

He sighed. "I don't like for that guy to feel like he's got one over on me."

Summer rolled her eyes. "I know. I almost drowned in all the testosterone over there. Can't you two play nice?" She scooped some potato salad onto her plate. "That was all a long time ago."

Luke grumbled. "He's still a jerk." Maybe he was over-reacting. But seeing Jefferson after all this time brought up all the insecurities he thought he'd put behind him. And who wore seersucker anyway? So pretentious.

The sound of silverware clinking against glass rang through the yard.

"Could I have your attention, please?" Mr. Rutledge called.

Vivian walked over to join her husband. "Thanks for joining us today," she said. "We're here to celebrate a special occasion." She smiled broadly.

Luke glanced at Summer, and she shrugged.

"That's right," Thomas said, putting an arm around his wife's shoulders. "We invited you here to tell you that our daughter Chloe has given us some news we've been waiting to hear for a long time."

Luke caught sight of Chloe and her husband, Preston, standing just beyond Thomas and Vivian. Chloe looked like she was about to burst into song.

"What'd they do?" he whispered to Summer. "Cure cancer?"

She elbowed him. "Shh."

"We're pleased to announce that in six months, we're going to have new titles," Vivian said dramatically. "Nana and Poppa." She threw her arms out with excitement.

The crowd burst into applause.

Luke felt Summer stiffen next to him.

She thrust her glass of tea at him, nearly spilling it, and hurried off toward the house.

He froze, unsure of whether he should follow or not.

Gram caught his eye and nodded her head toward the house. She rose and moved as quickly as she could to the french doors.

Luke looked at the abandoned glass of tea in his hand, once again filled with the sense of helplessness that had plagued him for months. Ever since that cold day in early December when he and Summer had learned that she'd suffered a miscarriage.

Even though it had been years since Summer had lived in her parents' home, her bedroom hadn't changed much. The ornate white furniture and pale pink bedding had been fit for a princess. Today, though, they were a painful reminder of all she'd lost.

She sank onto the bed and ran her hand over the soft bedspread. The irony of the situation wasn't lost on her. Her sister, Chloe, had always hated kids. She'd never babysat like Summer had. Never been the one the little kids at church flocked to.

And yet here she was, pregnant.

Not that it should be any surprise. Summer had always heard that when you're trying unsuccessfully to have a child, everyone you know gets pregnant. And that had certainly rung true for her. She couldn't count the number of high school and college friends who'd come out of the woodwork over the past months to share their happy news with the world. It was almost to the point that she hated to log on to Facebook, because she knew she'd be faced with a bevy of new profile photos depicting protruding bellies and ultrasounds.

Maybe things would be different if she'd shared her news with everyone. Then they'd be more sensitive to her feelings. But she and Luke had taken so long to get pregnant, she'd wanted to wait until she was past the first trimester. She'd lost the baby right at the end of the three months, so very few people ever even knew of her loss.

"I had no idea about Chloe, or I would've warned you

first," Gram said quietly from the door. Gram had been her lone confidante in the family. She'd promised not to say anything but had urged Summer to tell her parents what she'd gone through.

Summer looked up, tears in her eyes. "I know you would've." She managed a smile. "Maybe I should've listened to you and told them the news months ago." She'd had this great plan to announce her pregnancy at Christmas, thinking it would be such a wonderful surprise for her parents—and had hoped it would be just the thing to bring them close again. But then she'd miscarried just before Christmas and hadn't the heart to tell them. She had seen no reason to share the grief.

Gram came and sat down next to her. "That was your decision to make." She patted Summer on the knee. "And I understand you wanting to protect them. But sometimes there is strength in numbers. You might not be as close with your parents and siblings as you could be, but they would've stood by you as you were grieving. They would've grieved with you."

Summer shrugged. "Maybe. Or maybe Mother would've given me some speech about needing to take better care of myself or about how we should've started trying sooner." She sighed. "But mostly I didn't want them to look at me with pity." She refused to meet Gram's eyes. She knew how ridiculous she must sound. Even though she knew her family loved her, she never felt like she measured up to what they'd expected her to become. And failing to give them a grandchild seemed like one more way her best wasn't good enough.

"You get that streak of pride from your grandfather."

Gram shook her head. "He never could admit when he was hurting either." She clasped Summer's hand. "But darling, you might find that if you let people see your weaknesses, it will make you stronger in the long run."

"Maybe." Summer looked down at their entwined hands and felt the strength of the woman next to her. She'd always admired her grandmother so much. At least she had one family member who had always been in her corner no matter what.

Summer stood and walked over to the vanity where she'd gotten ready for so many important events in her early life. She traced her fingers over the smooth top, remembering when she and Chloe had sat in front of the mirror and tried on Mother's lipstick. Her gaze went to an ornate wooden box that she'd kept her treasures in since she was small.

She turned to Gram with a grin. "I can't believe this is still here after all these years. I think the first ring Luke ever gave me is in this box."

Gram looked at her curiously. "The first ring?"

Summer nodded and returned to her spot on the bed. She opened the box and began sifting through old letters, pressed flowers, and trinkets that had once meant the world to her. "Did I ever tell you that Luke proposed to me three times?"

Gram raised her eyebrows but stayed silent.

"The first time we were eighteen. It was the night of my debutante ball." She laughed and pulled out a tiny silver tab from a Coke can. "As soon as he saw me in that white gown, he stuck this on my finger and asked me to marry him." She shook her head at the memory.

She pulled a silver gum wrapper that had been folded and

taped and fashioned into a circle. "This one was during my sophomore year of college." She slipped the paper ring onto her finger. "Luke was in Nashville and I was at USC. We missed each other so much." She took the ring off and placed it gently back in the box. "He was home for Christmas, and he begged me to go back with him to Nashville. Said we could get married and get jobs."

Gram patted her arm. "But it all worked out. And the third time was the proverbial charm."

Summer nodded and put the lid on the box that held so many mementos of her past.

Gram cleared her throat. "I may as well tell you that there's something I've been worrying about." She peered at Summer with those crystal blue eyes that didn't miss anything. "I try not to worry—try to give my troubles over to the Lord." She sighed. "I don't mean to pry too much into your personal life, but I have this awful feeling that something is. . .off between you and Luke."

Summer had always heard that the first step to recovery was admitting there was a problem. And while she might be ready to finally admit to herself that something was amiss between them, she certainly didn't want Gram worrying about it. "We'll be fine." Now it was her turn to pat Gram's hand reassuringly rather than the other way around. "Dealing with Bobby's accident and then losing the baby have made the past year difficult. But Luke and I are fine." She managed a smile. "Really, we are."

Gram raised an eyebrow but didn't press the issue. "Well, just know that if you want to talk to me about anything, I'm here to listen."

"I know." Summer gave her a smile that she hoped was convincing.

"And I'll be praying for you both."
Summer's eyes filled with unexpected tears.
Prayer might be the only thing that could help them now.

Chapter 10

L uke stood in the grand foyer of the Rutledge home. It looked like no one else from the party had noticed Summer's abrupt exit. That was best for everyone. The last thing she needed was for a fuss to be made.

"Everything okay?" Jefferson asked from the doorway. "I noticed Summer rush off. I hope she's feeling okay."

Luke eyed him suspiciously. Surely Summer hadn't confided the truth in Jefferson when they'd seen each other earlier in the week. Gossip spread within Charleston society faster than the Confederate Jasmine that crept up the wrought iron gate leading to their house. If Jefferson knew about her miscarriage, Summer's family would, too. "She's fine." He took a sip of tea. "It's awfully hot out there today. I think she needed to come inside for a few minutes to cool down."

Jefferson raised an eyebrow but didn't comment on the feeble excuse. "Did she mention that I've moved back to town?"

Luke held his tongue. Somehow, even after all these years, Jefferson managed to bring out the worst in him. "We didn't really talk much about you." *Because you don't matter to us anymore, you arrogant man.*

"I'll admit, Summer choosing you over me was a huge part of the reason I left Charleston in the first place," Jefferson said. "But now that I've been around the world and had some wonderful experiences of my own, I figured it was time to come back home. I missed my family too much to let such an insignificant thing keep me away."

Luke's jaw tensed. Jefferson was clearly trying to bait him into some kind of argument. But why? "Well, I'm sure the welcome wagon will be wheeled out for you before long."

Jefferson laughed. "You still don't like me very much do you?"

Luke leveled his gaze on his old nemesis. "I don't give you much thought anymore."

"Well, maybe you should try this on for size: you may have thought you won back then, but really there was no competition." Jefferson's lips turned upward in a menacing smile. "Oh, I know you thought there was. And sure, I played along because you were so much fun to mess with. But if I'd have really wanted her, I would've had her." He shrugged. "It's that simple."

Luke took a step toward Jefferson. The other man might be taller, but Luke had broken up enough bar fights to know how to throw a punch. And there was nothing he'd like more than to wipe that smug expression off of Jefferson's face.

"How's it going in here?" Thomas Rutledge asked, coming into the room and looking from Luke to Jefferson. "The party seems to have moved inside. Is the heat too much for you boys?" The worry etched on his face belied his casual tone.

Jefferson chuckled. "No sir. I had to make a phone call, and Luke here was checking on his wife." He gestured upstairs. "I think she's in her room."

Thomas clasped Jefferson on the back. "Mitch is looking for you." He jerked his chin toward the french doors. "I think he wants to challenge you to a game of horseshoes."

"I'm never one to back down from a challenge." Jefferson

shot a parting look at Luke and walked out of the room.

Luke raked his fingers through his hair, suddenly uncomfortable at being left alone with his father-in-law. "Thanks for having us over," he said finally.

Thomas looked at him with eyes that looked remarkably like his daughter's. "I wish you and Summer would visit more often."

Luke stood silently. In the months since Bobby's accident, Summer's dad had reached out to him numerous times. And each time, he'd rebuffed. Those memories from when he and Summer had first met, and how her parents had disapproved of him, stung too much. If he hadn't been good enough then, he wasn't good enough now. "We stay pretty busy. Summer's business really picks up about this time of year, and it's hard for her to find a free weekend."

Thomas took a sip of his drink. "Well, you're welcome even if she can't make it. I'm always looking for a fishing partner."

A laugh caught in Luke's throat. All these years, and Thomas wanted to be friends now? Too little too late. Same as his own dad. "I appreciate the offer. Maybe we'll do that one of these days."

The words seemed to placate Thomas. "Is Summer not feeling well? I saw Mother go after her." He frowned. "That woman has a sixth sense when it comes to one of her children or grandchildren being sick."

So her exit hadn't been as unnoticed as he'd hoped. "I think she's just hot. And tired." He shook his head. "And she hasn't eaten anything yet." He forced a smile. "Bad combo."

Thomas nodded. "She needs to take better care of herself." He sighed. "Well, remember my offer. You have my number.

If you ever have a free Saturday, I'd love to hit the water."

"I'll keep that in mind." *Not a chance.*

An hour later, Luke had made small talk with several of Summer's relatives and family friends.

Alone.

He hated this kind of thing, but he forced a smile and turned on the charm.

"Please drag my sister away from work one night, and let's all go out to dinner," Summer's younger sister, Chloe, trilled. "Preston and I love Fig. We go there all the time, and I always say, 'We should ask Summer and Luke to meet us here,' because, you know, it isn't far from where you live." She paused for a breath. "And I'm thinking of getting Summer to help plan my baby shower. The big one, you know, the main one. Like the one that will be more of an event. Not just a tea or something, but a real sit-down dinner and celebration of our good news."

Luke watched her mouth, wondering how such a tiny person could use so many words in such a short time. Listening to her exhausted him. He glanced over at her husband, Preston. The man watched her adoringly and hung on to her every word. *It takes all kinds.* "I'm pretty sure that Summer is booked for a while." The last thing his wife needed was to have to plan her sister's baby shower. Not now.

Preston put an arm around Chloe. "We'll make sure you have the biggest, most fantastic baby shower this city has ever seen." He pulled her close and planted a kiss on her cheek. "Anything for my girl."

Chloe giggled like a teenager on her first date.

Luke fought to keep from rolling his eyes. "Great to see you guys." He jerked his chin toward the house. "I'm going to see if Summer's ready to go."

Thirty minutes later, he and Summer finally climbed into their SUV. She leaned her head against the seat. "Man. What a day." She glanced at him. "Sorry I left you to navigate the party alone." She reached over and patted his knee.

He pulled onto the main road. "No problem." He sighed. "Your dad invited me to go fishing with him. And I had a run-in with Jefferson. And Chloe and Preston."

She removed her hand from his knee. "Sorry."

They rode in silence for a few minutes. Luke wanted nothing more than to get home. He needed to mow the yard, and one of the flower beds could use some mulching. Sometimes it seemed like he could never get everything done.

He flipped on the radio and turned it to an '80s station. The sound of U2 filled the vehicle, and Luke felt the tension begin to leave his body. Until he felt Summer's eyes on him. He finally turned the volume down and glanced at her from the corner of his eye. "What? Is it too loud?"

"You don't think we should talk about things?"

He sighed. "I know we argued earlier, but can't we put that behind us?"

"You want to put everything behind us. Pretend like nothing has happened." She sniffed. "It doesn't work like that."

"I don't know what you mean."

"Don't you? Because if you're serious, then you really are the world's worst communicator." She crossed her arms. "You didn't want to talk about Bobby's accident. You didn't want to talk about our baby." Her voice shook with emotion. "But maybe *I* need to talk about those things."

Luke shook his head. He knew her well enough to know

that when her voice took that tone there was no reasoning with her. "You're upset about Chloe's pregnancy. You can take it out on me if you want to. I'm used to being the scapegoat."

"You're wrong. I'm not upset about Chloe. I'm *happy* for her. It was a shock, that's all. I wish I'd had some warning. Learning about it in such a public place was hard." She sighed. "You know how much I looked forward to making our own announcement."

He'd looked forward to it, too. He'd had this image of himself passing out those pink or blue bubblegum cigars to all the guys at work. He'd seen that once on some TV show, and it had stuck with him. But he could never tell Summer that. There was no reason to make her any sadder than she already was. "I know. And I'm glad you're happy for Chloe. Me, too." Maybe not, but he would be by the time the baby arrived. It's not like they saw her that much anyway.

Summer sighed. "I don't want to fight anymore. It's been such a long day."

"You want to go out to dinner tonight?" He glanced over at her. "We could go to Magnolia's." Her favorite restaurant was bound to lift her spirits. "I'll even spring for fried green tomatoes." He hated fried green tomatoes, but Summer had always loved them.

"Yeah. That sounds great." She reached over and turned up the radio.

The familiar strains of Bon Jovi's "Never Say Good-bye" filled the vehicle.

"No way." Luke chuckled. "Do you remember this?"

"Of course I do," she said. "How could I forget the first time you told me you loved me?"

Luke reached over and took her hand.

"What a night that was," he said. "And just think. . .if I'd have had my way, you would've married me as soon as we could get to a justice of the peace."

She looked down at their intertwined hands. She'd held on to his hand through so much. The first time he'd told her he loved her had been such a magical night.

"You were the most beautiful debutante I'd ever seen." Luke squeezed her hand. "And I still say that you could've passed for a bride in that white dress."

Summer's mouth turned upward in a smile. "I must've looked like some kind of crazy person sneaking out of Gram's house in that dress. But I wanted you to see it. When I got ready that night, it was you I wanted to impress." After the ball, she'd climbed down a ladder from the second floor piazza and hurried to the Battery to meet Luke.

"Have you been waiting long?" Summer hurried up the steps to the bandstand.

Luke let out a low whistle. "I'd wait on you forever." He grabbed her around the waist and pulled her close. "Don't you know that?" He leaned in and kissed her on the lips until they were both breathless.

"Sorry that it took me so long to get here. My parents kept questioning why I wanted to stay at Gram's tonight." She grinned. "Sometimes I think Gram knows that when I stay with her I sneak out and meet you, but she hasn't said anything about it yet."

Luke laced his fingers with hers. "I'm glad I have at least one fan in your family."

"You have two." She reached up and traced her fingers over his smooth face. *"I'm your biggest fan. I always will be."*

He raised his eyebrows. *"You sure you wouldn't rather be with Jeff?"*

She rolled her eyes. *"Jefferson doesn't hold a candle to you. How many times do I have to tell you that?"*

Luke knelt down and flipped on a tiny radio, and a Bon Jovi ballad filled the night air. *"May I have this dance?"* He pulled her close, and they swayed to the music. *"There's something I need to tell you,"* he murmured against her hair.

She pulled back so she could see his face. *"You're really a mirage?"* she asked.

He laughed softly. *"No. I'm totally real. And I love you, Summer Rutledge. With all of my heart."* He kissed her gently on the mouth. *"I always will."*

Luke squeezed her hand. "You okay? I don't think you've heard a word I said."

Summer glanced over at him. "Sorry. I was just thinking about that night. We were so young—"

"And so in love." He slowed down as they reached their street.

Summer nodded. *So in love.*

She wondered if Luke would've done anything differently if he had it to do all over. Would he have given up on his dreams to move back to Charleston to be with her? Would he have married her despite her family's misgivings?

She wondered those things, but she didn't have the guts to ask.

Chapter 11

Ashley poured herself a second cup of coffee. The phone at Summer Weddings had been ringing nonstop all morning. And with Summer out meeting a client, Ashley was manning the office by herself. She'd already had to talk a very grumpy bride off of a ledge. The young lady wanted to change her wedding colors at the last minute and hadn't been happy to hear the cost involved.

Adding to her stress was the fact that Justin was supposed to meet her for lunch today. She knew it wasn't a date. It was just business. But nevertheless, she'd taken great pains to look nice. Her bright pink wrap dress clung to her figure in all the right spots. With her hair pulled back into a smooth ponytail and her strappy black sandals, she'd felt pretty confident when she left the house this morning. She might be on the back side of thirty, but she could still pass for younger.

But as the lunch hour neared, her confidence waned. Friday night she'd felt cute and sassy and had even flirted with Justin. But she'd learned a long time ago that there was something about a warm Friday night, listening to music and laughing with friends, that made her feel light and free. Now, in the light of day and the middle of the workweek, she only felt foolish for even thinking a nice guy like Justin could be interested in being more than just her web designer.

She took a deep breath. Going through a divorce was hard for anyone. But when you had to sit by and watch as your husband chose another woman over you, it stripped away all of your self-confidence. It made you feel worthless and unlovable. Ashley had fought with those feelings of unworthiness for years. She'd thought she was over them. But today they were back with a vengeance.

The ringing phone jolted her from her walk down memory lane. "Summer Weddings, this is Ashley," she said into the receiver.

"Ashley," a male voice said. "It's Justin. Justin Sanders. We're supposed to meet today."

Her heart pounded so hard, she was sure he could hear it over the phone. She was so out of practice at this. "Y–yes. How are you, Justin?"

He laughed, a warm, rich sound that reminded her of summertime and lemonade and all the things she'd loved from childhood. "I'm just dandy." He cleared his throat. "Actually, somethin' has come up at the last minute. I was wondering if we could reschedule."

Disappointment washed over her. "Oh sure." She tried to tell herself it had nothing to do with him not wanting to spend time with her. He was a busy man. Something probably had come up.

"Well, I was thinking. . .maybe we might get together tonight?" Justin asked.

"Sure. I can stay late if you want to come by. I usually leave around five, but I can stay until six or so if that works for you." She wasn't crazy about staying late but would if she had to. Especially if it meant getting to know Justin a little better.

Justin laughed. "No. That's not what I meant. I was thinking more like maybe I could come pick you up at your place. Take you out to a nice dinner. How's seven?"

Was he asking her on a date? Because that sounded

awfully datelike. "Um. . .sure. That could work. Seven is fine." She gave him directions to her house and hung up.

Ashley was still staring at the phone when Summer walked into the store.

"You okay?" Summer asked, a concerned expression on her face.

"What? Oh yeah. I'm fine." She filled Summer in on the development with Justin.

Summer's eyes widened. "That's awesome. You'll have a great time. Justin is the sweetest, nicest guy, but he's always been painfully shy. I'm surprised he was so brazen as to suggest coming to your house. He's not making any effort to hide that he wants to get to know you on a personal level."

"I wouldn't normally give my address to some guy I only met once. But since you and Luke know him so well, it should be okay. Right?"

Summer grinned. "Definitely okay. He's the most respectful guy you'll ever meet."

Ashley couldn't hide her excitement. She was finally ready to move on with her life.

And Justin sounded like exactly the kind of guy she'd been looking for.

Summer was happy for Ashley, but she didn't envy her. The thought of dating at this stage in life didn't sound like much fun. "I'm going to run out and grab some lunch." She walked over to Ashley's desk. "Do you want to go? Or do you want me to pick something up for you?"

Ashley shook her head. "Thanks. But I think I'll just heat up a Lean Cuisine."

"Suit yourself." Summer grabbed her bag and headed out the door. She wouldn't have minded if Ashley had come with her, but since she was alone, she'd be able to stop by the cemetery. Ever since Chloe's announcement at the barbeque, Summer had felt the need to go and spend some time at the grave of the little baby who'd passed away so many years ago.

She slipped her sunglasses on and walked down King Street. Several shoppers milled around, their hands full of bags. She passed by a frozen yogurt shop full of college students from the nearby College of Charleston.

Summer peeked into the window of an antique shop. She'd always loved antiquing, even though Luke preferred brand-new things. Their home was decorated with an eclectic mix of pieces that had been in her family for generations and new purchases she and Luke had bought together. She kept going, enjoying the warm breeze. Charleston could be unbearably hot in the summer, but late May was perfect.

She reached the entrance to the church cemetery and walked through the iron gates. The shade made the temperature drop immediately. She inhaled, and the sticky-sweet smell of honeysuckle took her back to a childhood spent playing amid the gardens of Gram's friends.

She settled onto the stone bench and read the headstone for what had to be the hundredth time. A tiny life, only on this earth for a day. She wondered again about the child's mother. How had she survived the loss? Had her will to live died along with her baby? If she could find the energy, she could probably locate the story in the archives. But she knew it would be a story of sadness. Even if the woman had gone on to have ten children, that didn't diminish the loss of this one.

"I thought I might find you here."

She turned at the sound of Jefferson's voice. "Were you looking for me?" She hadn't spoken to him much at the barbecue, but Luke had confessed over dinner Saturday night that he and Jefferson had gotten into it a bit. No surprise there.

His face broke into a grin. "Yes and no." He nodded toward the bench where she sat. "Do you mind?"

She shrugged. "I guess not."

"I didn't set out to look for you, but I happened to be walking by and thought I'd pop in to see if you were here." He stretched his legs out in front of him. "My office is right down the street. It's amazing how things have stayed the same. There are more tourists though." He raked his fingers through his hair. "I was going to go grab lunch, and there are lines outside most of the restaurants."

She laughed. "Hey, tourism is good for my business, so I don't mind."

"I guess." He was quiet for a moment. "I want you to know how nice it is to see you again. I know I've done things in the past, things I'm not proud of." He peered at her. "But I've turned over a new leaf."

She raised her eyebrows. Jefferson had never been a bad guy, just a spoiled one. The kind of guy who was used to getting what he wanted and never knew how to handle himself when he was rebuffed. "I'm glad to hear that. Although I imagine it's just that you've grown up." She pushed a stray hair from her face. "We knew each other as kids. Not adults. We're both different now."

He shook his head. "Not that different. The same things that drew me to you back then draw me to you now."

Summer ducked her head. "Don't be silly."

"I don't mean to make you uncomfortable. At all." He shook his head. "But I do want to be your friend. We have a history that dates back to us in a playpen." He chuckled. "I don't want to throw away that kind of history just because we didn't work out as a couple."

Friends. With Jefferson. A part of her said it would be improper. But another part was happy to see him. Jefferson reminded her of being seven years old and learning to ride a bike. Of suffering through manners classes at the insistence of their mothers. And of going Christmas caroling in the sixth grade. She nodded. "I'd like to be friends."

He looked her in the eyes. "I'm glad. I wanted to talk to you at the barbecue. I was worried about you. The way you ran off like that."

"I wasn't feeling well." Even to her own ears, the excuse sounded flimsy.

He nodded. "That's what Luke said. But I could tell he was concerned." Jefferson rose from the bench and smoothed his gray suit jacket. "Just know that if you ever need an old friend to talk to, I'm right down the road."

"Thanks," she murmured.

With a wave, Jefferson headed toward the gate.

Summer let out a sigh and turned her attention back to the headstone in front of her. She should've brought flowers.

Maybe next week.

She walked slowly out of the cemetery and headed toward her office.

Chapter 12

Justin pulled up in front of Ashley's house in his brother's car. A fancy red sports car. He was going to put forth his best effort here. He hopped out of the car and hurried up the sidewalk.

The car wasn't the only thing borrowed for this date. He'd left behind his normal uniform of T-shirt and jeans and allowed his sister-in-law to choose his clothes for the night. Thankfully he and his brother were the same size. He tried to block the thought that the clothes he wore tonight probably cost more than the money he brought home in a month.

He rapped on the door and waited for Ashley to answer it. He hoped that the borrowed car and clothes would help him shed his normal self. Justin was tired of being the perpetual friend. The one girls told their problems to before they proceeded to settle for some jerk. Nope. That was the old Justin. The new Justin was going to be a different kind of guy.

The door swung open, and Ashley stood before him with a grin on her pretty face. She wore a pink dress that clung to her figure in all the right places.

"Wow." He smiled. "You look amazing." Her blond hair was pulled back into a ponytail, and her makeup was minimal. Which he appreciated. There was nothing worse than a woman who hid behind a lot of makeup.

She blushed. "Thanks." She motioned into the house. "Do you want to come in for a minute?"

He shrugged. "Sure." He glanced at his watch. "But we

have reservations, so we need to leave soon."

"Reservations?" Her green eyes were wide. "It isn't a fancy place is it? Maybe I should change."

He shook his head. "Not too fancy. And you look fine."

She wrinkled her forehead. "Okay. Well, let's go then." She grabbed a black purse and ushered him to the door.

Once they were outside, he hit the unlock button on the key fob. His own vehicle, an old pickup truck, didn't have one of those. Even the windows had to be rolled down manually. Daniel's car was much better suited for dating.

Ashley paused at the passenger door for a moment. He knew she was giving him the chance to open the door for her. Normally, he would've been all over that. He was nothing if not a Southern gentleman. But he'd seen the way it worked. Women always fell for jerks.

So tonight he intended on being one.

Ashley settled into the low leather seat of the sports car and buckled her seat belt. For some reason, she'd pegged Justin as a truck guy. The flashy red car surprised her.

But one thing she'd learned was that people weren't always what they seemed.

Justin hopped in the car and started the engine. He flashed her a smile. "Hope you're hungry. Our reservation is at the Peninsula Grill."

Ashley raised her eyebrows. She'd never been there but had heard good things about the place. It was a little more upscale and romantic than she was used to. And definitely not what she'd had in mind for a first date. "Sounds great."

He merged onto the interstate going south, cutting off another vehicle in the process.

Ashley cringed as he maneuvered the little red car through traffic like they were in a life-sized game of Frogger. She gripped the seat belt and prayed they'd make it safely.

"Not going too fast for you, am I, babe?" he asked, adjusting his sunglasses.

She furrowed her brow. Babe? "Um. Actually you *are* going a little fast. I didn't realize we were in some kind of race."

He chuckled. "Life's one big rat race, didn't you know?" But he slowed down some. "So tell me about yourself."

Ashley took a deep breath. She was really doing this—dating. Moving on. Getting to know someone new. It felt scary, but the good kind of scary. Like when she'd gone paragliding that time in Switzerland. "I'm originally from a small town in Alabama. I graduated from Auburn with a degree in business and lived in Birmingham for a while." She shrugged. "And I moved to Charleston three years ago."

Justin reached over and patted her on the leg. "I'm so glad you did."

She froze. It was way too early for any kind of physical contact. She wasn't a prude, but she did think the hand on the knee should wait until they at least knew each others' birthdays. She shifted in the seat, hoping he'd get the hint. "Yeah, it's been a good move. I enjoy working with Summer, and I've found a church I like." There. Surely a mention of church would shame him into taking his hand off her.

"That's great." He squeezed her knee again.

She jerked her leg out of his reach. "Please don't do that."

He pulled his hand away. "Sorry. You just look so good in that dress."

"Thanks." Relief washed over her as they got to the restaurant.

Justin pulled the car into a space and hopped out.

Ashley sat for a long moment, but he didn't open her door. How strange. . .and rude. He'd seemed so normal the other night. But now. . .he was another person. She got out of the car and walked over to where he stood on the sidewalk. "I'm starved."

"I'm glad to hear it. Most of the girls I go out with only eat salads." He looked her up and down. "But you look like you enjoy a real meal every now and then. Not like those stick-straight, skinny girls."

She widened her eyes in horror. She'd always been curvy, but she wasn't overweight. But to hear a guy she barely knew comment on her shape threw her for a loop. Still reeling, she followed Justin up the sidewalk.

They entered the restaurant, and Justin sauntered up to the hostess. "We have a reservation." He grinned. "For Sanders."

The girl returned his smile and scanned the list. She looked up with a puzzled expression. "I don't see that name on the list."

Justin leaned forward. "Can you check again? S-a-n-d-e-r-s."

The flustered hostess shook her head. "I'm sorry. It's not on here." She glanced at Ashley. "I'm really sorry about that."

"You're *sorry* about it? How exactly does that help us?" Justin sneered.

The hostess glanced down at the list. "We're not too busy

tonight. If y'all don't mind waiting a little while, we'll be able to seat you even without a reservation." She looked at them hopefully.

Ashley gave her an encouraging smile. She'd worked her way through college as a hostess and knew all too well what it was like to deal with rude people.

"How long will the wait be?" Justin asked.

The hostess checked the list again. "Probably about thirty minutes. Maybe forty-five."

"That's not acceptable," Justin said. "It isn't our fault that you messed up our reservation. Is there a manager I can speak with?"

Ashley couldn't take it any longer. She placed a hand on Justin's arm. "Actually, if it's okay with you, I'd like for you to take me home."

He whipped around and stared at her with wide eyes. "Take you home? But we haven't eaten."

She would've liked nothing more than to tell him exactly what she thought of him. But she wanted to make it home in one piece. "I'm not feeling that great. I'd appreciate it if you'd take me home now."

Ashley didn't even try to make small talk in the car on the way back to her house. There was no point. She wanted to get home and change into her comfy clothes and forget that this disaster of a night ever happened.

Chapter 13

W hat is wrong with you, man?" Luke asked. "Why would you ever think that was a good idea?"

"I'm a complete idiot." Justin put his head in his hands. He'd been so distraught, he'd asked Luke to meet him for lunch. Except that after last night's disaster, Justin had completely lost his appetite.

Luke shook his head. "Not usually. But this time, yeah, you were."

Justin cut his eyes at Luke. "Thanks for the brutal honesty."

Luke held his hands up. "I'm sorry, but pretending to be someone you're not is kind of idiotic."

"Yeah, she wasn't much of a fan. In fact, she asked me to take her home after the fiasco with our reservations." He made a face. "I should've come clean right then, but I knew how dumb it would sound."

Luke nodded. "It does sound pretty dumb."

"Cut me some slack, okay?" Justin asked. "You know my track record. I date women who end up leaving me for guys who treat them like dirt. It's a never-ending cycle." He took a sip of his Coke. "Look at Samantha. She'd rather exchange letters with a guy in prison than date me."

Luke almost spit out his drink. "I'm not sure, but I think the problem might be them. Not you." He shook his head. "I'm only going to tell you this because you've clearly gone off into the deep end here." He met Justin's gaze. "But I think part of the problem is the women you choose. I've watched you go through them. And Justin, these ladies have problems. Problems too big for you to fix."

Justin nodded. He did have a habit of getting involved with women whose lives were in shambles. "I like to feel useful."

Luke snorted. "Okay. So find a nice, normal girl who needs help mowing her yard. Or changing a tire. Not raising a child or bailing her mama out of jail."

Justin managed a smile. He had definitely gone out with some colorful characters. "Ashley seems like she's got it together."

"She does. At least as far as I know." Luke took a sip of his drink. "I'm thinking you might want to give that one another shot. Only without your alter ego."

"You think she'll speak to me again?" Justin asked.

"I have no idea. But there's only one way to find out." Luke glanced at his watch. "I have to run. I have a meeting." He pounded Justin on the back. "But good luck."

Summer paced the length of her office. "I'm really sorry. That doesn't sound at all like Justin." She couldn't believe the story Ashley had told her. "If I'd had any idea he would act like that, I never would've encouraged you."

"It's not your fault." Ashley looked up from her computer. "I thought I'd become a pretty good judge of character, but clearly I was way off the mark with this one."

"Well, if it makes you feel any better, I never would've thought he would act like that." Summer sat down at her desk and crossed her legs. "But then I've never been on a date with him." She was glad to see a smile finally brighten Ashley's face.

"Maybe it's me. I'm some kind of magnet for bad boy behavior. Clearly I can turn even the nicest guy into a world-class jerk." She shook her head.

"Don't say that."

"Seriously. My ex-husband had everyone snowed. Me especially. I didn't know what I'd gotten into until I was legally bound. And now with Justin. . ." Ashley trailed off. "I know I'd only met him once, but I thought he was one of the good guys."

Summer smiled. "Think of it this way—you're slowly but surely weeding out the guys who aren't right for you."

Ashley sighed. "I guess."

"Don't give Justin another thought." Summer locked eyes with Ashley. "Put him out of your mind. At least you didn't invest more than one night, right?"

"Right." Ashley brightened. "You're exactly right. I'll forget him and move on."

Summer motioned toward the door. "Now I'm going to run and grab some coffee from City Lights. You want me to bring you a muffin or something?" City Lights Coffee on Market Street was one of Summer's favorite spots. She adored local places where the barista knew her name and the coffee was served in a real porcelain mug.

Ashley shook her head. "No. Thanks though. I think I'll go out to lunch to cheer myself up." She managed a smile. "Maybe splurge and get a cupcake or something."

"A girl needs a cupcake every now and then." Summer grinned. She shoved her sunglasses on top of her head and hurried outside. Just as she was about to cross Meeting Street, she saw Luke standing outside of Toast. The restaurant was one of their favorites. If she'd known he was going to be around at this time of day, she would've offered to meet him for lunch.

"Lu—" The word caught in her throat as she watched him wave to a familiar redhead.

Sherry. The girl from the Sand and Suds.

Summer watched in horror as Luke held the door open for Sherry. She froze on the sidewalk, causing a woman to run into her.

"Sorry," the woman said. "I didn't see you stop." She shot an irritated look in Summer's direction as she passed by.

Summer struggled to keep breathing. She leaned against the brick building she was in front of, hoping her legs were steady enough to get her back to the office. Her knees wobbled, nearly buckling underneath her.

"Ma'am," a college-aged guy said. "Are you okay? Can I help you?"

"I–I'm not feeling well," she said weakly.

He peered at her through kind brown eyes. "You're white as a ghost." He jerked his chin toward a bench. "Let me help you sit down." He grasped her by the elbow and led her to the bench.

"Let me run inside there and get you a Coke." He pointed at the Subway restaurant across the street. "I'll be right back, ma'am. Just sit tight."

Summer had never been more thankful for well-brought-up Southern boys. Although she could've done without the "ma'ams." She took a deep breath and wondered what she should do next. Confront Luke? March right inside the restaurant and act surprised to see him?

"Here you go." The young man walked up clutching a fountain drink. "Maybe your blood sugar was low."

"Yes. . .maybe." She took the drink and smiled at him. "Thank you so much for your help." She dug through her purse and came up with a five-dollar bill. "Here you go—this should cover the drink."

He shook his head. "Don't worry about it. You can be my good deed for the day." With a wave, he was gone.

Her blood pumped so quickly, it thundered inside her head and drowned out the street sounds around her. The thought of Luke with another woman made her physically ill. Sure, they'd been going through a rough patch, but she'd never dreamed he might turn to someone else.

Summer kept her eyes glued to the door of Toast.

After what seemed like an eternity, Luke and Sherry exited the restaurant. They stood on the sidewalk, talking and laughing.

Sherry reached up and gave Luke a hug and hurried off down the street.

Summer stood. Had they made another date? She quickly crossed the street and stopped in front of her husband. "Fancy meeting you here."

She watched as Luke's eyes grew wide. And couldn't help but see the flicker of guilt flash across his face.

Chapter 14

Luke couldn't believe his luck. He must be cursed or something.

"Hi there, honey."

Summer narrowed her eyes. "Don't 'honey' me. Do you have lunch with groupies often? Or is the redhead special?"

He groaned, wondering if he could talk his way out of this disaster. "No. I ran into her, and we were both headed to the same place." He shrugged. "No big deal." He looked closely at Summer's face to see if she believed his fib. Clearly she did not.

"I saw you meet up with her on the sidewalk. It was a planned meeting. Don't lie to me, Luke. We've been through too much for that."

He swallowed. Maybe it was time to come clean. "I'm parked in the lot on Queen Street. Come with me, and I'll explain."

He put his hand on the small of her back to guide her, but she sidestepped away from him.

"I don't want to go anywhere with you." She looked at her watch. "Besides, I should be getting back to work."

Luke sighed. Her life revolved around work. "Ashley can cover for another hour." He faced her and put his hands on her shoulders. "Please. Trust me. There's something I want to show you."

She didn't speak for a long moment. "Fine. But I need to be back to the office in an hour." She locked eyes with him. "Promise?"

He nodded. "Come on."

They walked silently to his truck. It took all his restraint not to let his anger out. The idea that he was the kind of man who'd sneak around on the sly and meet up with random women really annoyed him. Summer had been the absolute center of his universe since he was barely seventeen. Seeing the accusation on her face and hearing it in her voice ran all over him.

"Where are we going?" she asked once they were in the truck.

He shook his head. "Nope. Just be patient." He cast a sideways glance at her. "Please?" This wasn't how he'd wanted to do it. He'd expected to have more time to plan. But he'd learned a long time ago to roll with the punches.

Twenty minutes later he slowed down and pulled into a parking lot.

"The marina?" Summer looked at him with narrowed eyes. "What are we doing here?"

He couldn't hide his smile. "You never were very good at patience, were you?"

"Might not be my best virtue, but I'm good at other stuff."

Luke chuckled and brought the truck to a stop. He walked around and opened the passenger door and held out a hand.

Summer accepted it and stepped daintily to the ground. "This had better be good. Because I haven't forgotten about you and that *woman*."

Luke shut his eyes. If he were still in the habit of praying, he would've prayed that the Lord would give him strength to tolerate her barbs without snapping. But instead, he'd just wish for it. "I have a surprise for you, actually. And that's

what my meeting with Sherry was about." He reached over
and grabbed her hand, hoping she wouldn't jerk away.

She didn't.

"Honestly. I wasn't having some covert affair with Jimmy's
cousin." He shook his head. "I would hope you know me
better than that by now."

Summer gripped his hand. "Sometimes I don't feel like I
know you at all anymore," she said quietly.

The words pierced his heart. His only hope was that the
anniversary gift he'd gotten her would help bring them closer
together. "Sure you do. I'm still the same old Luke." He pulled
her into an embrace. "I'm the same boy you fell in love with.
And the same man you married seven years ago." He'd missed
having her in his arms. They fit together perfectly. "I wanted
to give you this gift on our actual anniversary, but since you
caught me finalizing the deal, I'm going to go ahead and give
it to you today."

He led her down to the water where a line of boats sat
in a row.

They stopped at the third boat. "See that?"

She looked at him with a puzzled expression. "Yeah."

"Look at the name of the boat."

She took a step closer and peered at the side of the boat.
"No way," she said.

"The *Summer Girl*," Luke said. "I hope you love it."

Summer smiled. "I can't believe you did this." She shot
him a sideways glance. "We've always said we were going to
buy one."

"And spend our weekends out on the water, just the two
of us." He returned her smile. "I even got a life vest for Milo
so he can come, too." He chuckled. "Although he might have

to lose a couple of pounds first."

She joined in his laughter. "We'll have so much fun."

Fun. They hadn't had much fun together over the past year. It seemed like it had been one thing after another. Luke had hoped that purchasing the boat would bring them closer together again. "I'm glad you like it."

She threw her arms around his neck then pulled back. "But how does the redhead figure into things?"

Luke laughed. "She paints names and scenes on boats. It's part of her business." He rubbed Summer's back. "I mentioned to the guys several weeks ago that I'd bought the boat, and Jimmy told me about his cousin." He shrugged. "She's had some hard times and could use the business, so I hired her. I didn't want to have lunch with her at all. I'd just planned to drop off a check. But then she begged me to sit with her, said she hated to eat alone. So I did." He tipped Summer's chin. "Nothing more to it."

She at least had the decency to look sheepish. "Sorry." She drew her brows together. "But how did you manage to make a purchase this large without me knowing?" Summer kept the books for their accounts because she loved the satisfaction of seeing all the numbers balance.

He'd hoped she wouldn't ask. "Oh. That." He cleared his throat. "Well, I knew there was one account you wouldn't monitor."

Realization dawned on her, and the color drained from her face. "You didn't."

He swallowed. "It's not a big deal." He'd thought he'd have time to fix this before she found out.

"Not a big deal? Not a big deal?" Her voice rose with each word. "You used the money from the baby account, didn't you?" she hissed.

He nodded. He'd known she might be a little upset but hadn't counted on the venom he saw in her eyes. "Don't get so worked up. It was just sitting there, and I thought that would be the best way to keep it a surprise."

Tears rolled down her face. "I knew you didn't want to keep trying to have a baby. But I never thought you'd do something like this."

Luke paced in front of her. "We can replenish it." He reached out to brush a tear away, but she stepped back. "It's not a big deal."

"Quit saying that. It *is* a big deal. At least to me." She wiped her eyes and took another step backward. "You didn't even consider how this would make me feel, did you?"

"I thought I was doing something that would make you happy."

She shook her head. "You haven't made me happy in months. You tried to pretend that our baby never existed." Her tears started falling again, and this time she let them fall. "You wouldn't talk about it, wouldn't grieve with me." She sobbed in earnest now. "And I didn't have the energy to fight then. Not even when you emptied out the nursery and took all the baby stuff to the dump."

"I was trying to help."

She fished around in her purse for a tissue and wiped her face. "I'm done."

He sighed. "Do you want me to take you home instead of the office?"

Summer shook her head. "No. I'm done. Here." She pointed from her to him. "Us. I'm done."

Luke furrowed his brow. "I know you're mad, but don't

you think you're overreacting?"

She leveled a steely gaze at him. "Maybe. But I don't care right now. You like this boat so much? Then why don't you plan on staying on it for a while?" She turned and started walking toward the road.

Luke ran after her. "Summer, come on. Get in the truck."

"No. I'm too tired. Tired of pretending everything is okay. Tired of pretending like we aren't broken. I need some time alone."

Something in her voice stopped him in his tracks. "You want me to leave you here?"

She lifted her chin defiantly. "I'll call Ashley. She'll come pick me up."

He watched her walk toward the main road. There was no use in going after her.

If space was what she wanted, space was what she'd get.

Summer climbed into Ashley's Honda Accord. "Thanks for coming to pick me up."

Ashley looked at her with concern. "Are you okay?"

Summer shook her head. "No." She put her head in her hands. "Can you take me home?"

"Of course." Ashley turned the car toward downtown.

Summer tried to process everything, but her brain felt too foggy. "I'm sorry," she whispered. "I know I've been out of the office most of the day."

Ashley let out a sigh. "Don't you think you should focus on something besides work right now?" She slowed down for a red light. "Something has obviously happened, something bad." She looked at Summer. "Do you want to tell me what?"

Summer let out a shaky breath. She knew it seemed crazy to most people for her to be so focused on work, but that was what she'd clung to these past months. When everything else spun out of control, she could at least make sure her business ran smoothly. "Luke and I got into a fight. A big one." She filled Ashley in on what had transpired at the marina. "And the awful part is that he probably thinks it's about the money. It isn't." She shook her head. "He can buy all the boats he wants to buy. But that account was special."

"I knew things between you guys had been strained, but I didn't realize you were at the end of your rope like that." Ashley pulled into the driveway at Summer and Luke's house.

For the first time in a long time, Summer didn't admire the home she loved so much. Today it seemed more like a mockery than anything else. From the outside it looked like the kind of home a happy family inhabited. But inside it felt as lonely as a tomb. "I know he thinks I'm crazy for reacting like that." She shook her head. "I realize he was trying to give me a gift and do something nice for me."

Ashley nodded. "It sounds that way."

"But he's been so distant. First with Bobby's accident and then when I lost the baby." Ashley was one of the few people besides Gram who had known about Summer's pregnancy. "After I miscarried, he told me that he didn't want to keep trying. He said he didn't want to do the fertility treatments anymore. That maybe it would happen naturally, even though my doctor didn't think so." She shook her head. "So by using that money, money I'd set aside specifically for my child, it's the same as him saying that we will never have a baby of our own."

"And you're not ready to give up on that dream."

Summer shook her head. "We'd only done one round of treatments when I got pregnant. The doctor said there was no reason I couldn't carry a child to term, even after the miscarriage. But Luke wouldn't even discuss it."

Ashley sighed. "I don't know what to say. I had no idea what you'd been dealing with."

"Luke has slipped further and further away from me over the past months. It's to the point where I have no idea what to say to him most of the time. He doesn't listen to me, doesn't want to hear me talk about my day. And it seems like he finds reasons not to be home at night."

"But you love him."

Summer let out a bitter laugh. "Of course I love him." She met Ashley's eyes. "But for the first time, I wonder if love is enough."

Ashley didn't respond.

"Thanks for the ride. I'll walk Milo over to the office later and pick up my car."

"You're welcome. And if there's anything I can do for you, please let me know."

Summer paused. "Just pray. That's what I need the most."

She watched as Ashley backed out of the driveway and for a split second wished she could have her friend's life. It seemed so uncomplicated. No family around, no husband to argue with. That sounded perfect right about now.

She stumbled into the house and greeted Milo.

"Go outside, sweet boy." She opened the door and watched him run a loop around the yard, sniffing and marking his territory. In a minute, he was back. "Let's go to bed early, what do you say?"

Milo followed her up the stairs. With each step, her feet felt heavier and heavier, almost as if she'd accidentally stepped in wet cement. She made it into the large bathroom with its giant tub and expensive tile. She'd always thought of this as her sanctuary, but today it did nothing to calm her.

She sank onto the floor, and the tears began to fall in earnest.

Milo sat next to her and rested his head on her leg.

The gentleness of the big dog only made her cry harder.

"Lord, why are You letting this happen?" she asked. "What am I supposed to learn from this?" She didn't bother to wipe the tears. "I'm not the one who turned my back on You. Even when I lost my baby, I kept my faith." It had been Luke who'd lost his faith. Luke who'd refused to set foot in a church building after Bobby's accident. Luke who wouldn't pray with her after she lost their baby.

"Please. Please take my pain away," she whispered, hoping God was listening.

And there, huddled on the cold tile floor, Summer hoped she'd finally hit rock bottom. Because if things got worse, she wasn't sure how she would survive.

Chapter 15

Ashley walked into her house and promptly collapsed on the couch.

Work had kept her busy right up until nearly six. She'd taken care of several things that Summer had left behind. It seemed like the least she could do.

Although, the more Summer got distracted, the more Ashley felt entitled to a partnership in the business. Except that with the state Summer was in, it still didn't seem the right time to ask. But maybe there would never be a time that felt right. Maybe she would have to put aside her fears and go for it.

And as much as she hated to admit it, she took some satisfaction with the knowledge that if Summer turned her request down and she resigned, the business would take a hit. Summer didn't have time to find someone else who knew the ins and outs of their upcoming events, and despite all that was going on in her personal life, she would never let her business suffer.

Which gave Ashley leverage.

With that thought in mind, Ashley pulled on an old pair of yoga pants and a T-shirt from a long-ago 5K. She scrubbed the day's makeup from her face and twisted her long hair into a messy bun.

Tonight she would veg. Her DVR contained the entire last season of *The Bachelor*, and she had leftover pizza in the fridge. Perfect combo.

Ashley popped a couple of slices of pizza on a plate and

was about to put them in the microwave when the doorbell rang.

She groaned. Probably someone wanting to sell her something. Or a church group wanting to invite her to an upcoming revival. Not that either of those things was bad, but there were times she wished she lived in one of those big gated homes where no one could get to her door unless she wanted them there. Like a princess in a tower.

She peeked through the blinds and saw an unfamiliar pickup truck in her driveway. For the hundredth time, she wished she had a dog. It might give her a little security when there was a stranger at the door. Although she'd probably end up with a dog like Milo, who was more likely to lick someone than bark at them.

She pushed a wayward strand of hair behind her ear and gingerly opened the door.

Justin stood on the porch, holding a bag in one hand and a bouquet of flowers in the other.

You have got to be kidding me. "Justin." She forced a smile. "What brings you here?"

A sheepish expression washed over his boyish face. "I came to apologize."

She shook her head. "That isn't necessary. I appreciate you coming all the way out here though." Her North Charleston home was convenient to lots of shopping and dining, but getting here from downtown meant fighting traffic.

He hung his head. "I knew you'd probably say that, but I also knew that I'd always kick myself if I at least didn't try to explain my behavior."

She regarded him silently for a moment. "Go on," she said finally.

He gestured toward the old pickup. "That's my truck. It's my only vehicle. I've had it since I was in college. My daddy and I built it with parts we got from a scrap yard, but it runs just fine." He gave her a feeble grin. "It's not fancy, but I love it."

She opened her mouth to speak, but he cut her off. "And what I have on right now is the kind of thing I wear pretty much every day." He glanced down at his faded Gamecocks T-shirt and khaki shorts. "Unless I'm meeting a client, and even then I don't dress up much. I can't remember the last time I wore a tie, and I hated that suit I wore the other night." He met her gaze. "It was my brother's."

She smiled at his obvious sincerity. "Then what was that all about? The car, the suit. . .the attitude?"

He handed her the bouquet of flowers. "Can I come in and explain?" He held up a white bag. "I brought something to eat. Burgers from my favorite place."

She waved him inside. Even if she didn't plan to give him another chance, she could still hear him out. Besides, those burgers smelled yummy.

"This is a nice place. I didn't tell you that when I came to pick you up, but I thought it." He followed her into the kitchen and watched as she pulled two plates down from the cabinet.

"Thank you. It took a lot of years, but I was finally able to buy my own place." She'd been proud of the purchase. Living on a single income wasn't always easy. But she'd scrimped and saved after the divorce and finally had enough for a down payment. It might not be South of Broad like Summer and Luke's home, but it was perfect as far as she was concerned. Three bedrooms, two baths, and enough space in the backyard for a flower garden.

"I'm not quite there yet," he said. "I live in an apartment near downtown. It works for now, but I'm kind of at the point where I'm ready to have more room."

She held up bottled water and a soft drink from the fridge and looked at him with raised eyebrows.

"Water, please."

Ashley handed him a bottle and motioned for him to follow her back into the living room. "We can eat in there if that's okay." She paused. "If you're sure you don't mind something casual."

He chuckled. "That's more than okay with me. I'm just thankful you're giving me the chance to explain."

They settled on the couch, and he pulled out a burger from the bag and handed it to her. "I wasn't sure what you'd want—or even if you'd let me past the door—so both of them are the same. Mayo, lettuce, and tomato." He unwrapped his burger. "That's how I always get them."

"Sounds delicious." That was exactly how she liked her burgers, too, but she didn't see any reason to share that information.

Justin handed her a basket of fries. "Hope you like fries."

Ashley smiled broadly. "I'm a huge fan."

He cleared his throat. "Mind if I say a blessing before we eat?"

Wonders never cease. "Please."

He thanked God for their many blessings and asked Him to watch over them.

Ashley met Justin's gaze after he said Amen. "Thanks for praying."

"I know I probably gave you the wrong impression the

other night." He shook his head. "None of the stuff that came out of my mouth was stuff I'd ever say or think." He gave her a sideways grin. "Except the part where I said you looked nice."

"Well played." She returned his smile.

He chuckled. "I'm not playing. This isn't a game, I promise. I'm honestly sorry. It's just. . ." He trailed off and put his head in his hands.

Ashley might not have always been the best judge of character, but she knew in her gut that Justin was remorseful for the way he'd acted. "It's okay." She sighed. "But how about you tell me why you did it?" Nothing about his actions the other night added up.

He raised his head and met her gaze. "I'm the perpetual friend. The nice guy." He shrugged. "Since I was in high school, I've been the one women call when they need help or want a shoulder to cry on."

"That all sounds nice to me."

"Well, it's been a world of hurt for me. Because inevitably I'll get close to the girl, and then once her heart is all healed from whatever wound she carries, she moves on to another jerk."

Ashley gave him a tiny smile. "I've seen that kind of thing happen before. I've even been one of those girls actually."

"Yeah?"

She nodded. "And you know what? Those are always the guys I look back on and wish I'd have given a real shot." She'd learned a long time ago that playing "what if" only led to trouble. But there had certainly been some nice guys she'd let slip away, and sometimes she couldn't help but wonder how her life might be different if she'd made better choices.

"I guess I was tired of being that guy. My brother advised me to be someone else this time. So I did." He shook his head. "I could see the repulsion on your face at the restaurant when I was giving that poor girl a hard time. I almost came clean then but wasn't sure how you'd react."

"I admit, I was shocked. And Summer was so surprised when I told her what had happened. She'd told me that you were this wonderful, sweet, respectful guy."

"And then I acted the exact opposite."

She dipped a fry into ketchup. "Pretty much."

"I apologize. And I'd like it if you'd consider giving me another chance."

Ashley sat back on the couch and regarded him for a long moment. She felt certain he was telling the truth. But still, doubt lingered. "I appreciate you coming to explain things to me. Your little act the other night didn't do a lot to restore my faith in men." She met his curious gaze. "Because you're not the only one who has been hurt in the past."

Justin hadn't been sure dropping in unannounced was a good idea, but he felt certain it had been the only way to explain himself. And now, sitting on Ashley's couch, he knew he'd made the right choice. "I think a certain amount of past hurt is to be expected. Otherwise, you haven't really lived." He glanced over at her. "Right?"

She nibbled on her burger, lost in thought. "I guess." She gave him a slow smile.

"So what's your story then? What happened to diminish

your faith in men?"

Ashley cocked her head and gave him a sideways look.

He had the feeling she was still sizing him up, still deciding if he could be trusted. That was fine. He'd be happy to prove that he was one of the good guys, no matter how he'd acted on their date.

"I'm divorced. It's been a little over three years since it was final." She sighed. "No kids. Sometimes I see that as a blessing, because I know how difficult it is to watch your parents get divorced. And sometimes I see it as a curse, because I'm afraid that was my chance at being a mom and I didn't take it."

Justin couldn't help but think how beautiful she was right now. He was pretty sure this was more real than any date they could have gone on. There was something intimate about a conversation over burgers in her living room that was better than any loud, fancy restaurant could ever be. "I can't imagine dealing with a failed marriage. That must've been tough."

She nodded. "And my family sided with my ex, at least for the most part. That's what brought me here. I needed to start over and reinvent myself."

Her family sided with her ex? Justin hoped he hid his shock at that statement and resisted the desire to ask why they would do such a thing. Might be best to leave the topic for another time. "Well, Charleston is a great place to live, so you made a good choice. I grew up here and don't plan on ever leaving."

"Yeah. I've been happy here. I love what I do." She gestured around. "I found a home that suits me." She shrugged. "That's my story. Now how about you?"

Justin shook his head. "I told you most of it already. I guess

I have this habit of choosing women who have problems." He grinned. "Luke gives me a hard time about it." He glanced at her. "That's one of the things I liked about you. You seem to have it all together. Even Luke says what a help you are to Summer's business. That's not exactly what I'm used to." Even his own mama got on his case about the women he chose to date. Samantha had been the one who'd caused his family the most grief though. They'd been friends in college, even though they didn't have much in common. She'd always been fun to hang out with. And when they'd reconnected a couple of years ago, she'd been pregnant with Colton. She said she didn't know who the father was, and Justin could tell she was terrified at the thought of raising a child alone. She'd considered putting the baby up for adoption but had changed her mind at the last minute.

Justin would readily admit that the two of them were more friends than sweethearts, but he'd chosen to stick beside her as she adjusted to motherhood. She'd been totally overwhelmed. Then he'd fallen in love with the baby and had stayed a part of Samantha's life so he could have a relationship with Colton. These days Samantha had moved on, even had another child, but Justin had remained her friend.

He wondered how Ashley would react to his relationship with Colton. The guys gave him a hard time about being a pseudo daddy to the child. But he figured he was still on shaky ground with Ashley, so this was no time to bring it up.

"I haven't always had it together. But over the past couple of years, I've worked hard to simplify my life. I enjoy work, have a few close friends, and am involved with my church." She grinned. "I think I've finally found that ever-elusive balance."

Justin appreciated her outlook. "That's great. I think so many people search for that their whole lives. They put work in front of their family and in front of their spiritual life. And really, without those things, how do they enjoy their success?"

Ashley looked at him with surprise. "Exactly."

"So. . ." He trailed off with a grin. "Any chance you'd be able to put the other night behind us and consider going with me to a movie or something this weekend?"

"I'd love to. As long as you leave your race car driving skills at home."

"It's a deal."

Chapter 16

L uke sat on the boat and stared out at the water. He'd been expecting his phone to ring and to hear Summer's voice on the other end, asking him to come home.

But his phone had been silent all night. Not even a text.

He knew he'd done a lot of things wrong in his life. And the past year had been one of the toughest he'd ever endured. It ranked right up there with the year he was ten and his mama died.

Grief did funny things to a person. Luke learned that lesson more than twenty years ago. After Mama died, his dad had turned to the bottle, and it had almost been as if he'd died, too. Rose had started staying at their aunt's house most of the time, and Luke and Bobby had been left to fend for themselves. *"I've always got your back, little brother."* How many times had he said that to Bobby? He'd covered for his brother through the years, taking the blame for everything from breaking a lamp to forgetting to mow the yard. He'd protected Bobby from as much pain as he could.

But he hadn't been able to protect him from the semi whose driver had fallen asleep at the wheel and drifted into the wrong lane.

People kept saying the pain would go away in time.

Luke felt certain those people had never experienced sudden loss, never received that phone call that blares out in the middle of the night, and before you even answer it, you know bad news is on the line.

Mama's death had been expected. Still hard. Still

life-changing. But expected. She'd fought her cancer like a warrior, but in the end she'd been too tired to fight anymore. Knowing she was finally at peace gave him some comfort, though he was only a child.

But Bobby's accident had blindsided him like a bullet from a sniper's gun. There'd been no preparation. No last good-byes or final words. His brother was there one day and gone the next. Luke had called Bobby's phone out of habit many times over the past few months. As soon as it would ring, he'd remember. Bobby would never answer his calls again.

Luke had been tough his whole life. But putting his brother in the ground had been the hardest thing he'd ever done.

The cell phone rang beside him, and the light from the screen lit up the darkness.

"Hello," he said, not even bothering to check who was on the other end. He was ready to go home to his wife.

"Luke," Rose said. "I can't believe I actually connected with you. I've been trying for weeks. Don't you ever check your voice mails?"

He sighed. "Sorry. Things have been a little crazy. How are Dave and the kids?"

"They're great. Of course, you would know that if you ever came for a visit. Katie Beth asks me all the time why her uncle Luke doesn't come see her anymore."

He had all but lost contact with his sister and her family after Bobby's accident. It made him too sad to be around them. "Sorry." He sighed.

"Well, I need you to come out to the house soon." Rose's voice sounded identical to Mama's. She'd even acquired that tone that told him there was no declining her request.

"I'm not sure when I can make it out there."

"Find the time. You know we've moved into the house. Not that you offered to help us, but we finally got all moved in. And I've got to get rid of some of the stuff that's here. I don't think Daddy ever threw anything away."

"Why do you want me to come out there?" Luke asked. He'd avoided his childhood home for years.

"Bobby's stuff is here. If you want anything of his, you need to come look through it."

"Can't you just store it somewhere?"

"I've been storing it," Rose said sharply. "It's been almost a year. I've got to do something with it." She let out a loud sigh. "It's been hard on all of us, Luke. But we've got to deal with his belongings."

"I can pay for a storage building."

"You don't get to throw money at this and make it go away," Rose said quietly. "Come out here and look through it. Besides, there's still a ton of your old things here anyway. I don't want to toss it all without you at least seeing it."

He knew it was time to man up. "Okay. I'll come out Saturday if that's okay."

"Perfect. I'll cook lunch, and you can stay for a visit. I hope Summer can come, too."

Luke let out a breath. "She's probably busy, but thanks." His sister would hit the roof if she thought there was trouble between him and Summer. She'd often told him over the years that Summer was the best thing that had ever happened to him.

And she was right.

"See you Saturday. The kids will be thrilled."

They said their good-byes and hung up. He looked at the clock on his phone. It was after ten. If Summer had planned to call him, she would've done it by now.

Guess it was time to see if the living quarters in the boat were as nice as the salesman had promised.

Summer peeled herself off the tile floor and looked at the clock. She couldn't believe she'd slept there most of the night.

"Come on, boy," she said to Milo.

The big dog opened one eye and rolled over.

Summer went into the bedroom where she'd dropped her purse and phone yesterday. She picked up her phone. No missed calls.

She sank onto the bed, wide awake. Even though she'd never been angrier at Luke, she couldn't help but worry about him. Had he slept on the boat? Checked into a hotel?

She considered calling Justin to see if he'd stayed there but thought better of it. There was no reason to involve anyone else in their problems. She already regretted telling Ashley what had happened yesterday.

She'd always been a private person and had never liked people to know when she had problems. Even in high school when she'd struggled with math, she'd hired a tutor from a different school so none of her friends would ever know.

Today she felt better though. More at peace. She'd woken up a couple of times and each time had prayed that God would see her through. Today's peace was undoubtedly a result of those prayers. She still had a lot to deal with and knew that she and Luke had problems to face—but she didn't feel alone anymore.

She got up and quickly got ready for work. She and Milo would walk to the office, hopefully before Luke came to the house. She knew he'd have to come home to get a uniform. And she didn't plan on being there when he did.

An hour later, she and Milo walked through the deserted downtown streets. She'd forgotten how peaceful it could be. At this hour, the tourists were still sleeping, tucked away in their historic bed and breakfasts. The residents were just beginning to wake.

And she and Milo had the city all to themselves.

Chapter 17

"Y ou sure do yawn a lot," a little boy said, peering at Luke from his spot next to a cannon.

Luke gave him a smile. He'd just delivered what might be the worst ranger talk in park service history. It was a good thing none of his coworkers had listened to him stumble through. "I didn't get much sleep last night."

The child looked at him with wide eyes. "My bedtime is eight. Maybe your bedtime should be eight, too."

Luke chuckled despite himself. "I'll keep that in mind."

"Sorry," the boy's mother said, walking over and putting an arm around her son. "Tommy has never met a stranger."

"Not a problem." Luke smiled at the boy again. "Hope you enjoy the rest of your tour." He watched them walk off, hand in hand. Kids sure kept you on your toes. A pang of sadness hit him hard. Not a day went by that he didn't think of the child he and Summer had lost.

He reached into his wallet and pulled out a tattered black and white ultrasound picture. The edges had become frayed, but the picture was clear. That tiny speck of life frozen in time on the page had once given him such happiness. He couldn't count the times he'd stared at the photo, wishing things had turned out differently. When Summer miscarried, they'd been close to finding out if it was a boy or a girl. Luke would've been happy with either but had secretly longed for a son of his own.

"Everything okay?" Walter Young asked.

Luke jumped at the sound of his boss's voice. "Yes sir."

He hurriedly stuffed the photo back in his wallet, but not before Mr. Young had seen it.

The older man peered at him. "Are congratulations in order?" he asked. "The idea of becoming a father for the first time is certainly enough to distract a man."

Luke frowned. "No sir. Summer's not. . .she's not pregnant anymore."

His boss clasped him on the back. "I'm sorry to hear of your loss." He motioned toward the museum. "Listen, if you need to take some time off, say the word."

Mr. Young's obvious concern touched him. "Thanks. I don't need time off, at least not right now." Would time off give him the chance to fix his crumbling life? Probably not. "But thank you."

Mr. Young nodded. "We like you here, Luke. You do a good job. The visitors enjoy your programs." He furrowed his brow. "But I've noticed that these past weeks you've been struggling." He gestured toward the wallet in Luke's hand. "And I think this is probably why."

Luke didn't say anything. He'd thought his emotions were pretty well in check. But maybe not well enough. Embarrassment washed over him. He hated the thought of his coworkers thinking he wasn't doing a good job. "I'm sorry, sir."

Mr. Young drew his brows together. "Don't be sorry, son. Dealing with real-life stuff happens. We don't expect you to be a robot." He smiled. "Actually, now that I know what's going on, I feel better about the opportunity that's about to come your way."

"What's that?"

"Well, it's clear that you have a talent dealing with the

school groups who come through here. I'd like for you to consider tacking that onto your job responsibilities permanently. I know it's something we normally share between rangers, but I think we might be better suited if you take sole responsibility." Mr. Young peered at him over round glasses. "And there'd be a pay grade increase to go with it."

Luke couldn't hide his surprise. "Really?"

Mr. Young chuckled. "Think about it for a few days and let me know. You may not want more responsibility." He glanced at his watch. "Nearly quitting time. I'll let you get back to work."

Luke nodded. He'd never been readier for the day to be over. Summer may have been able to avoid him this morning by leaving early, but she would have to face him tonight.

Two hours later, he pulled into the driveway. It looked like she wasn't home yet. That was fine. He could wait.

He went upstairs and pulled a duffel bag from the closet. He threw in a few changes of clothing and some toiletries. He opened the linen closet and grabbed a couple of towels and the extra-soft blanket someone had given them as a wedding gift years ago.

That should just about do it. Luke zipped the bag and grabbed the pillow from his side of the bed. He cast one last look around their bedroom and headed downstairs. As he reached the bottom step, the front door swung open.

Milo bounded inside and jumped onto the couch.

Luke set down his bags and steeled himself for what he knew would come next.

The workday had been a struggle for Summer. She'd wanted to call Luke so many times but had decided against it. She was still angry, but she felt like she owed him an apology for telling him to stay on the boat last night. And that apology needed to be made in person. They weren't the kind of couple who gave up when things got tough.

She knew he was probably furious with her, but seeing his truck in the driveway had been a huge relief. She followed Milo inside the house, trying to figure out what her first words should be.

Luke stood in the entryway at the bottom of the stairs.

As soon as she saw him, her eyes filled with tears. "Luke." She dropped her purse and planner inside the door and walked toward him.

Then she saw his duffel bag and pillow sitting next to his guitar case.

She stopped in her tracks. "What's that?" she whispered, already knowing the answer.

Luke sighed. "I can't very well stay on the boat without some of my things. I don't want to have to drive over here every morning before work."

She locked eyes with him. "You don't have to do that. I don't expect you to stay there."

He raked his hands through his hair. The dark circles under his eyes told the tale of a sleepless night. "Let's talk." He motioned toward the living room.

She felt her heart drop to her stomach. This couldn't be happening. This wasn't what she meant to happen. "Okay," she whispered. She perched gingerly on the couch next to a sprawled out Milo.

Luke sat down next to her but didn't touch her. "I didn't sleep last night. Not a wink. I've had a lot of time to think."

She nodded but didn't say anything. She was afraid if she said a word, she might burst into tears.

"You were right to leave me there yesterday." He gave her a sideways look. "I don't understand how it's come to this. But I know that I don't want to be this guy. I don't want to hurt you any more than I already have."

She focused on her breathing. "What are you saying, exactly?"

"I hear the things that come out of my mouth." He shook his head in disgust. "That's not who I am. Or at least, who I want to be."

Summer let out a hot breath. "Luke. Just spit it out, okay? What's going on?"

"I need some time to get myself together. I'm not the guy you married. You didn't sign up for this." He shrugged. "Me not realizing how upset you'd get about that money was the icing on the cake. I've felt for a long time like we were headed down the wrong path. And it hit me last night. You've been walking on eggshells around me. Haven't you?" He peered at her, his brown eyes serious.

"Yeah, maybe. I mean, I know how tough things have been for you. I shouldn't expect you to bounce right back from two awful tragedies."

Luke shook his head. "I'm so sorry. Really. But I can't do this to you anymore. I remember what it was like to live in a house where you had to walk on eggshells. I don't want that to be your life. So I think it would be best if I stayed on the boat for a little while." He refused to meet her eyes.

She sat in shock. She hadn't anticipated this ever happening to her. "So that's it? You're just walking out?"

He furrowed his brow. "You told me to stay on the boat. You told me you needed some space."

"Yeah, for a few hours. I didn't think you'd—I didn't think you'd. . ." She looked at him in horror. "So you're done? Is that what you're saying?"

"No." He leaned back and rested his palms on his forehead for a second, then sat up and faced her. "I'm saying I think you were right. We do need some space. I need to get it together. You don't deserve what I've been putting you through."

"What about counseling? The church has a counselor on staff. I could make an appointment."

He glared at her. "I don't want counseling from someone at your church. I want time to work things out on my own." He stood.

She stayed frozen to the spot. Her mouth felt dry, like cotton. She put a hand to her forehead. Did she have a fever?

"Summer?"

She looked up at her husband. Her husband who was moving out.

"Okay," she whispered. "Will I see you ever?"

"Yeah. I want to take care of the yard. And see Milo." He shrugged. "If you're here, I'd like to see you, too. But if you'd rather me come when you're gone, that's fine."

She nodded.

Luke bent down and nuzzled Milo. He was rewarded with a lick on the face. "Bye, boy." He locked eyes with Summer. "Maybe I can take him sometime? The boat's not that big, but it would be nice to have him as company."

"You're not taking him on the boat. He belongs here."

Luke held his hands up in defeat. "Sorry. Just asking." He slung his bag over his shoulder and picked up his guitar. "Take care."

She watched her husband walk out the door without a backward glance.

Chapter 18

Ashley put the finishing touches on an itinerary for an upcoming wedding at the Mills House Hotel. From what she could tell, this one would be spectacular. She loved working with brides who had similar taste as her. It always made it a little more fun.

Summer came through the door, a stoic expression on her face.

"Mornin'," Ashley said. "I just made a fresh pot of coffee."

Summer gave her a tiny smile. "Thank you."

"Everything okay?" Ashley asked. Ever since the day she'd picked Summer up from the marina, she'd been worried about the couple. She hoped their fight had been resolved.

Summer poured herself a cup of coffee and sat in the ornate chair in front of Ashley's desk. "Since we work together, I may as well tell you. Luke and I have separated."

Ashley set her coffee cup down and walked over to Summer. She knelt down next to the chair. "I'm so sorry. Is there anything I can do?"

Summer closed her eyes. "There's nothing anyone can do. This is all my fault." She looked up, her eyes brimming with tears. "I practically pushed him out."

Ashley sat in the chair next to Summer's. "There is no point in assigning blame. Just focus on what you can do to fix things."

She listened as Summer filled her in on all that had transpired.

"And he wanted to take Milo. Like share him." Summer

wiped a tear away. "He won't even consider counseling. Says he wants to work things out on his own." She shook her head. "How does he think he can fix this on his own?"

Ashley frowned. "How are you dealing with it?"

Summer shrugged. "That's the thing. I'm not angry. I'm mainly numb. I don't feel anything." She took a sip of coffee. "It's kind of weird, actually. Last night after he left, I watched TV. Like nothing had happened. I ordered a pizza and took a bath."

Ashley narrowed her eyes. That didn't sound like Summer at all. "Really?"

Summer rose from the chair and walked over to her desk. "What was I supposed to do? It's not like there's a book called *How to Act When Your Husband Leaves* or something." She flashed a feeble smile. "So I'm going to do the best I can and trust that this will all work out somehow."

Ashley remembered saying the same thing back before she and Brian split up. Although, in some ways it had worked out. She was much better off without him. But she hoped and prayed Summer and Luke could work it out. "I'm sure it will."

Summer sat down at her desk. "It has to."

Justin paced the length of the sidewalk in front of his apartment. They were going to be late for the show if Luke didn't hurry up. He knew he should've driven separately. Although without a lead singer, it's not like the band could do much. Jimmy was pretty good at backup vocals, but he wasn't a front man.

Luke's truck finally pulled into the parking lot.

Justin jogged over and hopped inside. "We're going to be pushing it to make it on time."

"I know. Sorry." Luke pulled onto the road and headed toward Folly Beach. He flipped up the volume on the radio.

Justin glanced over at him from the corner of his eye. He'd hoped to fill Luke in on his upcoming date with Ashley. But the strain on Luke's face was evident.

"Any change to the set list?" he finally asked after several minutes of silence.

Luke shook his head. "Nope. I figure we should stick with what we know, especially since we didn't practice this week." He'd called and canceled their midweek practice, saying that something had come up.

"Sounds good."

Luke pulled into the parking lot and killed the engine. "Right on time." He jerked his head toward the restaurant. "Let's go."

Justin followed his friend up the stairs that led to the Sand and Suds. Something was off. He wasn't sure what had happened, but Luke wasn't acting like himself.

Jimmy and Will were already there, getting things set up.

"Thanks for showing up, guys," Jimmy said. "I was starting to think I was gonna hafta put on my Garth hat and put on a show."

Justin chuckled.

"Sherry wanted us to find out if your wife was happy with her artwork," Will said to Luke. "She said it was the prettiest palm tree she'd ever painted."

Luke nodded. "Yeah. She loved it."

"I forgot about the boat. So you've already given Summer

the present? I didn't think your anniversary was until later in the summer."

Luke scowled but didn't say anything.

"Man, I don't blame him for giving it to her early," Jimmy said. "It's a sweet boat. This way they can start enjoying it now."

The night passed in a blur for Justin. Even though he still wasn't completely comfortable on stage, he'd at least gotten to the point where he enjoyed himself. They sounded pretty good tonight, too. At least for the most part.

"Thanks guys," the restaurant manager said after they were through with their final set. "The crowd loves your music."

Jimmy and Will loaded their equipment into Jimmy's SUV.

"We're having a cookout on Monday for Memorial Day if y'all are interested," Jimmy said. "I have a new grill, and the pool is ready." He nodded at Luke. "And Martha told me to make sure you told Summer not to worry about bringing anything."

"Thanks," Luke said. "But I don't think we can make it. Maybe another time."

Jimmy glanced at Justin. "How about you? You already have plans?"

Justin hoped to have plans with Ashley, depending on how tomorrow night's movie went. "My family is cooking out, so I'll probably head over there."

"You might be the two biggest party poopers in the state of South Carolina," Jimmy said. "But that's okay. Every party has to have one." He chuckled and climbed into the vehicle.

Justin followed Luke over to his truck. "So what do you

and Summer have planned for the long weekend?" he asked. "Are y'all going to take the new boat out?"

Luke sighed. "No. At least not together." He climbed into the cab of the truck and started the engine.

Justin followed suit. "Does she have a wedding?"

"No. But we're kind of going through a rough patch right now."

"Oh." Justin glanced over at Luke's profile. He'd figured something must be wrong. "That why you forgot the words to three songs tonight, including one that you wrote yourself?"

"Yeah. My heart wasn't in it tonight." Luke let out a sigh.

Justin hated to see his friend hurting but had no idea how to help. "Y'all have been through a lot. You think maybe a weekend away or something would help?"

"I think we're past that." Luke gripped the steering wheel. "I moved out. I'm staying on the boat for a little while."

Justin let out a breath. He'd had no idea things might be that rocky. "Sorry, man." He shook his head. "Listen, if you need to sleep on my couch for a few days, you're welcome to it."

"Thanks. But the time alone is giving me some time to work through things. Summer shouldn't have to put up with my moods. I don't want to put her through more than I already have."

"I'll be praying that it all works out."

Luke's jaw tightened, but he didn't say anything.

Chapter 19

After a few nights of sleeping on the boat, Luke's entire body felt like one big knot. He'd been sure some time apart from Summer was the right thing, but it seemed like it might be at the expense of his health. He rubbed a kink out of his neck and climbed into the truck.

If he didn't show up today, Rose would send out a search party. He didn't know why she was so insistent that he look through Bobby's stuff.

He headed toward North Charleston and couldn't stop his thoughts from turning to Summer. They'd been a permanent, daily fixture in each others' lives for so many years, it seemed like part of him was actually missing. Like his arm was gone. He reached for his cell phone but drew his hand back. What would he say? It wasn't as if he'd thought about anything else. Talking to her would probably only bring him down more. There was a time when they'd had a routine on Saturday mornings. If Summer didn't have a wedding, the two of them would sleep in and then laze around in their pajamas until noon. They'd talk and laugh and argue over whose turn it was to choose that night's restaurant. And then Milo would jump right in between them until they'd finally get up and take him for a walk down to the Battery.

Luke sighed. Those were some great times. But they hadn't had one of those Saturdays in months.

He slowed the truck as he neared the neighborhood where he'd grown up. A few of the houses were more rundown than he remembered, but for the most part the place looked the same. He drove past a group of kids playing in a sprinkler in their front yard, a little boy on a bike on the sidewalk, and an old man out mowing his yard. It was nice to know the area hadn't gone downhill.

Luke pulled into the driveway and found himself flooded with memories. Mama had taught him to roller-skate right there on the pavement. He couldn't have been more than four, but still he could clearly remember holding her hand and sliding his feet back and forth in his skates.

"Uncle Luke," Katie Beth called from the doorsteps. She ran out to his truck, and he scooped her up into his arms.

"I can't believe you're all grown up," he said, groaning like she was too heavy to lift.

She giggled. "I'm five now. That's not a grown-up, silly."

Luke set her on her feet, and she took his hand.

"Come on. Dale is probably up from his nap now."

Luke let his niece lead him into his childhood home.

Rose met them at the door. "Hey, Bubba." She leaned in and kissed him on the cheek. "How are you?"

He glanced around the living room. Not much had changed. The same pictures still lined the walls that were covered with the same flower-printed wallpaper. Daddy hadn't changed anything in the years he'd lived in the house alone. "I'm okay."

She cocked her head and locked eyes with him. "No, you're not. But you can tell me what's wrong later on." She motioned toward Katie Beth. "Sweetie, why don't you go see if Dale is up?"

Katie Beth nodded and ran toward her brother's room.

"Dale's in your old room," she said. "We've barely moved in, so your old stuff is still in there all over the walls."

He wrinkled his forehead. "Still? I figured Daddy would've cleaned that out a long time ago." When he left home after high school, he hadn't taken much with him. Just the clothes he could fit into his old duffel bag.

Rose grinned. "It's all there. From your honor society certificate to your Bon Jovi poster."

Katie Beth and Dale ran into the room giggling.

"Hey, little man." Luke knelt down to see his nephew face-to-face. The child was the spitting image of Bobby at that age. He held out his hand for a high five, and Dale slapped it.

"Kids, do y'all want to watch Dora?" she asked. "I need to talk to your uncle Luke."

Katie Beth nodded and grabbed her little brother's hand. "Come on, let's go." They went into the den where the TV had always been.

"They're growing up so fast," Luke said.

Rose nodded. "I know." She motioned toward the kitchen. "You want some coffee or something?"

He wrinkled his nose. Coffee had never been his morning beverage of choice. He started his day out with a tall glass of milk. Summer used to always tell him how cute it was. "Do you have any milk?"

She chuckled. "Of course. I could put that in a sippy cup for you if you'd like."

He laughed. "A regular glass will be fine. I promise not to spill." He followed her into the kitchen and propped on a stool while she poured milk for him and coffee for her.

They settled at the old kitchen table that had been in the same spot since Luke could remember. He traced his fingers over the yellow Formica top. The corner of the table was cracked and peeling, just as it had been when Luke sat at the table as a boy.

Rose met his eyes over her coffee cup. She looked so much like Mama. Quick math told him she was about the same age Mama had been when she'd been taken from them.

"Dave had to work today but said to tell you hello," she said finally. "He said y'all need to go fishing sometime soon."

Luke nodded. He'd always liked Dave. He and Rose had been sweethearts practically since they were in elementary school. "Tell him hi."

"I'm glad you came out here today. I sort of expected you to bail at the last minute." She sighed. "I didn't want to be solely responsible for getting rid of Bobby's stuff."

His jaw tensed. "I'll look through it, but I have no idea what I would want that was his."

She shrugged. "There are lots of T-shirts, books, CDs. . . you know, stuff like that."

"Yeah, okay. I'll go through it. And then what? You're giving it away?" Luke hated the thought of Bobby's stuff loaded into bags and tossed in the Goodwill bin.

Rose sighed. "We don't have the room for it here. Daddy's and Mama's stuff is here, too. And there are four of us. We need all the space we can get."

Luke finished his milk and set the glass on the table. "I don't understand why you'd want to live here anyway."

"Things were tight in the apartment. This house has been a huge blessing to us." She frowned. "I know you have bad memories of the place, but this is a great neighborhood for the kids to grow up in."

"I guess."

She raised an eyebrow. "Besides. The nursing home isn't

far from here. Just down the street. Something you would know if you ever bothered to visit."

He sighed. He should've known she'd shame him about that. Their daddy had been in the nursing home since Bobby's accident.

And Luke hadn't stepped a foot in the door to check on him.

Summer pulled her dark hair into a ponytail and leaned closer to the mirror. Her eyes still looked puffy. She'd never been a pretty crier, never been one of those girls who cried dainty tears and then looked perfect. Her face turned red, her eyes swelled, and her nose ran for hours. Super attractive.

"Come on, Milo." She headed downstairs, the big dog padding along behind her. "Let's go for a good long walk."

Milo shook with excitement as she clipped the leash onto his collar.

They set out down the street, Milo pausing to sniff every few steps.

She loved the way things slowed down on Saturdays. Even the breeze coming from the water seemed to waft by slower, as if it knew it was the weekend. She and Milo walked down Legare Street and headed toward the Battery. The park there allowed dogs off leash. She wasn't sure if she wanted to try to handle Milo alone, but she might give it a try if there weren't too many other dogs around. Luke always let Milo off leash with no problem, but it made her a little nervous.

"Summer?" a voice called from the other side of the street.

She flipped her sunglasses to the top of her head and

glanced over to see Jefferson waving.

He jogged over to where she and Milo stood. "Hey there, Sunshine."

His old nickname for her might've been cute when they were sixteen, but now it seemed silly. "Please don't call me that." She watched as Milo sniffed around the gate where they stood. "What are you doing over here anyway?"

Jefferson's eyes twinkled. "Just moved in." He pointed to a home across the street. "I'm actually renting a carriage house right now. I don't want to buy until I've had time to look around." He shrugged. "And I haven't decided if I want to be here or somewhere like James Island."

She nodded. "I don't blame you for wanting to look around. Plus you've been away for so long, it's probably best to kind of get your bearings before you put down roots."

"You and I always have thought alike." He walked closer to Milo. "And who is this handsome fellow?"

"Milo. Luke and I rescued him off the highway when he was a puppy."

"I'd love to get a dog, but right now isn't the time." He absently scratched Milo on top of the head. "So where are you headed?"

"The Battery." She suddenly remembered her puffy eyes and put her sunglasses back on.

Jefferson shook his head. "Too late. I already saw those red eyes. And I'm pretty sure it's not an allergy." He raised his eyebrows but didn't question her tears. "Come on. Let me walk with you to the Battery. I haven't been down there since I got back."

They walked toward the park, Summer feeling more unsure with each step. The last thing she needed right now was an old friend who could get her to let her guard down. Because no one could know that Luke had moved out. Word would spread like kudzu. "I'll bet your mama is glad to have you back in town."

"Sure is. We're already gearing up for the annual Boudreaux family beach vacation. We still go to Kiawah Island every year." He glanced over at her. "But you probably remember. I think you came with us a couple of times."

"I know I went the year you'd gotten your driver's license. Because my parents were so worried about me riding in your convertible."

He chuckled. "I remember. I drove over to pick you up, and I thought your daddy was going to have a fit. But that was a fun trip."

She'd forgotten about those lazy beach days. She didn't make it to the beach much anymore. She and Luke went every now and then, but they'd been so busy last summer. At the thought of Luke, she grew somber.

"You okay?" Jefferson asked as they walked into the park.

Her eyes landed on the bandstand where she and Luke used to meet. "Yeah, fine." She pulled a dummy out of her pocket. "Look what I have, Milo."

The dog let out an excited bark and sat so she could take his leash off.

"Now, you'd better mind me." She unclipped the leash and tossed the dummy.

Milo bounded after it and scooped it up.

"Bring it here," she called. She glanced at Jefferson. "I don't usually let him off leash. That's Luke's department. But Milo needs some exercise."

"He definitely shops in the husky dog department."

Milo ran toward where she and Jefferson stood but veered off course. He dropped the dummy and charged full speed after a squirrel.

"Milo, no!" Summer ran after the big, brown dog. A busy street surrounded the park, and she wasn't sure if he'd stop before he got to the road. "Milo!"

The squirrel darted around the bandstand and past a trash can then crossed South Bay Street.

Milo followed behind.

"Milo, stop right now," she called as she ran.

The dog ran into the road, oblivious to traffic.

Summer's heart pounded. She gasped for breath and said a silent prayer for the dog's safety.

An SUV screeched to a stop, nearly hitting Milo.

She waved at the driver and reached the sidewalk where a startled Milo now sat. She sank to her knees and buried her face in the dog's fur. Her quiet sobs racked her body.

"He's fine now," Jefferson said, putting a hand on her shoulder.

She stroked Milo's coat, trying to stop her tears from falling.

Jefferson knelt down next to them. "Hey," he said in a low voice. "Do you want me to call Luke to come pick you up?"

Summer shook her head and wiped her eyes. "No," she whispered. "Luke's not at home."

Jefferson furrowed his brow. "Is he working?"

"No. I don't know. It doesn't matter." She searched her pocket for a tissue and came up empty-handed.

Jefferson held out a handkerchief. "Take this."

She managed a smile. Jefferson might be the only guy she knew who actually carried handkerchiefs. "Thanks."

"Now fix your face and tell me what's wrong." He took the leash from her hand and clipped it onto Milo's collar. "Come on, boy."

They walked toward Legare Street, the silence punctuated by Summer's sniffles.

"Well?" Jefferson said finally. "Spit it out. I may not have seen you in fifteen years, but I still know you well enough to know when something is wrong."

"It's nothing I want to talk about." As soon as she said the words, she realized they weren't true.

"Is it your business? Is it in trouble?"

She shook her head. "Nothing like that. Business is booming." If only her problem were business related. It would be much easier to rebuild a business than a marriage.

"Then what? Luke?" Jefferson peered at her closely.

She fought to keep her face neutral. "It's nothing."

"Sunshine, I know when you're lying." Jefferson directed Milo around a tree. "Your secret is safe with me."

"Whatever. You'll tell Mitch, and he is the mouth of the South. My parents will be at my front door before I can even blink."

"That's not true. If you want to unload on me, I'll keep it to myself. Promise."

Her eyes filled with tears. She was becoming one of those weepy girls she'd always hated. "There's a lot to the story, and it's very complicated. I don't want to get into it right now. But Luke and I have some things to work through. He's staying on our boat for a few days."

Jefferson drew his brows together. "I'm sorry." He raked his fingers through his hair. "I mean that. I am sorry that you're going through any pain."

"Thanks. I think it's been hard for him to bounce back after Bobby's accident." She didn't mention the miscarriage. But she knew in her heart that it had been both things together that had been too much for Luke to handle.

"That's tough." Jefferson shook his head. "I'm sure he'll get things worked out though." He glanced at her. "And I know he doesn't mean for you to be hurt in the process."

She widened her eyes. She'd expected Jefferson to rip Luke apart, not defend him. "Yeah. I know you're right. I just hate this unsteady feeling."

They stopped in front of her house.

"Thanks for your help." Summer reached over and took Milo's leash from Jefferson. "And for your handkerchief."

He chuckled. "You're welcome. And you can hang on to that handkerchief."

She managed a tiny smile. "What, you don't want it back?"

"Consider it my gift to you." Jefferson grinned. "I hope things get better soon. And I'd be glad to lend an ear if you need to talk."

"Thanks." Summer and Milo went through the gate that led to the house. She waved to Jefferson over her shoulder and went inside.

Jefferson might not be her first choice for advice, but at least he seemed to think things for her and Luke would be back to normal soon. And that was oddly comforting.

Chapter 20

The ringing phone blasted Justin out of a very sound sleep. "Hello," he mumbled.

"I need your help," Samantha said, her voice barely audible. "I think I'm getting strep throat, and the baby has the stomach virus. Mom's coming to get Allison, but she can't handle her and Colton both."

"You need me to come get him?"

"Please. Can he stay with you for a few days? I don't want him to catch this."

Justin sat up. "Sure. Of course." He held the phone back to see what time it was. Not even ten. After the late night, he hadn't bothered to set an alarm. "I'll have to run over to my parents' and switch cars with my mom." He felt safer putting Colton's car seat in Mom's Taurus than in his old pickup. "I'll be there in an hour."

He clicked off the phone and hopped out of bed. He didn't have groceries suitable for Colton. He'd have to swing by the store and pick up some stuff. Colton had spent the night before, but never multiple nights.

Thirty minutes later, he had showered and called his mom to tell her about Samantha. He headed toward his parents' house to switch cars. Just as he flipped on his blinker to turn into their subdivision, an awful thought hit him.

Tonight he was supposed to have his first official date with Ashley.

After the way he acted last week, he was afraid canceling would be the death of any potential relationship. But he hadn't told her how involved he was in Colton's life.

He pulled into his parents' driveway and turned off the engine.

Mom met him at the door with her keys in her hands. "Hey, hon." She gave him a kiss on the cheek. "Does this mean we'll have a little one at the cookout on Monday?" she asked.

Justin nodded. "Probably. Hope that's okay."

"Of course. I might have your dad pick up one of those little pools for Colton to play in."

His parents were past ready to become grandparents. But Justin's brother and sister-in-law were focused on their careers right now, and he hadn't met the right girl yet. "That sounds great. I know he'd love it."

"I guess this means you'll get to bring him with you to church," Mom said.

He nodded. "Yeah. I'm excited about that. I've thought about seeing if she'd mind if I pick him up every Sunday, but I'm afraid of overstepping my boundaries."

Mom put an arm around him. "You have to do what you think is best. It seems to me that she'd probably be happy for you to take him off of her hands."

"Maybe." He was never sure. Sometimes he honestly thought Samantha would give Colton to him if he asked. But the child needed a mother, even one who wasn't totally involved in his life. Right?

"Either way, we'll be happy to see the two of you tomorrow at church and at the cookout on Monday. I'm proud of you, son. Colton isn't your responsibility, yet you step up and care for him when he needs you. Not a lot of guys your age would do that."

He blushed. Her kind words made him feel awful considering what he was about to ask. "Thanks. I'd do anything for the little guy. He needs a man in his life." He raked his fingers through his hair. "But is there any way you and Dad could keep him for a few hours tonight? I already had plans, and hate to cancel."

Mom raised her eyebrows. "Your dad and I already have plans to have dinner with a couple from church. Why? Do you have a date?" Her voice rose at least an octave as she asked the question.

He groaned. His mother worried nonstop about his love life. "Yes. I do. A date that I've already gotten off on the wrong foot with. I'm pretty sure canceling because I have to babysit an old girlfriend's son isn't going to win me any points."

"Is she a nice girl?" His mom sounded so hopeful.

He chuckled. "Yes. Very nice." Ashley was the kind of woman he'd always hoped to find. But he'd hoped to get to know her better before springing his relationship with Colton on her.

"Well, then she should understand." His mom smiled and held out her keys. "Now go pick that sweet boy up before he gets sick."

He kissed his mom and got into the older model white Taurus. He pulled his cell phone out of his pocket. May as well get this over with. He scrolled to Ashley's name and hit the button to call her before he lost his nerve. He hit the SPEAKER button as he backed out of the driveway.

"Hello," Ashley said on the other end.

"Hey, Ashley, it's Justin." He took a deep breath. Would this end things for good? Only one way to find out.

"I've got some bad news." He forced the words out. He'd

disappointed her with the way he'd acted last week. And now he was disappointing her by canceling.

Justin felt certain he would never regain her trust after this.

Ashley furrowed her brow. "What's wrong?" She set down her coffee cup and waited for the bomb to drop. Getting a "bad news" call from a guy on date night never ended well.

"I'm not going to be able to make it tonight," Justin said. "Something's come up."

Ashley waited for him to explain, but he didn't. "What do you mean? Do you guys have a show tonight or something?"

"No, nothing like that. It's a favor I have to do for someone."

She could hear noise in the background. He must be in the truck. "A favor?" She knew she sounded like a parrot. But what was the deal with this guy? First he acted like a jerk. Then he apologized and she totally bought his explanation. And now he was canceling because of some kind of vague favor? Something didn't feel right about this.

"I'm so sorry. I hope you'll let me make it up to you. Maybe one night next week?"

She furrowed her brow. "Next week? I'm free tomorrow night after church. And off work on Monday for the holiday." She hated this position. If she gave him a hard time for canceling, she would come across as unreasonable. But if she let him get away with it, it would set the wrong tone for any future relationship that might happen.

"Oh, well. . ." He trailed off. "I'm actually going to be busy for a few days."

Right. Busy. "You know what, Justin? Maybe we should forget it. If you can't give me a reasonable explanation for canceling, then I'm not sure we should bother rescheduling." As soon as the words left her mouth, she felt proud of herself. The old Ashley would've let him get away with canceling and treating her badly. But not anymore. It was time to find a backbone. No more doormat.

Justin sighed. "Okay. Tell you what. I'll be there tonight. But there will be something we have to take care of. I'll need you to have an open mind."

She had to admit she was curious. "Fine. See you at six?"

"We'd better make it an earlier night if that's okay. Can you be ready at four?"

Four? What had she gotten herself into? "Yeah, I can do that." She clicked off the phone and wondered what Justin had up his sleeve.

He was clearly up to something.

Chapter 21

So how is Daddy anyway?" Luke asked.

Rose pinched the bridge of her nose and closed her eyes. Finally, she looked up. "Not well. Not well at all." She sighed. "He couldn't recover from Bobby's accident."

Luke at least could identify with that. "So his memory is. . .gone? Like he doesn't know you at all?"

She shrugged a shoulder. "Not exactly. Alzheimer's is a tricky thing." She tucked a strand of blond hair behind her ear. "He's best in the morning. Sometimes he will know who I am then, and we can have lucid conversations. But there are days he doesn't know, days he thinks I'm Mama."

"Really?" He knew the resemblance was strong. It made sense that Daddy would think that.

"I let him hold my hand and talk to me. He talks about us and Bobby. And sometimes work." She smiled. "I used to try to correct him and explain who I am. But it seemed to make it worse. This way he stays calm."

"How often do you visit?"

She met his eyes across the table. "Daily. And quite frankly, you should be ashamed. I know you haven't been there even one time, because there's a guest book in his room."

He leaned back and rested his head in his hands. He and Daddy hadn't gotten along when the old man was lucid. Why should it be any different now? "I'd probably only upset him."

Rose narrowed her eyes. "He's our daddy, Luke. He

147

provided for us for all those years. I don't care that you didn't have the best relationship with him. He's still the only daddy you're ever gonna have."

Luke nodded. Summer had said much the same thing to him in February when he turned down Rose's invitation to Daddy's birthday celebration. "I know. But he wouldn't want to see me anyway."

Rose shook her head. "He talks about you. And it isn't anything bad either. I think you should go."

"Maybe."

"Well, I need you to change that 'maybe' to an 'I promise,' because I need to be out of town for a few days."

He raised his eyebrows. "Where to?"

Rose smiled. "We're taking the kids to Disney World in Florida. They're so excited. At Christmas this year, we gave them little Mickey Mouse ears with their names on them. Katie Beth knew immediately."

"That will be awesome." Luke had always envisioned that kind of family vacation. But they hadn't had the funds when he was growing up, and now he and Summer didn't have a family and probably never would. "When do you leave?"

"It hinges on your promise." She reached out and gripped his hand. "I can't leave town for five days without knowing you'll go visit him."

"So you are saying that if I don't go visit Daddy while you're gone, you're gonna disappoint your kids?"

She nodded. "Yep. And I'm going to tell them it's because Uncle Luke is so selfish."

He scowled. "Sis, I think you might be a little evil. You know I don't want to be the reason your kids don't meet Mickey."

"Then you'll do it? Just an hour or so a day?"

"Fine. But some of it will have to be after work."

She jumped up and came around the table to throw her arms around his neck. "Thank you so much."

He laughed. It had always been impossible to stay mad at Rose. "When do you leave?"

"Two weeks from today." She jerked her head toward the living room. "Now why don't you go on in Bobby's room and look through his stuff while I get lunch fixed?"

He set his milk glass in the sink and made his way toward his brother's room, not sure he wanted to look through Bobby's things.

Somehow divvying up his stuff made everything feel too final. It was time to let his little brother go, and Luke still wasn't ready to do that.

He walked into the room and sat on the bed, remembering when it had been decked out with a Star Wars comforter.

Unexpected tears filled his eyes, and he angrily batted them away. He hadn't cried. Not when the call came. Not at the funeral.

Summer had tried and tried to get him to talk about his feelings, and each time he'd pushed her away.

But today, in the silence of Bobby's room, he wished she were there holding his hand.

Summer sank onto the leather couch and flipped through the DVR to see what she had saved to watch. It was hard to believe there was a time when the DVR was the source of most of the fights between her and Luke. He'd store as many shows as they had memory for, but she liked to keep the list pared down. Especially old sporting events. What was the point of having an old football game saved? He knew the outcome. When he'd find out she'd deleted some old game, he'd get so upset.

Most of their fights had ended in laughter and kisses. Not like now. But she didn't feel like they were fighting as much as they were simply no longer connecting. Ever since she told Jefferson about their temporary separation, she'd been wondering if it was really temporary.

They'd promised to stay together until death parted them. And she'd always thought those vows were serious. But maybe they weren't as binding as she'd expected.

She took off her wedding ring and looked at it. She still wore the same ring Luke had given her nearly seven years ago. Even though he'd offered numerous times to buy her a bigger ring, she refused. This one was her. Was them.

She wondered if Luke was still wearing his ring. It had been days now since they'd talked. She'd expected him to call by now.

But her phone stayed silent.

She clicked off the TV and went upstairs. When she got to the top of the stairs, she turned right instead of going to her bedroom. She opened the only closed door down the hallway.

The room that was to have been the nursery.

A wooden rocking chair was the lone piece of furniture in the room. Luke had gotten rid of everything from the nursery except for the rocker. It had been the one his own mother had rocked him in.

She sat in the chair and slowly rocked back and forth, just as she'd always imagined rocking their baby. Even though they'd never found out if she'd carried a boy or a girl, she'd always thought the baby was a boy. She never told Luke though. When he'd ask, she'd smile and say they'd have to wait and see.

But she'd known how much he wanted a son, and she felt in her heart that a son was what they'd lost.

And even though they hadn't had a real memorial service, there wasn't a day that Summer didn't remember her baby. Even if Luke tried to pretend it never happened, Summer knew better. She'd carried that tiny life inside of her, and that was something she could never forget.

Chapter 22

"You okay?" Rose asked from the door of Bobby's room. Luke looked up from the papers and books he was sifting through. "Yeah. I found a couple of mementos. One of his high school yearbooks and a tattered copy of *The Old Man and the Sea*."

Rose smiled. "You want any of his old T-shirts?"

Luke shook his head. "No. I wouldn't wear them. And then they'd be in my closet staring at me, reminding me that he's not here anymore." He met her gaze. "Not that I need reminding."

She sat next to him on the bed. "You've had a tough time with it. Tougher than the rest of us, I think."

"I still wish we would've fought harder for a prosecution."

She sighed. "It was an accident. That other driver was so upset, he didn't know what to do." She patted Luke's back. "You know that."

He let out a breath. No one else had seen it like him. Not even Summer. He'd pushed everyone to go after the other driver, certain the guy had been doing something wrong. But everyone had tried to get him to drop it.

Summer had even mentioned him seeing a grief counselor. They'd had a huge argument about it. She'd thought it would do him a world of good, but he couldn't stomach sitting in a room with some stranger and sharing his feelings.

"You sure that's all you want?" Rose asked, motioning toward his paltry stack.

He nodded. "Yeah." He didn't need material things to

help him remember Bobby. He'd remember him when he saw a Ford Mustang drive past or when he heard a Kenny Chesney song or when he saw two little boys with their fishing poles at Folly Beach. Memories like that were worth more than material possessions anyway.

Rose walked over to Bobby's dresser. "There's something I'd like for you to have."

"What's that?"

She opened a drawer and pulled something out. She walked over and handed him a tattered blue leather book. "His Bible. He had the same one since he was thirteen and got baptized."

He recoiled then accepted the Bible from her. Bobby's full name was engraved in gold down in the right-hand corner: ROBERT JAMES NELSON. Luke ran his fingers over his brother's name. He hadn't cracked his own Bible open in nearly a year. "Thanks." He refused to meet Rose's gaze.

"Luke, some people let a tragedy tear their whole life apart. Grief is one thing. But letting it eat you up is another. Do you think Bobby would want that?"

"How do we know what Bobby would want? He's not here to tell us, and we sure shouldn't answer for him."

Rose sighed. "I can answer for him. So can you. We knew him. We knew what he was all about. Bobby was fun and love and laughs. Do you think he'd like it if he knew the brother he adored, the guy who practically raised him, was sitting here looking like a shell of himself?"

Her words stung. He didn't want to think about what Bobby would think or say. That only made him miss his brother more. "I'm fine. I don't know why everyone keeps thinking otherwise."

Rose raised an eyebrow. "So Summer agrees with me?"

He dropped his head in his hands. "I moved out." Saying the words out loud pierced his heart, but he knew Rose wasn't going to let up before she got it out of him.

She sat beside him on the bed. "Tell me. Tell me everything."

Ashley paced the length of her living room. It was nearly time for Justin to be there, and her nerves were starting to get the best of her.

The other night over burgers, she'd felt like they had a connection. It seemed like he was truly remorseful for his bad judgment on their first date.

But now, she wasn't sure what to expect.

A knock sounded at the door.

Showtime.

Ashley pasted on a smile and flung the door open.

Justin stood on the steps with a big grin on his face, a tiny blond-haired boy at his side. He held on to the child's hand. "Hi, Ashley." He nudged the little boy. "Like we practiced," he whispered.

"Hi, Miss Ashley." The child's face lit up with a smile.

Ashley shot Justin a puzzled look and knelt down to see the little boy. "What's your name?"

"Colton," he said. "I'm this many." He held up three fingers.

She couldn't help but laugh. "Nice to meet you, Colton." She stood and motioned toward the living room. "Come on in."

Justin pulled a truck out of his pocket and handed it to Colton. "Sit right here at the coffee table and play with your truck while I talk to Miss Ashley, okay?"

"'Kay." Colton sat down and started running the truck along the length of the coffee table.

Justin motioned for Ashley to step into the kitchen. "I'm sorry. His mom and little sister are sick. He didn't have anywhere to go, so he's spending the weekend with me."

"Are you his. . .dad?" she asked. It seemed like Justin would've mentioned being a father.

He shook his head. "Nope. His mom, Samantha, and I only went out a couple of times. We knew each other from college. But we stayed friends. And when she had Colton, I sort of stepped in to help care for him." He shrugged. "Strange, I know. But that kid has a piece of my heart. His situation isn't his fault, and I want to make sure he has a man in his life."

She felt her heart melt right then and there. "You should've told me. I would've understood."

"I wasn't sure how to bring it up. And then I was afraid it would sound like an excuse not to see you." He touched her arm. "And I did want to see you. But I hope that a date night with both me and Colton is okay."

"It's more than okay. It sounds perfect." She returned his smile and felt a flutter in her stomach she hadn't felt in a long time. "So what do you have in mind?"

"Is someplace kid friendly good with you? And then maybe we'll drive out to the beach and walk around or something."

"My kind of day." She glanced down at her denim capris, red tank top, and flip-flops. She'd had a feeling it would be a casual date and hadn't been wrong.

"Let's go, little man." Justin scooped Colton into his arms, and the little boy giggled.

Ashley couldn't tear her eyes away. Was there a sight cuter than a man and a child sharing a bond? If her biological clock ticked any louder, everyone would hear it. She followed them outside and locked the door. "Third time you've been here, and third car you've driven." She laughed.

Justin smiled. "When I have Colton with me, I borrow my mom's car. I don't feel safe otherwise." He lifted Colton into the car seat and buckled him in then opened the passenger door for her.

"Wow. So that was part of your act the other night, too, then?"

He flinched. "Yeah. Sorry. It just about killed me to not open the doors for you." He climbed inside the Taurus and glanced back at Colton. "Are you hungry?"

"Yes!" Colton exclaimed.

Justin turned to Ashley. "Is Chick-fil-A okay with you? I think there's one not too far from here."

She nodded. "Sounds perfect."

He started the car, and the music blared a children's tune. Justin turned down the volume. "Sorry."

She burst out laughing. "I didn't peg you for a 'Wheels on the Bus' kind of guy, but I like it."

He backed the car out of the driveway and headed toward the restaurant.

Ashley listened to Colton's sweet voice singing along and couldn't help but smile. She'd never gone on a date quite like this one.

But she was having the time of her life.

Chapter 23

"I don't want to talk about it." Luke stood up from where he'd been sitting on Bobby's bed and walked over to the chair in the corner. He sat down and crossed his arms, wishing he hadn't told his sister that he'd moved out.

"For someone so smart, you can be really dumb sometimes," Rose said. "Just tell me what's happened. Maybe I can help."

He shook his head. "No one can." He filled her in on the fiasco with the boat.

She furrowed her brow. "But why does the account matter so much to her? You guys have plenty."

He'd hoped to avoid telling Rose. "The money was what we'd set aside for the baby."

Rose's brown eyes lit up. "Is she pregnant? That's such wonderful news. The last time I saw her, she mentioned that you guys were hopeful it would happen soon."

Luke scowled. "No. She's not." He sighed. "But she was."

Rose came over and put a hand on his shoulder. "Oh Luke. I'm so sorry. You should've told me."

He scratched his head. "Nah. We'd planned on announcing it to everyone at Christmas. But she didn't quite make it that far."

"I could've helped her."

He drew his brows together. "How?"

She sat down on the end of the bed, facing him. "I've been through it. Before we had Dale, we lost a little girl. Susanna Elyse."

"You named her after Mama?"

Rose nodded. "That was the name I had picked out all along. We'd just learned that we were having a girl when it happened. It was the lowest point in my life."

He met her eyes. "How'd you get over it?"

She shrugged. "Just by grieving. We talked about her a lot. Still do, actually. It always gave me comfort to think that she was with Mama. But that didn't stop the hurting."

Luke shook his head. "Summer always wants to talk about our child. She wanted to guess what he or she would've grown up to be and who the baby would've looked most like." He frowned. "But I didn't think talking about it was a good idea."

"That was her baby, Luke. She carried that baby inside her body. Of course she's not going to forget about her child. She probably felt really guilty, too. When something like that happens and you're so powerless. . .all you can do is wonder if you somehow did something wrong."

He wondered if that's how Summer had felt. He hoped not. She was certainly not to blame. She'd been so cautious, following all the rules the doctor gave her. She always followed the rules. "I know that she isn't going to forget the baby. But I wasn't sure if talking about the loss was healthy for her."

"You sound like a chip off the old block. Daddy's never been able to talk about his feelings either."

Luke hated to be compared to his father. "I thought it would be best for everyone if we moved on from what happened."

"Best for everyone or best for you?" Rose asked.

He let her words soak in for a minute. "Everyone."

She shook her head. "Well, you're welcome to look at Susanna's memorial stone. It's in the front of the house in the flower bed." She patted him on the leg. "Sometimes remembering what we've lost is comforting."

"Mama," Katie Beth said from the doorway, "Dale needs to go potty."

Rose glanced at Luke. "I'll be right back."

Luke picked up Bobby's things and stood. "Don't worry about it. I should go anyway." He kissed her on the cheek. "It's been great to see you."

She clutched his arm. "And I can count on you to check on Daddy? Because you know I'm going to expect you to let me know how he's doing."

He nodded. "You can count on me." He headed out the front door and stopped at the sidewalk. There amid the flowers was a stone with Susanna's name on it.

"She's our angel, you know," Katie Beth said, coming up behind him.

He jumped at her voice. He hadn't realized she'd followed him outside. "Yeah."

"Just like Mommy's Mommy. They're in heaven together watching over us. And now Uncle Bobby is with them. Like a family reunion except without the Kentucky Fried Chicken."

He smiled down at her. "When did you get to be so smart?"

She shrugged. "Kindergarten, I guess." She grinned, revealing a missing front tooth. "Are you sad, Uncle Luke?"

"Why would you say that?"

Katie Beth grabbed his hand. "Because Aunt Summer couldn't come with you today."

He knelt down in front of her. "Aunt Summer would've loved to have seen you. She loves you a lot."

"And Dale, too?"

"Yes. Dale, too."

Katie Beth tugged on his hand. "Next time can you bring Aunt Summer and Milo with you? I think he would like to see us, too."

He couldn't help but smile. Last year right before Bobby's accident, they'd all gotten together, and Milo had been a huge hit with Katie Beth. By the end of the day, they'd been best buddies. "He'd like to see you, too."

"But not Dale, because he pulled his tail last time."

Luke chuckled. "Milo is pretty forgiving, so I think he'd be happy to see both of you. Now I'd best get going."

Katie Beth flung her arms around his neck and gave him a kiss on the cheek. "Bye."

He kissed her on the cheek. She smelled like cherry Kool-Aid and sunscreen. "Bye." He climbed into his truck and tossed Bobby's things in the passenger seat.

Luke headed toward the marina, realizing it wasn't even five. The long weekend stretched out ahead of him, and for the first time since he could remember, he didn't have any responsibilities.

The logical side of him said that should make him happy. That's what he'd wanted, after all. Peace and quiet to sort out his thoughts without anyone making any demands on his time.

So why was it that the weekend felt more like a prison than like the freedom he'd expected?

Memorial Day dawned bright and clear. Summer had to admit she felt pretty proud of herself. She'd finally remembered to set the timer on the coffeepot last night.

She hadn't realized how much she depended on Luke to brew her coffee. The first couple of mornings after he left, she'd stumbled down the stairs and stared bleary-eyed at the empty coffeemaker, saying words unbecoming of a lady.

But today she sipped her coffee at the table as Milo snored at her feet. Even though she still felt like she was on rocky ground, that simple act of independence gave her a sense of control.

Control.

Luke, Ashley, and pretty much everyone who'd ever met her had accused her at one time or another of being a control freak. She didn't see it that way though. Summer appreciated it when things made sense. And order made sense to her. Her books were alphabetized on their shelf and sorted by paperback and hardback. She arranged her closet by color. Her filing system at work was so pristine, anyone could come in and find a file even if they'd never opened her file cabinet before.

Order made sense. And when things made sense, she didn't feel as tense as she did when things felt out of control.

She'd always figured it was one of the reasons she and Luke worked so well together. He dreamed the dreams, and she put the foundations underneath them. Without him, she'd be completely without imagination. And without her, he'd drift aimlessly.

At least that's what she'd always thought.

But he must be getting along okay, because he hadn't called her.

And she might not be doing okay, but at least she'd re-membered to make the coffee. Baby steps. That was all she could ask of herself.

Today, though, would be a test. Her parents' annual Memorial Day get-together had always been her family's way to kick off the summer. She and Luke went every year.

Going solo to the party could be dangerous. There would be landmines everywhere. Well-meaning relatives jumping out of the azaleas to ask where Luke was or when she was planning to start a family. Chloe would be there with her pregnancy glow to make Summer feel like a complete failure. Gram would take one look at her and know something was wrong.

Not to mention the usual dealings with her mother, who would be oblivious to her pain and probably want to talk about planning an upcoming shopping trip.

Yes, the landmines would be impossible to dodge. But she couldn't hide from them forever.

Thirty minutes later, she turned her SUV toward Isle of Palms. She rolled the windows down and turned the radio up. The blue sky and bright sunshine made it a perfect Chamber of Commerce day. It looked like the brochures they sent out to tourists to entice them into visiting.

Except that Summer knew what was in store for her. Each mile brought her another twinge of anxiety.

She parked in her parents' driveway and walked up the steps that led to the porch. She took a deep breath. These people were her family. They had her back no matter what. Or at least that was how it was supposed to work.

She opened the door. The foyer was empty. Everyone must be outside. She walked into the living room and tucked her purse underneath a chair.

"I wondered if you'd make it today," Jefferson said from behind her.

She jumped at the sound of his voice. "Sneak up much?" she asked, turning to face him.

"Sorry." He grinned sheepishly. "Everyone's outside. Even my parents."

"Thanks again for helping with Milo the other day."

She followed him into the kitchen and let him open the door for her to go outside.

"No problem." He leaned down. "And your secret is safe with me," he said softly.

Summer nodded. "It had better be." She waved to her dad, who stood next to the grill. He must've talked Mom into letting him do the cooking today.

"Hey, baby doll," Dad said, kissing her cheek. "Where's that son-in-law of mine?"

"Sorry he couldn't make it," she said. "You know how crazy things can get."

"Did he have to work?" Dad asked.

Before she could answer, Jefferson jumped in. "That smells delicious. I think you could get a job at Five Guys if you tried."

Dad laughed. "Thanks, but I believe I'd prefer to keep my amateur status."

Summer shot Jefferson a silent thanks. "I'd better go say hi to Gram." She hurried toward her grandmother, leaving Jefferson to talk to her dad.

She bent down and hugged Gram's neck. "Hi there."

Gram smiled and patted the seat next to her at the patio table. "Have a seat, hon."

"It's a beautiful day for this, isn't it?" Summer glanced around the spacious backyard.

Gram raised an eyebrow. "Don't you try to make small

talk with me. Where is your husband, and why did it look like you came out here with Jefferson?"

Summer felt the heat rise up her face. She'd known Gram wouldn't miss anything but hadn't bargained on her broaching the subject so soon. "Jefferson and I ran into each other in the foyer."

"He must've been waiting on you then, because this is the first I've seen of him."

Summer shook her head. "I'm sure it was a coincidence. He probably arrived right before I did."

"And Luke?"

Summer couldn't lie to her grandmother. Besides, knowing Gram was praying about the situation would give her a lot of comfort. She quickly filled Gram in on what was going on. "No one else in the family needs to know though. I feel sure we'll get everything all worked out in no time."

Gram gripped her hand. "I'm sorry to hear this, honey. Do you know how Luke is holding up?"

Summer furrowed her brow. "This was his decision. He's the one who felt the need to pack a bag and go."

"But honey, I know how much he loves you. You've practically been his whole world since he was a teenager. Being without you must be killing him."

Summer scowled. "I'm sure he's fine. If not, I would've heard from him by now." Gram's words made her feel guilty. As if this were her fault. She'd certainly not wanted this to happen.

"Okay. Well, keep me posted. I'll be praying for a quick reconciliation."

Summer leaned over and kissed her grandmother on the cheek. "Thanks," she whispered.

"Anyone over here up for a little volleyball?" Mitch asked, walking over to the table where Summer and Gram sat. "How 'bout it, Gram? You in?" He displayed a dimple that had been making girls swoon since he was in junior high.

Gram chuckled. "I believe I'll sit this one out. Maybe next time."

Summer joined in her laughter. "I'm in." She followed Mitch out to the section of beach behind the house.

Jefferson waved as she walked up. "Well, well. I didn't think Mitch could talk you into playing."

She slipped her sandals off and grimaced at him. "I happen to be a stellar athlete. I could practically be on the Olympic team."

Mitch tossed her the ball. "I forgot how competitive you were." He shook his head. "Or maybe it's more like I blocked it out."

"You're just mad that your sister used to beat you at everything," Jefferson taunted.

Summer cocked her head. "Not everything. Mitch always beat me at Ping-Pong."

"Of course. Because Ping-Pong requires such athleticism."

Mitch glared at Jefferson. "I don't remember you being crowned Athlete of the Year in high school either."

Summer threw the ball at Mitch. "Okay, you two. Enough. I think we've established that *I* was the sportiest one of the three of us. Tell me again. . .how did y'all feel about always getting beat by a girl?"

"That was years ago. Everything's different now." Jefferson winked. "Besides, if I remember correctly, you are a little older than us. So let's see if you can still keep up."

She wrinkled her nose. "I'm only a month older than you.

I doubt that gives you much of an advantage."

Preston and two of the neighbors walked up.

"Let's do this," Preston said.

They quickly divided into teams.

She took her place in front of the net. Every year for as long as she could remember, they'd all played beach volleyball at her parents' cookout. She and Luke always made sure to be on the same team. She blinked back unexpected tears. What was Luke doing today? Did he miss being here with her?

She looked up to see Jefferson's eyes on her from his spot directly across the net.

"You okay?" he mouthed.

She nodded and quickly wiped her eyes. She turned to look at Preston who stood ready to serve the ball. "Let's go." She clapped her hands and got into position.

Nothing like a little fake enthusiasm to chase the blues away.

Chapter 24

Ashley pulled into Justin's parents' driveway and put the car in PARK. She had butterflies the size of eagles in her stomach. She knew it was probably way too soon for a "meet the parents" situation, but when Justin had asked her over for a cookout, she hadn't been able to resist.

Their date on Saturday night had been perfect. She'd enjoyed Colton's antics and had especially liked watching how Justin interacted with the child. After dinner they'd gone to Folly Beach and collected shells.

Ashley didn't allow herself to dream about the future anymore, but Saturday night had given her a glimpse of what a life with Justin might be like. And it would be a good life.

But it was way too early to be thinking long term. She knew she needed to slow down. After her divorce, she'd been certain she'd never have feelings for anyone ever again. And even though she and Justin had gotten off to a rocky start, she knew he had all the qualities she'd been looking for.

"Hey there," Justin said, walking out to meet her in the driveway. "I thought you were just gonna sit in your car all day."

"Sorry."

"Nervous?" He raised his eyebrows.

She shrugged. "A little bit. What if your parents hate me?"

He shook his head. "No way. But don't worry. I told them we've only just met. No one is going to ask you any tough questions." He grinned mischievously. "They'll save that until the second time you come out."

"Second time? What makes you think there'll be a second time?" she asked teasingly.

He put a hand on the small of her back and guided her through the front door. "Wishful thinking," he said softly.

A shiver of excitement ran up her spine. He was a keeper—she just knew it.

Justin nodded his head at the patio door. "They're out back."

She followed him outside and glanced around. A small crowd stood around the grill and another group around a swimming pool where Colton was splashing around, clad in green swim trunks and a baseball cap. His pudgy little belly was so cute, it was all Ashley could do not to go lift him out of the pool and blow raspberries on it until he laughed.

"Everyone, this is Ashley." Justin slung an arm around her shoulder. "Ashley, this is everyone."

Once she had made the rounds and met his relatives, she settled into a chair near the pool. Justin's family didn't make a big fuss over her. Instead, they made her feel right at home. After three years of barely seeing her own family, it was nice to be around what was obviously a tightly knit group.

"Are you enjoying yourself?" Justin's mom asked, taking the seat next to her.

She smiled. "Yes, ma'am. Thank you for having me over."

"We're glad to have you," Mrs. Sanders said. "Justin never brings girls to the house. I think he's afraid we'll embarrass him."

Ashley chuckled. It felt good to hear that she wasn't one of many. Maybe it meant he thought she was special if he'd been willing to risk embarrassment for her.

Colton squealed as Justin sprayed him with the water

hose. He bent down and splashed water at Justin.

Justin grabbed a towel and scooped the laughing child up in it.

"They love each other to pieces," Mrs. Sanders remarked. "Justin would raise Colton as his own if he could."

Ashley found the situation puzzling to say the least. From what Justin had told her Saturday night, Colton's mom wasn't neglectful, but she wasn't very engaged in the child's life either. Still, Colton seemed pretty well adjusted. "I know. He'd make a great dad." As soon as the words escaped her lips, she wished she could take them back. *Scary girl who only just met you wants to have babies with your son.*

But Mrs. Sanders smiled. "He sure will."

"Hey, you two," Justin called to them. "You'd better not be talking about me."

His mom stood. "Don't flatter yourself. We have far more interesting things to talk about." She gave Ashley a wink. "I'd better go see if Jim needs help with the grill."

An hour later the food was almost all gone. "It was delicious," Ashley said to Justin's dad as she tossed her paper plate in the garbage.

"Glad you liked it," he said.

Justin lifted his empty glass. "I'm going to get more Coke. Do you want anything?"

Ashley shook her head. "Nope. I'm fine."

He looked her up and down. "You sure are."

She felt the blush rise up her face. "Shh. They'll hear."

"Sorry. I just call it like I see it."

It had been so long since a guy she liked gave her a compliment. She loved Justin's obvious appreciation for the way she looked. "Thanks."

"Why don't y'all get out of here for a little while?" Justin's mom asked. "Colton is down for his nap, and we'll be glad to watch him if he wakes up."

Justin raised his eyebrows at Ashley. "Sound good to you?"

She nodded. "Sure."

"Thanks, Mom." Justin kissed Mrs. Sanders on the cheek. "We'll be back soon." He put a hand on the small of Ashley's back and led her inside the house.

"So where are we going to go?" she asked.

He thought for a second. "How about I show you a piece of my childhood? You mind walking?"

"I could certainly use some exercise after that meal." She chuckled.

"Whatever. I think you're perfect."

She beamed. "Thanks." She followed Justin out the front door. Once they got to the end of the driveway, he took her hand.

"This okay?" he asked. "Or are you not a hand holder?"

She laughed. "It's more than okay." And it was. The way her hand felt in his was so comforting, so normal. It was almost as if they'd been doing it their whole lives.

They walked in silence for a few moments.

"Thanks for being so understanding about Colton," Justin said finally. "I was a little nervous that you'd be weirded out about it."

She squeezed his hand. "I think it's fantastic. Honestly. I can't imagine many guys so willing to rearrange their lives for a kid who isn't even theirs."

"You make me sound like some kind of saint. I'm certainly not."

"So tell me your flaws."

Justin took a deep breath and blew it out. "You really want to know? I don't want to chase you off so soon."

She giggled. "Try me."

"I forget to put the top on the toothpaste. I eat a lot of takeout because I'm a terrible cook. I never ask for directions. And I have kind of a tender heart."

"How's that one a flaw?"

He bumped his shoulder against hers. "I cry at stuff. I know it's not manly. Weddings. Movies. Even big sporting events. Some girls hate that. And my friends make fun."

"A sensitive man. I didn't know those existed except for in books and movies." She grinned. "I won't hold any of that against you, I promise."

"Good to know." He motioned toward a park. "Here we are." Justin led her through the gate and onto a sidewalk that wound around the park. "I can't tell you how many hours I spent here growing up."

"Looks like paradise." The giant trees scattered along the perimeter of the park were heavy with Spanish moss. The lush, green grass conjured up images of running barefoot and picnics and all the things that made summertime special.

Justin tugged on her hand. "Come on." They walked past a water fountain to a set of bleachers in front of a deserted baseball field. "After you," he said.

She climbed the bleachers and sat down.

"I learned to hit a baseball right there," Justin said, sitting down next to her and pointing at home plate. "My dad coached my T-ball and Little League team. This is where we practiced and played."

"I'll bet you were adorable in your little uniform."

He blushed. "My mom thought so." He chuckled. "She

came out here every day with a cooler of cherry Kool-Aid and those little paper cups." He pointed at an old wooden dugout. "She'd set it up in there, and by the time we got finished, we'd all have red Kool-Aid mustaches."

"Sounds like a perfect childhood." Ashley's own parents had split up when she was in kindergarten. Her dad hadn't been in the picture, and her mom had always been too busy searching for her own "happily ever after" to worry too much about her only child.

"Some people might think my parents were too involved in my life, but I realize now how blessed I was. And still am."

She tilted her head and admired his blue eyes. "Is that why Colton's so important to you?"

Justin nodded. "I've always wanted a family of my own. Since I was a kid. Most guys are looking for freedom and making conquests. I've always prayed that God would lead me to the kind of woman who would make a good partner and who wanted a family as much as me."

Her heart fluttered. She'd looked for that same thing. Prayed for the same thing. But had settled for Brian. She'd been terrified that he was her only shot at marriage and family. And when it didn't work out, she'd assumed that real happiness wasn't in the cards for her. "That's an amazing dream. Most guys are so worried about being successful, they don't give much thought to their family life." She squeezed his hand. "At least the guys I've met, up until now."

Justin locked eyes with her. He reached out and traced the back of his hand along her face. "I'm going to kiss you now. And it's going to mean something."

She gave him a tiny smile and leaned forward to meet his lips. The kiss was soft at first. Tentative. It grew deeper, more passionate, and by the time she pulled back, they were both breathless.

"Well then," Justin murmured. "That was. . ." He trailed off.

"Nice?" she asked.

He burst out laughing. "I guess that's one way to put it. I was hoping for something a little more enthusiastic."

She wanted to keep her enthusiasm to herself, at least for the time being. The last guy she'd kissed had been her husband. And there'd been a time she thought those kisses were pretty great.

But they didn't compare to kissing Justin.

"How about amazing?"

He nodded. "Amazing will do."

"Well, how would you describe it?"

He took her hand. "I'd say that was the best kiss I've had in all of my twenty-nine years on earth."

Ashley almost fell off of the bleachers. Twenty-nine? He was only twenty-nine? Her heart—that had been so full of hope for their budding romance—dropped.

She knew herself. And at thirty-six, she knew there was no way she could date someone who hadn't even reached the thirty milestone yet.

No way.

Even if she'd never been kissed quite like that before.

Luke pulled into the driveway at his house. Disappointment washed over him at the sight of Summer's empty parking space. He'd hoped she'd be home by now.

Her parents' traditional Memorial Day party must've run long, because usually Summer was aching to get away from their house. Although maybe she wasn't looking forward to coming home to an empty house. Just like he hated going to the quiet loneliness of the boat.

He let himself into the house and turned off the alarm. At least she'd started remembering to set it.

Milo looked up from his spot on the couch. The big dog rose and stretched. He padded over to Luke and looked up at him.

Luke knelt down and gave Milo a pat. "Hey, boy. Have you missed me?"

Milo sank lower onto the floor and rolled onto his back.

Luke scratched Milo's stomach, and the dog wriggled with happiness. "Let's go outside and take care of the yard."

Mowing the yard made him think of meeting Summer for the first time. He couldn't help but grin to himself. His buddies had told him that someone like her would never go for a guy like him, but he'd been smitten from the first time he saw her.

They'd started out as friends. He'd looked forward to the weekly visit to her grandmother's house, because after a few weeks, Summer was always there. She'd bring him something cold to drink, and after he'd finished working, they'd sit on the porch and talk about books and music and what they wanted to do with their lives.

"Someday you're going to hear my songs on the radio," Luke told her.

Summer gave him a slow smile. "I'd be your biggest fan."

"Yeah, well when that happens, maybe your daddy won't mind if I ask you out." Luke's ego still stung from learning that

Summer's dad wouldn't hear of letting her go out with him.

She shook her head. "What he doesn't know won't hurt him."

Luke had asked her out to a movie, but she'd balked at the thought of him picking her up in his old truck and said her daddy wouldn't let her go with someone whose family he didn't know.

"So you'll meet me then? Even though you might get in trouble?"

Summer tossed her dark ponytail. "I'm staying at Gram's tonight. I'll tell her I'm meeting a friend for a movie." She grinned. "Which is totally true."

"Awesome. Meet me at the bandstand at the Battery at seven." She nodded. "I'll be there." She stood. "I'd better go inside."

He grabbed her hand and felt a twinge of excitement. "I'll see you tonight."

At the time, it had seemed like it was them against the world. Luke had tried to make a good impression on her dad when they'd finally met, but Mr. Rutledge had always been cool toward him.

His own family had loved Summer from the beginning. She'd even broken through his dad's gruff exterior. The elder Nelson had told his son that hanging on to Summer was the smartest thing he'd ever done.

And if he remembered correctly, Daddy had also warned him not to mess it up.

As he finished mowing the yard, he wondered if he'd messed up bad enough that they couldn't come back from it. Nothing irreversible had happened. He'd just packed a duffel bag and spent a few nights away.

He sat on the porch steps and took a swig of water. He'd wait for her to get home. Give her an apology. She was the most important person in his life. And she deserved to be treated better.

He leaned back and stretched his legs out in front of him. Just those few days apart and he'd realized that he needed to do whatever it took to get them back to where they used to be.

And if that meant going to counseling with some guy at Summer's church, then he would have to man up and do it. The talk he'd had with Rose had made him realize a lot of things. Number one being that he'd crumbled under the grief of losing Bobby and the baby, and Summer had been the one to suffer because of it. He would have to figure out a way to make it up to her.

Milo barked at the gate.

Luke looked up to see Summer's SUV pulling slowly up the driveway, Mitch's red Porsche following behind her.

Summer climbed out of the vehicle and walked over to the porch. "I didn't expect to see you here." She looked good. Her khaki shorts and green polo shirt showed off her trim figure.

He stood. "I wanted to get the yard done and see Milo." He met her gaze. "And you."

Hope flickered across her face. "Yeah?"

Luke wanted nothing more than to run to her and take her in his arms. Kiss her until she couldn't think straight and then carry her up the stairs to their room. But he knew they had a lot of talking to do first. "Yeah."

"Luke, we missed you at the cookout," Mitch said.

He looked up in surprise. He'd been so happy to see Summer, he'd forgotten that Mitch had followed her into the driveway. Much to his chagrin, Jefferson stood next to Mitch, an amused expression on his face. "Yeah, sorry I missed it."

"Your wife put us to shame on the volleyball court,"

Jefferson said. "That's why we're here. We promised to take her out to dinner tonight if her team won two out of three."

"And they won three out of three," Mitch grumbled. "So here we are."

Summer locked eyes with him. "Why don't you come with us? I think we're headed to California Dreaming. You know how I love their crab cakes."

He shook his head. "I'd better not. But you go on."

She climbed the porch steps and stood next to him.

His hands ached to touch her. But he didn't.

"I'll go get changed. Be right back." Summer brushed past him and went into the house, Milo at her heels.

The three men stood in silence for a long moment.

Mitch cleared his throat. "Well, this is a tension convention. I'm gonna go in and grab a bottle of water. You boys play nice." He trotted up the stairs and into the house.

Luke eyed Jefferson. "So have you settled in yet?"

"I'm renting a carriage house a few houses down from here." He raised an eyebrow. "That should make you feel better, knowing that if Summer needs anything, I can be over here in a few minutes. Especially now that she's living all alone."

So he knew Luke was staying on the boat. She'd told Jefferson of all people. Luke would've rather been sucker punched than betrayed by his own wife. "Yeah. It makes me feel loads better."

Jefferson chuckled. "Now, now. It sounded to me like you brought all this on yourself."

"Have I mentioned how happy I am that you're back in town?" Luke asked. "Just gives me a warm, fuzzy feeling inside." He glowered.

"Oh, I can imagine." Jefferson smirked. "And believe me, I'm thrilled to be back."

Luke stood. "If you'll excuse me, there's something I need to take care of inside." He pushed the door open with a vengeance, almost knocking Mitch down. "Sorry, man," he mumbled, walking past his brother-in-law and into the entryway.

He took a deep breath and headed up the stairs.

Summer stood in front of the mirror, twisting her hair into a bun.

"Can we talk?" he asked, sitting down on the bed, admiring the way her skin glowed from a day in the sun.

She turned to face him. "Luke, they're waiting downstairs. I don't think this is the right time."

"When will be the right time then?" He rubbed his jaw.

"I don't know." She turned her attention back to the mirror. "You can't just stop by and expect me to drop everything. I waited days for you to call and didn't hear a word. So the way I see it, our talk can wait a little bit longer."

"I've known you for a long time. I can tell you're upset."

She turned back around, fire in her blue eyes. "You think? My husband moves onto a boat that he purchased with money that I had earmarked for the child that I hoped to have someday." She narrowed her eyes. "The child I *still* plan on having someday. And now you show up like nothing happened and expect me to forget it?"

He shook his head. "It's not like that, and you know it. Besides, *you're* the one who first suggested that I stay on the boat." He sighed. "And you know I don't expect you to forget everything that has happened. But we need to talk about it."

"All those months. All those months I wanted to talk.

Begged you to talk." She grabbed her purse from the foot of the bed. "And you acted like I barely existed."

"I know I have a lot to apologize for."

She paused at the doorway. "Luke, I do want to talk to you. We definitely need to. But right at this minute, I don't have it in me. Do you hear me? I am not capable at this point in time to have this conversation with you. It's been a long day. A longer week." She shook her head and sighed. "And at this moment, all I can handle is going to eat some crab cakes and letting Mitch and Jefferson make me laugh. At this moment, I want to forget for a couple of hours that I'll be coming home to an empty house."

"I'm sure Jefferson would be glad to walk you home and check the place out." Luke glowered. "I can't believe you told him that I left. What were you thinking?"

"What was *I* thinking?" She closed the bedroom door and turned to face him. "I don't know—I guess I was thinking that it was the truth. You left. And to top it off, you haven't called. Haven't come by. I haven't heard so much as a peep from you." She narrowed her eyes. "Jefferson happened to see me out for a walk with Milo, and I was upset. I didn't intend to tell him, but I'm not sorry I did."

"He happened to see you out, huh? Don't you think it's a little weird that he shows up all of a sudden, and now he practically lives next door?"

Summer groaned. "Seriously? I thought we'd gotten over the Jefferson hurdle years ago when I married you."

"Is that a hint of regret I hear in your voice?"

She furrowed her brow. "Don't be stupid. Do I need to remind you again that this whole thing—"

"What? Is all my fault?" He shook his head. "Right.

And you are totally blameless. Except for the whole walking around like a robot for months, forgetting the simplest things and working sixty-hour weeks at the office. But besides all that, you're perfect." Luke could admit that many of their problems stemmed from him. But it had taken both of them to reach the point where they were now. The breaking point.

"I know I'm not perfect." Her eyes filled with tears. "I know that better than anyone."

Luke took a step toward her, but she held her hands out to stop him.

"Don't." Her whisper carried as much force as any yell.

He sighed. "I didn't come here to argue. I just wanted to see you and Milo."

"Milo is downstairs and needs to be walked. Stay as long as you like. But I'm going to dinner now." She walked out without another word.

Luke buried his head in his hands. Summer had never rattled easily. But he could see that his presence had thrown her. Angered her even. Maybe a surprise visit hadn't been the smartest thing. He should've called her last week and checked in. He should've kept a lid on his anger over Jefferson's presence. He should've done a lot of things.

He got up and watched out the bedroom window as Summer, Mitch, and Jefferson drove away.

So maybe apologizing to Summer and getting things back to normal wouldn't be as easy as he'd expected. He'd keep trying until he won her trust back, even if it took him forever.

Because the idea of not getting back on solid ground with Summer was too painful to even consider. And the fact that his old nemesis had somehow weaseled his way back into her life made him very uneasy.

Chapter 25

Ashley had been replaying that kiss with Justin over and over in her mind ever since Monday. Followed quickly by the reminder that he hadn't reached his thirtieth birthday yet and she was knocking on forty's door. Okay, so maybe she had four years left until forty, but that didn't seem all that comforting right now.

Summer tapped her fingers on Ashley's desk. "I don't think you've heard anything I've said. Are you okay?"

"Huh?" Ashley looked up to see Summer standing in front of her desk, an amused expression on her face.

"I asked you if you're going to go with me to the new bridal boutique over on Calhoun Street. I want to officially introduce myself. Jennifer St. Claire is getting her dress and bridesmaids' dresses there. She's been really pleased."

The St. Claire–Wentworth wedding was coming up in the fall. Ashley had met with Jennifer what seemed like fifty times already. She hadn't seen the dress though. "I'd love to go with you. I wonder if they can show us Jennifer's dress."

"Only one way to find out. Let's go." Summer grabbed her purse and a binder from her desk and led the way out the door. "Are you okay though? You've been quiet all week."

Ashley hadn't been sure what to tell Summer, so she'd opted to keep her mouth shut. But it would be nice to unload it. She quickly filled her in on her outing with Justin and Colton, the cookout, and the kiss. "Why didn't you tell me he wasn't even thirty?" she whined.

"Honestly, I didn't think about it. I guess I always forget

that Justin is younger. He was actually one of Bobby's friends first, but he and Luke hit it off." Summer unlocked her SUV and climbed inside.

Ashley got into the passenger seat and buckled her seat belt. "I can't imagine continuing the relationship now."

Summer waited for a car to pass before she pulled out of her parking space. "I think you're silly. Justin is a great guy. Very mature for his age. And you don't look a day over twenty-five."

Ashley laughed. "I know he's a great guy and all of that. But as soon as I found out his age, I felt so self-conscious. I have little laugh lines around my eyes."

"Maybe if you look with a magnifying glass."

"At twenty-nine, that means some of the girls he's gone out with over the past year have probably barely been in their twenties. I can't compete with that."

Summer let out a huge sigh. "I can't believe you're this insecure. You look amazing. You're a smart, interesting *woman*. Twentysomething girls have nothing on you."

Ashley wanted to believe Summer. But after what happened with Brian, she couldn't let go of the fear. "He might be happy with me for a few months until some tanned, flat-bellied girl-woman saunters by and turns his head."

Summer groaned. "What's this really about? Because if that kiss was as good as you say, I can't believe you're going to let a little something like age keep you away from him." She pulled into the parking lot at the boutique.

"Just some stuff I've gone through." Ashley sighed. "I agreed to go out with him again this weekend, but I'm thinking of canceling."

Summer turned off the engine and looked at Ashley.

"Does he know how old you are?"

Ashley shook her head. "No. I don't want him to know."

"I can guarantee you that he doesn't care if you're a few years older than him. He might even find you more attractive." Summer grinned. "You never know."

Ashley followed her into the store. She wasn't sure she wanted to know. Because her self-confidence couldn't take it if the opposite was true.

"It's so nice to meet you," Madelyn Ashworth said. "Jennifer has said such wonderful things about Summer Weddings." She smiled.

"Likewise," Summer said. "We wanted to come over and introduce ourselves and take a look around your beautiful shop."

Madelyn beamed. "It's a lifelong dream of mine. I have four daughters, and let me tell you, helping each of them choose a wedding gown is one of my favorite memories." She gestured to the rows of pristine gowns. "Wedding dresses are so personal, aren't they? I try to make sure that each of my clients tries on several different styles. Sometimes a girl comes in here thinking she wants one thing and realizes that something else is better suited for her."

Ashley thumbed through an old issue of *Modern Bride* from a nearby table. "I was one of those girls. I always said 'no way' to a princess-style dress. But wouldn't you know it, I tried on a poufy, lacy thing and fell in love with it." She laughed.

Madelyn turned to Summer. "How about you? Did you

wear the dress you'd always dreamed of or were you surprised by what you wound up with?"

Summer grimaced. "Actually, I got married at city hall." She shook her head. "I never even tried on a wedding dress."

Madelyn drew back, her eyes wide with horror.

"Don't worry though. I've been doing this for a long time. Just because I didn't have my own fairy-tale wedding doesn't diminish my ability as a wedding planner." Summer tried to laugh it off, but she could see her credibility had fallen as far as Madelyn was concerned.

Madelyn looked over at Ashley. "Are you thinking what I'm thinking?"

Ashley nodded. "I am."

"Come on." Madelyn pointed at a row of dresses in the back of the store. "This is the new collection for the fall. Try one on. Just for fun."

Summer drew her brows together. "Oh, I shouldn't." She didn't want to appear unprofessional. But she had always wanted to try on a wedding dress. Last year she'd picked up a dress from the cleaners for one of her brides. It had absolutely been Summer's dream gown and in her size, too. It had taken all her self-control not to try it on. She'd held it up in front of herself in the full-length mirror at the back of Summer Weddings and imagined what it would've been like to float down an aisle toward Luke.

"Come on," Ashley said. "Seeing you go all princess will cheer me up."

Summer twisted her mouth into a smile. "I'll try one on. But only if you promise not to cancel your date with Justin."

"If it means you doing something spontaneous and trying on your dream gown. . .I'm in." Ashley smiled and held up her iPhone. "And I'm totally willing to document this little fashion show."

"What style do you have in mind, Summer?" Madelyn asked.

Summer thought for a moment. "My dream gown used to be a ball gown with a full skirt. But now I think I like a straighter, column style. But not strapless." She chuckled. "I get so tired of seeing strapless dresses all the time."

"Maybe a high neck?" Ashley asked, pulling one off the rack and holding it up. "Like this?" The white chiffon had intricate beading at the bodice.

Summer inhaled sharply. "Oh that's beautiful."

"Go try it on," Madelyn said, pointing at a fitting room. "If you need help, let me know."

Summer carried the gown into a lavish dressing room. The A-line chiffon dress had a high halter neck in the front and a deep V in the back. It might not be as traditional as a poufy, strapless dress, but it fit Summer's sophisticated style perfectly. She slipped it over her head. "Can someone zip me?" she called.

Madelyn opened the door and carefully zipped the dress. "Oh my. It's like it was made for you. Come step up on the platform and look in the mirror."

Summer tentatively walked out of the dressing room and stepped up on the block that was in front of a floor-length mirror.

"It's perfect," Ashley breathed. "Just perfect." She sighed. "You make a beautiful bride."

Summer laughed. "Okay, simmer down. I've already been a bride, remember? Now I'm just an old married lady."

Ashley raised an eyebrow. "Please don't mention the word

old to me today."

Summer turned to face herself in the mirror. She might be married, but her husband was living on a boat. Without her. So much for the fairy tale. "This is a gorgeous dress."

Madelyn walked over with a tiara and veil. "Try this, too. You want to get the full experience."

Summer bent down, and Madelyn placed the headpiece on top of her head. She stood upright and looked back in the mirror. "I look so—so. . .bridal."

They burst out laughing.

"That's kind of the point," Ashley said. "Here, smile." She held up the phone and snapped a couple of pictures.

Summer turned back to the mirror. She'd never told Luke, but not having a real wedding had always bothered her. She'd dreamed of a church wedding at St. Michael's. Chloe's wedding had taken place in the historic building, and it had been so beautiful. Every time Summer planned a wedding at St. Michael's, she imagined what her own would've been like. But it was too late now. "This has been fun. I guess now I know how I would've looked as a bride."

Madelyn smiled. "Hon, with your looks and figure, you could model those dresses. Be a bride every day."

Summer stepped down from the platform with a laugh. "This was enough. Besides, if I were dressed like a bride every day, it wouldn't be special anymore."

"Um, I'd take that job," Ashley said. "Any day that includes a tiara sounds like a great day to me."

Summer paused for Madelyn to unzip the dress. "Thanks for this. It was fun." She smiled. "The most fun I've had in a while."

"I'm glad you were a good sport." Madelyn smiled. "I love

to see that look on a girl's face when she sees herself in the dress for the first time. You were no different. For a minute, even the toughest girl turns into Cinderella."

Summer closed the fitting room door behind her and glanced in the mirror one last time.

She was nobody's Cinderella. But it had been fun to pretend for a few minutes that everything was perfect.

Chapter 26

L uke sat in his truck in the nursing home parking lot. He hadn't seen his dad since Bobby's funeral almost a year ago. Almost exactly a year ago.

And even then the old man had been feeble. Broken. A lifetime of regret had been etched on his weathered face.

Luke hadn't tried to contact Summer since he'd seen her on Memorial Day. He hadn't known what to say. Her eyes had been so full of anger and hurt. He'd never dealt that well with emotions, so he wasn't sure what he could say or do to take away her pain.

But today he wished he'd called her. He wished he'd asked her to come here with him. She would've known what to say, how to act. Her presence would've put him at ease.

He climbed out of the truck and walked slowly toward the entrance. Rose had warned him that Daddy might not recognize him. She'd given him so many instructions on the phone last night, his phone battery had almost given out. He walked inside the building and glanced around the big hallway.

A few elderly people shuffled past in robes. A teenage girl pushed an older woman in a wheelchair.

He inhaled. He must be near the cafeteria, because there was a distinct food smell in the air. It didn't seem as much like a hospital as he'd expected. It was a little homier with nice décor and wallpapered walls.

He glanced at the sign on the wall. His dad's room should be down the left corridor. He walked to the room and stopped in the doorway.

Roy Nelson sat in a recliner next to his hospital bed, staring straight ahead. His gray hair was longer than the buzz cut he'd worn most of Luke's life.

Luke tapped gently on the door. "Hello," he said.

Daddy looked up, and his face brightened. "Pete," he said with a grin. "It's great to see you."

Pete Nelson had been Daddy's older brother. He'd passed away fifteen years ago while Luke was in Nashville. Everyone in the Nelson family had always thought Luke resembled Pete more than he'd favored his own father. "Hi," Luke said. Rose had warned him, but even so, the situation made him uncomfortable.

"It's been such a long time. How are Lucille and the kids?"

Luke smiled. "Fine. How is your family?" He wondered what year it was in his dad's mind.

Daddy shook his head. "You know how hard it's been since I lost Martha."

Luke nodded. "I know."

"But the kids are doing well. Rose stays with Martha's sister a lot. She's turning into such a good little cook. And so sweet. And Bobby is my athlete." Daddy grinned. "Even though he's just in junior high, I think he might end up playing football someday for the Gamecocks."

Bobby had played for a year until he'd torn his ACL. Luke had been so proud of his little brother and had gone to every home game. "That's great." He leaned forward. "How's Luke?" He steeled himself against his dad's response.

Daddy's face lit up. "Luke's my pride and joy."

Luke's eyes filled with unexpected tears. "Yeah?"

"He's so smart. That boy can be anything he wants. He's

in Nashville right now, trying to make it as a musician." The older man chuckled. "But his heart's here. Her name's Summer."

"She's a nice girl?"

Daddy nodded. "She comes from money, but that doesn't matter to Luke. First time I saw them together, I knew. He'd found someone to love like I loved Martha." He sighed. "I've been so hard on him over the years. I've always been so proud of him, but I wanted him to want more than the life I had. Sometimes I wish I'd handled things with him differently."

Luke gripped his daddy's hand and forced back the tears. "It's not too late. I'll bet he'd love to hear from you."

"Oh, I wouldn't do that. I don't want to bother him. He's got his own life to live now."

Luke nodded. "They do grow up quick, don't they?"

Daddy's face grew sad. "Too quick. I blinked, and they were gone. Bobby's the only one at home now, and the next couple years will fly by."

"Make the most of it." Luke couldn't stay in the room any longer. The pain was too much.

"Oh, I will. I'm hoping to have all the kids back in the house for Christmas."

Luke remembered that Christmas. He'd stayed in Nashville instead of coming home. And right now he'd give anything to be able to go back and accept the invitation his father had offered. "That sounds so nice."

Daddy beamed. "Oh, it will be."

"I'd better get going." Luke stood.

"Tell Lucille and the kids hello."

Luke nodded. He turned to go then turned back around and threw his arms around Daddy's neck. "I'll be back soon."

Daddy smiled and patted him on the back. "Okay. Bye, Pete."

Luke rushed out of the room, almost knocking down a nurse. He had to get to the truck. As soon as he hit the exit door, he broke into a run. He climbed into the truck and hunched over the steering wheel, his body racked with sobs.

Luke hadn't cried in years. Not when Bobby died. Not when Summer miscarried. Not even the night last week on the boat when he'd realized he might not be able to put his life back together again.

He'd heard of people hitting rock bottom. But this was the first time he'd experienced it for himself. He'd waited his whole life to hear those words from his dad: *I'm proud of you.* They'd never come. Not once. Not when he'd graduated second in his class and spoken at the ceremony. Daddy had made some comment about how he should've worked harder and been first. When Luke married Summer, Daddy had just warned him not to mess up. And when he'd graduated from college and begun working for the National Park Service, Daddy had only shaken his head and muttered that Luke hadn't reached high enough.

But today, as Daddy thought he was talking to Uncle Pete, his pride had been evident. Maybe it had been there all along and Luke had been so sullen he hadn't noticed it. He thought about all the times Summer had tried to persuade him to visit Daddy. Luke had given her a million reasons why he didn't have time.

And now time had run out. Even if he visited Daddy every day for the rest of his life, it wouldn't matter. He couldn't turn back the clock.

Luke leaned back and rested his head against the seat, his

eyes blurry with tears. He glanced over at the passenger seat. He'd tossed Bobby's things there and left them. He reached over and picked up his little brother's Bible. He flipped it open, surprised by how many passages were highlighted and how many pages were dog-eared. He stopped in Ecclesiastes where nearly all the text on one page had been underlined and began to read in chapter 3:

> *There is a time for everything,*
> *and a season for every activity under the heavens:*
> *a time to be born and a time to die,*
> *a time to plant and a time to uproot,*
> *a time to kill and a time to heal,*
> *a time to tear down and a time to build,*
> *a time to weep and a time to laugh,*
> *a time to mourn and a time to dance.*

He looked over the words again. How had he missed it? He'd looked at everything that had happened in his life over the past year as a personal attack. But that wasn't it at all. It was just life. Unpredictable and unsteady. But God must know what He was doing even if Luke didn't understand.

And even though his pain was fresh, that thought gave him comfort.

Summer flipped through her planner. June was flying by. Maybe it was best that this was one of her busiest months, because she'd barely had time to think about her problems. She'd spent the day being all too aware of the significance of today's date though.

Bobby's accident had happened exactly a year ago.

She'd been expecting Luke to call her all week. After the way he'd stopped by the house on Memorial Day wanting to talk, she'd thought he would seek her out. But maybe he'd expected the same thing from her. Or maybe he was so mad at her for letting Jefferson know about their problems that he didn't want to talk to her.

She leaned back in her chair and sighed. She'd been thinking lately that their relationship problems were a two-way street. He'd alluded to it on Memorial Day. It might be easy for her to blame Luke for pulling away and being distant, but she knew she'd done the same thing. After the miscarriage, she'd felt so lost. Luke didn't want to talk about it, and only Gram and Ashley knew the truth. So she'd tried to handle her feelings herself.

Over the months, she'd been so distracted, so foggy. No wonder Luke hadn't known how to respond to her. He wasn't the only one who'd acted like a different person. She had, too. It had taken some time alone to see her part in their problems more clearly.

"You okay?" Ashley asked.

Summer startled at the sound of her voice. "I'm fine. Just thinking. Today is the anniversary of Bobby's accident."

Ashley furrowed her brow. "I'm so sorry. I know that's got to be tough. Have you talked to Luke?"

Summer shook her head. "No. I think I'm going to call him. Although I doubt he'll tell me how he's really feeling about everything."

"Why are men so much trouble?" Ashley dramatically put the back of her hand to her forehead. "Is it them or us?"

Summer couldn't help but laugh at her friend. "Probably a little of both." She shook her head. "Any news on the website launch?"

Ashley nodded. "Yep. It's finished. Justin says it will be live come Monday."

"Awesome. Thanks again for your work on that."

A shadow crossed Ashley's face. "You're welcome."

Summer tried to read Ashley's tone. Something was off with her. "Everything still okay with Justin? You went out last week, right?"

"I did. But all I could think about was that I clearly remember the year he was born. I was in the first grade for Pete's sake. Then I realized that when he was seven, I was fourteen. Which means I could've been his babysitter."

"I think you're overthinking it."

Ashley sighed. "Maybe. Probably. But I still can't shake that feeling. He is great though."

"You kissed him again, didn't you?"

"I sure did. And man, that boy can kiss. I swear, he makes me feel sixteen when he kisses me."

Summer couldn't hide her smile. "I still think he's a keeper."

Ashley shook her head. "I've made up my mind. We're going out this weekend, and I'm going to tell him I can't see him again." She frowned. "I wish I could handle it, but I can't. I'm too scared he'll start to think of me as old and want to trade me in for a younger model."

Summer could only surmise that had been what happened in Ashley's marriage, but she wasn't certain. "You might be surprised."

"Or I might be heartbroken. I'd rather be alone than have

my heart broken by Justin."

"There are no guarantees. On anything." Summer had learned that lesson the hard way.

Ashley raked a strand of blond hair from her face. "I know. But I'd rather be safe than sorry."

Summer stood up from her desk. "I'll be out for the rest of the afternoon. I'm going to the boat to wait for Luke to get home from work. I want to see how he's doing. Maybe he doesn't realize what today is."

"Okay." Ashley turned her attention back to her computer.

Thirty minutes later, Summer pulled up to the marina. Luke should be here soon. She turned off the engine and went to sit on the dock next to the water. It was so peaceful. Water had always calmed her. She glanced over to where the *Summer Girl* sat. Had she been too hard on him for buying it? Maybe they would've had a great time on the boat this summer.

She glanced at her watch. He should be here by now. She picked up her phone and dialed his number.

Voice mail.

Where would he go? She took a deep breath and tried not to worry.

After fifteen minutes, she tried the call again and still got his voice mail. Her heart pounded. What if something had happened to him? It had been her constant thought over the past weeks. That something would happen and no one would know.

Until it was too late.

Summer picked up the phone and tried Rose's number. Maybe Luke had decided he needed to be around his family today.

"Hello," Rose said.

Summer quickly explained why she'd called.

"I haven't seen him, but I'm glad you called me," Rose said. "He told me what was going on. He told me everything. I'm so sorry for your loss."

Summer's eyes widened in surprise. It wasn't like Luke to confide in anyone. "Thank you. I'm surprised he told you though."

Rose chuckled. "Oh, I had to drag it out of him, and he kicked and screamed the whole time. Getting that man to talk is almost impossible."

Tell me about it. "Well, I'm sorry to bother you. I hoped you might know where he was today."

"Hang on. I think you and I should get together. I've dealt with the loss of a child, too. I'd love to talk to you about it. See if I can help any. I wish I'd known when it happened. I know how lonely the experience can be."

Unexpected emotion washed over Summer. She'd always gotten along with Rose, but Luke had wanted to keep his distance from his family. "Thank you. I'd like that."

"No problem," Rose said. "I'll call you in a week or two, and we'll make plans to meet."

"Okay."

"And Summer? You might try the cemetery. I went out earlier this morning and took some fresh flowers. I have no idea if that's a place Luke would go, but it might be."

Summer ended the call and sat in the SUV for another minute. As far as she knew, Luke hadn't visited the cemetery since the day of Bobby's funeral. Maybe today had been the day he'd finally faced it.

She headed to North Charleston to the cemetery where

Bobby had been laid to rest. Her mind reeled with the news that Rose had also lost a child. She and Luke should've known about it. And they would have if they were closer to his side of the family. She resolved to strengthen that bond once she and Luke got things worked out.

If they did.

She drove the SUV through the cemetery gates and spotted Luke's truck in the distance. She quickly parked next to it and set out toward Bobby's grave. It seemed like just yesterday when they'd been out here for the burial. Luke had been stoic, unwavering. At first she'd admired his strength, but soon she had begun to worry that it was unhealthy.

And then she'd miscarried and had been so focused on herself, she hadn't the time to make sure he was dealing with his grief.

"Hey," she said quietly as she approached Bobby's grave.

Luke rose from where he was kneeling and turned to face her. "How'd you find me?"

"Lucky guess." She stood next to him. "You okay?"

He raked his fingers through his hair. He still wore his park service uniform but had left his hat in the truck. "I'm not sure." He reached over and took her hand. "I've made a mess of things, haven't I?"

She squeezed his hand. "Let's focus on remembering Bobby today."

"He's at peace," Luke said quietly. "It took me a long time to realize it."

She glanced over at him. Something seemed different, but she couldn't put her finger on it.

Luke continued. "I think the accident was so violent, I couldn't imagine him being at peace. You know?"

Violent was the only word that could be used. Bobby's car had been unrecognizable as a car. And an open casket hadn't been an option. In a lot of ways, she knew that had only made it more difficult for Luke. "He knew the Lord. Had his life in order. So yes, I believe he's at peace."

Luke nodded. "I'm trying to find my own peace with the situation."

"It's hard. But you know Bobby would want you to let go."

Luke knelt down and brushed a speck of dirt from the headstone. "I'm getting there." He rose and faced her. "I'd like to take you out to dinner. Would you go with me?"

His uncertainty surprised her. After years of dating and marriage, she wouldn't have expected him to be so unsure about asking her. "I'd like that." She smiled. "A lot."

"Saturday? Pick you up at seven?"

She nodded. "Sounds good." She jerked her chin toward her vehicle. "I'm going to go and give you some time alone." She turned to go then walked back to him. "I'm glad to see you." She reached up and cupped his face with her hand. "I miss you."

His lips curved into a smile, and he put his hand on hers. "You, too. See you Saturday."

She walked to her SUV feeling much lighter than she had when she'd arrived. Luke's dinner invitation told her that he was willing to work on their relationship.

And that gave her more hope than she'd felt in a long time.

Chapter 27

Justin paced in front of Samantha's townhouse. She'd called and asked him to stop by, but no one was home. He glanced at the clock on his phone. If he didn't hurry, he'd be late picking up Ashley.

They'd gone out on a date once since the Memorial Day cookout. He'd taken her to dinner at his favorite little hole-in-the-wall restaurant, and they'd finally made it to a movie. The kisses had been fiery, but he'd had a suspicion Ashley was upset about something. She'd been quiet at dinner, but when he'd asked why, she claimed to be tired.

He couldn't help but worry he was going to mess up their budding relationship. Ashley was easily the best girl he'd ever dated. She had every quality he'd been looking for. Hopefully tonight would go better.

Samantha's older model car pulled into the driveway. She climbed out and lifted eight-month-old Allison out of her car seat. "Hey."

"You need some help?" Justin walked over to the car.

She shook her head. "Nah. Allison and the diaper bag are all I've got." She held her keys out to him. "You can unlock the door though."

He quickly unlocked the front door and held it open for Samantha. "Where's Colton?" he asked.

"At Mama's. He's staying the weekend."

Justin narrowed his eyes. Each time he learned that Colton was staying with Samantha's mother, he cringed. The older woman was in no shape to care for an active toddler.

Her poor health kept her bedridden much of the time, and she definitely had a hard time keeping up with Colton. "Oh."

Samantha set Allison on a blanket on the floor. "Sorry to call you over here like this, but I didn't want to talk on the phone."

"Do you need money? Because if the kids need something, I'll do what I can."

She smiled. "You might be the nicest guy in the world. Honestly."

He blushed. "I just want to help if I can."

"Actually I just wanted to let you know that I'm moving."

An icy vise gripped his heart. He'd known this day might come, but he hadn't realized how it would impact him. "When? Where?"

Samantha sighed. "As soon as I can get packed. Carl and I want to make a fresh start."

He didn't say anything about the wisdom of making a fresh start with a felon. He believed in second chances as much as the next guy but hated to think of Colton being raised by a less-than-stellar role model. "I see."

"Don't judge. Carl was in the wrong place at the wrong time. He's not a bad guy."

Justin held his tongue. He wasn't so sure about that but didn't want to get into it now. He was much more concerned with Colton.

"He's got some family near Atlanta. So it looks like we're Georgia-bound." She tucked a strand of platinum blond hair behind her ear. "We're not taking Colton." She glanced at him. "He'd just be more than we can handle, with trying to find jobs and day care and all."

Justin narrowed his eyes. "Where is he going to live?"

"With Mama," Samantha said. "I wanted you to know because I hope that you'll still be involved in his life. She'll need all the help she can get."

He frowned. He knew he should be relieved that he'd still be able to be part of Colton's life. But he wasn't sure it was the best situation for the child. He didn't want to get into that with Samantha though. "Thanks for letting me know. If you need me to help move his stuff over to her house, I'll be glad to."

She smiled. "Thanks. That would be great."

Justin said his good-byes and climbed into his pickup. His mind whirled with possibilities he wanted to talk through with Ashley. Maybe she could help him figure out how to handle the situation.

Ashley glanced in the mirror one last time. She'd opted for low-key tonight. A simple yellow V-neck top, jeans, and flip-flops were a lot more casual than she normally wore on a date. But she knew tonight was the night she had to end things with Justin.

She went into the living room and peeked out the window.

Justin slammed the truck door and started up the sidewalk to her porch. He looked adorable. As usual.

But she had to be strong. She couldn't get distracted by his surfer-boy blond hair and blue eyes. And she certainly couldn't look at his mouth and wish it were on hers.

Because that would only make things tougher.

She flung the door open, unable to keep a smile from her face. "Hey." She heard the excitement in her voice and hated herself a little bit for being so weak. When she was around him, she could actually feel herself glowing. That didn't bode well for her decision to walk away from him.

Justin beamed back. "Sorry I'm late." He pulled her into a big hug.

She relaxed against him for a second and inhaled his soapy scent. "Don't worry about it." She pulled away and met his gaze. "You ready? I'm starved."

He hesitated. "Actually I wondered if you'd be okay with ordering a pizza. I need to get your opinion on something."

She shrugged. "Of course. Pizza is good." She stepped back and ushered him inside, thankful she'd spent time that morning cleaning.

Justin sank onto the couch and looked up at her. "It's not too soon for a night in, is it?"

She adored quiet nights at home. But the knowledge that he was going to be in her personal space unnerved her. A restaurant would've been safe. It's easy to keep distance in public. But a night at home, on the couch, eating and talking? It would be impossible for her to keep her hands off him. She felt drawn to him like a magnet. "It's not too soon. Plus I love pizza." Instead of going to sit next to him, she grabbed a phone book from the end table. "Any certain brand?"

He grinned. "I'm a Domino's kind of guy, but we can order whatever you like."

"Domino's it is." After a brief discussion, they settled on a large, thin crust pepperoni. Ashley called for delivery then sat down in the recliner next to the couch.

Justin looked at her with a puzzled expression. "I took a shower before I came over. What gives?"

She shrugged. "Nothing. Sorry. Just habit, I guess." *And*

*the fact that I'm afraid when you find out I could've been your
babysitter, you'll run away.*

He twisted his mouth into a smile. "Okay. As long as it's
not me." He sighed. "So I've had a weird day. That's part of
why I wanted to stay in."

"What happened?"

She listened to his story about Samantha's impending
move. "How do you feel about it?" she asked.

"Torn. On the one hand, I'm glad she's not taking Colton.
But on the other, I'm worried about him living with his
grandmother." He shook his head and sighed. "Samantha's
mom means well, but she's in poor health. I can't imagine
what kind of life Colton will have growing up there."

Even though she'd only seen Justin and Colton together
twice, she still had a pretty good idea of how much Justin
cared for the child. And it was clear that Colton was crazy
about Justin. "I guess you need to decide how far you're
willing to go for Colton. And what kind of sacrifices you're
willing to make."

Justin met her eyes. "Am I crazy? Single guy, about to turn
thirty, and considering raising a child who isn't even mine?"

"Like I said. It will be a huge lifestyle change. I think
you'd better be sure you're ready for that kind of commitment
before you start down the path. Because Colton certainly
doesn't need to be displaced again."

He leaned his head back against the couch. "Decisions
are hard."

She chuckled. "Some decisions are easy. But life-changing
decisions take a little more thought. And a little more prayer."

Justin sat up and looked at her. "You're right. I should pray
about it. Talk to my parents." He raked his hands through

his hair. "Because they would be part of the commitment. Obviously I would need help."

"For what it's worth, from what I saw at the cookout, they're crazy about Colton." She was pretty sure Justin's parents would be completely supportive. She couldn't help but wonder what that kind of family support felt like. Maybe she'd never know.

Justin nodded. "They sure are. They've known him since he was a tiny baby."

"Do you think you're ready for that kind of commitment?" she asked.

He chuckled. "I've never been one of those commitment-phobic guys. I've never been scared of settling down, just scared of settling down with the wrong person. And in my mind, kids were always going to be part of the picture."

"So you think going from a couple of visits a week to being responsible for him full-time is something you want?" Ashley wasn't trying to discourage him. But she wanted him to realize that commitment should mean forever. Not until something better or more fun came along. She'd been on the wrong end of that once and had been devastated.

He nodded. "I do. I think anything worth having is worth making changes for. And Colton makes my life more complete."

"Well then, I think you should talk to your parents to see what they think. And you don't know for sure that Samantha would be on board, right?"

Justin nodded. "True. But over the past year, I've started getting the impression that if I even broached the subject, she'd be ready to give me custody of him on the spot." He reached over and took her hand. "But I need to know what you think."

She regarded him for a long moment. "I think this is something you have to figure out for yourself."

Justin's face fell.

The doorbell rang and saved her from more questions.

She grabbed her purse and took some bills from her wallet.

"Let me get it." Justin walked over to her.

She shook her head. "Nope. It's on me. You might be raising a child soon." She patted him on the arm. "I hear that's expensive. You should save your money." She motioned toward the kitchen. "You can go get us drinks and plates though."

She paid the delivery guy and put the hot pizza on the coffee table. She sat on the floor in front of the coffee table and opened the box.

"That looks great." Justin set down the plates and two bottles of water.

Once they'd filled their plates, Justin said a quick prayer.

Ashley flipped the TV on to a rerun of *Seinfeld*, and they ate in silence.

"That was good stuff." Justin tossed a sliver of pizza on his plate and sat back on the couch.

She nodded. "Good call on the takeout." She took a sip of water and watched Justin out of the corner of her eye.

He leaned forward and caught her gaze. "I'm just going to throw this out there, Ashley. I'm sorry to do this to you at this point, because it's not like we've known each other long enough to think about the future. . .but what do *you* think about the possibility of Colton being a permanent part of my life?"

There it was. The question she'd been hoping he wouldn't ask. Except that there was a tiny part of her that was glad he cared. "I think you'll be a great role model."

Justin narrowed his eyes. "That's not what I mean, and you know it. I don't usually lay all my cards on the table so soon, but I really like you. And I could actually see a future for us."

Her heart pounded. It would be so easy to tell him she saw the same thing. Or at least she would if he were a few years older. Or even better, if she were the same age as him and still had a fully functional biological clock on her side. "Justin. . . I don't know what to say. I mean, we've only been out a few times. I've had fun and all, but I don't think you should take me into consideration at all when you're deciding what to do about Colton."

He flinched.

She wanted to take it all back. She wanted to take his hand and pull him to her and tell him that he was exactly what she'd been looking for. But she couldn't do it. She couldn't risk her heart on someone who would end up disappointed in her in a few years.

"You're right. I'm sorry. It was too much too soon." He stood. "I shouldn't have put you on the spot like that." He jerked his chin toward the door. "I should probably go."

She stood and followed him to the door. "Bye," she whispered.

Justin reached out and smoothed her hair. "I'll call you soon," he said softly.

Ashley ached to kiss him until it was okay.

Instead, she watched him walk out the door.

Chapter 28

Summer smoothed glossing cream through her hair. She'd decided to wear it down tonight because she knew Luke liked it that way. She'd even gone shopping earlier and bought a new dress to wear to their dinner.

She glanced at herself in the full-length mirror, confident Luke would appreciate the results of an afternoon of pampering. She dabbed on a touch of pink lipstick and put the tube in her purse.

She was ready.

It might seem weird to be so excited about a date with a man she'd known for half of her life. But over the past months, she'd felt like Luke was looking right through her. Ever since the miscarriage, Luke had barely touched her. Tonight she wanted to turn his head, just like when they were teenagers. She wanted to show him that she was still the woman he'd fallen in love with. The woman he used to not be able to keep his hands off.

The ringing doorbell announced his arrival.

She took a deep breath and walked slowly down the stairs. *Please, Lord, help us get back on the right track.* Summer paused at the door then flung it open.

Jefferson stood on the other side, a grin on his face. He let out a low wolf whistle. "You are smokin' hot." He looked her up and down. "Sorry to be so blunt, but wow."

Her face flamed. "Thanks." She smoothed her dress, suddenly self-conscious. "What are you doing here?"

"Clearly you've got plans. I don't want to keep you." He

held up an empty cup. "I know it's cliché, but I actually need to borrow some milk. I'm making mac and cheese and was right in the middle of it when I remembered I'm out."

She raised an eyebrow but didn't say anything. She'd never known Jefferson to do anything domestic. In fact, she had her doubts he could even boil water, but she didn't have time to get into it now. "Wait here." She left him standing on the porch while she went to the fridge. She grabbed the milk and walked back to where he stood. "Just take the whole thing. It's only half a gallon, and I've barely used any."

He took the jug from her. "Are you sure?"

She nodded. "Yep. Enjoy your mac and cheese." She started to shut the door, but Jefferson stopped it with his hand.

"Hang on."

Summer sighed. "What?"

"Where are you off to all dolled up?" He indicated her dress with a jut of his chin.

"Dinner with Luke." She steeled her gaze on him, daring him to say anything.

Jefferson raised his eyebrows. "Well, that's great news. I'm glad you two are trying to work things out."

She nodded. "Me, too." She shooed him off the porch. "Now leave. Seeing you here will only put Luke in a bad mood."

Jefferson wrinkled his nose. "Fine. Have fun." With a wave, he walked through the iron gate that led to the sidewalk.

She swung the door closed and leaned against it. Jefferson wasn't all bad. It was kind of nice to see him again after all these years. But she knew Luke didn't share her opinion.

She glanced at the clock on the end table. He should be here in five minutes. That would give Jefferson plenty of time to get home unnoticed. The last thing she wanted was for Luke to have another run-in with Jefferson.

Milo stretched and jumped down from the couch. He walked over and sat down at her feet.

"You're looking fit, sweet boy." She reached down and scratched him behind the ear. She and Milo had been going on lots of walks lately, and he'd already dropped some of his extra weight. He seemed happy even though she'd taken away his off-leash privileges. After the squirrel incident, she'd decided not to risk it.

The doorbell rang.

Better be Luke this time. Summer paused then opened the door slowly.

Luke stood on the other side. He held a bouquet of roses in his hand, but his expression was strained.

"My favorite," she said, taking the flowers. "Come inside."

She waited for him to comment on how she looked, but he went straight for Milo. "I'll put these in a vase, and then we can go." She walked into the kitchen and tried to chase away her disappointment. Maybe he no longer found her attractive.

She filled a vase with water and put the roses inside. She carried the arrangement into the living room and set it on a table. "Perfect." She smiled at Luke. "Ready?"

He nodded. "Starving." He held the door open for her, and they stepped out onto the porch. "The yard looks pretty good, but it's getting a little high. I'll come over and mow soon."

She glanced at him. He looked good but tired. "If you'd rather me get someone else to do it, I'd be glad to."

His jaw tensed. "Maybe Jefferson would like to take care of it. Except for that whole manual labor thing."

She furrowed her brow but didn't say anything.

"My car or yours?" he asked.

"Yours."

Luke opened the passenger door and helped her inside. "Magnolia's okay?"

"Perfect." She watched as he walked around the truck and climbed into the driver's seat. "So did you stay long at the cemetery after I left the other day?"

He backed slowly out of their driveway. "Not too much longer. I left there and went to see Daddy."

She turned to look at his profile. As far as she knew, Luke hadn't seen his father since Bobby's funeral. "How's he doing?"

Luke shook his head. "Not well. Not well at all. His mind is wandering. He thinks I'm Uncle Pete."

She reached over and rubbed his leg. "I'm sorry. I know that's got to be tough."

"I waited too long." Luke slowed the truck to a stop at a red light. "He doesn't even know it's me." He reached down and covered her hand with his. "It's one of many regrets."

She hated to hear it. She'd always hoped Luke and his daddy would somehow make amends. When she was pregnant, she'd foolishly thought the baby would be the bridge that healed the relationship. But it sounded like that wasn't going to happen.

Luke parked the truck and came around to help her down. He didn't let go of her hand as they walked toward the restaurant.

And even though there was still a distance between them

at least a mile wide, Summer held on to his hand for all she was worth.

Luke wasn't sure which was the biggest surprise of the evening so far. The fact that Summer looked more beautiful than he could ever remember her looking or that he'd seen Jefferson leaving the house as he pulled into the driveway.

That dude was really on his nerves. Jefferson had held up a half gallon of milk and pointed to it as Luke drove by. But Luke wasn't stupid. Jefferson had no more needed to borrow milk than Luke needed a hole in the head.

He wasn't going to mention it to Summer though. Sweet Summer. She'd never think Jefferson had an ulterior motive for anything. She'd always believed the best in people. And he could hardly complain about it, as that was one of the things that had drawn him to her in the first place. But it really chapped his hide to see Jefferson with that smirk, sauntering out of the driveway like he'd just won a ticket to paradise.

Luke knew he'd only look like a jealous fool if he said something, and he didn't want a repeat of their Memorial Day argument. So he'd keep his mouth shut. "You look pretty tonight." He tugged on her hand as they walked into the restaurant. "Even prettier than the day we met."

She beamed. "Thanks."

They followed the hostess to a table for two and ordered their standard fare.

"Is it boring that we always order the same thing here?" Summer asked.

He shook his head and admired the way her dark hair fell

in waves around her face. "Not at all. It's comforting. Like a warm blanket on a cold night." He grinned.

"So what made you decide to go see your daddy?" she asked.

He filled her in on his visit to see Rose and go through Bobby's things. "I couldn't be the reason Katie Beth and Dale didn't get to go to Disney."

Summer nodded. "I'm glad you stepped in. I actually spoke to Rose on the phone earlier in the week." She locked eyes with him. "I think we've messed up by not being more involved with their lives."

"You mean *I've* messed up." He took a deep breath. "I've had a lot of time to think. A lot of time to consider the wrong decisions I've made. I don't know why I always thought everyone was against me, but I did."

"I've never been against you," Summer said quietly. "You know that."

He reached over and took her hand. "I know. You're the reason I'm not completely screwed up."

Summer gave him a tiny smile. "Glad I could help." She sighed. "What are we going to do here?"

"Eat?"

At her steely glare, he chuckled. "Sorry. I'm trying. But this whole getting in touch with my emotions thing isn't exactly easy for me."

"No. Emotions have never been your strong point."

He sighed. "I've been really focusing on letting go of my anger. I don't know how you stood it for so long." Ever since he'd opened Bobby's Bible, he'd been thinking about where his anger was coming from and how to get rid of it.

"I kept thinking you'd snap out of it. But you never did."

The waitress set their food on the table.

Summer caught his eye. He knew she was waiting on him to pray for their food. But he hadn't quite worked up to talking to God yet. "Dig in," he said with a smile.

"Summer," a petite blond woman said, coming up to their table. "It's nice to see you again."

Summer smiled at the woman. "Thanks, you, too." She glanced at Luke. "This is Madelyn Ashworth. She's just opened up a new bridal shop over on Calhoun Street." She turned to Madelyn. "This is my husband, Luke Nelson."

He stood and shook Madelyn's hand. "Nice to meet you," he said.

"Did you tell him about the dress?" Madelyn trilled.

Summer shook her head.

"What dress?" he asked.

"Your beautiful wife had never tried on a wedding dress before. But you probably know that." Madelyn giggled. "We had her try on her dream gown the other day just for fun. She looked like a princess."

He raised his eyebrows at Summer. "I'll bet."

"You'll have to get your friend to show him the pictures." Madelyn patted Summer on the back. "Well, I don't want to keep you from your dinner." She smiled at him. "Nice to meet you."

"You, too," he said.

Once she was gone, he looked at Summer. "Your dream wedding dress, huh? You're not planning on running off with some other guy are you?" As soon as the words left his mouth, he had a vision of her with Jefferson.

She shook her head. "It was stupid. But Ashley and Madelyn were so persuasive. And the dress was beautiful."

She shrugged. "I guess I've always wondered what I'd look like in a fancy bridal gown."

"I already know what you'd look like. I don't need a picture to tell me. You were the most beautiful bride I'd ever seen on the day I married you, even if we were just at City Hall in church clothes."

She gave him a half smile. "Thanks." She sighed.

"Are you upset?"

Summer shrugged. "Just trying to process things here." She chewed on her bottom lip. "I know you're working through things. But I think maybe there's stuff with us that needs to be worked through, too."

"I don't want to lose you. To lose us." He raked his fingers through his hair. "I'll do whatever it takes."

"You mean that?" She looked at him hopefully. "Counseling even?"

He slowly nodded. "Yes. Whatever it takes. You make the arrangements, and I'll be there."

Her lips turned upward in a smile. "It means a lot that you're willing to do that. I think after the year we've had, we could both use some help dealing."

He nodded. "I'm sorry I didn't see it sooner. I kept thinking I could handle everything on my own. Kept thinking that if I didn't talk about things, they'd go away." He shook his head. "I don't want to turn into my daddy."

She reached out and squeezed his hand. "Why do you say that?"

"I get the feeling that he wishes he'd done things differently and not been so distant from us, especially after Mama died. And it hit me the other day that I was doing the same thing. I watched grief eat him up. Watched it turn him into someone I didn't recognize. And then I almost let it do the same thing to me." He shook his head. "I need to learn from his mistakes. At this point, I think it's the only way to be the son I never was."

Summer's blue eyes glistened with tears. "I've been praying that you'd come to that conclusion."

He gripped her hand. "Keep praying for me, Summer. It helps me sleep better at night, knowing you're praying for me."

A tear trickled down her face. "Let's go."

He pulled some cash out of his wallet and put it on the table then stood and held out a hand to her.

They walked slowly to his truck.

He paused before he opened the passenger door. "We'll be okay. Right?"

She nodded. "Hope so."

He pulled her tightly to him and inhaled the sweet scent of her shampoo.

Chapter 29

Ashley listened as Summer filled her in on the events of the weekend. "What do you think changed his mind about counseling?"

Summer shrugged. "I have no idea. Rose. His daddy's condition. Having time to think." She sighed. "Honestly, I don't care who or what the catalyst was. I'm just thankful he wants to give it a try."

Ashley had been surprised when Summer started the day by telling her something personal. Since Luke had moved to the boat, Summer had started to open up more. It was almost as if she'd been letting things build up inside her until she couldn't help but let them out. "Me, too. I know I saw a counselor after my divorce. The thing that helped the most was for me to talk through my feelings. It sounds like that's what y'all need, too."

"Luke's never been much on sharing the way he feels. I think that's one reason why he writes songs. They help him express things he can't say out loud in conversation."

Ashley doodled on a pad in front of her. "He's that way even with you? I mean, I can see that he might not be all touchy-feely with other people, but I figured it was different where you're concerned."

Summer chuckled. "I wish. Just getting him to say, 'I love you,' is a big deal. He usually says 'Me, too,' or something like that." She sighed. "I *know* he loves me. But it would be nice to hear it verbalized every now and then."

"I guess that doesn't come easy to everyone." Ashley

couldn't help but think of Justin. He might be the exact opposite of Luke in that regard. Justin wasn't afraid to express himself.

"So how about you? Have you gotten over the age difference with Justin yet?"

Ashley shook her head. "It's more than the age difference. I mean, that's the driving force behind my uncertainty. But then there's that awful feeling of vulnerability that goes along with letting someone into your life."

"And you're not ready for that?"

Ashley didn't know if she'd ever be ready for that again. "I love spending time with Justin. But he seems like he's ready to jump in with both feet, and I barely have a toe in the water. You know?" She sighed.

"So how did it go the other night? Did you tell him that you couldn't see him again?"

Ashley shook her head. "Not exactly. He'd had a tough day." She explained about Samantha and Colton. "And then he wanted to know what I thought he should do. I could tell he was implying that his decision to take on more responsibility for Colton would impact me. It's kind of flattering that he'd even take my feelings into consideration. Except that it adds another dimension to the situation." She sighed. "Because then I would be involved with Colton's life, too. And then if things didn't work out or whatever, that's one more hurt to add to the pile."

Summer frowned. "It still seems like a lot of excuses to me. Are you sure you're not just looking for a reason to write him off in order to protect yourself?"

"No. At least I don't think so." Ashley rifled through some papers on her desk and refused to meet Summer's gaze.

Maybe her friend was right. Were the qualms she had about Justin legitimate? Or was she just scared of getting hurt again?

Justin wasn't used to carrying around so much anxiety. But between trying to figure out what to do about Colton and trying to guess what was going on inside Ashley's head, he was a basket case.

He'd spent Sunday afternoon talking to his parents about the situation with Samantha and Colton, and they'd been very supportive. He was supposed to talk to Samantha tonight, and he had no idea what to expect.

"I'm not going to pray for Samantha to agree to Colton living with you," Mom had said. "Instead, I'm going to pray that the situation will work out according to God's will."

Justin liked that outlook. Some people might think it was crazy to have that kind of faith. But he couldn't imagine living any other way.

He pulled up in front of the townhouse and thought about what he wanted to say. He'd decided that either way, he'd make the best out of the situation. And even if Samantha was firm in her decision for Colton to live with her mama, Justin knew he'd still get to hang out with the little boy often.

He closed the door on his pickup and walked up the sidewalk to the townhouse. He rapped on the door and waited.

The door swung open, and Samantha stood on the other side. She smiled. "Come in. But please excuse the mess." She ushered him inside.

Boxes in various stages of being packed were piled around the living room. He stepped over two boxes labeled KITCHEN and sat down on the couch. "Looks like you've been busy."

She nodded. "Yeah. I'm ready for a fresh start." She knelt on the floor next to a bookshelf and began to stack books in a box.

"Can I ask you something?"

Samantha looked up. "Sure. What's up?" She set down the books and looked at him with tired eyes.

Justin sighed. "I'm here about Colton. Have you told him that you're leaving him behind?" It broke his heart to think of Colton feeling unwanted.

"Look, it wasn't an easy decision." Samantha picked at a loose cuticle. "But I think it's the best one for everyone."

"Do you see this as a permanent arrangement?"

She shrugged. "I don't know. Maybe. I guess it depends on how Mama does with him."

"So you realize that she might not be able to care for him forever?"

Samantha narrowed her eyes. "Of course I do. It's just that. . ." She trailed off. "Carl doesn't like Colton too much. I mean, Allison is his own flesh and blood, so he dotes on her. But Colton gets on his nerves. You know how much energy he has."

Justin had suspected as much. "And this is your chance to get out of here and start over as a family."

"Well, yeah." She buried her face in her hands. "Honestly, sometimes I think it would've been better for all of us if I'd have given Colton up when he was born. I never feel like I give him what he needs anymore. Allison ends up getting my attention, and he has to do his own thing." She wrapped her arms around herself. "And then I start to feel like I must be the worst mother in the world."

Samantha had always been plagued by insecurities about her mothering skills. That was one of the reasons Justin had gotten so involved in the first place. When Colton was newborn, she'd been terrified she'd hurt him somehow. Justin had ended up doing a lot of bottle and diaper duty as a result.

"In light of that, there's something I want you to think about." He took a breath. "I'd like for Colton to live with me." He leveled his gaze on her. "Permanently."

Her eyes widened. "No way. You don't mean that."

He nodded. "I'm serious."

"But he requires a lot of attention. I mean constantly. And soon he'll be in preschool, so there'll be all that stuff to contend with." She narrowed her eyes. "Why would you want to do that? Don't you think it will mess up your life?"

Justin rarely got angry. But with each word she spoke, he felt his blood boil. "I know he needs attention. And I don't mind giving it to him. And contending with stuff like preschool and T-ball and homework wouldn't be an imposition, because I love him and want what's best for him."

Samantha's head dropped. "Sorry. I can't fathom someone voluntarily choosing that life."

He stood. "I know I don't have a claim to Colton. But I want what's best for him. If you decide that's being raised by your mama, that's fine. But if you think he'd be better off with me, my offer stands." He turned to go.

Samantha walked him to the door. "Would it be just a trial basis?"

"No." He paused in the doorway. "Colton doesn't deserve to be some kind of guinea pig that lets me figure out if I'm ready for the responsibility. If I didn't think I was ready on a permanent basis, I wouldn't have offered." He turned to go.

"Wait," she called, following him down the sidewalk.

He turned to face her. "Yeah?"

"You're right." She gave him a tiny smile. "Colton would be better off with you than he would with anyone else. Even me. You've been there for him when no one else was." She bit her lip. "He'd be lucky to have you."

"No. . . I'd be lucky to have him," Justin said.

She smiled. "Maybe you'd be lucky to have each other."

"Then it's settled?"

Samantha nodded. "I'll talk to Mama about it tonight. I think she'll be relieved. But you'll take him to visit her, right?"

"Of course."

"And I'll want to see him when I come to town to see Mama."

Justin nodded. "I'm glad to hear it."

He waved good-bye and climbed into the truck. He'd tried to tell himself he was going to be okay no matter the outcome of the conversation with Samantha. But the relief that washed over him now told him that only one outcome would have satisfied him.

He didn't know how it would go when Colton moved in. But he knew that with his parents' help and lots of prayers, they'd be fine.

Chapter 30

Summer tossed a rawhide chew onto Milo's dog bed at the shop. He'd seemed depressed this morning, so she'd decided to bring him to the office.

She sat down at her desk and flipped open her planner. As she turned the page to today's date, her heart dropped. The words DUE DATE written in bold jumped out at her. She shut the planner tightly and sat back in her chair.

How had she forgotten?

"Morning," Ashley said. "You're here early."

Summer looked up. "I'm supposed to meet with Jennifer St. Claire tomorrow." She shrugged. "You know how picky she is. I was trying to put together a couple of possible itineraries for her out-of-town guests."

Ashley nodded. "Yes, being overprepared is the best bet where Jennifer is concerned." She smiled. "Otherwise she'll start trying to take over, and everything goes downhill from there."

Summer managed a smile. It was silly to be so upset over a date that didn't mean anything anymore. But telling herself that didn't take away the sorrow.

"You okay?" Ashley asked. "You look pale. Do you think your blood sugar is low or something?"

Summer shook her head. "I probably just need some sunshine." She turned her computer on. "I might walk down to Marion Square later on and get a little sun." The historic square was a gathering spot for college students, tourists, and businesspeople who worked along nearby King Street. She'd spent countless hours there as a teenager, watching college boys play Frisbee or football. Now that her office was within walking distance, it was a favorite place for an outdoor lunch or quick afternoon break.

"Sounds nice. I'd offer to go, too, except that Justin is supposed to drop by around lunchtime. It's our final meeting about the website." She sank into her office chair. "But if you happen to stop in at Cupcake, I'd be glad for you to bring me a sample." The little bakery across from Marion Square was one of their favorite places to go for an afternoon pick-me-up.

"Of course." Summer glanced up from her computer. "And I hope things go well with Justin."

A shadow crossed Ashley's pretty face. "It's strictly business." She shrugged. "At least mostly."

A little before noon, Summer grabbed her purse. "I'll be out for a little while. But I have my phone if you need me."

Ashley nodded. "Okay."

She headed North on King Street, lost in thought. She considered calling Luke but thought better of it. He was at work. Besides, he probably wouldn't realize today had been her due date anyway.

"Summer," a voice behind her called.

She turned to see Jefferson hurrying toward her. "Hi."

He grinned as he reached her. "Sorry to sneak up on you. I went by your office, and your assistant told me where you were headed." He chuckled. "Of course I had to really turn on the charm to get her to tell me."

"I'll bet. I feel certain that once you found yourself in the presence of a beautiful blond, the charm automatically turned on."

He laughed. "You've got me there."

She rolled her eyes, certain that Jefferson had laid it on thick with Ashley. Thankfully she was too suspicious to fall for any of his lines. "What did you need? You in the market for an event planner?"

"I was going to see if you wanted to grab lunch."

She furrowed her brow. "I'm not hungry. I'm actually on my way to Blue Bicycle Books."

"Oh. Well then, will it annoy you if I tag along?"

She wanted to be alone for a while to sort things out in her head. But if she said that, Jefferson wouldn't leave her alone until she explained why. "I'm going to browse around the bookstore and then maybe pop over to Cupcake for a treat. I doubt that's the way you want to spend your lunch hour."

"You underestimate me. I happen to love books *and* cupcakes. So it's a win-win."

They walked in companionable silence the rest of the way.

"I love this place," she said once they reached the bookstore. "The bicycle outside and the quirky window displays. . .such a great little store."

Jefferson nodded. "I've only been in it a couple of times, but I've been impressed."

She always tried to support local businesses over chains when she could. Whether it be the farmer's market or a bookstore, it always made her feel good to do business with local owners.

Jefferson held the door open for her, and they went inside.

She browsed the new release section while Jefferson went to check out the literature room. She picked up the new Mary Higgins Clark and took it to the checkout counter.

Once she paid for her purchase, she poked her head into the back room. "I'm going to get a cupcake."

He followed her outside. "Is everything okay?"

She nodded. "Just having one of those days."

"Tell you what. . .why don't you go find a place to sit in the park. I'll go grab some cupcakes. There's probably a line."

She should say no. The less Jefferson did for her, the better. But for just a moment, it would be nice to let someone take care of her. "Okay. Thanks."

"Chocolate, right?" he asked with a knowing smirk.

She nodded. "You got it. And get an extra one for Ashley."

He hurried off.

Summer found an empty bench in Marion Square and sat down. She tilted her face toward the sunshine and closed her eyes, not even caring if she looked silly. The warm rays bathed her face, and she began to relax.

"You know they say that's bad for you," Jefferson said.

She jerked her head down. "I need to put a bell on you so you'll stop sneaking up on me."

He chuckled. "Sorry." He held up a bag. "Maybe this will make up for it. Prove my usefulness." Jefferson sat down next to her. "We were in luck today. I didn't have to wait in line."

She reached for the bag. "Thanks." She pulled out a chocolate cupcake piled high with icing and bit into it. "So good."

He watched her eat. "How was your dinner the other night?"

She glanced up. "Good. Thanks for asking."

"I'm concerned, that's all."

She took another bite of her cupcake and watched a group of kids toss a football around. On this day in particular, she wished she could be like them. Light and carefree. Lately she'd felt like the weight of all her problems might crush her.

"You sure there's not anything else going on?" Jefferson asked. "Because you don't seem like yourself."

She glanced at him. "You don't even know me anymore. So maybe this *is* me being myself."

"Maybe. But I don't think so."

She finished her cupcake and brushed the crumbs from her skirt. She felt his eyes on her but refused to look at him. She wished she were somewhere else. Preferably the kind of place where no one would pry into her life and ask her what was wrong. Except that she'd learned the hard way that no matter how much you closed yourself off, the memories still managed to hitch a ride. They went wherever she did. No matter what.

Jefferson pulled out a handkerchief and handed it to her. "You'll feel better if you get it off your chest."

Summer took a breath. If she were thinking more clearly, she probably could've bluffed her way out of the situation. But as it stood, she did want to talk about it. Even if it was to Jefferson.

"This was supposed to be a really special day," she began.

Luke wasn't the kind of guy who called in sick to work when he wasn't actually sick. But this morning, he hadn't been able to get out of bed. And while he knew that the thing that plagued him wasn't contagious, he was still thankful for a generous sick leave policy.

Because he couldn't imagine facing the day as if it were

just a normal day.

Today was supposed to have been their baby's birthday. He'd typed it into the calendar on his phone months ago and hadn't thought about it again. Until he happened to see it last night.

His fingers had itched to call Summer, but he'd resisted. She had enough grief of her own without dealing with his.

So instead he'd called in sick today and had taken the boat out. It was a beautiful day, but it may as well have been raining to match his mood. Finally, he realized the only thing that might help him was talking to Summer.

He drove by the grocery store and picked up a bouquet of flowers. It had been ages since he'd shown up at her office to surprise her. He smiled to himself as he thought about her reaction.

Traffic snarled as he turned off of Cannon Street to King Street. He should've gone a different way. He tapped on the steering wheel as he waited for the red light to change. He hated traffic. He rolled down his window and tried to relax, despite the bumper-to-bumper cars.

He finally made it to Marion Square. Not too much farther now. He glanced out at the park. When he was in high school, he and some of his buddies used to play pickup football games there. It looked like not a lot had changed.

A familiar figure sitting on a bench caught his eye. He peered closer. Summer sat with Jefferson, engaged in what looked like an intense conversation.

His heart dropped. So this is what it had come to. Having a rendezvous with Jefferson on her lunch break. He fought the urge to park the truck right there and confront them.

Instead he kept driving.

An hour later, he found himself parked in front of Gram's house on Isle of Palms. His mind reeled. He trusted Summer. But he didn't trust Jefferson. And right now he was having a hard time rectifying those things in his mind.

A knock on his window made him jump.

Gram peered at him through her bifocals.

Luke cut the engine off and opened the door. "Hello." He climbed out of his truck and hugged the elderly woman.

"This is a surprise." Gram smiled. "And I can't say it's a bad one." She motioned toward the house. "Come inside and let me pour you a glass of fresh lemonade."

He followed her inside.

Gram's house was as nice as Summer's parents' home but on a much smaller scale. When she'd turned the family home on Legare over to Summer and him, she'd said it was because it was time to downsize.

He walked into the living room where large windows provided a spectacular view of the water. Gram might've moved into a smaller space, but the price tag on the property must've been enormous.

"Here you go," she said, handing him a tall glass of lemonade. "Let's sit out on the deck." She led the way outside.

He sat down in a comfortable chair on the deck opposite Gram.

"What brings you here?" she asked.

He sighed. "I'm not sure."

She smiled. "Oh Luke. I know what's going on. Summer told me you'd moved onto the boat." She reached across the table and patted his hand. "I know how difficult this year has been for y'all."

He nodded. He'd assumed Summer had confided in her

grandmother. And in a way he was glad, because that made his visit easier. "I need to know how to fix things."

Gram raised her eyebrows. "I don't think that's anything I can tell you. You'll have to figure it out all by yourself."

He shook his head. "It's so messed up. I have no idea how to make things right." He sighed. "And now she's spending all this time with Jefferson."

Gram met his gaze. "I've noticed."

Luke bristled. He'd hoped she would tell him he was crazy. "You have?"

"At the Memorial Day cookout. I noticed that he seemed to have an eye on her." She shook her head. "I've never cared for Jefferson, you know. He's just like his grandfather. Manipulative and vindictive."

"That's not a good combination." He sighed. "I'm trying hard not to be mad at Summer though. What is she thinking?"

"She's not thinking. I've spoken to her a few times over the past few weeks. You know how she is. Summer likes everything to be on schedule and everything to run smoothly. And when it doesn't. . ." She trailed off.

"When it doesn't, it's hard for her." He nodded in agreement. "But still, that's no excuse."

"I'm going to be blunt here, Luke." Gram raised an eyebrow at him.

He took a deep breath. "Please do."

"I've watched you and Summer drift apart this year. It hasn't been pretty. You went from being the kind of couple who could finish each other's sentences to the kind of couple who has no idea what the other is thinking." She shook her head. "I know there've been tough times. Your brother's accident and then Summer's miscarriage. And I know that sometimes after high stress events like that, relationships can take a hit. But you've got to decide if your marriage is worth fighting for. And if it is, then you're going to have to give it all you've got. And that might mean sacrifices and compromises and asking forgiveness."

He nodded. "I know it's worth fighting for. But what if she doesn't feel the same way?"

Gram furrowed her brow. "She's crazy about you. When she was here on Memorial Day, she looked so defeated and so lonely."

Although that sounded an awful lot like him these days, Luke hated to hear Summer described that way. "So what do I do?"

"Prove to her that you're on her side. What is it that I've heard the two of you say so often? That you're on her team?" Gram smiled. "That's the answer. Make sure she knows that you still want to be on her team. . .no matter what."

He nodded. He could only think of one thing that might prove to Summer that he wanted to stay in it for the long haul.

But he was going to need help to pull it off.

Chapter 31

Justin paused outside of Summer Weddings. Ashley was expecting him, but that didn't squash his nerves. Their last date had left a lot to be desired, and their last couple of phone calls had been awkward.

He opened the door, and Milo jumped up to greet him. "Hey, boy." He scratched the dog behind the ears.

"Hi," Ashley said, coming through the archway that separated the front of the shop from the kitchen. "Perfect timing. I just finished lunch."

He tried to mask his disappointment. He'd thought he'd ask her to have lunch after their meeting. But it looked like that would have to wait until another day.

She motioned at the chair across from her desk. "Have a seat."

He sank into the plush chair. "Well, I have great news."

She raised her eyebrows. "The site is ready?"

"Well that, yes. But I was actually going to tell you that Samantha agreed for Colton to live with me. We're still working out the details, but I guess I'm going to be his legal guardian." He grinned. "I'm a little nervous, but I know a lot of people were praying for the outcome. So I feel really good about the situation."

Ashley smiled. "That's great news. I'm happy for you." She turned her attention to the computer. "So about this website. . ."

He frowned. She wasn't making any effort to hide that she wanted to keep things professional today. "It's live. People can log on and create an account then build their 'dream' wedding out of the choices you've given them. They'll put all those things into their cart and submit it. The information will come to you, along with their contact information," he explained. "The cool thing is that since all the components have a price attached to them, it's possible for them to pay right online."

"So I'll get an e-mail?"

He nodded. "Yes. You'll get an e-mail whenever someone submits an event. It will tell you all of the specifics, and then you can reply either by phone or e-mail and go over everything. But this lets them narrow down and make choices without having to actually come to Charleston and do any legwork."

"I think this is going to be so cool."

"Me, too." He winked. "Whoever thought of it must be a genius."

She blushed. She'd confided in him that the project had been her brainchild. "There's also the possibility that no one will use it and it will be a huge waste of money."

"You might need to work on being a little more optimistic."

She brushed a loose strand of hair from her face. "I know."

He cleared his throat. "So what would you think about having dinner this weekend?"

Uncertainty flitted across her face. "I'm not sure. I've got a wedding on Saturday, and by the time that's over, I'll be exhausted."

He nodded. It had been his experience that people found time for the things they thought were important. So if she couldn't carve out any time over the whole weekend to see him, that spoke volumes. "Maybe some other time then." He liked her a lot. He thought they could actually have a future together. But he wasn't going to beg.

He stood. "If you have any problems or questions with the site, don't hesitate to call me."

Ashley nodded. She walked him to the door.

His instinct was to hug her, but he held back. She seemed to be drawing a line that she didn't want him to cross.

And even though he didn't like it and didn't understand it, he would respect it.

Ashley sat back down at her desk after Justin left. She couldn't remember ever feeling so conflicted. Part of her wanted to throw caution to the wind and see where things with Justin could go. But the more practical part of her knew that wasn't a good idea.

The front door opened, and Summer walked inside, followed by Jefferson. Ashley hadn't been especially charmed by the guy when he'd stopped by earlier to see Summer. There was something about him that she didn't trust. "Hi," she said.

Summer set a bag from Cupcake on her desk. "For you." She grinned. "It's chocolate. I already had mine, and let me tell you, it was worth the calories."

Jefferson laughed like that was the funniest thing he'd ever heard. "I'd better get back to the office," he said. He glanced down at Summer. "Chin up, Sunshine. Things will get better." He turned to Ashley. "And it was nice to meet you." With a wave over his shoulder, he walked out the door.

Summer sat down at her desk and turned her attention to her computer.

Ashley bit her tongue. It probably wasn't her place to tell Summer what she thought about Jefferson, but holding it back didn't feel right either. "So what was that all about?"

Summer looked up with wide eyes. "What was what all about?"

She jerked her head toward the door. "Jefferson. Swooping in and giving you cupcakes and a pep talk."

Summer made a face. "You make it sound like something inappropriate happened. We've been friends since we were in diapers. He moved back at the beginning of the summer. I see him every now and then around town or at my parents' house."

Ashley stood up from her desk and walked over to lean against Summer's file cabinet. "I know you've been through a lot and all that, but do you really think spending time with another man is a good idea?"

"You make it sound like I'm sneaking around and doing something I shouldn't." Summer's normally calm face flamed with anger.

Ashley raised her eyebrows. "I want you to recognize that the path you're on could be dangerous. I've seen it happen too many times. It starts out innocently, but soon you're confiding in someone who isn't your spouse." She met Summer's narrowed eyes. "That's what happened in my marriage. Brian told me later that he'd never intended on being unfaithful. That he'd run into an old friend and they'd caught up. And then that turned into them talking about their problems. And eventually it turned into something more." She sighed. She knew she was jumping to conclusions, but Summer wasn't in a good place right now.

"I'm sorry that happened to you, but just because it

happened to you doesn't mean that's what is going on in my life."

Ashley nodded. "There was something odd about the way Jefferson sauntered in here looking for you. I get the feeling that he sees you as some kind of prize. I think you should keep your guard up."

Summer didn't say anything. Finally, she stood. "You're entitled to your opinion. But there's nothing to worry about. In fact, I'm meeting Luke this afternoon at the counselor's office." She slung her bag over her shoulder. "See you tomorrow."

Ashley watched her walk out. Were they good enough friends that they could be totally honest with each other and it not have a negative impact?

Only time would tell.

Chapter 32

Luke carried his bag and guitar into Justin's apartment. "Thanks for letting me stay here. I was going stir crazy on the boat."

"What, it's not a luxury liner?" Justin asked.

Luke set his things down in the living room. "It's nice, but it was starting to get a little cramped. I honestly thought the walls were going to close in sometimes."

"I can't imagine. That's the kind of thing that probably sounds like fun until you actually do it."

Luke nodded. "So when is Colton going to be moving in?" He'd been surprised when Justin had filled him in on what was going on with Samantha. Talk about a lifestyle change. Going from being a single guy to a full-time guardian would be an adjustment.

"Actually, next week. I'm trying to get the spare room turned into some kind of kid's room," Justin said. "My mom has a big plan to paint the walls with pictures of animals playing sports." He chuckled. "I have no idea how that's going to turn out, but I told her to do whatever she wanted."

Luke had to admire his friend for his willingness to step in and do what needed to be done for Colton. "Is Colton excited?"

Justin shrugged. "I'm not sure that he even understands what's going on. I suspect I'm going to be in for a difficult time at first. I'm not the only one whose world is about to change, you know?"

Luke nodded. "Kids are resilient though. He'll probably adjust just fine."

"I hope so."

Luke tapped his watch. "We'd better go."

"I think we're getting better, don't you?" Justin asked. "Last week I actually thought we sounded as good as some groups on the radio."

Luke nodded. "Yeah."

They walked out the door and got into Luke's truck.

"You given any more thought to that songwriting contest I mentioned awhile back?"

Luke bristled. He had given it thought, but it wasn't going to be the answer Justin was hoping for. "I'm not interested. I have too much other stuff going on in my life right now." He merged onto the James Island Connector. "Honestly, I'm starting to regret even signing on to play at the Sand and Suds on a regular basis." He shot a quick glance at Justin to gauge his reaction.

"Fine by me. I was just along for the ride anyway. And now that I'll have Colton, that means either finding a babysitter every Friday night or depending on my parents to keep him. And honestly, if I'm going to have to do that, I'd much rather it be because I'm going out with Ashley."

Luke sighed with relief. He'd been afraid Justin might be upset. Now if Jimmy and Will felt the same, he could tell Charlie to find a replacement. "How are things with Ashley, anyway?"

"We seem to have hit a brick wall. I'm not sure what happened. One minute I thought we were on this really good track, and the next we veered totally off course." Justin sighed. "It's so frustrating."

Luke was all too familiar with veering off course. When he saw Summer and Jefferson together earlier in the week, he'd felt like someone punched him. And even though Gram tried to assure him that nothing was going on, he'd still been so upset that he'd called and canceled their counseling session. Summer had acted as if she understood, but he had his doubts.

His plan to win her back had already been set into motion though. All he could do now was wait.

Summer walked into the office on Monday resolving to make it a good day. She and Ashley had talked things out on Friday, and there were no hard feelings. Granted, Ashley's accusation that Summer might be getting too close to Jefferson had stung, but she knew her friend's concern was coming from a genuine place.

Still though, the conversation had played heavy on her mind all weekend. Jefferson did have a habit of popping up out of nowhere and saying the right thing. Ashley thought his moves were more calculated than spontaneous.

But Summer couldn't imagine him being that vindictive. Even so, she'd decided that it might be best to curb their friendship. Because if Ashley thought it was suspicious, others might as well. And Summer never wanted to give anyone the wrong impression.

"Morning." Ashley walked into the office wearing a frown.

Summer held up her coffee cup. "Surely it's nothing a little coffee can't cure."

Ashley flung herself into the chair across from Summer's

desk. "I had a date this weekend. And it was *awful*."

"What happened?"

"You know how I said Justin was way too young? Well, this friend of mine from church called me last week and asked if I was dating anyone. When I said no, she said she had someone she wanted me to meet." She shook her head. "I should've said no. But I thought maybe this would be the guy to make me forget all about Justin."

"But he wasn't Mr. Right?"

"That's an understatement. He wasn't even Mr. Someone I'd Be Friends With."

Summer couldn't help but smile at Ashley's dramatics. "That bad?"

"He's forty. Which I thought was great at first. But that means his children are almost grown, and he made it very clear that he has no interest in having more. And then he proceeded to explain his fitness regimen in detail and ask me how I planned to stay in shape as I age."

"Wow."

Ashley nodded. "I know. The whole night made me sad."

"Because it was such a bad date?"

"No. Because it reinforced how strong my feelings are for Justin." Ashley leaned forward and put her head in her hands.

"I still think you should be totally honest with him. You might end up pleasantly surprised."

Ashley shrugged. "Maybe you're right." She got up and walked to her desk. "But I do have some good news at least."

"Oh yeah?"

"We got our first client through the new website." She smiled broadly. "Cool, huh?"

Summer nodded. "Very. What's the deal?"

"You're not going to like it, but I think we can pull it off."

"Why does the sound of that make me nervous?"

Ashley giggled. "It's a pretty quick turnaround."

"How quick?" Summer raised an eyebrow. She liked to have as much time as possible. In fact, she preferred six months to a year.

"Two weeks from Saturday."

Summer stopped what she was doing and looked up. "You have got to be kidding me."

Ashley shook her head. "Nope. But the place where they want to have the ceremony is available. You know that resort over in Mt. Pleasant? The same place the Jennings wedding was earlier in the spring?"

Summer nodded. "That's a nice place."

"Well, it just so happens that it's available," Ashley said. "And get this—the couple who wants it is giving us free rein to plan the details. As long as we come in within their budget, they don't want any input. Their *generous* budget."

Summer's eyes widened. "Seriously?"

Ashley nodded. "They say they've looked at some of the weddings we've done and can tell we have great taste. So since they're from out of town, they want us to take care of all the details." She grinned. "Can you imagine? All the details. So we get to pick out the flowers, the colors, the food, the cake. . .the whole nine yards."

"Cool."

Ashley stood and brought the information sheet over to Summer. "And I think *you* should be the one to do it. Since you and Luke tied the knot at city hall, this will be like your chance to put your dream wedding together."

Summer took the sheet of paper from her. At least it would take her mind off of things. Like why her husband had really skipped out on their counseling session. And how it was possible that he'd been on the boat for four weeks yet she still missed him as much today as she had on the first day.

Chapter 33

L uke finished his explanation of Civil War artillery pieces and hung around to take questions.

"Thanks for your time," an older man said to him. "That was a great talk. Do you have any idea what time I have to be back on the boat? I think they announced it, but I didn't hear."

"Enjoy the rest of your visit here. You still have fifteen more minutes until the boat departs." The only way to get to Fort Sumter was by boat and they were very strict about departure times.

"Luke," Mr. Young called. "Can you come over here for a second?"

Luke made his way over to where his boss stood. "Yes sir?"

"I wondered if you'd thought about the position we talked about."

He'd been thinking about it a lot. He nodded. "I'd like to accept the responsibility. I think it's something I'm really going to enjoy."

Mr. Young nodded. "I'm very glad to hear that. I know you're going to do a great job."

"Thanks."

Mr. Young walked toward the museum with a wave.

Luke wondered what Summer would say about his new responsibilities when she found out about them. These days he wondered what she'd think about a lot of stuff. She was the one big piece missing from his life now.

Even after Rose and Dave had come back from Disney,

Luke had continued to visit Daddy. He'd even had a moment of clarity the other morning and had known Luke was there. It seemed like many of the pieces of his life were starting to fall into place. But the missing piece was Summer.

He'd finally started talking to God again. At first he'd mainly apologized for being such an idiot. But soon he'd started praying specifically for things in his life. And then he'd started to thank God for his blessings and to praise His name.

And even though he didn't expect life to be perfect, Luke knew that he had the tools to deal with the disappointments and the failures that were inevitable parts of life.

He couldn't wait to share the changes in his life with Summer.

And he hoped and prayed that she'd give him the chance.

"Have you seen the weather?" Summer asked as soon as Ashley walked in the door.

Ashley nodded. "Yes. But according to my e-mail, the wedding is still a go in spite of the hurricane watch."

Summer's stomach churned. "Do they realize that our ability to pull off this wedding totally hinges on the weather? Because if this thing hits, we won't be able to have a catered dinner and flowers brought in from a flower shop. We'll be lucky to keep a roof over our heads and maintain electricity."

Ashley shrugged. "It was all very clear on the site, and they sent me an e-mail last night that stated everything was a go."

"Okay." Summer tapped her pencil against her desk. She

flipped through her planner and penciled in a couple more items on her to-do list. "You know what? This wedding is the same day as my anniversary." She frowned.

"Do y'all have plans?"

Summer shook her head. "Not exactly. Luke came over yesterday to mow the yard. We ended up talking for a while. I came super close to asking him to move back in the house." She sighed. "But I'm a little scared. I'm afraid if he moves in, we'll never actually deal with any of the problems. I don't want to sweep them under the rug. I want to face them together and then move on."

Ashley smiled. "I think you'll get there."

"I hope so." Summer lifted her hair off her neck. It was so miserably hot outside today. "He moved off the boat and moved in with Justin. And Colton."

"Whoa. I'll bet that's an interesting household."

Summer chuckled. "Luke said Justin and Colton are like two peas in a pod. He says that considering Colton isn't Justin's biological child, it's uncanny how alike they are."

"I hope the situation is working out."

"Seems to be." Summer glanced over at Ashley. "Except that Justin is still really sad. I ran into him at the grocery store a couple of days ago. I can tell he's happy to have Colton with him, but he asked about you right off."

"He did?" Ashley asked. "I figured I'd sabotaged any chance I had because I was so scared."

Summer shrugged. "You'll never know until you try."

Chapter 34

Friday afternoon, Summer looked out the window from her room at the resort. The clouds were rolling so fast they looked like they were from a time-lapse video. If the TV weather guys were right, things didn't bode well for tomorrow's wedding.

"You worried?" Ashley asked. She was perched on the sofa, tapping away on the keys of her laptop.

She let out a breath. "A little bit. It's not a good sign when the Weather Channel has someone stationed at your hotel, is it?"

"I guess not. But they probably have people stationed all over the coast. Just because we're in the cone of uncertainty doesn't mean we're going to get hit."

"My whole life is a cone of uncertainty." Summer managed a smile at Ashley's amused expression. "What? It is."

Ashley rolled her eyes. "Haven't you figured it out yet? Life is uncertain. Thankfully we can be certain of what comes after that."

"Has anyone ever told you that you have a good perspective on things?"

"A time or two." Ashley twisted her mouth into a smile. "Or maybe it's that wisdom comes with age."

"Speaking of age. . . I meant to tell you that Justin's birthday is coming up in August. His thirtieth birthday." Summer raised her eyebrows. "Does that push him over your mysterious threshold and make it appropriate for you guys to see each other again?"

Ashley sighed. "I don't know."

"If it's honestly that you don't see the possibility of a future with him, that's one thing. But if it's because you're scared of taking a chance, that's another."

"I never thought I'd be in this position, you know?" Ashley tucked a stray hair behind her ear. "Starting over with someone new. Trusting that this time love will work out for me." She sighed. "It's a lot harder than I expected it to be. So yes, I'm scared."

"I wish I could give you a guarantee," Summer said. She sat down on the plush king-sized bed and toyed with her wedding ring. "But obviously I can't. I will say that some things are worth the risk. Worth the hurt."

Ashley nodded. "I know. And I believe that, too. I have to find that courage to take a leap of faith."

Summer smiled. "I used to have trouble with that. You know what a perfectionist I am."

"You, a perfectionist?" Ashley giggled. "No way."

"I'm serious." Summer sighed. "It's hard for me to do things that I might fail at. Whether it's planting a garden or expanding the business. But a few years ago, I realized that in the end I'd rather regret something I did than something I didn't do." She shrugged. "It's that simple. I don't want to look back and have to wish I'd taken a chance or wish I'd told someone how I felt. So I started living that way."

"That's actually really good advice." Ashley looked up from her laptop with wide eyes.

Summer grinned. "Sometimes I do have good ideas."

Ashley closed her laptop and looked seriously at Summer. "Okay then. In light of that, I have something I've wanted to talk to you about for a few months." She took a deep breath.

Ashley willed the words to come out of her mouth. She tried to remember all the points she'd planned to make if she ever got the nerve to make this little speech. But for the most part, they eluded her. "I've put in a lot of hours over the past six months," she said finally.

Summer nodded. "And I'm so appreciative."

"And with the new website launch, we're only going to get busier. I even have some ideas on ways we can expand from weddings to parties and general events." Ashley met Summer's curious gaze. "You know I'm a good employee. I'm dependable and responsible, and I get along well with our clients."

"I know. Finding you has been such a blessing to me and the business."

"Well, I've been thinking lately that I'd like to play a bigger role in the business side of things." Her heart beat faster, but she plunged ahead. "I'd like for you to consider making me a full partner."

Summer's eyes widened. "I guess that should have occurred to me already, huh?" She shook her head. "I'll need to talk to my accountant and to Luke, but I don't see any reason why we can't make that happen."

"Are you sure? Because I don't want you to feel like you have to say yes just because we're friends."

Summer smiled. "I'm positive. I'm sorry you had to ask though. I should've thought of it myself. I know how hard you've worked over the past months, and I know how good you are at what you do." She sighed. "Honestly, I think it will be a relief to share responsibilities with someone. The business is at the point where we're either going to have to expand or start turning down work. There's only so much two of us can do without literally working around the clock."

"Thanks." Ashley couldn't hide her surprise. She'd fully expected Summer to be upset at the very idea of being partners.

"It might be the answer to a prayer actually. I'm hopeful that Luke and I will have things back on track soon. And honestly, I don't want work to be my primary focus all the time. But if we restructure some things and hire some support help, I think you and I can both have real lives outside of work."

Ashley nodded. "That sounds perfect." A real life. She knew that's what she'd have with Justin. The kind of partnership she'd always wanted. Everything she knew about him told her that he'd be committed to her and to their future.

The only thing holding her back now was her own insecurity.

Chapter 35

Luke stopped at the front desk of the resort. "Could you tell me if Summer Nelson from Summer Weddings is on site?"

The receptionist gave him a shaky smile. "I think so. She was in the east ballroom earlier. The flowers didn't get delivered, and she was pretty upset." She glanced around and leaned forward conspiratorially. "To tell you the truth, I feel sorry for her. What kind of people insist on having their wedding during a hurricane? I mean, honestly." She sighed. "I wouldn't be here except that I figure this building is safer than my house, plus I'm making overtime. I don't even normally work the desk here, but everyone else headed out of town. My boyfriend loaded up our dog and is driving west."

He nodded. "I'm sure it will be fine. It's not supposed to hit for several hours, and maybe by then it will have weakened."

"You sound just like my daddy. He refuses to evacuate. I guess I'm a big old chicken."

Luke's daddy had the same philosophy. His only concession to a potential tropical storm had been to put the plastic lawn chairs in the garage. "About Summer. Do you know where she might be now?"

"She has a suite reserved. You want me to ring it?"

He thought for a minute. "Actually, can I make a reservation? But not on the same floor as her."

The girl narrowed her eyes. "You're not some kind of

stalker are you? Because I don't want any drama." She smiled. "I'm hoping that if I do a good job, they'll offer me a position at the desk permanently. And if I end up letting a psycho in the building, that'll never happen."

"I'm her husband," he said quietly. "I'm trying to surprise her for our anniversary. That's all." He raised his hands in surrender. "I promise."

She seemed satisfied by his answer. "Well, okay. We do have a lot of rooms available. Just a few guests are riding out the hurricane. And that crew from the Weather Channel." She sighed.

He paid for a two-night stay and went outside to his truck. He needed to call Ashley and see if everything was in place.

And he didn't want to risk running into Summer before it was time.

Justin lifted Colton from his car seat and carried the sleeping child into his parents' house.

"Just put him in your old room," Mom whispered.

He gently put Colton on the bed, and the little boy curled up in a ball. He was such a good sleeper. He smoothed Colton's blond curls, covered him up, and shut the door behind him. He took two steps and turned around. What if Colton got scared and Mom couldn't hear him? He opened the door a crack and made his way to the living room.

"Thanks for letting me bring him by. I appreciate it so much." Justin leaned down and kissed his mom on the cheek.

She looked up with a smile. "Anytime. But I wish you'd

stay. They're saying it's only a matter of hours before the storm rolls in." She nodded at the weather coverage on TV. "Your daddy has gone to get gas for the generator in case we need it."

He shook his head. "Thanks. I'm hoping it's going to miss us completely. I'm glad you're going to be with Colton though." He sighed. "Luke has concocted some crazy plan to win Summer back. He won't let go of it. I'm headed down to Folly Beach to help him. I have to go by their house and pick up their dog and take him down there."

"Can't you tell him you don't want to be out in a tropical storm? It could turn into a hurricane, Justin. That's not anything to play around with."

"I know. But I'll get there in plenty of time to hunker down. You know that after the last one came through here, most of the buildings were built to withstand high winds."

"Okay. You need to go on then. I don't want you out when it hits." She stood and gave him a hug. "And don't worry about Colton. He'll be fine."

"Thanks, Mom." He headed out the door and climbed in his truck. The sky looked ominous. Not at all the kind of weather he wanted to be out in.

The only upside to the situation was that Ashley was with Summer at the resort. And even though things hadn't worked out the way Justin wanted them to, he still held out hope that she would have a change of heart.

Chapter 36

A knock at the door startled Summer. She wasn't expecting anyone. After Ashley rushed off to take a phone call, Summer had tried to get some e-mails answered. But she kept a wary eye on the sky.

Even though she'd been a little girl when Hurricane Hugo hit, she still remembered the destruction. It had taken days for them to get power back and years for the area to return to normal.

The pounding continued, and she peeked through the peep hole. *You've got to be kidding me.* She opened the door. "What are you doing here?"

Jefferson stood in the doorway clad in a red polo shirt and khakis. "I came to check on you."

After her talk with Ashley the other day, his appearance made her uncomfortable. "You didn't need to do that. I'm fine. This place is solid. And the wedding I'm working on should go off without a hitch." *If I can find a flower shop willing to deliver during hurricane conditions. And a photographer. And if the bride and groom actually make it.*

"Without a hitch, huh?" He cleared his throat. "I'm actually here because I was worried about you. I thought you might need some help. You know, some muscles to move things or somebody to corral a rogue groomsman." He winked. "Or console a bridesmaid."

She narrowed her eyes. "Thanks for the offer, but I'm sure I'll be fine."

"You just gonna leave me standing here in the hallway, or

are you going to invite me inside?"

She frowned. Two weeks ago she wouldn't have thought twice about inviting him inside. But now. . .it seemed inappropriate. "I have a lot of work to do."

Jefferson cocked his head to the side. "Come on, Sunshine. I haven't seen you in over a week. You didn't come out to your parents' the other night for game night. I even knocked on your door a couple days ago, and you didn't answer." He comically furrowed his brow and stuck out his bottom lip in a pout. "Are you avoiding me?"

She shook her head. "Fine. You've got ten minutes. I'm working. And you shouldn't be here." If Ashley came back and saw Jefferson in the suite, she would hit the roof. And probably retract her desire to become business partners. Summer felt like an idiot for not thinking of it herself. She was proud of the business, but there was no denying she could use the help. Relinquishing control would be a challenge, but it would be good for her.

Jefferson plopped down on the plush sofa. "Man, what a spread you've got here." He looked appreciatively around the room. "This looks like a honeymoon suite."

"Don't act like you've never been in a nice place before." She sat down at the desk and shuffled through her itinerary for tomorrow's festivities. "I know good and well that you spare no expense when you travel."

He chuckled. "Okay, you've got me there. But it's only because I want the best."

"Of course."

Jefferson patted the cushion next to him. "Come sit down. Take a break."

She reluctantly stood and made her way over to the sofa.

If focusing on him for five minutes would get him to leave, then that's what she'd do. "I can't take much of a break. And you need to be hitting the road. It looks like the bottom is going to drop out any minute." She narrowed her eyes. "I'd hate for you to get stuck here."

"Would you hate that? Really?" he asked. "Because I don't think you would."

She sighed. "What are you getting at?"

Jefferson turned toward her. He reached out and lightly ran his finger down her arm. "We're alike, you and me. We come from the same background. We want the same things out of life."

She got to her feet. "Please don't touch me!"

"These last weeks have been nice. You confiding in me. Me putting a smile on your face." He stood, tipped her chin up so she'd have to look at him. "Luke never deserved you. And he still doesn't."

So Ashley had been right. Summer started to turn away, but Jefferson grabbed her hand. "Don't deny it. You've wondered over the past weeks if you made a mistake in letting me go, haven't you?" He pulled her close until they were face-to-face. "No one ever has to know. This can be just between us."

Bile rose in her throat. She pushed him away as hard as she could. What a fool she'd been. "That day in the cemetery." She glared at him. "You said you wanted to be friends. I should've said no. But I wanted to believe that you were a good person."

"I am a good person. And I know a good thing when I see it. What was I supposed to do? I come to town and find out you and Luke are having trouble, and I'm supposed to walk away? How could I do that?"

"He's twice the man you are. Without even trying." She walked to the door and flung it open. "It's time for you to go. Whatever you thought was going to happen between us isn't happening. I'm a married woman. And in a moment of weakness I might have confided in you. But that doesn't change the fact that I love my husband. And I will always honor him."

Jefferson shook his head. "Your loss, Sunshine." He shrugged. "But it was worth a try."

A sudden blast of rain pounded against the windows, startling her. It looked like the storm had arrived early. "If you won't leave, I will." She pushed past Jefferson and ran to the stairwell. She didn't want to chance being stuck on an elevator with him.

She pushed the exit door open and sank onto the top step. What was wrong with her? She'd come dangerously close to betraying her husband. Not because she was tempted by Jefferson. But because she never should've allowed herself to confide in him in the first place. No matter what was going on in her life. *Lord, please give me the right words to apologize to Luke. And guard my heart in the future.* She slowly made her way down the stairs.

She reached the first floor and took a deep breath. Had Jefferson had time to leave? She hoped the blinding rain outside didn't mean he'd have to stick around. She pushed the door open and looked both ways. All clear.

She went down the long corridor toward the reception desk. Maybe the girl there could tell her if the wedding party had made it yet. She rounded the corner and stopped in her tracks. Her hands rose to her mouth and muffled the sound of her gasp.

Jefferson and Luke stood facing each other in the grand lobby. And from the look on both of their faces, they might need a referee.

The hurricane-force winds outside had nothing to do with Luke's bad mood. He'd been so excited about the prospect of surprising Summer for their anniversary. He had it all planned out. From the words he was going to say, to the gift he was going to give her.

Yes, it should have been perfect.

But when he walked into the resort lobby carrying a huge bouquet of roses and his suitcase, he ran right into Jefferson.

"Fancy meeting you here, Jeff." Luke forced a smile.

Jefferson looked from the roses to Luke and sneered. "You're a little late." He nodded toward the elevator he'd just stepped from. "Those would've looked great up in Summer's suite. Number 432, in case you didn't know."

Realization hit Luke like a brick. "I don't know what kind of game you're playing, but I feel like you might need to be reminded again that Summer's my wife. She made her choice a long time ago."

"Maybe. Or maybe she finally came to her senses and realized she chose wrong." Jefferson smiled a slow, menacing smile. "She's too good for you. Always has been."

Luke glared. "There might've been a time when you could get to me with those jibes. But not anymore. It isn't worth it. You're not worth it."

"Summer seems to think I'm worth it. In fact, she's spent a lot of time over the past weeks telling me how unhappy she is. Because of you." Jefferson shrugged.

Luke's blood boiled. "Why are you here?"

"Summer and I had some unfinished business." He met Luke's eyes. "She's a feisty one, isn't she?"

Luke flinched. He fought the urge to knock the smirk from Jefferson's face. The idea that Jefferson might have acted inappropriately with Summer made him nauseous. "You'd better not have laid a hand on her."

"Her skin's as soft as it was when she was sixteen."

Luke had worked all summer to let go of his anger. He'd promised Summer. So he had no choice right now but to turn the other cheek. No matter how much it hurt. He calmly rolled his bag to the reception desk and carefully placed the bouquet on top.

Then he turned and walked right out into the storm.

Chapter 37

Justin sat in the lobby and watched as Luke had a very heated conversation with some preppy-looking guy. Luke was normally so laid-back. But whatever the tall guy was saying was causing Luke's whole body to tense up.

Justin had already snuck Milo up to Luke's hotel room and was waiting on his friend to fill him in on what the big surprise was supposed to be. It had better be good to justify all the trouble he'd gone to. Thankfully it had been easy to distract that girl at the desk while he led the big dog onto the elevator.

"Justin?" A familiar voice said from behind him.

He turned to see Ashley with her laptop under her arm. "Hey." Man, he'd missed her.

"It's looking bad out there." She motioned toward the big windows. Rain pounded against them, and the sky outside was dark even though it was daytime.

He gestured toward Luke. "It's looking bad in here, too."

Ashley made a face. "Ugh. I can't stand that guy." She filled him in on Jefferson and his history with Summer and Luke. "He's so smarmy. I don't understand why Summer doesn't see it."

He sighed. "Some things are easier to see from the outside looking in, I guess."

She sat down next to him. "Yeah. Maybe." She jerked her chin toward the two men. "Do you think we should go over there?"

He shook his head. Whatever was going on, Luke needed

to handle it himself. "Nah. It'll be okay." At least he hoped it would. Luke wasn't a fighter. And that preppy guy didn't look like he could throw much of a punch even if he tried. Probably wouldn't want to mess up his manicure.

"I guess you got Milo here okay?" Ashley asked.

Justin raised his eyebrows. "You know about that?" He was always the last to know about stuff.

She giggled. "Yeah. Luke and I have been working together."

Before he could ask her what the big surprise was going to be, he spotted Summer hovering in the hallway watching Luke. He leaned over to Ashley. "There's Summer. She looks really upset."

Ashley halfway stood then sat back down as they watched Luke put his things down and walk out the lobby door.

Summer took off running. She pushed against Jefferson and said something that made him glare, then ran outside after Luke.

Ashley raised her eyebrows at Justin. "Should we be worried that they've both gone out into a huge storm?"

He shrugged. "I'm sure they won't go far. Maybe to the parking lot. They'll be back in a minute."

The lights flickered in the lobby.

"That's not good." Ashley looked around nervously. She stood. "I think there's a TV in the restaurant over there. I'm going to check to see if there's any update on the weather."

He nodded. "Mind if I come with you?" He wanted to talk to her and see if there might still be a chance for them. But he didn't want to come across as a creep who wouldn't leave her alone.

"Yeah. I'd like that." She smiled.

They walked past an empty bar then an empty section of the lobby. No one was in sight.

"It's kind of eerie how deserted it is here."

Ashley nodded. "Most of the guests left yesterday. There are a handful who chose to stay. I met a couple of older ladies this morning who are here from the Gulf Coast." She laughed. "They said they were too old to drive back and fight the evacuation traffic, so they were staying put."

"My family decided to hole up at Mom and Dad's. Colton is there with them." He frowned. "I hated to leave him, but I wasn't sure what to expect here. Luke's been so evasive about everything."

They stopped at the restaurant entrance.

"You think there's anyone there?" he asked.

She nodded. "Yeah. This is the only place to get anything to eat. I think some of the resort employees are staying here tonight with their families." She shrugged. "You know, people who are afraid their homes might not withstand the storm."

"It's good that they have a place to go."

They walked inside, and a harried woman waved to them. "Just sit anywhere. We're short staffed, as you can imagine, so the menu is pretty limited. Soup, salad, or sandwiches."

He held out a chair for Ashley.

"Thanks."

He sat across from her. "Even though this is some kind of crazy situation, I'm glad to see you."

Ashley's eyes filled with tears.

Justin peered at her. "Do you want to tell me about it?" he asked quietly. Though she'd made her lack of feelings for him clear, he still didn't like to see her upset.

"There are things I should have told you. Things that are hard for me to talk about." Ashley angrily wiped a tear away. "You've always been so open and up-front with me. About who you are and about where I stand with you." She gave him a shaky smile. "And I was never able to do the same."

Justin regarded her with serious blue eyes. "I disagree. I'd say you were pretty clear about where I stood."

She shook her head. "Yeah, but not for the reason you think."

"Okay. You can tell me anything. I think you know that."

She took a breath. She'd gone out on a limb by telling Summer she wanted to be business partners, but that was nothing compared to this. "You know I'm divorced."

He nodded.

"My husband left me for another woman. I know. It's the oldest story in the book. But when it happens to you, it feels different." She grimaced. "I was never totally convinced he was 'the one,' but in the town I lived in, there weren't many options. We got along pretty well, and I thought we wanted the same things." She hesitated.

Justin reached over and took her hand. "Go on."

"And soon after we married, he cheated on me. I'm not sure when the affair started or if there was more than one."

"One is enough."

She nodded. "She was several years younger. One of his sister's friends. They reconnected online of all places." She made a face. "I noticed that she'd posted on his Facebook page a couple of times but didn't think anything about it.

But apparently there was more to it than that." She looked into his sympathetic eyes. "And then one night he came to me and told me he loved her. There was no discussion. Nothing I could do."

Justin squeezed her hand. "You're better off."

"It was difficult though. I know I'm better off. I know I don't want to be treated disrespectfully. But my family, especially my mom, thought I should look the other way. She actually made a comment about how I wasn't exactly in the prime of youth anymore." She sighed. "And I think that's been part of my problem with you."

Justin furrowed his brow. "What do you mean?"

"I know you're not even thirty yet. And I'm thirty-six."

He looked at her with wide eyes; then his face broke into a smile. "That's what this is about? Our age difference?"

"You knew I was older?"

Justin looked sheepish. "Well yeah. I saw your diploma on the wall. And I figured based on the dates that you must be a few years older. Either that or you were some kind of prodigy."

Ashley swallowed. "And that doesn't bother you? I mean, technically I could've been your babysitter."

He burst out laughing. "I really don't want to lose you over a technicality. Besides, if you'd been my babysitter, I would've had a crush on you and hoped that someday I'd grow up and be able to take you on a date."

She couldn't help but smile. "But don't you think you'd be better off to date someone younger than you?"

Justin laced his fingers through hers. "Ashley. I've dated girls younger than me. And you know what? They aren't serious. They want to go out and have a good time, and that's it. I'm looking for more than that. I thought you knew that."

She nodded. "I know, you say that now. I guess I'm worried that you'll get tired of me and want someone more exciting."

"Are you kidding? Do you know how amazing you are? You're smart and kind and funny. Not to mention beautiful." He squeezed her hand. "I was an idiot who messed up from the beginning and then brought a toddler on a date." He laughed. "If anything, I expected you to tell me that I wasn't even in your league."

She looked at their joined hands. Maybe she shouldn't throw away their obvious connection because she felt insecure. "Thanks. I might have overreacted a bit." She gave him a tiny smile. "But you have to remember that it's been a long time since I've met anyone I could actually see a future with. And things seemed to happen so quickly." She sighed. "I guess in my experience, things that happen fast don't always work out in the end."

"That's my bad. I was so excited to finally meet someone like you that I jumped the gun. I know I started talking about the future way too soon. Part of that was because of the situation with Colton. And part of me wanted to hear you say you'd want to be a part of both of our lives. But I can see that it was probably too much too soon."

She nodded. "Can we take things slowly? Are you okay with that?"

Justin lifted her hand to his lips and kissed it gently. "If it means I get to have you in my life, I will move as slow as molasses."

She smiled. "Sounds perfect." She raised an eyebrow. "Although I probably wouldn't complain if you kissed me a time or two."

"I'm more than happy to oblige."

Chapter 38

Luke, wait!" Summer ran after him through the parking lot. The pouring rain soaked her clothes and plastered her hair to her face, but she didn't care. "Luke!" He'd almost made it to his truck.

He turned around. "Summer? What are you doing out here? Go back inside."

She could barely see him with the rain coming down so hard. A gust of wind sent a plastic pool float whizzing past her.

Luke grabbed something out of his truck and ran toward her. "Come on. We've got to get inside." He pointed at a building just off of the parking lot.

She ran toward the building, fighting the wind as she went. The hard rain stung her skin, and she tried to shield her face with her arms.

The Weather Channel reporter and a cameraman opened the door just as she got there.

"We're heading to the main building," the reporter said. "But this place is for authorized personnel only."

Luke came up behind her. "It's okay. She's the wedding planner."

The reporter looked at her for a minute then shrugged. "Whatever. Be careful."

The two men ran toward the hotel.

She couldn't stop the laugh from escaping her lips. "It's okay, she's the wedding planner," she mocked. "Like that means anything."

He joined in her laughter. "Use your powers for good and all that, right?" He held the door open for her. "Hurry. It looks like the storm is almost here."

She ran inside the building. "Looks like this is where they keep the beach chairs and supplies."

Luke grabbed a white pool towel from a shelf and tossed it to her. "Here."

"Thanks." She toweled off her soaking hair then wrapped the towel around her wet clothes.

Neither of them spoke for a long minute, and the only sound was of the wind and rain outside.

Finally, Summer turned to Luke. "I'm sorry," she said softly.

"You shouldn't have followed me." Luke attempted to mop up some of the water that fell around him in puddles.

Her mouth quivered. "I didn't want you to leave without hearing me out. Jefferson being here is not what it looks like. I didn't know he was going to show up, I promise."

Luke walked over to her and took the plush towel from her hands. He gently wiped her face, a mix of water and tears. "I wasn't leaving," he whispered. "Just getting a little air."

She met his gaze. "I saw you talking to Jefferson. I need to explain."

Luke lifted a beach chair from a stack and set it on the floor. He guided her to it and motioned for her to sit. "We might be here for a while. May as well get comfortable." He sat next to her.

She swallowed, hoping the right words would come out and not the mixed-up thoughts that were rolling around in her head. "Why are you here in the first place?" she asked. While Jefferson showing up had been unexpected, Luke being here in the middle of a potential hurricane was totally out of the blue. He was supposed to be at home with Milo, boarding up their windows in case the storm hit.

He shook his head. "I came to see you. I admit, I was surprised to run into him. And I wasn't too happy to hear him insinuate that you might be falling for him again." He frowned.

"He said that?" She closed her eyes. "Ugh. I'm sorry. I can't say it enough. Nothing happened between us. I honestly thought he just wanted to be my friend. And I somehow convinced myself that a friendship would be okay, because at first he seemed genuinely concerned about you and me." She sighed. "I was an idiot not to see him for who he really is."

She'd never thought she might be one of those people who did something that could be construed as inappropriate. She was a firm believer that an emotional affair was as bad and as damaging as a physical one. And even though things hadn't gone that far with Jefferson, she could see how easy it would've been to go down that path.

To her surprise, Luke took her hand.

"You believe the best in people until they give you a reason not to. From where I sit, that's a good quality." He half smiled. "Although I could do without you thinking the best of Jefferson."

"You're not mad?"

Luke shook his head. "I was pretty upset a couple of weeks ago. I saw the two of you together at the park."

"You did?" That explained a lot. "It wasn't planned. At least on my part. Looking back, I wonder if maybe those chance meetings weren't so much chance after all." Summer sighed. "Honestly. I planned to go to Blue Bicycle Books and then over to get a cupcake. I needed a little time to decompress. I'd barely left the office, and then there he was. I sat at Marion Square while he went and got cupcakes. And of course, he insisted on staying with me and walking me back to the office." She hung her head. "He could tell how upset I was."

"I passed by there on my way to your office. I knew it was supposed to have been your due date, and I wanted to see how you were doing. But when I saw you with him, I got mad and left."

"That's why you didn't show up to the counseling appointment later that day?"

He nodded. "I know I gave you a flimsy excuse about work. But I actually went to see your grandmother instead."

She raised her eyebrows in surprise. She'd spoken to Gram on the phone that very day, and Gram hadn't mentioned Luke's visit. "Well, if it makes you feel any better, Ashley tore into me when I got back to the office. She said I was playing with fire and not even realizing it. She had Jefferson pegged all along. I guess everyone did but me."

"As far as I'm concerned, that's all over now."

Summer gripped his hand. "Thanks." She'd never expected to be in this situation. "You have to know that I never would've done anything to jeopardize our marriage. Not with Jefferson or with anyone else. I love you, Luke. And the vows I made to you are sacred."

He nodded. "I believe that. But honestly, I don't even think Jefferson is one of our problems. He doesn't have anything to do with what's been going on between us."

"I know."

"There are a lot of things I wish I'd done differently. I know I shut down on you. Not that I was ever that open to begin with."

"I should've tried harder," she said.

Luke shook his head. "I don't think there was anything you could've done. This lesson was one I had to learn on my own. I'm sorry I hurt you in the process."

"So what did you learn?" Summer knew she'd learned her own lessons over the past months, but she wanted to know what Luke had gleaned from their separation.

"The first time I went to see Daddy in the nursing home, I fell apart. I didn't know where to turn and felt like I was completely alone. Bobby's Bible was in my truck, so I picked it up and flipped through. He'd highlighted a lot of pages, so I started reading to try to calm myself down. The first one I came to was that passage in Ecclesiastes that talks about how there's a time for everything. It helped me to put things into perspective, you know?"

She nodded. Luke had struggled with his faith ever since Bobby's accident. So for him to finally open his heart again was a big step.

"I was so selfish. I looked at all these things that had happened in my life as being things that had happened just to me," he said, pointing toward himself. "But I started to realize that I'm not the only one who was impacted. It's not all about me." He shook his head. "I might not understand why Bobby was in that accident or why you had a miscarriage. But I can accept those things now without feeling like I'm being singled out."

She squeezed his hand. "I'm glad you can accept things."

"And then I realized that I might have talked the talk, but

I didn't walk the walk. I went with you to church. I prayed. I tried to do what was right. But the moment things got tough, I turned my back. I stopped praying. I stopped being the man I know I'm supposed to be." He shook his head. "I see now how foolish I've been."

She hadn't seen that honesty in his brown eyes in a long time. "I haven't been perfect either. Even before Jefferson came back to town, I'd started to pull away from you. I was exhausted. I didn't have it in me to try to fix whatever was going on with us, because I felt like I was broken myself. The miscarriage is the worst thing I've ever gone through, and I felt like you wanted me to get over it and move on. And I wasn't ready to do that." She sighed. "So I felt stuck, you know? I wasn't able to handle it the way you wanted me to, so I did nothing. I turned into this scattered, foggy version of myself."

Luke put an arm around her and pulled her close.

She sat like that for a long minute, relishing the nearness of her husband and shutting out the storm that had been raging in their marriage. And the storm that was raging outside the door.

Luke had missed her even more than he'd realized. But he hated to hear that he'd hurt her. "I'm sorry," he murmured against her hair. "I wanted both of us to move past losing the baby because it was so painful." He pulled back from her so he could see her face. "But there hasn't been a day when I haven't grieved."

"Why didn't you share that grief with me? I felt like

it was mine alone."

He rubbed his jaw. "I wanted to be strong for you. I saw how hurt you were, and I didn't want to add to that by making you watch my own pain." He shook his head. "But I guess I didn't realize how it would come across."

"Like it didn't matter."

The words stabbed him. "I think about our little boy all the time. What his laugh would've sounded like. How proud I would've been watching his first step. What he would want to be when he grew up."

"You say it like you were certain it was a boy." She looked at him curiously.

He laced his fingers through hers. "I'm pretty certain."

"How?"

He smiled. "I read this article right after we found out you were pregnant. It told how to figure out if you were having a boy or a girl. It said that when a woman is carrying a girl, she's sharing her beauty, so she's not as attractive as when she's carrying a boy. And I knew right then that you must be having a boy, because you were more beautiful than I'd ever seen or even imagined."

Tears filled her eyes. "You really thought that?"

He reached out and tenderly wiped a tear away. "I sure did. Sometimes you would literally take my breath away." His mouth turned up in a smile. "And you still do."

"Thanks," she said softly.

The wind howled outside the building.

"It's getting nasty out there," he said.

She smiled. "Good thing we're warm and dry in here."

The power flickered and went out, leaving them in total darkness.

He put his arm around her. "Are you scared?" he whispered.

She turned her face toward his. "A little. But it has nothing to do with the weather."

He pulled her to him, and his lips found hers in the darkness.

Chapter 39

Ashley paced inside the ballroom. It was the interior room and supposedly the safest. But she wasn't crazy about being there. She felt trapped.

"You okay?" Justin asked. He'd brought Milo down, and the big dog was curled up in a ball next to him.

"It's the waiting I hate. Will it hit, will it not hit? If it hits, what category will it be. . . ?" She trailed off and sighed. "The uncertainty is a pain."

"If it makes you feel any better, I talked to the weather guy a few minutes ago. He thinks we're going to dodge a bullet." He patted the floor next to him. "Sit down. Milo and I will keep you safe."

She had to admit, having him here was a comfort. She sank down onto the floor. "Thanks." A loud cackling laugh came from the other side of the wall. "Those ladies I was telling you about found a Monopoly game in the library. I guess the game is going well."

"You want to go join them?" Justin asked.

She nodded. "I think that might help take my mind off the storm. This is my first tropical storm, so I guess I'm extra nervous."

He stood up and shook his legs out. "Come on, Miles." He tugged on the dog's leash, and Milo slowly rose from his spot on the floor.

She led them into the next ballroom.

Two elderly women sat hunched over a table, a Monopoly game between them. They were glowering at each other.

"Hi, ladies," Ashley said.

One of the women stood up. She had to be close to six feet tall. Her bright orange hair, while not a color found in nature, somehow suited her. She grinned at Justin like a schoolgirl. "I'm Mavis Bunch," she said. She stuck out a manicured hand as if she were royalty.

Justin never missed a beat. He took her hand and lifted it to his lips. "Charmed to meet you, Miss Bunch. I'm Justin Sanders."

She giggled. "If I didn't love Alabama so much, I would move to Charleston just for the Southern gentlemen."

The other woman stood up and smacked her on the arm. "We have Southern gentlemen in lower Alabama." As if remembering her manners, she batted her eyes at Justin. "I'm Mary Bunch. Her sister." She motioned her head toward Mavis. "Although sometimes I think there may have been a mix-up at the hospital."

"She's my *older* sister," Mavis said with a wink.

Justin shook Mary's hand.

"Ashley from Alabama, how's the wedding planning going?" Mavis asked. They'd met yesterday as Ashley was attempting to carry an arch through the double doors. Once they found out they shared a home state, the two women had wanted to talk to her until they found someone they knew in common.

"Pretty good." She sighed. "Of course the storm might be a problem."

Mary shook her head. "Here we thought we were so smart. That Jim Cantore keeps saying that the Gulf Coast might get hit hard by the tropics this year. So we decided to come to Charleston. And now here we are right in the middle of a hurricane."

"So we have y'all to blame for this, I guess," Justin said.

Mavis giggled. "Our daddy used to say we went through the house like tornadoes. So maybe there's some truth to that."

"That's not what he said. He said we went through the house like whirlwinds," Mary chided her sister.

Mavis shrugged. "Same thing."

Justin met Ashley's eyes. She could tell he was as amused by them as she'd been yesterday.

"I've got to sit down. I've had a bad knee ever since we hiked the Grand Canyon a couple of years ago." Mary sat down, clutching her knee.

"Y'all hiked the Grand Canyon?" Justin asked.

"We sure did." Mavis wiggled her hips. "We stay in shape. I'm the oldest certified Zumba teacher in the country."

Mary groaned. "Don't encourage her. She'll have us up doing the rumba or something, and I tell you, my knee can't take it." She patted the chair next to her. "Y'all sit down. You're makin' me nervous."

Ashley, Justin, and Mavis sat down in the empty seats.

Milo collapsed into a heap on the floor.

"That is one big dog," Mavis observed. "Yours?" she asked Justin.

He shook his head. "I'm watching him for a friend."

At the mention of Luke, Ashley furrowed her brow. "Do you think they're okay?" she murmured.

"They're fine. That reporter told me they went into the pool house."

Mavis and Mary looked at them with identical quizzical expressions.

"Our friends went out into the storm earlier and haven't

come back," Justin explained. "But we got word that they're safely holed up in the pool house."

Mary raised her eyebrows. "Why did they go out in the storm? That seems like a dumb thing to do."

Justin burst out laughing. "I like you. You tell it like it is, don't you?"

"Once I hit eighty, I decided it was time to stop holding back." Mary motioned at her sister. "Now Mavis has never held back. She was born telling her opinion about everything. I used to hold my tongue because I didn't want to ruffle any feathers." She shrugged. "Until I realized that holding it in was only hurting me. I used to worry and fret about things. Now I just get it off my chest and feel all kinds of better." She winked. "Of course, the trick is to speak your mind with tact."

Mavis sighed. "I have tact, too. I just forget to use it sometimes." She winked. "So, Justin and Ashley from Alabama. . .How long have the two of you been an item?"

"Don't pry into their personal business," Mary chided.

Mavis shrugged. "I'm just trying to pass the time."

"Actually, we aren't technically a couple, I don't guess," Justin said. He glanced at Ashley. "Or are we?"

She cringed. There was nothing like being put on the spot, especially in front of people she barely knew. She smiled at the women. "We haven't really had that conversation just yet."

Justin enjoyed watching Ashley squirm as she tried to explain to Mary and Mavis exactly what their relationship was.

"Do you like her?" Mary asked.

He nodded. "Very much."

Mavis turned to Ashley. "And do you like him?"

"I do." She blushed.

"Well, at least you're on the same page about that," Mary said. "Now let me give you two some advice."

"We need all the advice we can get," Ashley said.

Mary chuckled. "Well, we love to give advice. Now, the most important thing is to remember that your relationship isn't a competition. If one of you is always trying to win, it will never work."

Justin nodded. That made good sense.

Mavis patted her hands on the table. "And you can take it from me, because I was married for fifty-one years. You have to believe that you're equal partners. And don't hold back anything, even when you fight. If you're going to be partners, then be partners in every sense. Which means the good, the bad, and the ugly." She chuckled. "But try not to go too heavy on the ugly."

He glanced at Ashley across the table. He knew he didn't want to leave the resort without knowing exactly where they stood. "Ladies, it's been a pleasure," he said. "But I've got to go feed Milo and check on my family." He stood.

Ashley rose from her seat. She bent down and hugged first Mary and then Mavis.

He waved to the women and grabbed Ashley's hand as they made their way out of the ballroom.

"Do you really have to feed Milo?" she asked once they were alone in the deserted lobby.

He grinned. "Soon. But first I wanted to do this." He pulled her to him and kissed her gently.

Ashley smiled against his lips.

"Does this mean that from this day forward if someone asks us how long we've been an item, we can pinpoint now?"

She nodded. "Yes. I think that sounds like a good story. It happened in the middle of a hurricane."

"Kind of romantic." He kissed her forehead.

"Definitely." She furrowed her brow. "Do you think Luke and Summer are okay?"

Justin took her hand and led her to the couch. "Yes. I do. I hope that being forced together like this is exactly what they needed."

"Me, too," Ashley said softly.

He settled onto the couch and held her hand. The rain pounded on the roof, and the wind continued to howl, but he felt as peaceful and calm as he could remember feeling.

Chapter 40

Summer had just dozed off when she felt Luke's breath against her face.

"Summer," he whispered. "Are you sleeping?"

She lifted her head from his shoulder. "I was resting my eyes." They'd been in the dark for at least an hour, but the lights had finally come back on. The resort must have some kind of backup generator or something.

"Why are you so tired?" he asked.

"I've been working on a wedding that's kind of been thrown together at the last minute. And you know how I like stuff like that."

He laughed. "I know."

"Plus it's not really coming together because of the storm. The florist didn't deliver, the photographer canceled, and the last time I checked, the bride and groom weren't even here." She sighed. "So maybe I've been working for nothing."

He shifted on the lounger. "I think I need to tell you something."

She looked at him. "What's wrong?"

"Nothing's wrong. . . . It's just that I have a confession to make."

Her stomach tightened. Things were finally starting to smooth out between them. She wasn't sure she wanted to hear a confession.

He stood and got the large white box he'd gotten out of his truck earlier. He brought it over and set it in front of her. Then he got down on one knee.

She cocked her head to the side. "What are you doing?"

"Do you know what tomorrow is?"

She laughed. "Saturday?"

He took her hand. "Seriously. Tomorrow?"

"It's our anniversary."

He smiled broadly. "The wedding you've been planning these past weeks. The one where you had free rein to plan however you wanted? That was for us."

Her jaw dropped. "No way." She'd never suspected a thing. She smiled at him. "You wanted to renew our vows?"

"I did."

She bit her lip. "But now you don't? I don't understand."

Luke handed her the box. "First I want you to open this. It's an anniversary gift. A little more personal than a boat." He smiled.

Summer lifted the lid off of the box. The wedding gown she'd tried on at Madelyn's boutique, her *dream* gown, lay inside ensconced in white tissue paper. "Luke," she breathed. "I can't believe you did this."

"You like it?"

She felt tears spring into her eyes. He'd put so much thought into this surprise. "I love it."

"I wanted to renew our vows on our anniversary. . .but I think I'd rather wait."

She furrowed her brow. "Why?"

Luke sat down next to her. "Summer, I meant my vows when I said them seven years ago. Till death do us part. I still feel that way today." He smiled. "So I know we don't need to have another ceremony for any reason other than symbolically. But I don't think we should renew our vows here at some resort with only a couple of friends present," he said. "And Milo."

"Milo's here?" She couldn't believe the length he'd gone to in order to make her happy.

He chuckled. "Probably giving Justin fits as we speak." He took her hand. "This time around, I want it to be different. I want our families around us. And I want to say those vows in a church."

Summer couldn't stop the tears of joy that trickled down her face. "You do?"

He nodded. "This year has taught me that we need God at the center of our marriage. And I don't want to leave Him out of the ceremony."

Just hearing Luke say those words gave her such comfort. They'd been married for seven years, most of those good years. But she couldn't help but believe that the future was going to be even better.

Luke smiled as her face lit up. "What do you say?"

"I'm speechless. You surprise me so much sometimes. I don't guess I ever told you that my dream had always been for us to get married at St. Michael's. Did I?"

He shook his head. "No. But I started thinking about it on my way here today. I realized I'd planned the perfect surprise, but it didn't feel right. Even if the florist and the photographer had made it, I still would've asked you to wait until we can invite our families and make arrangements at a church." He reached out and stroked her smooth cheek.

Her mouth quirked into a smile. "I think it sounds amazing." She gripped his hand. "I think we're back on the right path, don't you?"

He nodded. There was one more thing he knew he had to talk to her about, and he had no idea what she would think. "I do. I know we're both committed to this marriage. And that makes all the difference." He pushed a strand of hair from her face. "But I think we need to talk about having a family."

She frowned. "Is this where you tell me that you don't think we should keep trying?"

He shook his head. "I know that's what I said before. But I didn't mean it. If you want to meet with the doctor again and see what he thinks our best bet is, then I'm on board."

"Really?" she asked.

He nodded. "You know I've always wanted a family. That hasn't changed."

"But you said. . ."

If he could go back in time and erase any conversation, it would be that one—the night he told Summer he wasn't sure if they were cut out to be parents. His own words had haunted him almost since the night he'd said them. "I know. I was so scared we would go through losing a child again. And at that point, I knew I couldn't handle it. Do you know that the reason I took the things from the nursery to the landfill instead of giving them away was because I couldn't stand the thought of another child using the stuff that had been meant for our baby?" He shook his head. "But I've had a lot of time to think about things."

"And what have you decided?"

"Our life is full of kids. Chloe's baby will be here before we know it. Katie Beth and Dale adore us. Even Colton has become part of our world. And watching Justin step in and be like a dad for Colton has made me realize that there are a ton of kids out there who need someone to care about them." He rubbed his jaw. "So yes, I want to have a baby of our own. But I'm prepared to find another way to be parents if that doesn't work out."

"Like adoption?"

He nodded. "Sure. We have that big house and plenty of money. And a lot of love to give."

Her face lit up in a smile. "That sounds amazing."

"Besides. . .I've made a decision about my music. A decision that will give me more time to devote to a family."

Her blue eyes narrowed. "What do you mean? Are you finally going to pursue music full-time?"

He chuckled. "Actually, just the opposite. The band is breaking up." He'd weighed his decision carefully and prayerfully, and in the end, he knew he was making the right choice.

"I don't understand. You love to play."

Luke nodded. "I do. I love the music. I love to write songs." He shrugged. "But over these past few weeks I started to question why I felt the need to halfheartedly pursue music." Summer had told him more than once that she'd be behind him if he wanted to give his music another shot. But he'd always found an excuse why it wasn't a good time.

"Yeah?"

"I wanted to make something of myself. I guess I always had this idea that if I made it in Nashville as a musician or if I actually had some of my songs recorded, that would mean I was really somebody." He shrugged. "But you know what? I'm *already* somebody. And I have a great life with you. My career with the park service has gradually morphed into something I love. This fall I'll be handling all the school groups that come through, which is something I'm really excited about."

Summer beamed. "Really? That's awesome. I know you'll be great at it." She paused. "But won't you miss playing?"

"I'll still play. At home. Or we'll do a show every now and then." He shook his head. "But weekly practices and shows aren't for me. Not anymore." He raked his fingers through his hair. "Music will always be part of me. I'll always tinker with my guitar and write songs. Maybe I'll record them and put them on YouTube or something."

"So I'll still get to hear you sing, but I won't have to share you with screaming groupies?" She chuckled.

"Something like that, yes."

She glanced at the tiny window above their heads. "I think the storm has stopped, at least for now."

"Should we make a run for it and check on Milo? It's getting kind of late."

Summer leaned forward and kissed him square on the mouth. "How about we stay here for a little while longer? Just us."

He pulled her to him. "Just us," he whispered. "That sounds wonderful."

Chapter 41

Three months later

Summer took one last look at herself in the mirror. The Mori Lee wedding gown looked like it had been designed with her in mind. Madelyn had made a couple of alterations, and it was the most perfect article of clothing Summer had ever worn. She glanced at the clock on the wall. It was almost time.

It was hard to believe three months had passed since she and Luke had celebrated their anniversary. Thankfully, the hurricane had spared them. By the time the storm reached land, it had been downgraded to a tropical storm. There was a lot of wind and a lot of rain but none of the devastation that easily could have happened. They'd spent their actual anniversary at home with a low-key celebration for two.

Since the storm hit, they'd made a lot of good progress as a couple. The counselor stood behind Luke's idea to renew their vows, and Summer had gone into full wedding-planner mode. And loved every minute of it. And now, on the third Saturday in October, it was time for their vow renewal ceremony.

"You ready?" Ashley stuck her head in the door. She stopped in her tracks. "Wow. You look incredible."

Summer took in Ashley's red Grecian-style, floor-length gown. "Likewise. Justin's eyes are going to pop out when he sees you in that."

Ashley beamed. "Thanks." She walked over and stood in

front of the mirror next to Summer. "Thanks for having me as your bridesmaid." She chuckled. "A few months ago, the idea of being a thirty-six-year-old bridesmaid would've had me drowning my sorrows in a bucket of Ben and Jerry's. But honestly, I'm honored to stand beside you as you renew your vows."

"It doesn't hurt that you're totally in love with the guy who'll be standing opposite you either." Summer grinned.

"That's just a bonus." Ashley returned her smile. "But do you think Britney can handle things out there?"

She thought for a second. They'd hired Britney, fresh out of college, to work as an associate at Summer Weddings. She was energetic, overly enthusiastic, and sometimes made Summer feel about eighty. But she also came with great references and so far had been an asset. "It's time for her to sink or swim, I guess." She sighed. "I officially relinquished control yesterday. Today I'm just the bride. I'm not solving any problems. Not putting out any fires with a florist or a musician. I'm focused on Luke and our vows."

"Good girl."

"Summer?" Britney whispered from the door. "Are you ready?"

"I sure am."

Britney walked in and closed the door behind her. "Everything is going smoothly so far. The church is filling up, and the music is perfect." She glanced at her watch. "In five minutes, it will be time for y'all to take your places."

"Did Luke's dad get here?" Summer asked.

Britney scrunched her face up in thought. "Is he the one in the wheelchair?"

Summer nodded.

"Yeah. I saw Luke talking to him a few minutes ago." She smiled. "By the way, I think it's very cool that y'all scheduled this so he could come."

They'd talked to Luke's daddy's doctor and had all agreed that if the ceremony was held in the morning, his daddy might be able to come. Summer was relieved to hear that Mr. Nelson was out there. She knew it meant a lot to Luke. Even if his daddy didn't remember the occasion tomorrow, Luke would remember it forever. "I'm just glad it worked out."

"And a postwedding brunch is such a fun idea," Ashley said. "You might start a trend."

Summer nodded. "Gram is excited because brunch is her favorite meal of the day. And my mom is determined to have a write-up about it in the society column."

Before she knew it, it was time. Her dad waited for her in the foyer. "Darling, you look amazing." He kissed her on the cheek. "I know you're technically already married, but it's always been a dream of mine to walk you down the aisle. I'm thankful to get this opportunity."

One of the biggest surprises of all had been how close Luke and her dad had grown. It seemed like the two of them had put their old differences aside and had become something that looked a lot like friends. And Summer had even gone on a shopping trip to Atlanta with Mom and Chloe. She'd come away realizing that even though she didn't have a ton in common with them, they could still enjoy spending time together. "Thanks, Daddy. I'm glad you're here."

Katie Beth, Dale, and Colton stood with Britney by the door. Katie Beth wore a white dress with a red ribbon tied around her waist. The little boys were in matching tuxes.

Summer knelt down to their level. "Everyone know what to do?"

"I do." Katie Beth smiled proudly. "We're going to walk down the aisle all the way to the front where Uncle Luke is standing. If we get tired, we can sit down on the front row."

"That's right, Katie Beth."

Summer walked back and took her dad's arm.

"Think they'll be okay?"

She nodded. "Katie Beth is a girl after my own heart. She's got it all under control." She chuckled. "Plus Colton and Dale know that Rose and Mrs. Sanders are on the front pew with prizes for them if they cooperate."

She watched as Britney opened the door for Ashley.

Ashley glanced back with a wink and then proceeded down the aisle.

"She's a good friend, isn't she?" Dad asked.

"Yes."

Britney knelt down and gave the little ones last-minute instructions then sent them on their way, pulling the door closed behind them.

Summer gripped Dad's arm. "I've planned what seems like hundreds of these and always chide the bride for feeling jittery. But this is kind of nerve-racking."

He smiled. "But when you see Luke waiting at the end of the aisle, it will be worth it."

"It's time," Britney whispered. She opened the door as the "Wedding March" began.

Summer and Dad paused in the doorway. Seeing the familiar faces of family and friends made the moment so special.

Then her eyes found Luke's, and everyone else faded away. As the music swelled around her, she walked toward him. She knew this was one of those moments she'd remember forever, surrounded by her friends and family and proclaiming her love for Luke. The past year had been tough, but they'd come through stronger than ever.

And as Summer took her place next to Luke at the front of the church, she knew the next leg of their journey together would be even better than the last.

Luke could count on one hand the number of times he'd been overcome by emotion. Watching Summer walk down the aisle toward him today would go on that list. She took his breath away.

It was more than her physical beauty though. He'd known her for so long that he was well aware that she possessed much more than just looks. The way she treated people, the way she cared, the way her first instinct in any situation was to pray—those things made her so much more than just a pretty face.

He took her hand as they faced the minister.

"Luke and Summer have written their own vows," the minister said with a smile. He nodded at Luke. "Whenever you're ready."

Luke turned to face Summer and took both her hands in his.

She smiled.

He took a deep breath. "Summer, I told you a long time ago that you were the best thing that ever happened to me. And that is even truer today. Seven years ago, I pledged to love, honor, and cherish you. I promised to stand by your side through the good and the bad." He sighed. "And I know we've dealt with some difficulties over the past year. There've been things that have almost pulled us apart. But I stand here before you today promising that my love for you has never been stronger." He gave her a tiny grin. "I know I might not say it enough. But Summer, I love you. I love you more than anything."

Her lip trembled, but she returned his smile.

"A few months ago, we were trapped in the middle of a storm. Literally. And we held on to one another and made it through. I know that in our life together, other storms will come. During those times, we will need to cling to each other and to God." He paused. "From this day forward, I promise to put God at the center of our relationship. Summer, you make me want to be a better man. The kind of man you respect and the kind of man who will make our children proud. I come here today and pledge to you my love, affection, and honor as long as we both shall live." He squeezed her hands.

"Summer," the minister said with a nod to her.

She smiled. "Luke, I've known you for half of my life. In some ways, that seems like a really long time, but then there are moments when I feel like we're still seventeen and meeting up at the bandstand at the Battery." She took a breath. "The past year has tested us. There were times when I didn't know what would happen. But there was never a time when I doubted my love for you. I've always told people that I'm blessed because I'm married to my best friend. You're the first person I want to share news with, both good and bad. You're who I want to talk to about big decisions. You're the one who can make me smile even through my tears."

She paused and looked deeper into his eyes. "We've both made mistakes. We've both put other things in front of our relationship. But I know in my heart that we've learned from those mistakes." A tear trickled down her face. "Over the years, I've joked that you're on my team. And I still feel that way. I choose you. Always. You are the one I want to go with on this wonderful, crazy journey called life." She smiled. "I promise to love you, honor you, and cherish you until the end of time."

The rest of the ceremony passed quickly. The minister finally said the words Luke had been waiting to hear. "Luke, you may kiss your bride."

Luke pulled her to him and gently kissed her lips.

They turned and faced the crowd and were met with applause as they walked down the aisle, arm in arm. A horse-drawn carriage waited for them out front.

He helped her into the carriage and whispered, "I love you."

She smiled. "I love you, too."

He leaned over and kissed her as the carriage began to move slowly through the streets of downtown Charleston.

"I feel like a princess." She grinned. "Thanks for letting me plan my dream wedding. It would've been just as easy for us to renew our vows right back at city hall."

He took her hand. "Nope. I wanted the world to know how we felt. No hiding this time. There's no reason to be scared someone won't approve of us."

She nodded and then glanced around. "Do you mind if we make a stop before we get to the brunch?"

"Sure."

"Thanks," she said. She leaned up to the driver. "Can you go to King Street, please?"

Luke wondered what she had in store but didn't question the detour. As long as they were together, he'd sit back and enjoy the ride.

Chapter 42

Summer took Luke's outstretched hand and let him help her out of the carriage. She turned to the driver. "This will only take a second."

"What's this about?" Luke asked.

She led him through the gates that led to the Unitarian Church Cemetery. "There's someone I need to visit."

A few moments later, they arrived at the stone bench next to the unknown child's grave. Summer glanced at Luke. "I come here sometimes to remember. Not just our baby, but all of those whose lives were cut short." She sat down on the bench.

He sat beside her. "It's a beautiful cemetery. I don't guess I've been here for years. Not since some long-ago elementary school history trip."

She slipped her hand in his. "I wandered in one day while I was on my lunch break. I found this spot and felt drawn to it." She motioned toward the headstone. "I guess it gave me a tangible place to come to in order to think about our child and to pray for healing."

"Thanks for bringing me here."

She stood. "I think it's time for me to say good-bye." She knelt down and placed her bouquet of roses at the foot of the grave. "We can go now."

Hand in hand, they walked down the pathway that led to the cemetery gates.

"Your carriage awaits," Luke said with a wave of his hand. "I've always wanted to say that and mean it."

Summer climbed back inside the carriage, thankful for the peace she'd finally found.

"Please welcome Mr. and Mrs. Luke Nelson," Justin said from the stage.

Ashley turned from her spot at a table near the front of the room to watch a beaming Summer and Luke walk inside, holding hands. They made their way into the large banquet room and were surrounded by well-wishers. She shifted Colton in her lap.

"Do you want me to take him?" Mrs. Sanders asked, gesturing to Colton.

She smiled. "No, he's fine." She leaned forward so she could see his face. "Aren't you, sweetie?"

Colton nodded and banged his toy truck on the table.

"We're going to eat some pancakes in a minute, okay?"

"Okay."

"Is this seat taken?" Summer asked, coming over to the table and pointing at a chair.

Ashley smiled. "Please sit." She gestured around the room. "This is awesome, by the way."

"I can give you my wedding planner's card if you'd like." Summer laughed.

Ashley joined in her laughter then noticed movement on the stage. "What's he doing?" she asked.

Luke stood center stage and took the microphone from the stand.

"I have no idea," Summer confessed.

"Ladies and gentlemen, we'd like to thank you for coming

today to celebrate the renewal of our vows," Luke said. "Everyone in this room is special to us, and we appreciate your prayers and support. But it wouldn't be right if we made this day totally about us." He motioned for Justin to join him. "And now I want to turn the floor over to my best man, Justin Sanders."

Ashley shot Summer a questioning look.

Summer shrugged.

"Everyone loves a wedding, don't they?" Justin asked with a smile. "But a wedding is more than a nice ceremony and pretty flowers. It's about the joining of two lives. It's about two people who are going to stand together through thick and thin." He took a breath. "And I have to confess, I've always wondered if I'd ever find someone of my own. Someone who would be my partner and my companion. Someone who would love me no matter what."

He gripped the microphone and stepped down from the stage.

Ashley watched, mesmerized, as he walked right toward her. Her heart pounded, and she clung to Colton like he was a lifeline.

Justin stopped once he reached her and dropped to one knee. "Ashley, I know it hasn't been that long since we met. But I also know that my whole life has changed for the better because of you. The moments that we spend together are the best I've ever had."

She wiped away a tear.

"I've fallen in love with you, and I can't imagine my life without you in it." He smiled. "Ashley Watson, will you marry me?"

"Yes," she whispered. "Of course." She stood and hoisted

Colton to her hip.

Justin pulled both of them into his arms, and the crowd cheered.

He kissed her lightly on the lips. "I'm going to make you so happy," he whispered.

"You already have." She smiled.

He headed back to the stage and put the microphone back on the stand.

Summer walked over, a huge smile on her face. "Congratulations."

"Did you know?"

Summer shrugged. "I suspected. Luke told me that there would be a couple of surprises."

"A couple? I wonder what the other one is."

Summer nodded toward the stage. "I'm thinking this might be it."

Justin, Luke, Jimmy, and Will were on the stage gearing up to play.

"I didn't know they were playing." Ashley was surprised Justin hadn't mentioned it.

"Me neither."

Luke tapped the microphone. "There's one more thing I need to do today." He smiled broadly. "I started writing this song when I was seventeen but didn't finish it until recently," he explained as he strummed his guitar. "This one is dedicated to my beautiful Summer Girl."

Summer gasped. "I don't believe it."

The opening chords of an unfamiliar song filled the room.

Ashley glanced over at Summer. Tears flowed down her face as she listened to the song written just for her. She hugged Colton and glanced down at the beautiful ring Justin had slipped on her finger.

There was a time when she would've been wary because everything was going too well. She would've been expecting something to happen to mess it up.

But today, all she felt was joy. She'd been given a second chance at happiness, and even though life wouldn't always be perfect, she was surrounded by people who cared about her and who would always stand by her.

The Lord had blessed her with a beautiful life, and she wasn't going to miss another minute of it worrying.

A Wedding Transpires on Mackinac Island

by Cara C. Putman

Dedication

To my kids—praying you allow God to direct you to the future and the ones He has for you. The greatest adventure is seeking Him and living for Him.

Acknowledgments

Mackinac Island is a wonderful place our family loves to visit. A couple of years ago, I had an idea to write a romance mixed with mystery and suspense that would be set on the island. When we returned, my husband went to Fort Mackinac while I went to the police department to talk to the police chief. He spent time answering all of my questions about what would happen if someone was murdered on the island without offering to let me spend time in their cell, for which I will always be grateful. While writing the book, I also realized that I needed to understand how a gunshot wound would be handled on Mackinac Island. Dr. Jennifer Shockley very patiently answered my questions and did all she could to make sure I understood what would occur on the island and at a mainland hospital. Many thanks to these gracious people. Any mistakes are mine.

Thank you to my agent who let me know there was an opportunity to write a book for Barbour, and Rebecca Germany, who read my proposal and gave me a chance to write this story.

I was also blessed to have several friends read the book and help me. Initially, Colleen Coble, Robin Caroll, and Sabrina Butcher helped me brainstorm the idea and flesh out a plot. Then as I wrote, Sue Lyzenga read the book not once but three times, while Sabrina and Casey Herringshaw gave input on the manuscript. Lastly, thanks to my stellar editor, April Frazier, who helped me fix the details and make the plot work. I also want to thank my husband and kids who make Mackinac Island such a great place to escape. I love walking the island, exploring the trails, and riding bikes around the island with you. I love you!

Chapter 1

*D*on't do it. Don't do it. Don't do it.

The refrain beat a steady tempo through Alanna Stone's mind as she dragged up the gangplank to the ferry where it rocked in the early morning light at the St. Ignace dock. She avoided gazing to her right in the direction of Mackinac Island. A place of beauty and peace to many, it symbolized all the harshness that could shimmer beneath the surface in a small town. She'd sworn never to return and had honored that vow for eleven years.

Now? Now she abandoned her firmly held avoidance to help her parents. A wave rocked the boat, and she bobbled as she struggled to stay steady on more than her feet.

A man in the green polo that bore the Arnold Transport Company logo steadied her with a smile. "You'll find your sea legs in no time."

"Good thing, since the trip's so short."

He laughed and nodded. "About fifteen minutes."

How could she tell him she wished it lasted fifteen months or years? That time would freeze, and she'd stay on this side of the lake?

Seagulls cawed as they took to the air and swooped around the boat.

Fifteen minutes. That's all it took to start a new life.

Diesel fumes rolled around her as the ferry's engines roared into gear. With a grinding stop and jerk, the boat eased away from the dock and powered across the lake. Alanna sucked in a deep breath then coughed as fumes settled in her lungs. She clenched her jaw and pivoted until she faced east as the boat pushed through the water toward the sun. She needed to face her new reality and the hidden embarrassment. All represented by one tiny spot on the map.

Mackinac Island.

In the morning light, it looked like an emerald emerging from the lake with the Victorian cottages and Grand Hotel popping out like embellishments against the forest backdrop.

The wind blew across Alanna's face, misting it with a fine spray as it tangled her hair. The strands whipped around her neck, but she let the wind do its worst. Even then, it couldn't reflect the chaos churning inside her. Tension tightened her body again. It had been her constant companion during the Menendez murder trial. The case had faded from the front page of the newspapers, and the reporters had finally abandoned their posts at her home and the office. Not the first time media had hounded her, but at least this time it involved a client rather than her brother. She'd thought she had shed the constant headache, but now it roared back to full strength in her temples.

Going home did that to her.

The catamaran shifted beneath her, the engines grinding.

When Mother had called begging for help after Daddy's stroke, Alanna had two choices: return to the island to keep her parents' art shop open or let their lives' work close.

Maybe things had changed in the time she'd been away. Memories shortened. Ugly innuendos against her brother faded. If only the island could transform into an oasis for her. One she needed after the lengthy, brutal civil trial tied to a murder between feuding neighbors. She still felt the fatigue from a hard-fought victory, one that consumed almost as many of her nights as days.

Her jaw clenched as the boat shifted further and the engines reversed direction. The shuttle chugged toward the island, slowing as it approached. The Arnold dock bustled with activity, but it was the kind propelled by men pushing caddies and horses stamping their hooves. Alanna collected her thoughts and softened her knees to rock with the ferry as it slid next to the dock.

At first glance nothing had changed. Bicycles and horse-drawn taxis lined Huron Street at the end of the dock. Men wearing hotel logo-embellished polos wove between groups of tourists. Their intent gazes focused on destinations while the tourists ambled from fudge shops to knickknack stores.

Alanna stumbled against the railing as the boat stopped. Her feet anchored in place. The other passengers disembarked. She needed to move. Tackle whatever waited for her.

It's just a few weeks, two months at most. She could do anything for that long. Get the store open again. Find someone to run the shop. Return to Grand Rapids before the partners missed her too much. That's all she had to do. Grabbing her briefcase, Alanna hiked over the short gangplank. A taxi could take her to the cottage first. No, if she did that, she might not make an appearance at the shop today.

She marched to the trolley lined with suitcases, handed over her claim ticket, and took the handle on hers. It was big, but she could maneuver it the few blocks to the store. She slipped into the flow of visitors pouring off the dock. With her suitcase rolling behind her, maybe no one would recognize her. Even with that hope, her sunglasses stayed firmly in place. If any of her opposing counsel spotted her hiding behind the glasses, they'd laugh. Her reputation as a tiger in the courtroom would lay shredded at her feet.

She ducked behind a group and followed them up the street. She crashed off a hard surface—no. . .somebody—and fell.

"Are you okay?" A rich baritone, eerily familiar, spoke the words.

Alanna nodded from her position on the sidewalk but kept her chin tucked. She couldn't let him get a good glimpse at her or her embarrassment. What if he remembered her? Eleven years might not be long enough to make her anonymous to the man who first claimed her heart.

"There are too many people on the sidewalks not to pay attention. Can I help you up?" The man offered her a hand.

Alanna peeked up then tilted her head back farther and saw the man she'd hoped most to avoid on the island. Her pulse picked up speed, a nod to their long-ago high school summer romance. Her gaze slipped to his mouth, and she jerked it back up as heat flashed up her neck at the thought of their twilight kisses on the dock by her parents' home years earlier. In an instant, the memory morphed into the panicked thought Jonathan might recognize her. She longed for something—anything—more substantial than glasses to hide behind.

His face had matured. The jaw squared, the nose bent like he'd broken it, the eyes green with a tinge of blue—matching the calm waters of Lake Huron. He still towered over her a good six inches or more. Her gaze traveled down his fit form, but he waved his hand in front of her face.

"Help you up?" Mischief danced in his sea-green eyes as if he knew she'd stared at him from behind the glasses.

Alanna hesitated a moment then accepted his hand, finding hers dwarfed in his. A shock raced up her arm. He pulled her to her feet, and she two-stepped backward. "Th–thank you."

"Sure you're okay?"

"Yes." She had to get away before he recognized her. Of all the people to run into! She hadn't prepared for the memories and what-ifs to assault her the moment she stepped on Mackinac Island. Her breath hitched, and she tightened her grip on the suitcase. "Thank you again."

Alanna skirted around him and hurried down Huron, gaze fixed in front of her. She knew he must think her ridiculous, but she couldn't look back. If she did, she'd be lost in his gaze, and he'd recognize her in an instant. If Spencer hadn't ended their year-long relationship, she'd have some defense to Jonathan. Instead, she felt vulnerable to the memories.

If the first moments together, when he didn't know her, were any indication, her long-buried attraction to him would chase her right off the island.

Shadowy memories chased questions through Jonathan Covington's mind as he watched the woman hurry down the street, the suitcase bumping over cracks in the sidewalk. Her willowy form reminded him of someone, only the short blond hair didn't fit the image. He wondered what color her eyes were, but she'd hidden behind the large sunglasses. Her suitcase bobbled on one wheel, but she didn't slow. If he didn't know better, he'd say a wildcat or black bear chased her—only the island didn't have any. No, the only big wildlife was the tourists. Almost as entertaining but not quite.

Her thin form glided around a mother leading a toddler down the street. At least this time she was more attentive to others on the sidewalk. She hopped as the suitcase bounced against her ankles.

He watched her a moment more, a distant memory tugging at him. Something about her seemed familiar, but he couldn't tell as she hid behind those huge Jackie O sunglasses, useless on a cloudy morning.

"You getting her number, Covington, or getting back to work?" Mr. Morris watched him with a hint of amusement defying his stiff posture as he braced his arms alongside his trim waist.

Jonathan snapped his fingers. "Knew I forgot something." He pulled his attention from the retreating woman and pasted a grin on his face before turning back to his client. The man expected him to work, not daydream. Besides, he had a relationship. . .of sorts. "Ready for the best pancakes in town?"

Edward Morris snorted, his nostrils flaring. "There isn't much competition."

"Part of the island's charm."

"So Bonnie says." Humor lightened Edward's eyes and eased the lines on his tanned face. Didn't look like the man missed many opportunities to walk a golf course. Jonathan filed the detail for easy access as he prepared an itinerary for the Morrises' event. He needed to nail this event and get the referrals that had to come from them. Otherwise Jonathan stood dangerously close to losing his event-planning business and returning to another job working for someone else.

"That woman has been intent on a celebration of a lifetime for our fortieth. Says, with the way couples divorce, we have to make a splash. I hope this works for her."

"That's why I'm here." Jonathan opened the door to Mike's and inhaled the rich aroma of roasting coffee. Everyone else could purchase overpriced brew at the chain down the block, but he enjoyed the hearty coffee served here. The small restaurant was a new and welcome addition to the morning offerings. "Right this way."

"Morning, gents." Mike's deep voice bellowed from behind the old-style counter. "What can I get you this morning?"

Jonathan grabbed a stool at the counter. "Coffee and a stack of your blueberry pancakes."

"Black and Michigan maple?"

"Of course."

"And for you?" Mike looked at Edward, who studied the simple menu as if it were the *Wall Street Journal* he usually tucked under his arm.

"A plain stack and doctored coffee."

"Plain, really?" With all the options on the menu, Jonathan couldn't imagine settling for plain. "Try the apple or cherry. Both are great."

"I'll stick with good ole syrup."

Jonathan shook his head and winked at Mike, who'd watched the exchange with his trademark easy grin. "So what do you envision for this party?"

"We'll need somewhere for the kids and grandkids to stay. Then recommendations for friends who make the trip. And someplace that accommodates a moderately sized group. Maybe forty, though if Bonnie has her way, she'll break the bank and invite everyone she's ever greeted."

"Formal or relaxed?"

"Casual. It's easier for everyone that way."

"Hope you brought your appetite today, Jonathan. I don't want to throw food away this time." Mike plopped a plate of steaming pancakes in front of him. A dollop of butter melted in a pool on the top cake with three slices of thick bacon lining the plate's edge.

"I didn't order the bacon."

"I know. Thought you'd need the extra sustenance." He nodded his head toward Edward. "And here's some link sausage for you. You look like that kind of guy."

"Really?" Edward hiked an eyebrow as he examined the tower of pancakes.

"Most definitely. Someone who's only here because his wife told him to come. What I don't get is where's the missus?"

Jonathan winced. There'd been no way to warn Mike, but the sudden pallor in Edward's face made him wish there had been.

"She'll be here later in the season." Edward pushed the bite of pancakes he'd cut through the syrup but didn't shovel it to his mouth.

Mike shrugged, but Jonathan caught his gaze and shook his head, a small movement to keep Mike from inserting his foot deeper in his mouth. As he watched Edward choke down his emotions with a swig of coffee, Jonathan thanked God he'd remained single. The pain that shadowed the man's eyes when he thought about his wife and her battle with cancer left Jonathan determined to avoid that depth of pain.

Love traveled a path that led directly and unavoidably to heartache. The only question was how long the journey took. He had to look no farther than his parents' caustic marriage or his own string of tepid relationships.

Guess that's what happened when the gal you believed was the love of your life walked away without a glance. Showed how much he understood love. Even now he couldn't convince his heart to engage with the lady he enjoyed. Something was wrong with him, or love wasn't meant to be part of his life.

The only way to evade the issue was to bypass love.

And as the strong, gruff man swiped under his eyes and cleared his throat, Jonathan determined to maintain his present course and dodge that fate.

Chapter 2

A passing glance at her parents' art studio left the impression its owners had abandoned it without notice. It languished between a store filled with knickknacks and a photography studio. Across the street sat a bike shop with an attached Internet café. Alanna shook her head as two teens leaned close to monitors. . . . The Internet invaded even this quiet spot.

She looked at the jumbled mass of keys her mother had handed her the night before at the hospital in Grand Rapids. Mom's hands had shaken as she delivered a brief primer on the keys. Here, in the light of day, standing in this place, Alanna's mind refused to remember which key did what. As she stared at the mess of keys, the monstrous suitcase collapsed on its side into her knees.

"Ouch." Alanna jumped away from the case then righted it, balancing it when it teetered again. Finally, it rested against the wooden wall. She rubbed the back of her knees. The morning couldn't get much worse.

She selected a key, tried to cram it into the hole, and then flipped to another. Alanna didn't know whether to be relieved or disappointed Jonathan Covington didn't remember her. Time had passed, but she hadn't changed that much. Tears filled her eyes as the hopes she'd held for them overwhelmed her. She rammed another key into the keyhole.

"Work. Please work." She had to get inside where she could hide her meltdown. She'd known it wouldn't be easy to return to Mackinac, but the flood of emotions so soon caught her off guard.

The key swiveled in the hole followed by the door creaking open. Alanna stumbled into the dim interior. The air hung heavy, tainted by mustiness rather than the soothing lavender that usually saturated the space. Shadows filled the room, the eerie images playing on the walls flung from the modern art statues standing in the middle of the room. She might not be able to do much about the lavender until she got to the cottage, but she could turn on the lights and fill the silence. Mom must have left the jazz CDs that usually piped through the music system somewhere.

"Hey, lady."

Alanna startled at the deep voice. She turned and stopped at the red GRAND HOTEL insignia on the shirt. One of the best nights of her young life had occurred when Jonathan took her to an amazing dinner at the grand lady of the island. She'd dressed up, and he'd looked so handsome in his suit. She shook her head to clear the memory.

"Need help with your bag?" He gestured to the black monolith that languished where she'd left it.

"Thank you. Could you pull it inside the door?"

He did, taking it behind the counter. "Unless it's your latest sculpture, I doubt you want it left by the door. Need me to carry it upstairs?"

"No, I don't live there. Thanks for your assistance." She dug a single out of her wallet and handed it to him. The man left with a smile splitting his ebony face. If only she could generate that kind of response from everyone she encountered. Without the money tied to it.

She considered the back stairway. Mom used to use it as a studio then had converted it to a small apartment. So far, the space was empty for this season. Alanna guessed she could stay there, but she wanted the comfort and familiarity of the house. The privacy, too.

A sigh shuddered through her. If she truly wanted her privacy, she should have stayed in Grand Rapids and continued braving the media. All the regulars here knew her. Knew the past. Knew the pieces she'd kept separate from the life she'd created on the mainland. There people didn't remember Grady Cadieux's death and tie it to her younger brother, Trevor Stone. There may not have been enough evidence to prosecute him, but she'd seen the questions and anger in her neighbors' eyes. The popular mayor's son had captained the basketball team and had dreams the island's residents adopted as their own. Then he died, and their grief transferred to anger that targeted Trevor.

She parted the lace curtains and peeked at the street. Even though it was barely 8:00 a.m., people strolled up and down the sidewalk. If she wanted the opportunity to sell anything today, she needed to open. Mom had relayed what sounded like a never-ending list of tasks she must complete each day before unlocking the door.

A sigh burbled from the depths of her soul. It was Monday morning, and she should be an hour into case reviews. Maybe at the courthouse preparing for a trial or hearings. Instead, she stood on the one place she swore she'd avoid until her dying days. It helped that her parents lived here only during the tourist season and abandoned the island for the holidays. She'd wondered if they did it for her and Trevor. Her brother wanted to return to the island even less than she did.

She shook her head before the thoughts took over.

She couldn't afford to descend into the past. Not when tourists—potential buyers—peeked in the windows. If Alanna wanted to ensure there was sufficient money to pay her father's hospital and rehab bills, she had to get the Painted Stone open and sell some art.

After she flipped several switches, light filled the space. Spotlights highlighted paintings at regular intervals, with smaller works featured in between. Lights she hadn't noticed on the floor emphasized the sculptures. And each wall was painted a rich shade—crimson, eggplant, gold, and midnight blue—that served almost as an extra mat to the paintings. Her mother's artistic touch filled the studio. And her father's fingerprints would dot the office.

Walking behind the counter, Alanna flipped the switches to turn on the computer that served as a cash register. It hummed to life, and she crouched and rummaged through a box for CDs. Finding one that looked promising, she popped it into the CD player and hit PLAY. Soft notes from a piano filtered through the room. Add some lavender and everything would be perfect.

"Hello?"

Alanna popped up, ramming her head against the counter with a yelp. She rubbed her hand across the back of her scalp, biting her lip to keep from saying the words that rushed to escape.

"Are you open?" A woman's soft voice edged into the studio followed by the sound of heels clicking against the hardwood floors. "The sign isn't flipped, but I saw lights and the open door."

Alanna smiled around the pain and finished standing. "I'm almost ready, but feel free to look around while I finish."

"Thank you, dear." The older woman had soft white curls that wisped around her face. She wore a lavender spangled shirt over linen white capris, the picture of a visitor. She wandered in front of one of Alanna's mother's large oil paintings. She stood in front of it, edged to the right, then the left. She cocked her head like a seagull eyeing a treat someone had dropped. "This scene is quite vibrant. Do you know where it was painted?"

"Let me see." Alanna slipped from behind the counter and joined the woman. The location couldn't be clearer—the Grand Hotel's long white porch lined with rockers, the yellow awnings peeking from the ground level and first level of the porch. The colors were right. The setting appropriate. But somehow the painting felt off. Different. Not quite like her mom's usual work. The woman turned to her, a question reflected in her gray eyes. "This is the Grand Hotel. I'm sure you'll see it during your stay. It's quite the landmark for the island."

"Of course. How could I miss that?" The woman turned with a soft smile. "I'll just have a look around."

While the woman stopped to admire each painting, Alanna hurried to the supply closet to get the items she needed to finish preparing the store. Even as she dusted the paintings and turned the sign to OPEN, her gaze wandered back to the painting.

The plates held lingering puddles of syrup but otherwise stood empty with every last blueberry and crumb consumed.

Mike smiled as he whisked the plates behind the counter. "Can I get anything else for you gents?"

Edward shook his head, and Jonathan grabbed the bill before the other man could.

"Ready to explore possible sites?" Jonathan handed Mike a twenty and then pulled out his portfolio. He shook the image of the woman who'd collided with him from his mind again. To accomplish all he'd promised, they'd need to maximize each moment. And that meant ignoring all distractions, especially the ones that made no sense. Mackinac might be small, but it was filled with event and lodging options. "Several bed-and-breakfasts could be perfect for your family and might even have openings since it's still early in the season. But we don't want to wait long. Better to check them today and make your decision quickly."

Edward's focus had returned, his eyes clear of the lingering pain that had stained them during breakfast. The athletic man pulled out a smartphone and clicked away.

At times Jonathan wished technology hadn't invaded the island to the degree it had. Now everyone had BlackBerries, Droids, and iPads, all the things that invited the world they escaped to assault the protected beauty up at the tip of Michigan.

"What are the names of the B&Bs?"

Jonathan laughed. "You're eager to get to it."

"Time's a wasting, my man." Edward shrugged, that silly light creeping back into his expression. "I promised Bonnie I'd give her a full report tonight. That means pictures, notes, details. She's really the one who should be here with you." He swallowed hard. "But I'll do the standing-in part then let her make the decisions."

Jonathan clapped Edward on the shoulder. "No problem. Let's head to my office. Get you oriented and collect some brochures you can take notes on."

As they walked the block west along Huron, Jonathan watched for the woman. He tried to corral his thoughts, but they insisted on returning to the way her head had tilted like a bird trying to decide whether he was a friend or enemy. They turned onto Market, and he picked up the pace. He slowed at the Painted Stone's door. It stood tucked between a photography studio filled with amazing images of the island and a unique flag shop. The art studio had been closed since the owner had a stroke a week earlier, though it looked like someone had opened the store. He'd have to check on Mr. Stone's status later.

Mr. Morris studied the window, his hands shoved in his pockets, an intense gaze on his face. "You think they could commission something?"

Jonathan startled and glanced at the man. "A painting or a sculpture?"

"Naw. It's a crazy idea. Let's get moving."

"All right. We're almost there." He said a quick prayer for Mr. Stone as he led Mr. Morris down the street. Jonathan led Edward to a side door tucked among the storefronts. It opened to the stairs to his second-floor office. Edward took in his office. It was small with one main room, a kitchenette, and a bathroom tucked at the back. The walls reflected the rich green of the evergreens on the top half with white paneling on the bottom. The white kept the green from shrinking the room but showed every ding and bang. Jonathan made a mental note to touch it up.

"Why don't you take a seat." Jonathan settled at his cherry

desk while he grabbed the folder he'd slapped a label on and filled with brochures and maps of the island. "We'll start at Haan's 1830 and explore a few of the other smaller B&Bs. Then we can look at several restaurants. If you think you'll have more than forty people, we should consider an outdoor venue. One far away from sidewalks." As Edward's eyebrows rose, Jonathan hurried on. "Don't worry, there are plenty of great locations. And several of the hotels have meeting space. But depending on the timing, we could create a fun event outdoors. Plenty of space for the kids to run around and more flexibility in setup."

They reviewed the map and plotted the best way to get from place to place. Edward stood, and Jonathan grabbed his keys and cell phone. He ushered Edward toward the stairs and followed him down.

They had one day to find exactly what Edward and Bonnie imagined for their event. He needed to focus on hitting as many spots as possible while helping Edward define exactly what they wanted. If only he could convince the morning's mystery woman not to return to his thoughts.

Chapter 3

The sun sat poised to rise above the pine trees dotting Jonathan's property the next morning. A bird's muted chatter broke the silence surrounding him. He moved around the kitchen as he started a fresh pot of coffee. He rehashed the prior day while he waited for his first cup. Edward had seemed pleased with Jonathan's suggestions as he took copious notes at their many stops.

When the coffeepot beeped, Jonathan grabbed a mug from the rack beside the sink and filled it. He carried it to the front porch and sank onto the rocking chair his grandfather had made. He blew on the steaming coffee as his gaze searched the spindly pines. Maybe this morning he'd catch a glimpse of the elusive Kirtland's warbler.

He'd tried hard to keep the cowbirds away but hadn't seen any activity to suggest the warblers had returned. If Jonathan's ears didn't deceive him, maybe this fellow was one. The only problem was the bird could be anywhere in a quarter-mile radius. If he was right, the bird had found a good home in the jack pine habitat.

Chip-chip-che-way-o. That's how the bird guides described the sound of the yellow-bellied warbler. To Jonathan's ears, its song rang more melodious in the early morning silence.

Jonathan sipped the strong coffee. There wasn't a better way to start the morning than sitting on his cabin's porch surrounded by God's creation, even the hidden ones. He might not see the warbler yet, but he would.

The alarm on his watch shrieked, wrecking the morning's peace. The trees rustled as birds took flight. He jabbed the buttons on the watch, and it fell silent. So much for a calm start to the day. How could he have forgotten to turn it off when he woke before the alarm? Jonathan shifted against the porch railing, the day's demands replacing the fleeting peace. Might as well face reality. It promised to be another busy, stress-filled day. Better tackle it head-on instead of wasting another moment worrying about how to land the Standeford wedding account and keep another couple, the Wenzes, happy with their anniversary plans. All the meetings with local hotels and associations to gain new business. His mind spun with the details and ideas. Business looked ready to pick up, but he needed to clone himself if he wanted to keep up.

At times like this, he wondered if he'd ever find a way to add an employee. Maybe if he pulled everything back to his cabin. He could always meet people at local spots like Mike's. The problem was his cabin was small. It'd be tough to find space for all his supplies. His office might not be huge, but it did provide the extra space and a bit of separation from his home. Still, working with someone as part of a cohesive team sounded great. Then he could work on the events while someone else focused on marketing to prospective clients. Then his business could really grow.

The steady clop of horses' hooves on the packed road running in front of the cabin invaded his thoughts. People rarely traveled the out-of-the-way road, especially this early.

The taxi passed, containing one passenger, a woman whose short hair turned golden when the sun's rays reached through the trees to touch it. Only a couple of homes dotted the road beyond his small place. Where was she headed?

He blew on the coffee again then sipped.

"Morning, Jonathan." The soft words carried across the short distance echoing from his past.

He spewed the coffee. She knew his name? Two words. Yet with them hope and anger spiraled through him.

It couldn't be Alanna. Not after all this time. Surely not. Would her father's stroke pull her back to the island when he hadn't been enough? The coffee churned in his stomach. He dumped the rest of the brew on the lilac standing by the steps. His grandmother had babied that bush, yet it seemed to do okay with his occasional coffee bath. Though it never flowered like it did under his grandmother's care.

So he didn't have a green thumb.

Jonathan set the mug on the railing and took a step off the porch. The taxi had disappeared down the narrow lane. Unless he wanted to follow it and risk looking the fool, he'd better stay put. His watch beeped again. He didn't have time to hunt down an elusive woman who knew his name. Maybe it had been a lucky guess. He snorted. *Yeah right.*

Jonathan—one of the top three names on the tip of beautiful women's tongues. Especially when they saw him.

Only one woman had said his name with an inflection that felt like a caress.

He jumped down the steps and hurried to the road. Looked down it. Saw the taxi stop at the path leading to the Stones' cottage. With a glimpse of a beautiful woman hiding behind Jackie O sunglasses, it hit him he'd run into Alanna yesterday. If she'd arrived then, why hadn't she come home last night? He hadn't seen lights when he'd checked the house for the Stones. Maybe that was all the excuse he needed to confirm the woman in the carriage truly was Alanna.

His watch beeped its warning again.

Time to get moving. He'd drop by tonight. See if she had a good explanation for the way she disappeared, cut him out of her life.

He shook his head, trying to free himself of the immediate hold she'd reestablished. What would Jaclyn think? Jaclyn Raeder, the woman who'd worked her way into his life along with that precious little boy. Sure, he'd never felt the flashes of attraction with Jaclyn, but she was a good woman. And she'd been here. Consistently.

He couldn't go there. Not now, and not after two mere words.

His clients didn't care about the overpowering desire he had to abandon the day's agenda and rush to the house, but Jaclyn would. Clients only focused on whether events ran without a hiccup, snag, or noticeable problem. As long as he was the one losing sleep and weight over the details, they'd sign the checks.

The slow *clop-clop* of the taxi echoed in the quiet. Jonathan smiled when he saw the empty passenger seats. She was back. Now he had to run or he'd miss his first appointment.

Alanna leaned against the door. What had she been thinking? *Hello, Jonathan?* It was bad enough they'd live next door to each other. She'd prayed he'd moved, but the moment she bumped into him yesterday, she knew he still lived in the small cabin. So she'd been a coward and spent the night in an anonymous bed-and-breakfast. Finding an open room had surprised her—even this early in the season—but it gave her the retreat she'd needed as she formed a plan.

From the moment Mom called with her plea, Alanna's prayers had included the request for Jonathan Covington to be far removed from Mackinac. That he would be anywhere but here. Why couldn't God have answered that prayer? It would have simplified her emotionally complicated return. Enough strands existed on the island to capture her in the spiderweb of the past. She didn't need her heart involved, too.

Not after she'd worked so hard to pretend she never cared for Jonathan. That their relationship had never proceeded past a weak adolescent shadow of love. But as she hid in the B and B, she had to admit she'd fooled herself. It wasn't the pressure of law school and starting a career that kept her from relationships. She couldn't even blame the uninteresting men she ran into. Maybe they'd been uninteresting because they weren't Jonathan.

In the early light of morning, she decided to attack the mess of emotions head-on. After finding a taxi, she headed to the cottage. Home. It hadn't been that for years. Alanna stood on the porch, bag next to her, key in hand. One jab and twist and she'd fall inside. She hesitated, listening for the sound of heavy footsteps across the lawn. A bird jabbered angrily somewhere near her, but she didn't hear the sound she anticipated and feared.

Alanna took a steadying breath and twisted the key, opened the door, and pulled her bag into the small sitting area. Dropping the suitcase's handle, she marched to the kitchen and stood at the window. A dock angled from the backyard into the small pond the house shared with Jonathan's cabin.

Heat curled through her at the thought of the nights she and Jonathan had sat at the end, toes dangling inches above the water, shoulders touching.

Before she got lost in more what-ifs and unfulfilled hopes, she spun on her heel and headed to her small bedroom. As soon as she stepped inside, she groaned. Nothing was as she remembered from high school. Every scrap of pink had transformed into the perfect guest bedroom rather than a teenage girl's dream escape.

If she hurried, she could shower, change, and hike to town before the studio opened. Tonight she could wallow in the past. Now she had to survive the present.

By noon she couldn't wait to leave the art studio and join the tourists staring in the fudge shop windows. The four walls had closed in as she answered questions about the island, none leading to sales. People wanted free tourist advice. Didn't they understand that if she didn't sell art, she couldn't keep the studio open to answer their questions? Maybe she needed to talk to Mom about lower-priced items that were accessible to more checkbooks.

She merged with the melee on Huron. Today several tour groups stood out in the crowds with their matching ball caps or guides wielding umbrellas. She stepped against Doud's Market's tan wall to let a group of smiling senior citizens pass. Their guide steered them to Fort Mackinac. One lady teetered on spiky heels that weren't designed to navigate the steep hill and stairs leading to the fort. Maybe Ste. Anne's Church would be a better destination for her.

The last tour member smiled as she passed. Alanna nodded at her then continued to the Yankee Rebel. The mix of cleanly painted wood buildings smashed against brick storefronts gave the street a touristy, village feel, her favorite part of the island.

She entered the restaurant and waited for the hostess to acknowledge her.

"Alanna Stone. Over here."

Alanna longed to disappear as the boisterous voice bellowed. A man her daddy's age waved at her from the back corner.

"Come join me."

She glanced around and didn't notice anyone she recognized, though after eleven years she wasn't sure she'd recognize many. In fact, the idea he knew who she was after all this time seemed incongruous. Still, the tables had started to fill. Maybe she should join him.

The man stood and headed her way. He took her arm and escorted her to the table. "This way. It's time you returned, young lady. Sorry it took your daddy's stroke to get you here. This may be a good that comes from it. Time to return, face the past, and clear the air, so to speak."

Alanna watched him out of the corner of her eye as they crossed the room.

"Here, let me help you." He pulled out a chair next to his, waited for her to sit, then scooted her to the table. "Remember me?"

"No."

"Not surprised. I've lost a lot of weight. Had the gastric bypass. Worked like a charm." He patted his waist then brushed a lock of salt-and-pepper hair out of his eyes. "Gerald Tomkin."

"Mr. Tomkin?" The principal? No wonder she'd blocked him. The man always acted as if the whole world wanted to hear every word he said, no matter how inconsequential or irrelevant. But swiping the hair out of his face was classic Mr. Tomkin. She'd graduated with his son Brendan, who had seemed destined to follow in his father's pompous footsteps. After the graduation party accident, he'd been even more unbearable, like he had taken Grady's death personally.

"Your mom kept me up-to-date on your progress. Impressive, young lady. But I knew you had it in you to change the world."

Alanna studied her hands, unused to praise from him. "Are you still at the school?"

"No. Retired last year and now working with the island's foundation. You should get involved. Right up your alley as an attorney. In fact, I have a project to discuss with you. One important to the foundation's future."

"I don't think I'll be here long enough for a project."

A waitress stopped by the table.

"We'll talk more after we order. I'd get the pot roast sandwich. You won't be disappointed." He rubbed his stomach.

Still bossy as ever, but it did sound good. "All right."

The waitress collected their drink orders, and Alanna glanced around. The door opened, and sunlight streamed through the opening.

"Doris, where are you hiding?"

Jonathan Covington—here? Alanna slouched in her chair. She picked up a menu and pretended to study it intently, holding it in front of her face. Footsteps clomped across the wooden floor in her direction. She kept her head buried, refusing to look up.

"Gerald Tomkin. Just the man I wanted to see."

Alanna stifled a sigh and glanced up. She forced a smile

on her face, one that froze when she noticed the funny way he looked at her. He clutched the chair across from Gerald. "Still rent your flower garden for photos?"

"Another wedding?" Gerald gestured at the table. "Why don't you join us?"

"Of course." Jonathan took a seat then frowned.

"Flower garden?" Alanna jolted as she felt something on her shoulder. Mr. Tomkin had placed his hand there. She started to scoot her chair away, but that would put her closer to Jonathan.

"I rent it out occasionally for the right event." Mr. Tomkin grinned. "When it's in full bloom, it's a spectacular backdrop." He looked at Jonathan. "When would you need it?"

"I'm not sure yet. But would like to add it to a wedding proposal." Jonathan shifted his attention and quirked his head as if trying to decide if it was really her. "Alanna Stone?"

"Hi, Jonathan."

"What brings you back to the island? Your father's stroke?" His eyes searched her face, wariness keeping a safe distance between them.

"Yes." She tried to meet his gaze but couldn't.

"Is he improving?" Genuine concern lined his voice.

She found his gaze, saw the concern mirrored there. "Not much change. That's why Mom asked me to come."

"Aren't you a high-powered attorney? Can't imagine you staying here long." Jonathan played with the napkin-wrapped silverware at his place.

"I can't. Just long enough to find someone to run the store. Shouldn't be too hard." She hoped. Then she'd run to the ferry as fast as she could.

Mr. Tomkin nodded then turned to Jonathan. "So tell

me about this wedding."

Alanna tuned the two out as they talked details and locations.

"Then you can help me talk Miss Stone into helping with the foundation. As an attorney, she's exactly what we need to wade through the tangled mess of finances."

Jonathan shrugged, a shuttered look clouding his face. He served on the board? Another reason for her to avoid it if they pressed her to serve. She couldn't get involved, not when a legal dispute here could delay her return to Grand Rapids.

The waitress returned and set waters in front of them, somehow knowing to add a third for Jonathan. "What can I get you today?"

They rattled off orders, and the waitress disappeared in the back.

Alanna took a sip of water, watching Jonathan from underneath her eyelashes. His jaw tightened, and then he took a deep breath and seemed to make a decision.

"Maybe we can catch up tonight."

"Maybe."

Gerald guffawed. "I see you two still have something between you. Good thing Jaclyn's not here." He leaned toward Alanna, like he could get any closer. "That mama wouldn't be happy. And her little boy is latched on to Jonathan. You're a regular daddy figure."

"Gerald." Jonathan's frown should have stopped Gerald.

"Let me warn you. . . . Nature Boy here spends his extra time scouring the trails for the Audubon Society. Don't see the relaxation in that, but to each his own."

Jonathan shrugged, an easy gesture that didn't dislodge the distance in his eyes nor the tightness around his mouth.

"Not all of us thrive on conflict."

"Touché." Gerald laughed, but hardness settled in his eyes. "Maybe I'm tiring of it. The mess with Hoffmeister is enough to wear anyone down. You know what that's like. Lots of conflict." He glanced up, and then a sharp grin twisted his face. "Lookie there. Isn't that Jaclyn, Jonathan?"

Jonathan glanced toward the door and nodded as the red-haired pixie made her way toward their table. "Sure is."

Maybe Alanna should be glad Jonathan didn't bound from his chair to welcome her. Instead, it felt like a load of rocks from the shoreline dropped in Alanna's stomach. The thought of eating anything left her nauseous.

Jonathan leaned toward her. "You okay?"

His sensitivity only made matters worse. Now tears and regret puddled with the debris from the past. "I'm sorry. I don't feel well. If you'll excuse me."

She bolted from her chair and fled before either man could say anything and before Jaclyn arrived at the table. Alanna didn't turn back, didn't glance in the window, didn't stop as she felt the past waiting to pounce.

Chapter 4

Alanna unlocked the door to the Painted Stone, her hands shaking and heart pounding. What was she thinking? The last thing she should do is spend one moment more than necessary with Jonathan Covington. When she abandoned the island, she'd left him behind, too.

What had Gerald meant when he threw out that comment about Jaclyn? It had been years. . . . Jonathan couldn't have waited. It was only normal for someone as good-looking and kind as Jonathan to find a woman to spend his life with.

He couldn't have waited. She knew that. Really.

But a father? She'd glanced, couldn't stop herself. He didn't wear a ring.

If he was a father, then she needed to stay away from him. Keep at least twenty feet between her and the first man to kiss her. The man who still made her pulse gyrate. She'd be crazy to spend one moment with him. . .especially alone at the pond. They shared too much history there. Summers roaming the woods. Stolen kisses on the dock.

"Come on." She twisted the key to the side and pushed the door open. It ricocheted off the wall, and she left the keys hanging from the lock. She hurried to the counter and shoved her purse beneath it before slipping into the tiny bathroom to check her reflection. Her eyes were wide, her cheeks flushed. She tried to pat her hair back into submission, but her hands trembled.

That settled it. She was a fool.

"Anyone here?" A woman's voice lured her back to the shop.

Alanna pasted on a smile and slipped from the bathroom. "Can I help you?"

The woman dangled keys in her hand. "You left these in the door."

Alanna's cheeks flushed hotter, and she stepped forward. "Thank you. I rushed in."

"I'd say. Looked like a woman with the past on her heels."

The woman had no idea. The past squeezed her from all sides. Alanna pulled her thoughts to the customer. "Can I help you find anything?"

"I'm all right." The woman gave the keys to Alanna then turned to the artwork. "Has this studio been here long?"

"My parents opened it twenty years ago, the summer I turned nine."

"Umm. What brought them to the island?" She cocked her head to the side as she studied one of Mother's richly detailed landscapes.

"Mom always wanted to paint but claimed no time and no inspiration. We vacationed here one weekend, and that changed."

"Any of these hers?"

"Only the best." Alanna pointed to the large four-by-five painting the woman stood in front of. "This one was painted from the side of the fort. Knowing Mom, she didn't take the road up—she would have hiked a back trail. She called it 'getting in the mood.' And a walk through the woods always worked. But that's why you see the fort and then the roofs of the buildings around here leading to the lake. Most people would paint looking up at the fort, but not Mom."

"She's very talented."

"Thank you."

"You might think I'm just saying that, but"—the woman reached into her bag and pulled out a slim business card—"I teach art at U of M. Her color use reminds me of a student of mine. It's quite distinctive."

Alanna studied the card. Janine Ross, associate professor. In her coral capris and white shirt, she didn't have the look of an artsy person. She wore no multicolored, dangling earrings or wildly swirled scarf. And with short blond hair missing any teal or purple highlights, Janine looked like a career woman enjoying a weekend escape.

"Not what you expected?"

Alanna chuckled. "I guess not."

"I've spent a lifetime breaking expectations." Janine moved to the next painting, giving it only a cursory glance before working her way along the room. "I like the bold use of color on the walls. They act as an additional mat."

"That's what Mom said, though you should have seen my father's face when she handed out the gallons of paint."

"Have you thought about printing note cards? Tourists would love them."

"True." Alanna moved to the counter to make a note. A customer didn't need to know she hadn't stood in the shop for eleven years. "I'm sure Mom's considered it. . . ."

"Tell her to call me if she needs a printer. I know one who does excellent work."

"Thank you."

Janine stopped when she came back to the first painting. "Are you certain this is your mother's work?"

"Yes." Alanna approached the painting and pointed to the squiggled signature in the lower right-hand corner. "That's her John Hancock."

"The resemblance to my student's work is uncanny. Huh." She stared a moment more then made her way to the door. "What was his name? Trevor?" she muttered as she exited onto the bustling sidewalk.

Trevor? Why would the professor mention Trevor? As far as Alanna knew, her brother hadn't taken any art classes, but really they'd drifted apart. It was possible. And with years watching Mom paint, it couldn't be unusual that he'd picked up her love and technique.

Alanna watched her progress up the street for a minute then turned back to the painting. It was ridiculous to think that the painting could be anyone but Mom's. Most artists approached Fort Mackinac from the front. The stairs were daunting enough from that perspective. Few people had the energy to work their way up the roads and then wind a path through the trees. It seemed too much work for an uncertain reward. Yet Alanna had helped Mom lug her easel, paints, and supplies through all kinds of narrow trails and switchbacks in the hunt for the perfect sunlight.

After Alanna entered high school and had to juggle its heavier course work, Trevor accompanied Mom on her painting hikes. He'd carried a sketchbook with him on those trips. Before she'd left for college, she'd snuck a few peeks at the pages. He had talent, but painting? Could he have taken classes from this professor after he followed Alanna to U of M?

Alanna studied the painting, this time breaking it into grids as she methodically examined it. Little things seemed off, but she hadn't accompanied her mom in so long, maybe she didn't know Mom's style anymore. How would Trevor make such detailed paintings without returning to the island, something Alanna was certain he hadn't done? Still, the woman's words raised a niggling doubt. It was her mom's signature, but was it her painting? It seemed an absurd thought. Why would Mom ask someone to create paintings for her to sign? Mom came alive when she held a paintbrush in her hand and studied a canvas.

The tinkle of the bell dancing against the door pulled her thoughts from the painting. A group of four women walked into the studio, their loud chatter bouncing off the floor and muting the smooth sounds of jazz. Alanna smiled at them then slid behind the counter, careful to stay out of their way as they wandered the room.

She doubted they would buy anything. And that's what she needed. Customers who had the interests and pocketbooks to make purchases. Daddy's medical bills wouldn't get paid by lookers. Especially if the art they sold wasn't by the artist claimed.

No amount of knickknacks and art by other Upper Peninsula artists could cover that kind of fraud.

Jonathan replaced the phone on the hook. Everything was lined up for Edward and Bonnie's anniversary celebration. The owners of Haan's 1830 would hold its rooms and suites for the family, and he had a couple of other B&Bs on notice that there could be overflow guests. The rest was up to Edward. If he got the word out in a timely fashion, this could become the wonderful event the man had envisioned.

It was after six, and Jonathan felt ready to escape to his

cabin. Maybe he'd spend some time fishing at the pond. There wasn't much to catch, but what was there always fried up nice for a quick meal.

And there was something about sitting in the middle of the woods by the pond that settled him at the end of a busy day. He could commune with God while he waited to see if anything bit on his bait. That led to peace in the midst of the chaos. With event planning, there was an abundance of that—almost too much.

He just had to fish and avoid Alanna and the complications she brought.

The thought tempted him to avoid the dock, but this long holiday weekend would fly by with a wedding and reception, so he'd better grab moments while he could. Jonathan locked up and hustled down the steps as he slipped his messenger bag over his neck then slid the bag to his back. At the side of the building, he unchained his mountain bike and straddled it. As soon as a gap appeared in the tourists on foot and bike, he pushed into the flow of traffic.

Where most tourists continued along Lake View Boulevard, he veered up Cadotte Avenue and then biked steadily up the hill. His legs pumped in a steady rhythm as he worked the bike around a few others. This was what made the island such an ideal place. You worked hard all day then released the day's cares and stress on the bike ride home. He couldn't think of too many other places that allowed the same release.

The yards evolved into thick woods, and still he biked. His cabin hid on a road that most visitors never discovered. So while the island's population swelled from a few hundred to several thousand during the summers, he still lived on an isolated patch of God's creation.

After fifteen minutes of steady pushing, he reached the turn to Scott's Road and then the cutoff for his cabin and the Stones' home. His house looked like it was constructed with a child's Lincoln Logs compared to the Stones' Victorian. His needed landscaping of some sort. Something to make it look like somebody who cared about the place lived there.

He snorted at the thought. Since when had things like flowers and grass mattered to him?

He parked his bike alongside the house and shook his head. Since a certain Stone had returned. He'd never bothered before because of the extra work it took to get anything onto Mackinac. It was difficult enough getting the groceries up from the dock or Doud's, but plants? He'd never bothered.

That settled it. He needed to get it out of his head that Alanna Stone was anything special. She'd left without a glance back only to return without warning. He stomped into the small living area. He bumped into the lone chair at the tiny table on his way to the refrigerator and growled. He had to evict her from his thoughts before she resumed permanent residence.

The pond beckoned, but he couldn't risk sitting on the dock. Not with his thoughts already filling with Alanna. Been down that road. Not willing to travel it again.

He fiddled with the cans in the pantry until he settled on clam chowder. That should banish any romantic notions if she deigned to wander by. Or maybe he should go by her house.

Stupid. He threw the can opener back in the drawer and dumped the soup in a bowl. While he waited for the microwave to work its magic, he stared out the window. Normally the view of the pond calmed him. Tonight all he could see was the past. Alanna and he laughing on the dock as they sat shoulder to shoulder. What had happened to that? To them?

The clop of horses' hooves and the jangle of harnesses along with the creak of wood reached him through the open window. A taxi bringing Alanna home?

The microwave dinged, and he pulled the steaming bowl out, his attention focused on the road.

"Hot dog." He whistled and placed the bowl on the table before hurrying to stick his burning fingers under the faucet's cold water. Fifteen minutes later, he placed the empty bowl into the sink when someone knocked at the door. Jonathan stared out the window a moment then brushed a hand over his hair.

Sooner or later, they'd have to say hi. It'd be awkward if they didn't.

"Get it over with," he muttered as he squared his shoulders. "She's only someone you used to know."

Really well.

Which she destroyed when she threw him away along with the island she'd learned to hate.

Chapter 5

Alanna hadn't felt this nervous since taking the bar exam. She tugged the hem of her shirt while she waited at Jonathan's door. As the silence stretched, her ire grew. If he didn't want to talk to her, fine. She wouldn't beg.

She turned from the door at the memory of Grady Cadieux's body being pulled from the frigid water. He'd looked so blue. So dead. The paramedics had labored over him, and she'd prayed he'd make it—especially when she saw Trevor's face as he struggled from the water. Brendan Tomkin's saunter looked forced, but no one else seemed to notice as everyone focused on a too-still Grady. The paramedics loaded him in the ambulance and zipped him to the clinic before boarding the ferry that transported him closer to a hospital, yet all their efforts failed, and he still died.

A stupid stunt by kids who liked to prove who was better than the other. And Trevor got pulled into their ridiculous cockfights. Then one kid died and another's life was ruined by accusations, spoken and unspoken. Somehow Brendan slipped into the background and avoided attention. She'd never understood how he managed that. Guess it helped when your dad was the principal.

To top off the memories, she'd left her keys at the Painted Stone. She fought the desire to disappear into the night and avoid Jonathan, but he had a spare key. She had no choice but to see him. . .after her embarrassing departure at lunch.

What a perfect example of the disaster her decision to return was.

Mom and Dad could have found someone else to run the studio. Then she'd be back in Grand Rapids in her well-ordered and controlled life rather than standing on Jonathan's porch.

The door opened, and she spun from the fence dividing the properties. Jonathan leaned against the door frame. Any concern that had been in his eyes at lunchtime was replaced with a studied distance.

"Alanna." He moved from the doorway and took a step toward her. "You're really back."

She nodded, the motion jerky. "For the moment."

"Your mom talk you into this?" There was something hard, almost cruel, in his voice.

"Mom said to see you if I needed help. Sorry to bother you. I'll break a window."

His shoulders slumped. "Look, I'm sorry. It's surreal seeing you. After all this time."

The words felt like an indictment. She didn't need that. Not on top of the memories that flooded her on every corner of this island. "Good night, Jonathan."

"Wait. Do you need the spare key?"

She nodded, wishing she could deny it. At this rate, he'd think she'd fallen apart. "I left mine downtown."

He ran a hand over the five o'clock shadow on his cheeks. "I've got a key in here." He disappeared into the house, but she didn't follow. A minute later, she heard what sounded like a junk drawer being dumped on a table. "Found it." Footsteps hurried toward her. "Here you go."

"Thanks." She stared at him, the weight of the past pressing against her.

His phone rang, and he glanced at the screen. "Sorry, I've

got to take this."

"Well, good night."

"Night, Lanna." Before she turned away, he'd opened the phone and said hello to Jaclyn. Her stomach lurched at the idea his girlfriend had interrupted their conversation.

She climbed the fence and like a fool hoped he'd follow anyway. Cut the conversation short and come after her. Instead, muffled conversation followed her as she hurried home. She should be grateful for the thick stand of trees that stood between them. That hid him. Then she might be able to forget the divide. One she'd allowed with her loathing of this place. Trevor didn't deserve the lies and tarring he received after Grady's death. The blame could have been placed on anyone. But the island's residents had thrust it squarely on his thin shoulders.

The muffled conversation ended, and she sighed. Why, now that it was impossible to have Jonathan, did she wonder what they could have had together?

When she entered her parents' home a minute later, she stood in the entryway taking in the living room. She'd return the key later. For now she wanted to relax. It didn't look as if her mom had redecorated any space but Alanna's room. If anything, she had added layers of paintings to the living room. Every square inch of wall was covered with landscapes in brilliant colors.

The paintings looked. . .right. The way she remembered. Her mother had a distinctive flair for putting colors together in a rich, eye-catching manner. The style was that of an Impressionist master, but the colors danced with life and vibrancy. She approached the paintings over the fireplace. They were stacked three deep on the mantel. And the closer she came, the more she knew they were her mother's work.

With that realization came an inkling. Maybe the art professor wasn't crazy to think someone else painted those at the studio. At least a few of them. She pulled a painting down and laid it on the couch. She repeated the process until artwork covered the couch and floor. Dusk filled the room, and Alanna flipped on one of the Tiffany floor lamps. The light splayed through the stained-glass shade, casting rose-colored shadows on the walls. No matter how she studied the paintings, she couldn't find the nebulous something she looked for.

There had to be some clue that indicated her mother and no one else painted them, but Alanna couldn't identify it. Then as she scanned them again, Alanna noticed the red geraniums painted into the art. A potted plant sat next to most of the front doors. Hadn't that been the flower Mom had used at her wedding reception to bring joy to each table?

Her cell rang, a Matthew West song about not wanting to waste life. She fished the phone from her pocket and opened it. "Hello."

"Hey, girl." Samantha Rice's bubbly voice brought a smile to Alanna's face. "Whatcha doing?"

"You wouldn't believe me if I told you."

"That good?"

"Better." Alanna didn't want to stir up all over again the crush of emotions she'd experienced in coming home.

"Aren't you going to tell me?"

"Let's just say I'm settling in."

"Not too well, I hope. This apartment is empty and dull without you." Sam's pout made Alanna laugh, something she hadn't done in too long.

"It's not like I've been around that much."

"Sure, the trial kept you busy, but you at least slept here most of the time." Sam made an oooing sound, like a ghost. "It's creepy here alone. You've never heard so many creaks and groans in one place."

"You could come here." Alanna clapped a hand over her mouth. Returning home must bother her more than she realized.

Sam snorted. "That would require me to have some idea of where you are. Tell me, and I'll get the time off."

She opened her mouth but couldn't do it. She needed the separation between her worlds. "Never mind."

"That's what I figured. Well, glad to know you arrived wherever it is you went. Let me know if you need anything other than forwarding your mail to your mom and feeding your cat."

"Thank you."

"That's what friends are for. Even if you're being overly secretive. I'm ready to believe you're a secret agent or something equally crazy!"

As Alanna hung up, she wondered why she couldn't just tell Sam the truth. Most people associated Mackinac Island with a relaxing getaway. Sam would probably think it was the perfect place to recover. Could it feel like a retreat? Maybe it should. The events that caused Alanna to run happened eleven years ago. Maybe it was time to stop hiding.

The next morning, Alanna awoke to light streaming through the eyelet curtains. Her room had transformed from Pepto-Bismol pink to white and pristine. She stretched then burrowed back under the covers. How long would it take her to get down to the Painted Stone? Taking the taxi yesterday was an expense she couldn't afford every day.

A cool breeze fluttered the curtains. Maybe her old bike still rested in the storage shed. If so, she'd ride it down. Otherwise she'd need to find one. The island was too big to walk everywhere.

Alanna got ready then grabbed the storage shed key from the junk drawer and walked out the back door to the storage building. It sat a few yards to the side of the house, surrounded by lilac trees. The paint peeled on the cream-colored building. She worked the key into the padlock then slid the door to the side. The early morning light penetrated the shadows in the small building. Cobwebs hung in strands from the rafters, making Alanna wonder when her parents had last used the building. Without a horse, she couldn't imagine either of them walking into town every day. The walking in wouldn't be a problem since it was primarily downhill, but returning was a doozy.

Back in a corner, she found her old bike with the large basket on the front. She pulled it out and tested the tires. She'd need to find a pump, because those flat inner tubes weren't taking her anywhere. After digging, she found a bicycle pump buried in a corner and got the tires filled. She hopped on and took it for a spin around the yard. The wide tires bounced across the lawn. She'd make it to the studio, no problem. She ran back inside, grabbed her purse, and headed down the road.

As she pedaled to town, the bite in the morning air made her wish she'd grabbed an extra jacket and gloves. By noon the sun would burn off the clouds and warm the air, but late May mornings held on to the cold, with the temperature hanging in the forties. She shivered as she chained the bike behind the Painted Stone and unlocked the door. The downtown area held the calm of a waking town. The tourists remained ensconced in their warm rooms, leaving quiet in their absence.

Alanna took advantage of the stillness to dust the paintings. The work of four or five artists dotted the walls. Everything from modern slashes of paint to her mother's Impressionist leanings.

Alanna considered rearranging the paintings to bring some order to the mismatched styles, but first she'd check the storage room. See if any paintings waited to replace any she sold. Somehow she had to get buying customers in the store while finding an employee.

The bell dinged over the door, and she exited the storage room with a smile. Her steps faltered when she saw who entered. "Mr. Hoffmeister?"

A short, balding man pivoted on his heel. His shoulders were slightly stooped from a lifetime of pushing fudge along marble tabletops. Gray curls ringed his head like a crown. The rich smell of chocolate flavored with mint clung to him. He appraised her with intelligent, chocolate-colored eyes, a cautious smile twitching the corners of his mouth. "Alanna Stone. I'd heard rumors you were back."

"The grapevine in action."

"This is a small place."

Alanna bit back a sharp retort. "Yes, sir."

"You here to help your parents?"

"For a bit."

He nodded. "Is that it?"

Alanna straightened the pens lined up on the counter, avoiding the old man's searching gaze. "Don't worry. I'll leave as soon as I can find someone else to work here."

"No one wants to run you off. I've missed seeing you around."

"Unlike. . ."

"No one ran you off then, Ms. Stone. You did that on your own."

It hadn't felt that way. "Everyone assumed we did it."

"No one ordered Grady to jump into the water."

"How do you know?"

"You young fools were down the hill from my house. Besides, Ginger filled me in."

Alanna's mind spun with the possibilities. As an eighteen-year-old, she'd never stopped to think who might have seen the party. They'd all assumed they were too sneaky to have adults notice. "You could see?"

"Of course. And with Ginger there, I kept an eye on things. How do you think the paramedics got there so fast? It would take a deaf and blind fool not to notice the bonfire."

The bell jangled as the door opened again. A couple walked in wearing the resort casual clothes indicative of guests at the Grand Hotel.

The woman, looking like a flamingo in her head-to-toe pink ensemble, approached the wall of Stone originals. "Honey, look at these colors. Can't you see this one over the fireplace?"

"Sure, darling." The man nodded with the bored air of someone who didn't know an original from a paint-by-number kit and would rather hit the links on the hotel's golf course.

If he was that indifferent, Alanna could taste the sale. She glanced at Mr. Hoffmeister and then at the couple.

He waved her off. "Stop by some night. I'll get you some of your favorite fudge, and we can catch up. Maybe Ginger can come over and you can reconnect. She needs more friends." He raised his fingers to his head in a salute. "It's good to see you."

"Thank you." She watched him leave then turned to the couple. Slight unease she couldn't shake tightened her shoulder blades. Ginger had dated Grady, been certain they would have a fairy tale come to life. Then Grady died, and she changed, altering the close friendship Alanna and Ginger had shared throughout school.

Alanna shook free of the thought. Maybe tonight she'd stop by Mr. Hoffmeister's shop. Eat fudge and hear him out.

"Ma'am, I think we'll take this one." The woman smiled broadly while her husband tugged at his back pocket.

Right now she'd sold a painting. A surge of hope pulsed through her.

Chapter 6

Jonathan hurried across the street and into the breach. Well, that's what it felt like as he rushed to reach the foundation meeting. Having a four-color, glossy presentation for each member of the foundation's board of directors wouldn't do him a lick of good if he arrived late. He wished his printer had fed the paper without jamming on every other page.

If Jaclyn hadn't called as the printer jammed on the last brochure, he still might have arrived on time. But she'd cried through another crisis, and he'd listened because he couldn't cut her off.

The squat white building with a bright red door and black shutters on each side of the windows sat next to the community building. He sidestepped a tourist and opened the door. He eased his shoulders down and hoped his face didn't reflect evidence he'd run across the business section to arrive late.

"Good morning, Laura."

The midforties brunette looked up from her computer monitor at her desk. "There you are. Mr. Tomkin's about to go into his late-is-unacceptable dance."

Jonathan sighed. "Guess it's good I arrived."

"You betcha. Go on back." Her fingers clicked against the keyboard as she spoke.

He followed the pine hallway to the conference room. The door stood open to reveal a battered oak table surrounded by eight chairs. A whiteboard on the wall had a dozen bullet points with various arrows connecting the ideas.

"Jonathan Covington." Mr. Tomkin leaned back in his chair, his arms crossed across his chest.

"I told you he'd get here." Bette Standeford, an older woman with blond highlights trying to cover her gray, leaned back in her chair. She'd been a regular on the island longer than he could remember, making it her year-round residence a couple of years earlier. A few months ago she'd sent her niece his way to plan her wedding. It was good to have her here and on his side. "We're eager to hear your ideas."

Jonathan strode into the room with his chin up and messenger bag at the ready. He might sit on the foundation's board, but the foundation had made it clear he wouldn't get the work without providing a proposal that wowed them. "Thanks for inviting me to share some ideas with you."

"Word's spreading that you've got good ideas." A man in a polo with one of the B&B logos on it studied him. "So what do you have for us?"

"Whatever it is, I hope it's good." Bryce Morris, the event manager at the Grand Hotel, studied Jonathan. "You've brought a few clients our way. I appreciate it, even if it doesn't take much effort. . . ."

Polite laughter circled the table, and Jonathan smiled. Moments like this energized him. Those on the island recognized his work. Now if he could get them to send referrals his way, it would help with his plans to expand.

Jonathan met Mr. Tomkin's appraising gaze. "Where would you like me?"

"Right there."

"All right." Jonathan opened his bag and pulled out the file filled with presentations. "I've brought preliminary ideas for a new festival." He handed out the sheets, and the next five minutes disappeared as he spun his vision for a swing event under the stars. "It's popular in other locales. Most important, it would complement the jazz festival without competing."

Gerald shook his head. "I don't see retirees going for it."

"Sure they will. It's music from their childhoods, and the younger crowd has rediscovered it. It's the perfect mix."

"Why not something like country?"

"Mackinac Island isn't exactly a big buckle, ten-gallon hat, and cowboy boots kind of place."

"Are you stereotyping, young man?" Bette grinned as she lobbed the question.

"I like being called a young man, but no. Not any more than fudgies do." She smiled at his use of the local term for tourists. "There might be a day to try an event centered on a country theme. But we'll ease our way there. Think where most people who visit come from—Chicago, Indiana, Michigan. Not exactly cowboy country."

The conversation ricocheted, disagreements surfacing only to have Gerald squash dissenting views. The more time Jonathan spent around him, the more Gerald's used-car-salesman persona grated on him. Did Jonathan really want to coordinate an event with that man reviewing his every move—because anything Jonathan did for the foundation ultimately had to please him.

"Bottom line, Mr. Covington." The formal words didn't elicit much hope. "We've got the music festival in August. If you can't give us new ideas, then we'll look elsewhere." Mr. Tomkin leaned back in his chair and crossed his arms. "We need something fresh."

"Remember, something completely new takes time. It

has to be branded and launched well. Otherwise you'll lose money on something more time could have saved."

Gerald studied him then looked at the other members. "Well?"

Almost an hour later, Jonathan escaped the small building. While the foundation members liked his ideas, Mr. Tomkin prodded to a point Jonathan didn't expect. Maybe Jonathan hadn't pushed enough. Or he'd been too honest. Still, he hadn't endured a challenge like that in a while.

He inhaled deeply, trying to shake the uncertainty that clouded his mind. Tomkin had made it clear the contract wasn't his—at least not without some major revisions to his proposal. Now Jonathan wasn't sure he wanted to try again. Not when it meant pleasing Tomkin—an impossible task. He needed to refocus. Fast. His afternoon calendar overflowed with conference calls for various clients, the kind who actually liked his ideas and paid for them.

When the Painted Stone stood in front of him, he stopped. The lights were on, but the store looked abandoned. A lingering guilt replaced the blasé feeling from the meeting. He'd been too harsh last night. Maybe their summers together hadn't meant as much to Alanna. He needed to let the past go. Good grief, she disappeared eleven years ago, and he had Jaclyn. The thought didn't bring the satisfaction it did even a week earlier. It didn't matter. Anyone else would have moved on years ago. It wasn't her fault his attempts had flopped. That he clung to the future he'd imagined for them. He needed to face facts. Real life didn't measure up to the ideal.

He needed to apologize but limit it to that. He straightened his back and walked into the store.

"I'll be with you in a minute." Alanna's alto carried across the room from the back. Didn't her mom have a studio of some sort tucked in there? It had been last season since he'd received an invitation to see Rachelle's latest work.

"There's no hurry."

At the sound of his voice, she popped around the corner. "Jonathan?"

He shrugged. "Bet you didn't expect to see me."

"Not after last night." She crossed her arms over her torso. "What can I do for you?"

"Look, I wanted to apologize for last night. I was a boor."

She nodded. "You were."

"Were you going to explain why you left without a word? Back then?"

Fire flashed in her eyes as her face paled. "Why do you care now? You could have asked then if it mattered." She glanced around the studio. "It's not like my parents left."

He studied her, pondering the right words to diffuse her anger. Maybe he shouldn't have been so abrupt last night. Now his frustration had transferred to her, and he couldn't really fault her. Maybe they could find a way to reach a truce and survive their time as neighbors.

"Look, I'm sorry for how I acted last night. I never expected to see you back on Mackinac after all this time. Guess I was unprepared." He shoved his hands deep in his pockets. "Sorry to bother you. I'll see you tonight."

Some of the stiffness evaporated from her posture. Did he make her feel like she had to protect herself from attack, or did the island do that? He turned toward the door then paused as a painting caught his eye. "You know, there's something about these new paintings of your mom's that's different."

She frowned and came to stand beside him. "What do you mean?"

The question wasn't nearly as hostile as he'd expected. How could he explain to her something indefinable? "I'm not sure."

"You'll have to be more specific. After all, don't you think an artist's style can evolve over time? She's painted for decades."

"Maybe."

"Maybe? You must have missed art appreciation in college. Just look at Van Gogh. His use of color and technique definitely changed."

Jonathan cocked his head to the side as he studied the painting. Mrs. Stone's perspective in her paintings tended to be different from other artists. Maybe because she lived on the island for months each year she saw things others missed. But still, she chose different angles. He studied the painting a moment more. It wasn't the angles that looked off. Was it the colors?

"See, you can't explain it." Alanna seemed happy, almost as if she forced the emotion. "You're hypercritical."

"Maybe, but I don't think so. You might ask her about it."

"And when would I do that? In between the doctor appointments and physical therapy? Or when she's meeting with contractors to try to figure out if they can reconfigure the house so they can return?"

She had no idea how attractive she looked when her eyes flashed like that. The cheeks that had drained of color earlier now had the flush of roses. Her lips parted as if she wanted to launch her next salvo. He placed a finger on top of them, and she froze.

"No need to take out your anger on me, Lanna." The pet name slipped from his mouth.

She sputtered a moment then stepped back. "Nobody calls me that."

"Nobody but me." He leaned closer, his breath catching. What was he doing? He cleared his throat and took a step back. He glanced at his watch. He needed to move or he'd have angry clients to deal with in addition to prickly Gerald Tomkin. "We'll continue this tonight. My place. Six o'clock."

"What? You think I want to spend time with you?"

"Yes."

"What if I have plans?" Something in her expression begged him to keep asking even as her words resisted the idea.

"Change them. We need to talk." He'd pull out the extra chair. "Six o'clock."

"I don't think I can leave here by then." She brushed her lips, as if still feeling his finger there.

He memorized the moment. Maybe they weren't through after all. The thought caught him.

"There's so much to do, and I can't afford to miss any moment that someone might come."

"Most stores close by six. Especially this early in the season." He leaned toward her, closing the space, feeling the pull to get closer to her. "Don't worry—it'll be painless. You don't have to cook, and I promise not to poison the food." He looked at the wall of paintings again. "And I have a client who might want to commission something by your mom."

The door opened, but he kept his gaze locked on Alanna. "Jonathan. Fancy seeing you here."

He closed his eyes then turned toward Jaclyn. "What

brings you here?"

"Need new artwork for the spa." Her words were light, but she studied him. "Introduce me?"

"Alanna, I'd like you to meet my. . ." What? Friend? Girlfriend? Neither word tasted right. ". . .Good friend Jaclyn Raeder. Jaclyn, this is an old friend Alanna Stone. Her family owns the Painted Stone."

"Uh-huh. Surprised I haven't seen you around." Her smile had a bite to it.

Alanna looked between the two of them, an ah-ha moment crossing her face. She covered it with a smile that didn't reach her eyes. "Nice to meet you, Ms. Raeder. I'd be happy to help you find the right art for the spa. Where is it located?"

"The Grand Hotel."

Alanna's eyes brightened, and her smile grew bigger. "Do you want to pick out some artwork now?"

"It's why I'm here."

"Nice to bump into you, Jaclyn. Tell Dylan hi for me." Jonathan turned to Alanna. "See you tonight, Alanna."

A small smile twitched Alanna's cheeks. "All right. If I can get away."

"If. . ." He backed toward the door. There'd be no "if" about it. If she didn't come home, he'd bring the food to her. A woman had to eat, and he could easily grab some sandwiches and salads at Doud's. She couldn't hide forever.

"Until tonight." He caught Jaclyn's eye and grimaced. He'd have a lot of explaining to do. Something that had to wait until he had a better idea what might develop between him and Alanna. One moment it felt like no time had passed between them, and other times he felt every year of the eleven.

Chapter 7

Traffic on the street never slowed through the afternoon. A steady flow kept her in the studio in case customers wanted to explore the collection. As a result, hunger gnawed in Alanna's stomach, but she didn't think she could leave. Not yet.

And it had nothing to do with Jonathan's invitation. She'd decided not to hide. Not from him.

Okay, maybe she'd look for every excuse she could find to stay away. Once Jonathan left, Jaclyn had straightened her petite frame and turned the full force of her charm on Alanna, but it had felt staged. The woman's auburn curls had bounced each time she tossed her head, and her smile had the edges of a cobra. Like the woman intended to learn everything she could about Alanna without giving much information about herself. Well, other than the fact she and Jonathan were more than friends.

The hour Jaclyn had stayed had passed with lots of awkward moments, times when Alanna looked up to catch Jaclyn studying her. Intently. Alanna had wanted to assure her she had nothing to worry about. But couldn't.

Jaclyn had taken her cute self from the studio without a painting. She'd promised to come back with a purchase order, but Alanna didn't plan on seeing her again. She should have told the twentysomething that she hadn't seen Jonathan in eleven years. That whatever they might have had disappeared a long time ago. But she hadn't. So the thick fog of discomfort remained.

Enough. She shook free of her unease and pulled up Google on the old computer and waited for the server to chug through cyberspace. Then she pulled up the *Grand Rapids Press*. There had to be a better way to find an employee, but at the moment she couldn't think of one, especially since she didn't want to hire a local. The last thing she needed was to answer the questions, *Where have you been? Why did you leave?*

A woman walked by arm in arm with an older man but pulled him to the window. She pressed her nose to the glass as she looked in. Alanna considered waving, but would that invite or intimidate her?

Instead, she clicked to the classified ad section of the paper and scanned a few for inspiration. She tried to frame an ad in her head. *Studio on beautiful Mackinac Island seeks summer help. E-mail your résumé to:*

To where? She entered the studio's general e-mail address then looked up as the bells danced.

So the woman had talked her escort into entering.

Alanna did a double take as the woman gracefully swayed across the floor. Her escort looked familiar. So familiar, Alanna fought the urge to dive into the back room and stay there until the couple left. After all, they wouldn't buy anything. Too bad her mama didn't raise a coward. Alanna raised her chin and squared her shoulders.

It wasn't every day the opposing counsel on the case that had splattered her image across every newspaper in the state for more than a month walked into her parents' studio.

He leaned against the door, his posture indicating he'd rather be anywhere but here. His gaze traveled the room, sliding over her before coming back. He pushed from the wall, a wolfish grin on his face. "Alanna Stone?"

"Hello, Bennett." She tried to hold a pleasant smile but couldn't.

"So this is where you ran. The legal grapevine's gone crazy wondering where the conquering heroine disappeared. Glad to see it's not a nervous breakdown."

Sure he was. "Nothing like relaxing here. Can't get much slower paced."

"Too much so if you ask me, but Tabitha likes it." He shrugged. "After the trial, I owed her."

"You sure did, baby."

Bennett smiled at Tabitha then turned to study Alanna. "Why are you here?"

"Having that nervous breakdown." She winked, even though it killed her to be nice to the man. He'd made her life miserable for the duration of the pretrial and trial. Anytime he could make an argument, he did. The annoying part came in the way the judge allowed him to do it. She'd fought so hard for her clients.

"Really? After that win—which I'm appealing."

Alanna stifled the groan that rose at the thought of more battles with him.

"Ready, Tabitha?"

"Not yet. I think I want this one." The blond, who looked a bit like a poodle with her bouncy, curly hair, pointed at one of her mom's largest paintings. "This would look amazing behind the dining room table, don't you think?"

Bennett rolled his eyes. "If that's what you want. . ."

"You promised I could have anything. This is it." She pointed a perfectly manicured finger at the explosion of color. "The fall shades are perfect."

"Fine." He turned to Alanna. "So how much is that beauty?"

Alanna forced back a grin. This could be the perfect payback for all the trouble he inflicted. "Let me look it up for you." She clicked a few keys on the keyboard to pull up the database. "Could you tell me the name?"

"Watercolor Sunsets."

"Really?" Interesting title since Mom only used oils.

Tabitha leaned closer to the small block of card stock next to the painting. "Yes."

"All right." Alanna clicked on FIND then entered the name. When the information popped up, she added five hundred dollars to the amount. "Five thousand five hundred dollars."

Bennett flinched. "For that piece of canvas and a bit of paint? I could make that in my sleep."

"You're welcome to try, but this artist's work sells quickly. I wouldn't wait too long, or it might disappear."

He led Tabitha into the corner and chatted for a moment, but by the set of the woman's jaw, Alanna knew the painting would leave with them. Five minutes later, she wrapped the painting like a mummy in bubble wrap before sliding it into an oversized box. "Be careful carrying this. The paintings are always heavier than you expect."

"My wallet's certainly lighter. We'll send a courier. Come on, Tabitha."

The woman sidled up next to him and practically purred. Alanna released the joy that had built inside. A sale—and to a man like that. She couldn't believe it.

"Thank You, Lord!" She breathed the words as she disappeared into the storage room to find a replacement. A few minutes later, she returned lugging a new painting. Jonathan scanned a wall of paintings. A picnic basket sat at his feet.

"Sorry, I didn't hear you come in."

"No problem. I brought the picnic to you." The smell of something sweet yet spicy wafted from the basket.

"It smells great." Alanna drew in a breath and smiled. She wouldn't hide her hunger, but the way she suddenly longed for time with Jonathan surprised her. She couldn't be swayed simply by a great-smelling picnic. "I can't tell you how glad I am I stayed. I just sold my first large painting. Since I was a teen anyway."

"Congratulations. Need help hanging that one?"

"Sure." In an effortless movement, Jonathan hefted it onto the hanger. "Thanks."

Jonathan brushed his hands on his jeans then glanced at the floor. "Do you have anything we can sit on? I forgot to grab a blanket."

Really? He didn't plan to mention Jaclyn? Fine, she'd play along for the moment. "I don't know. Let me check the studio."

The first time Alanna had walked back there, the lack of mess surprised her. It used to overflow with half-painted canvases and piles of sketches and tubes of half-used paint. Now it felt almost sterile with only splatters of paint dotting the cement floor and empty easels. Her mother must have done a deep clean before leaving Mackinac. But Mom never dealt with stress and uncertainty that way before. Instead, the house and back areas of the studio would get more chaotic as her stress increased.

Jonathan would follow her back here in a minute if she didn't find something and get out front. She opened the closet door and pulled out a folded canvas tarp. Bright paint splotches dotted it, making it a colorful swirl. Her low heels clicked against the floor as she hurried back to the front room. She slowed and watched Jonathan stroll the edge of the room. He seemed to carry a burden as he trailed from painting to painting. When she stopped, he turned toward her.

"Will this work?"

"As long as you promise me the paint's dry." He rubbed his thumbs down his jeans.

"I promise I haven't used it."

"Good enough for me." He walked over and took the bundle from her. A shiver slipped up her arms where his hands glanced against her. He stilled and looked deeply into her eyes. Could he read her thoughts? She hoped not as they ricocheted like colliding atoms without any order. He cleared his throat and stepped back. He flicked his wrists, and the tarp ballooned before parachuting to the floor. "How's this?"

"Good." The only good thing about having a picnic in the studio was anybody passing by could see. Alanna could only imagine the electricity that would leap between them if they were secluded in his little cabin. She'd spent years convincing herself there was nothing special between them. Now in minutes he'd eradicated that idea.

Jonathan crouched next to the basket and opened the lid. In a minute, he'd pulled out a tub of fried chicken and the fixings. Her stomach growled as the wonderful aromas filled the space. Then he pulled out a bottle of sparkling cider and a pair of champagne flutes. Her heart thudded as he set them on the tarp.

Rebound. That's all this was. If Spencer hadn't told her a couple of weeks ago he didn't plan to buy a ring, she wouldn't feel so vulnerable. So needy for love. She must stiffen her defenses. Fortify her resolve. Remember Jaclyn's slate eyes as she watched Jonathan.

"Is this okay?" Questions carved lines into the corners of his eyes.

"It's been awhile since I've had fried chicken."

"You used to love it."

"Still do," she assured him as she wondered if they'd keep things so surface.

"You got so quiet, I wondered."

"Just thinking."

"As long as it was good thoughts."

She nodded then sank to the edge of the cloth. "How long have you been on the island?"

"Since Gram and Pops decided the winters were too much for them. I usually abandon this area for the worst months of winter. But I love it here. Always have."

A shiver tickled her spine at the thought of the long, harsh winters. "Nothing like riding snowmobiles to get to school."

"Never did that, but you always said you liked it."

"When I was young and didn't know better." Winters in Grand Rapids might have tempered her. Now she couldn't imagine spending the winter in a place with as much snow as Mackinac Island endured.

Jonathan reached into the basket and pulled out a plastic plate and set of silverware. After a quick prayer, he handed them to her. "Dig in."

Silence settled over them as they filled their plates and ate. Alanna wondered if she should force conversation but didn't feel up to the challenge. Then Jonathan started asking questions. He probed what college had been like, shared some of his crazy college stories, then asked about the churches she'd attended. It seemed his faith had grown as hers had while they were apart.

"So what has God taught you lately?" Jonathan pushed his plate to the side and focused on her as he waited for her answer.

She shifted and picked at a piece of lint on her slacks. "That's a good question. One I'll need to think about. I know He's working but not sure I can articulate how on the spot."

Jonathan nodded. "Fair enough. It's a question one of my roommates in college still likes to ask. Always makes me think hard." A comfortable silence settled over them.

Could Jonathan become a trusted friend again, or should she keep him at arm's length? If only her parents' home didn't sit next door to his. The island was too small to avoid him anyway.

He wiped his fingers with a napkin and set it on top of his empty plate then leaned back on his hands and studied her. She swiped a strand of hair out of her face and behind her ear, fighting the urge to blush under his scrutiny. "What?"

"Would you have returned if your dad hadn't gotten sick?"

Alanna looked at a point beyond his shoulder, unable to meet his intensity. "Probably not. I got pretty good at avoiding it. Everything I loved died with that stupid party."

"You always talked about coming back after college. You wanted to be part of the future here."

Not anymore. Not after they betrayed her brother. Her posture tightened as she felt the familiar anger return. Someday she needed to move on, but being here on the island brought it all back to stark reality. She clutched it to her like a protective shield.

"Do you see Trevor often?" Jonathan's quiet question

jerked her from her thoughts.

"He's my brother."

Jonathan shrugged. "Sure, but I know lots of siblings who never see each other."

"That's not us. Or it shouldn't be. I always imagined that at some point he'd quit being my twerpy brother and become one of my best friends. Then we both left, and it felt like any time we spent together threw us both back to Grady's death. It was less painful to just not see each other." The relaxing, romantic evening spiraled downward with the trend of her thoughts. Romantic? She had no right to think in those terms—not with Jonathan.

"Have him come here."

"Back to Mackinac?" Alanna snorted, not caring what kind of impression that made. "He wants to be here even less than me."

"That night was more than a decade ago. How long will it control you?"

"Control me?" Her voice rose. "You don't know what you're talking about, Jonathan. Believe it or not, everyone brushed me with the same brush they applied to Trevor." Tears clogged the back of her throat, and she launched to her feet. "Thank you for bringing dinner, but I need to lock up and get home." If only that meant her apartment in Grand Rapids. Especially since the reporters probably had abandoned their nightly stakeouts.

Even if they haunted her doorway, anything would be better than staying one more moment on this island with the shadows of the past.

Chapter 8

Jonathan had known the past distorted Alanna's vision, but he hadn't expected her to order him out. The ease of their earlier conversation had surprised him. Now he'd collided with her erected barriers.

She stopped long enough to shove plates and containers filled with remnants of their meal back in the basket. Moisture filled her eyes and threatened to overflow. The oh-so-tough Alanna Stone looked ready to break.

It couldn't be simply what happened to Trevor. There had to be something more adding to the stress. Jaclyn? He wished he could have stuck around for their conversation. He'd explore that later, because now it was abundantly clear she wanted him out. Gone. Disappearing.

He touched her hand, felt it tremble under his. "I'll get this. You do whatever else you need to." As soon as she nodded, he stifled a yawn. He couldn't afford fatigue, not when he had several hours of work waiting when he got home.

In less time than he expected, he followed Alanna out the door and waited as she locked it. "I'll bike home with you."

"I have a stop." Her words were tight, almost strangled.

The island might be safe, but there was no way he was going to leave her to make her way on the roads by herself. It would be dark soon, and in the wooded areas it would already feel like night had fallen. Besides, the tourists had arrived, and with them came the typical round of drunk and disorderlies. In her frame of mind, she might forget how the island could be at night.

"I don't mind waiting." He'd make supercharged coffee in the morning.

She glanced at him a moment then threw her purse strap across her shoulder. "Whatever you like. You always did what you wanted anyway."

The way she said the words had a bite that made him almost change his mind. Yet his mother had drilled into him the need to be a gentleman when it came to ladies. Always. Regardless of how they treat you. He'd extend grace for now. He pulled back at that thought. Grace shouldn't be extended in dribs and drabs.

"Really, Jonathan. Go home. I'm fine." As if to punctuate the comment, Alanna threw a leg over the bike and pedaled into traffic.

The *clop-clop* of dray horses' hooves against the asphalt didn't distract him. He shoved the handles of the picnic basket over the handlebars and pumped to follow Alanna. If she didn't want him, fine. He'd stay behind, still her silent guardian.

Raucous music filtered out the open doors of the Man O' War. A young man stumbled out and right into Alanna's path. She swerved the bike, narrowly missing a woman on foot in her efforts to avoid the drunk. She pulled to the side in front of I'm Not Sharing Fudge Shop.

Jonathan eased to a stop next to her. "Want some dessert?"

Her hair flipped across her face as she turned toward him. "Go away, Jonathan."

"Not happening. Last time you disappeared for eleven years."

"I need to ask Mr. Hoffmeister a question."

"That old guy? He's nice enough. . . ." But why ditch him for Mr. H.?

"Really, Jonathan, go ahead. You've got better things to do than watch my bike. Where's it going?"

Her insistence made him want to demand he tag along. She was up to something, and he wanted to know what. Guess he was ultra-nosy at the moment.

"Come on, Lanna. I'll keep my mouth shut."

"No." She pushed at his handlebars, and he wobbled as the basket slid to the side. "I'll see you *later*."

How much rejection should he endure before he acquiesced? "If you're sure. . ."

"I can find my way home. Good night, Jonathan."

"All right then." No matter what his mom had told him, you couldn't be a gentleman if the woman refused.

Alanna watched Jonathan pedal down the street. He looked over his shoulder once, and she waved. She didn't need him acting like a burr attached to her side. She turned to I'm Not Sharing Fudge Shop. Maybe Mr. Hoffmeister still worked evenings. He'd always insisted that was his favorite time to man the shop since he could observe everyone pass by.

Maybe he knew something about what happened to Grady. How could she have forgotten his cottage faced the area they'd chosen for the bonfire and festivities? Between that and whatever Ginger knew, she needed to talk to him.

An electronic ding announced her arrival. The old man hunched over a paperback as he sat on a stool behind the cash register. He marked his page and then glanced up. A grin split his face, revealing stained teeth. "Alanna! I wondered when you'd stop by. Need some fudge?"

"Yes, sir. I haven't missed much but your fudge. Someday you'll have to share your special ingredient."

"No can do. If I did, nobody would need me anymore. Can't have that." He grabbed a piece of wax paper and a knife. "Now what would you like to sample?" He pointed at a couple of blocks. "How about the mint chocolate? Or the peanut butter? But if I know you after all these years, I'm thinking the peppermint tickles your taste buds."

"Sounds great." As soon as he handed her a thin slice, she broke off a corner and slipped it in her mouth. The sweetness melted against her tongue, and she moaned. "This is so good. I'd better take a pound and be grateful I bike and walk everywhere."

"I knew you'd like it." He sliced off a bigger chunk and wrapped it in a one-pound box. "What else can I do for you?"

He sidled back to the cash register and rang up her order while she considered how to proceed.

"I wanted to ask what you remember."

"About that day?"

"Yes, sir."

He slipped her money into the cash drawer then sank to the stool. "That was a long time ago, kid. You have to let go."

"You must have talked to Jonathan."

"Jonathan?"

"Covington. He told me the same thing."

"Haven't talked to him, but we're of the same mind. What good comes of stirring up that hornet's nest?"

Alanna clutched the box as if gripping a lifeline. "Because

I want the world to know Trevor wasn't involved."

"Everybody there was."

That stung. She'd been there. To this day she wondered if there was something she could have—should have—done to avert the tragedy.

"Look, you can carry this burden the rest of your life, let it color every day and everything you do. Or you can release it and trust those around here to move on with grace. You might try it yourself." He glanced at his watch and stood. "Time for me to close up."

"What's this about you and Mr. Tomkin?"

He frowned. "Nothing for you to worry about. He just wants to build a monstrosity next to my house. Seems shocked I think he should follow all the building rules."

"Being neighbors can be hard on a friendship."

"It certainly can." He glanced at his watch. "Suppose I should start working on closing duties."

Alanna nodded. She'd be back, but he'd made it clear he didn't want to talk—not now. His words about grace echoed in her mind as she left.

Grace wasn't a new concept, not after all the sermons she'd heard on the topic. But applying it to this situation? That seemed impossible. Not when she had an island's worth of people to forgive. Forgetting and moving on came easier, until her parents needed her to return.

The door clanged shut behind her, and she turned to watch him hit a light switch. She couldn't imagine how many times he'd closed the shop in his lifetime. Through all kinds of events on the island, he stayed. Thought she should have done the same.

It wasn't that easy. Never had been.

Her streak of justice ran too deep to ignore, especially when it involved family. Someday she wanted a family of her own, but not if what happened to Trevor could repeat. She needed to right this. Then she could pursue a family. Maybe she was stubborn, but now that she had returned, she needed to find the truth. See if there was any way to clear her brother.

She straddled her bike and looked up then startled. Talk about stubborn. There stood Jonathan Covington leaning against the wall of Doud's. "What are you doing? I saw you leave."

"Making sure you make it home." A thread of challenge rang through his words. Just like when they were teens and he insisted she let him do something—usually something completely unnecessary.

"Go home, Jonathan."

"That's exactly what I plan to do." He lifted the Coke bottle he held. "Needed something to drink."

She tucked her slab of fudge in the bike basket. "Sure you did. Come on, since I can't shake you."

He chuckled. "That's right. I'm going to watch out for you."

Her back stiffened, and she pushed down on the pedals. "I'm not a young teenager anymore. I am fully capable of taking care of myself. Especially in such a small, *safe* place."

"I'll sleep better knowing I didn't leave you to find your way in the dark."

"I think the Coke'll keep you up." No point mentioning the hundreds of times she'd biked these same roads and trails. She might have left eleven years ago, but that didn't erase a childhood spent exploring every inch of this island.

Silence fell as they biked through neighborhoods and into the woods. Alanna felt her lungs burn as she fought to keep up with Jonathan. He didn't break a sweat as she gulped oxygen. She pumped harder, refusing to let him stay ahead. Not after all the times they'd raced up and down the roads. Then he rarely bested her. She couldn't let him start now, no matter how much her body screamed in protest.

The trees acquired shadows as the sun sank beneath them. The shadows changed the way everything looked. She hadn't noticed the new houses and lanes on her couple of trips to the studio. Without Jonathan, she might have gotten turned around, but she wouldn't give him that gem to use against her the next time he insisted she allow him along.

He stopped at her driveway, and she skidded to a halt next to him. "You all right from here?"

"What? Your mama didn't tell you to walk the girl to her door? Isn't this the equivalent of honking the horn?"

"I didn't think you wanted me any closer." He reached out and caressed her cheek.

"I. . .don't."

He leaned toward her, closing the space between them. "Say it like you mean it."

"I don't need you."

"Don't believe you. I know you better." A strange expression flashed across his face at the words.

"You know the girl I was."

"I see the woman hiding in the shadows."

Her heart stilled as he stared into her eyes. Then his gaze traveled to her lips, his eyes hidden by the shadows. She clutched the handlebars but couldn't move. Years of history zinged between them. She had to break away. He had a girl, possibly a child, though she struggled to reconcile the Jonathan she'd known with a child out-of-wedlock. She couldn't interfere in that. She didn't want a reason to stay on the island one day more than necessary.

She slid her bike back and forced a smile. "Good night, Jonathan."

As she biked up the lane, it took all her willpower not to look back and see if he still watched her. She didn't need this attraction between them. Not now.

She parked her bike and then slipped inside the front door. She couldn't trust herself with any man, let alone Jonathan. Not after how easily she'd handed her heart to Spencer. The way he'd callously thrown it back proved she didn't know men and couldn't make a good decision. Not when in a couple of short days she was ready to jump back into Jonathan's arms after an eleven-year absence.

Only a fool relinquished her heart that quickly.

Chapter 9

Jonathan settled at his kitchen table, laptop open and loading spreadsheets while he scanned his calendar. The picnic basket sat unpacked at his feet. Alanna might fight him, but tonight had illustrated how much remained between them. Now to decide if he could retreat to friendship.

His phone rang. He looked at the display and grimaced. Jaclyn. How could he so easily think about Alanna when Jaclyn had remained constant? Would Jaclyn fight to keep up with him as he pumped his bike up the roads? She worked at the Grand Hotel for a reason. She liked things a certain way. A way he couldn't afford.

He flicked the phone. "Hey, Jaclyn."

"What're you doing?" Her sweet voice had a sultry edge to it, one that usually made him clear his calendar.

"Work."

"Now?"

"It never goes away."

She sighed. "Don't I know. When can we get together?"

No mention of this morning? Jonathan cleared his throat. He didn't want to clutter his calendar. Not right now. "Let me check some things tomorrow." Coward. That's what he was.

"Fine. Good night." Jaclyn hung up before he could say anything. He'd smooth things over tomorrow.

Tonight he had to get some work done or he'd have unhappy clients. And while he might look like his professional life was well established, he had bigger plans for his tiny firm.

He loved how God always provided, but he'd like to implement some of his ideas for growing. Before he could hire an employee or two, he had to buckle down and find the time to make his current clients' visions reality while finding new clients.

He nursed the half-empty Coke and berated himself. He really hadn't had time for Alanna. Not when she acted as elusive as the Kirtland's warbler.

From the first moment he saw her the summer before his freshman year, he'd known she was special. The girls at his high school on the mainland didn't interest him after a summer exploring Mackinac Island with Alanna. Each summer he returned, and the bond grew. He'd thought she felt the same, but then she'd left. He could have pursued her, but why chase someone who never called or wrote?

Now she'd returned.

And he had Jaclyn. The thought made his shoulders tighten. Until yesterday, he liked the idea of more days with Jaclyn. Now he felt a churning, uprooted sensation.

Maybe it indicated he had a chance to see if he'd imagined everything and expanded on it during the intervening years. Or a chance to shatter a good woman's heart while another woman broke his. Jaclyn was a kind woman, one he should be happy to spend his life with. But now that Alanna had arrived. . . He'd never imagined one day around Alanna after all this time would reignite what they'd had. He couldn't begin to imagine how to explain to Jaclyn. What if she'd walked by the studio, glanced in, and seen the picnic? How could he explain that what looked intimate wasn't? The worst part came from the realization he didn't want to explain it away.

One fact remained uncontradicted: Jaclyn didn't match the standard Alanna set. With her love of life and drive, Alanna had set the bar too high for anyone else to hurdle. And that wasn't because absence made the memories sweeter.

The computer dinged. Guess he had e-mail.

Time to get back to work and get those revised ideas ready for Tomkin.

The next morning, Jonathan took a few minutes on his back patio to listen for the Kirtland's warbler while he inhaled his coffee. No brew existed rich enough and caffeinated enough to get him through the day. He might as well set up an IV drip and drag it behind him.

The morning was pretty quiet. He couldn't hear the warbler, let alone scan for it with the binoculars that rested at his side. Maybe this weekend he could claim the time to stalk the little, impossible-to-find bird.

If he did that, he wouldn't have time between events to sit at home wondering what Alanna was doing next door. Though if she hadn't found an assistant by then, she'd be down at the studio. Her family couldn't afford missed income on what was usually the busiest day of the week.

Add in Memorial Day, and the weekend should hop with tourists taking advantage of package deals at the Grand Hotel and bed-and-breakfasts. Then he had a wedding to coordinate on Monday. Any peace he'd pulled around him evaporated at the thought. For someone who loved event planning, weddings weren't his thing. They paid the bills, but a part of him felt like he stole from the couples when he encouraged their vision of happily ever after.

Having Alanna back on Mackinac didn't change his position. Especially as they struggled to find footing as friends.

His mama had raised him to treasure one woman. The problem came when that woman walked away without a backward glance. Then she returned bearing scars. Oh yeah, he was ready to go plan the final details on someone's forever commitment. Could he pretend? *Help me, Lord.*

This wedding he hadn't prayed about first. Mistake number one.

Then the bride changed her mind every other minute, and he didn't say anything. Mistake number two.

Not answering her call last night? Mistake number three.

He'd have to talk her off the ledge today. An emotional bridezilla.

The sound of the door opening next door filtered across the space, jarring him from his downward-spiraling thoughts. Time to act rather than think. And if he happened to catch Alanna on the trail, all the better.

Five minutes later, water dripped down his neck as he pulled on khakis, a polo, and a fleece pullover. He shoved a couple of protein bars in a pocket and hopped on his bike. He didn't see Alanna or her bike as he headed out. The fact he checked made him chuckle. For a guy who didn't believe in true love, he sure wasted effort keeping tabs on Alanna. He could still catch her. He couldn't imagine her riding hard enough to glisten before she got to work. Coming home was different than getting there.

He steadied his breath, pumping just to the point of raising his heart rate but letting gravity pull him toward Lake

Huron. He hadn't gone far when he saw a hot-pink shadow on an old bike. Hot pink? Still her color after all these years, though he supposed she called it something fancy like fuchsia now.

He pedaled harder to help gravity's pull until he reached Alanna's side. A headband pulled her hair back from her face. The wind had pulled a few strands loose, and they framed her face in a way that left his fingers itching to tuck them behind her ears.

She didn't even glance at him. "Don't you have better things to do?"

"Going your way, ma'am." She must have caught his mocking tone, because she turned to him and made a face. "I'll slide around you then."

"You betcha." The way she said it with her mouth tipping up in the corner made him laugh.

"You haven't been gone that long."

"Feels years longer." Then she glanced at him with that same ole mischievous glint.

"Uh-oh."

"You have no idea."

Next thing Jonathan knew, he trailed a hot-pink streak flying down the road. No way would he let her win. Not when he'd invited himself, creating the race.

He pumped up-down, up-down. Alanna seemed to have a sixth sense—or maybe she had developed a mother's second set of eyes—because she knew exactly what he planned and slid into his way each time. He grunted as he braked hard, wheels locking to avoid her latest attempt to cut him off.

"You aren't playing fair." He gritted his teeth and tried again.

"Just trying to win." Her voice wasn't flirtatious or wry, just intense. They reached the point where Scott's Road intersected with Leslie Road and turned right, but then she surprised him by turning right on British Landing Road, extending the time before they reached the busier roads. Maybe she had eleven years of frustration to take out in one bike race.

But as the trees raced past them on British Landing Road, he wondered if she'd remembered where they'd intersect Lake Shore Drive.

Alanna's lungs strained to provide the oxygen her muscles demanded. Who's crazy idea was it to make an easy ride to work a race across the island?

At this rate she'd need a shower when she reached the studio, despite the May chill in the air. Guess it was a good thing the upstairs apartment stood empty. Who'd have thought forty-five degrees would fail her along with her Secret? Didn't matter. She was not giving up. If she had any control on the race, she'd win. Plain and simple.

But no matter how many times she swerved or swayed, Jonathan wouldn't back off. It made her think of the way he kept coming around. She'd only been on the island a few days, but already she'd gotten his message: he didn't plan to go anywhere.

She bore down and swerved around a fallen limb. The bike didn't have big enough tires to go over things like that. Not without bumping her off the seat and possibly giving her a flat. More broken branches had her steering in a crazy-eight pattern until she feared losing control. That wouldn't leave the image she wanted in Jonathan's mind. She flipped down a gear and hoped it helped. Next thing she knew, her back tire jolted, and she swayed to keep her balance.

An *oomph* from Jonathan made her want to look over her shoulder, but he bumped into her tire again.

"What are you doing?" Her voice rose, out of her control as adrenaline spiked her system.

"Trying to stay alive," he huffed. "What's with the pell-mell dive down the hills?"

"Just trying to get to work."

"In one piece?"

She snorted. "What other way is there?"

"Slow down, crazy woman." There was something in his voice that made her want to stop, ask for details. But she couldn't. She wouldn't.

"And let you slip past me? I don't think so." She leaned forward, pumping harder still.

"Watch out!"

The command in Jonathan's voice pulled her gaze up in time to see a branch loom in front of her face. It smacked her cheek, knocking her to the side. She fought for balance but couldn't find it as her bike rocked side to side. She inhaled, trying to tighten her core as her Pilates instructor harped.

Next thing she knew, she lay on the ground, her bike wheels spinning over her head. She made a mental note to tell her instructor that advice didn't work on bikes. Stinging erupted across her shins and palms where she'd collided with the ground.

Jonathan skidded to a stop and slid off the bike next to

her. "Are you okay?"

Alanna touched her cheek, feeling a lump and knowing the pain would kick in soon. "Does it look as bad as it feels?"

"Better." The concern in his eyes belied his words.

"I'm not sure I believe you."

"Do you think you can get up and bike home?"

"Nothing doing. I've got to work." She touched her cheek again. "I'll stop for ice."

"Let's get you up." He reached down and offered her a hand.

She accepted his help and moaned as he tugged her up.

He stopped instantly. "Did I pull too hard?"

"Nope." She grinned at him. "Just wanted to make you worry." He looked like he wanted to drop her hand. "Just kidding."

"No you aren't, imp." He searched her gaze. "I don't want anything to hurt you."

She stilled, lost in the intensity of his look. If someone asked her for directions, she knew she wouldn't know the first place to direct them on the small island that had been her home for nine years. And at the moment, she didn't care. Being lost in his green eyes seemed like the best thing she'd done in a long time. She inhaled a shallow breath. Would he kiss her? What would it be like after all this time?

He looked down, breaking their connection. He pulled his left wrist in front and showed her his watch face. "We'd better get moving. We can get you ice and still open in time."

She blinked. Had he caught her staring at his lips? She dragged her gaze to his eyes then over his shoulder to the pine trees towering over the trail. She needed to get away from this. . .thing. . .growing between them. She did not come here to resurrect ancient history.

She wouldn't sign up for that. Not willingly.

"You're right." She pushed her bike upright. "Can't have anyone thinking I'm not working today. The last thing Mom needs is a call from some helpful soul keeping tabs on me."

Alanna wobbled onto the bike. Taking a moment to let her equilibrium stabilize, she started pedaling without waiting for Jonathan. He'd catch up. The bottom of the road loomed. As it did, her heart hiccupped.

How could she have forgotten what lay at the end of this road?

Chapter 10

She skidded to a stop at the side of the road. Her breath hitched, and she couldn't get her lungs to expand. She couldn't breathe, and the realization terrified her.

She had to leave this place. But her legs wouldn't cooperate. She stood paralyzed, straddling the bike with the view of waves crashing against rocks along a rugged beach confronting her.

A woman slowed down, concern on her face. Not Ginger Hoffmeister. Not now. Yet there was no doubt the short, slightly rounded figure belonged to her high school friend.

In an instant, she transported back to that day in May.

The sun burned hot on her face as she joined the other high school students. Seniors for one more week. The words tasted as sweet as cherry preserves on her tongue.

In a couple of months, she'd head to University of Michigan, but before that a glorious summer of freedom stretched in front of her. She could spend every evening at the dock with Jonathan Covington. By Memorial Day weekend, he'd be back at his grandparents' for the first of many stays over the summer. She couldn't wait to see him.

But tonight her classmates celebrated. It had never felt so good to dance in the sunlight.

"Alanna?" Jonathan touched her shoulder. "Are you ready for this?"

"Ready?" She choked on the word. Who could be ready to revisit the place that changed their lives?

"Alanna Stone?" Ginger approached, her auburn hair

inches shorter than the long ponytail she'd worn in high school. Her nose still perked up at the end, but her emerald-colored eyes held concern. "You're back?"

Alanna sucked in air, trying to force it into her lungs. Black pricked the edges of her vision. She needed oxygen. Now.

"Lean over." Jonathan pressed against her back until her forehead practically kissed the handlebars. "That better?"

Alanna wanted to scream, "No!" Not while Ginger Hoffmeister stared as she panicked.

"What happened?" Ginger's soft voice conveyed concern, concern she couldn't possibly feel or she would have contacted Alanna after her freshman year of college. Three years on the same campus, and Ginger had ended their friendship with her distance.

"Nothing." She pressed the word past the knot tightening in her throat. Pushing back, she dislodged Jonathan's hand and straightened.

"You're sure you're okay?" Ginger studied her. "I heard you were back. Sorry I haven't stopped by the studio."

"I didn't expect you." Bitterness laced her words even as she gritted her teeth together.

Ginger seemed to absorb Alanna's indifference and shrank back. "It's good to see you." Ginger pushed off, leaving them behind.

Jonathan studied Alanna. "What was that all about? I thought you were friends."

"We were." This was too much. The scene of Grady's accident and now Ginger. They'd been inseparable growing up. She missed the history they'd shared.

"Ready to get going? We can be at the Grand Hotel in

minutes and by the library before you even notice you've started riding again."

He was right. Before the morass of pain and images sucked her under, she jerked from his touch and pushed the pedals. She hadn't noticed the bicyclers out for a ride in the early morning air, but she'd created a scene. One rider glanced away after making eye contact.

"I have to get away from here." She stepped forward, thrusting the bike into traffic between two cyclists and hurrying into the fray.

This wasn't a day to watch the last rays of the sun rising. No, today was a day to bury her head at the Painted Stone and pray for a quick escape. Nothing good happened to her here.

She never looked back on the ride around the perimeter of the island, yet she sensed Jonathan behind her. She didn't need him shadowing her every move. Discovering every secret she kept hidden. No, she needed to push him away. Keep a safe distance. And get off this island as fast as she could. Tomorrow if possible. The weekend, definitely.

Jonathan slowed down. He should head home and take a shower before slipping into the office. Good thing his first meeting wasn't until ten. He watched Alanna power around a couple out for an early morning ride.

Why did she run from the past? From him? The real Alanna was far different from the one he'd carried in his memories. Her return highlighted that. Much as he didn't like it, maybe he needed to see. How else would he move on?

Thirty loomed around the corner. He didn't want to live alone the rest of his life. He'd always imagined a passel of kids wrestling with him every night after work. Waiting for a mirage wouldn't make that dream a reality. He loved every moment with Jaclyn's little boy, Dylan, but he wanted kids of his own, too.

Until she confronted whatever demons chased her, Alanna wouldn't return to the strong, feisty woman he remembered. She had feisty in spades, but strength eluded her. Instead, she seemed worn down. Weary. Yet drawn to the past like a moth to the bug zapper on his porch.

His legs burned as he pumped home. A quick shower later and he again had dripping hair as he stood in his kitchen. His stomach growled. A protein bar wasn't going to fill him after that ride, but he didn't have time to make breakfast. He grabbed a browning banana and peeled it as he exited the small cabin. The cabin hadn't seemed too small before, but with dreams of Alanna floating in his head, he knew she couldn't be satisfied with a place like his. No room to make it her own.

He shoved the last bite in his mouth and headed down the hill, eventually taking Fort to Market. He avoided looking in the Painted Stone's window as he rolled past. The last thing he needed was another dose of Alanna's poison.

The moment he stepped in the office, the phone rang. He sucked in a deep, steadying breath then picked up the implement. "Mackinac Island Events."

"Jonathan Covington, just the man I wanted to talk to." The gruff voice rang with strength.

"Good morning, Mr. Morris."

"Edward, son. How many times do I have to tell you that?"

"A few more to overcome my mother's training."

The man's rich laugh tickled Jonathan's ear. "This is why I like you. Polite with a deadly sense of humor." A moment of silence descended, and then Edward cleared his throat. "Bonnie loves all your ideas, like I said the other day, but it's not enough. Any thoughts on how we can make it bigger? She's the love of my life for as long as the good Lord lets me keep her. I want to celebrate her in a big way."

"Well. . ." Jonathan's mind spun, thoughts engaged by the challenge of creating something client worthy on the fly. "She's a special lady."

"That she is."

"What does she like to do?"

"Mentor young moms. You wouldn't believe the number of times I come home even now to find her stretched out on the couch and a young mom and her baby sitting next to her. She's always giving." Edward cleared his throat.

"Do you want to add something to the events or find something she can take home?"

"It needs to be something that's a visual reminder of our love. I'm not the best at saying the words. Too much like my dad in that respect. But I don't want her to ever doubt me."

"Didn't you say she liked art? Maybe a painting from the island?" Edward had broached the idea earlier. Jonathan hoped he still liked it.

"Maybe." Jonathan could imagine the man stroking his chin. "But it needs to be extremely special. She's always loved art though. Before she got sick, she served on the local art council. I know she misses it."

"You liked what you saw at the Painted Stone. How about I talk to a local artist about a commission? I can send photos of her art—they're vibrant pieces, and I bet she could paint something that reflects a love like yours." Did the silence mean Edward didn't like the idea? Jonathan scrambled to come up with anything else. "Or we could. . ."

"I like it. E-mail me examples. Bonnie loves color. The more the better."

Jonathan exhaled. "Glad to do it. I'll stop by this afternoon. Hope there's enough time to make this work if you like her style."

"What's the artist's name?"

"Rachelle Stone."

"I'll Google her. See what I can find. Keep thinking in case this doesn't work out."

"Yes, sir."

Edward's rich laugh was back. "It's Edward. Talk to you soon."

Jonathan stared at the phone a minute before replacing it on the cradle. Now he'd done it. He would have to see Alanna. But he'd give it some time. He had a pile of work to tackle on the Lyster wedding first. Beginning with calling the bride. He pulled out the Lyster binder and looked up Theresa's number. He dialed and said a prayer for patience. The woman rode the emotional waves of wedding planning like an awkward first-time surfer.

The phone rang to the point he expected voice mail. At the last moment, he heard it click.

"Hello?"

"Ms. Lyster?"

"Yes?"

"This is Jonathan Covington."

"Well, it's about time. I'm driving to Mackinac right now."

Jonathan glanced at his desk calendar. Yep, there it was in bright red letters: *Theresa Lyster arrives.* "It will be great to have you back here."

"I don't know how we'll get everything done in time. The wedding is in four days, and there's so much to do."

"That's where I come in. Remember you hired me to make this a special event without burdening you."

"It's a nice theory, but it's still my wedding. My parents have invited all their hoity-toity friends, and it doesn't feel like my day anymore." She inhaled so deeply it sounded like she wanted to suck all the air out of her car and might stand on the verge of hyperventilating.

"Is anyone coming with you?"

"Rebecca Simpson, my maid of honor."

Perfect. Someone to help anchor the bride while he did the work. "How about I set up a spa session at the Grand Hotel this afternoon for the two of you? I'll make it right after tea so you can enjoy a relaxing afternoon. I'm checking in with the florist and caterer. Touched base with the party supply company yesterday, and they're set. Everything is coming together great."

"What will an afternoon like that cost?"

Jonathan stifled a chuckle at the thought. One didn't get married on Mackinac Island without a certain disregard for costs. It wasn't an easy place to reach, and everything had a price.

"Wait. Add it to Daddy's tab. After all, he's why I'm stressed."

He heard giggling in the background. Must be the maid of honor. "Come by when you get on the island, and I'll take care of the details. You relax. Tomorrow we'll cover what's left."

"All right, Jon. You're a lifesaver. Maybe I'll survive after all."

As soon as Theresa hung up, Jonathan dialed Jaclyn. Instead of looking forward to the excuse to talk, he dreaded hearing her voice. If he'd needed any proof he had let things get out of control with Alanna, he had it. Jaclyn had started as his contact at the Grand Hotel's spa but had grown to be a good friend. More than a friend when he was honest. Then there was Dylan, her two-year-old.

"Grand Hotel Spa." Jaclyn's voice held the professional tone of a busy manager.

"Hey, Jaclyn."

"Jonathan." Warmth crept into the word. Guess she'd forgiven him. "What's up?"

He chitchatted a few moments then got back to business. "I need a couple massages for a bride and her maid of honor. I'd like them to start with tea and then come to you. Assign your best masseuse."

"Sure, Jonathan. When do you need these?"

"Today."

"Today?" She groaned. He heard the rustle of pages in the background. "I'm not sure I can do that. Not even for you."

"This bride needs the special treatment, and I need the time to finish the work on her wedding." He pictured her chewing on the end of her pen as she studied the calendar. How many times had he seen her do that?

The page flipped a few more times. "All right. If you send

them up here for the final tea slot, I can squeeze them in with Analise and Nicole. But you'll have to tip well since they'll stay late."

"No problem. It's going on 'Daddy's' account, and he can afford it."

"You owe me dinner, too."

It wouldn't be the first time by a stretch. They always had a good time, but with Alanna back. . . Jonathan considered saying no. "You're right. I've got the wedding Monday. . . ."

"Jonathan, we miss you. I'd almost believe you have someone else."

Her words pierced him. "I'll call later."

"Fine. I'll talk to you then." Jaclyn hung up, and he hoped she didn't take an eraser to the appointments.

One crisis averted. Now to plan out the Standeford wedding proposal and then snap photos of Rachelle Stone's art. Which meant seeing Alanna. Again.

Chapter 11

The sun tried to poke through the cloud cover as Jonathan strode up Market Street toward the Painted Stone and Fort Mackinac. Just when he wanted to pull his jacket collar up to protect his neck from the cold, he'd step into a pool of sunshine and feel spring.

He whistled a flat tune as he ambled. He had too much to accomplish to walk slowly, but the thought of seeing Alanna held him back. He sidestepped another tourist as he approached the paned-glass front of the studio. It beckoned him, but he stood a moment checking for Alanna through the windows. The studio stood stark, nobody filling its space. The ridiculousness of his hesitation tensed his shoulders. He needed to get in there, get the information, and leave. If he hadn't promised Edward photos, he'd have called.

Space. He needed space to clear the hold Alanna's return had on him. He needed to get his head straight. Fast. If Rachelle Stone had created that web page like he'd suggested, he wouldn't have to approach Alanna now.

His phone buzzed against his hip. He snagged it and glanced at the caller ID. Since he didn't recognize the number, he let it slide over to voice mail and opened the door. The bells jangled their greeting. He winced. Alanna would round the corner in a minute then freeze when she saw him. Not the kind of reaction he liked to elicit in a woman, especially one he was attracted to. He strode to a painting. Maybe if he stood engrossed in one, he could miss her inevitable reaction.

Jonathan picked a painting that illustrated the view from

Fort Mackinac down across Lake Huron to the lighthouses. The artist had painted the field of grass a vibrant green—the color of cucumbers. Roofs poked through the trees until gentle waves rocked the island with a rich blue the color of a blue jay's feathers. Lower, the Round Island Lighthouse peeked from the bottom right-hand corner of the painting, looking like a squat, barn-red ice-cream cone topped with vanilla custard.

The painting held Mrs. Stone's scrawled signature in the corner but didn't look right. Jonathan studied it a moment but couldn't peg what bothered him. He snapped a photo with his phone then turned to the next painting. This one was a winter scene, the storefronts bursting with color against the blinding white of snow-covered streets.

The click of heels ricocheted against the hardwood floor. "Jonathan?"

He kept his gaze on the painting as he snapped a photo of it.

"What are you doing?"

"I have a client who wants to commission a painting for his wife in honor of their fortieth anniversary."

"Why take photos?"

He turned to look at her, noting the fine lines straining the edges of her eyes. "He liked your mom's art. Since she doesn't have a website, he asked me to take some photos to e-mail him. Can I have her current contact info?"

Her jaw worked, not the reaction he'd expected. Shouldn't she show some excitement that he'd made the recommendation?

"I doubt she has time right now with all Dad's problems."

Jonathan slipped his phone in his pocket. "Shouldn't she

make that decision? After all, aren't you here to keep the studio running? And doesn't that mean they need the income a commission like this could provide?"

The lines tightened as she frowned at him. "I don't like it."

"Okay. I don't like these paintings."

"What do you mean?"

"They're missing something."

Alanna fisted her hands against her hips in a tight stance. "Excuse me?"

"They don't quite fit Rachelle's style." The words sounded stupid as he said them.

Alanna felt heat flush her neck. It wasn't from his presence. Couldn't be.

Could her mom accept the commission? Even a few thousand dollars would help immensely. She watched Jonathan for a moment. He nosed closer to the painting until his schnoz almost touched the paint-layered canvas. He stepped back and squinted. He looked ridiculous, but she mimicked his motions. As she neared the layers of paint, she stilled.

That's what bothered her.

Mom didn't layer oils like she had in these paintings.

Sure, she liked to add a sense of texture, but these paintings seemed to have the oils caked. Maybe her style had evolved. It wasn't like Alanna had paid tons of attention since she bolted from the island. College then law school and launching a career had absorbed her.

Mom had given her small paintings of her favorite spots on the island for the occasional birthday and Christmas presents. The lighthouses. A favorite cottage. Altogether it formed a nice collage of the area. But she hadn't seen large paintings for a long time other than those at the cottage. Long enough for Mom's technique to change and get heavier?

Alanna didn't know, but she wouldn't admit anything. "You're ridiculous."

He shrugged. "Maybe, but your mom's one of the best artists around. My client has planned an anniversary weekend here for his wife. A painting that commemorates their love and the island is ideal." He squinted at the painting then turned to her. "But I want her to paint. Not some knockoff."

Alanna jolted at his tone. "How can you say that?"

"Because these aren't your mom's paintings. And I have proof." He turned to the winter scene. "See here. . ." He pointed at Ste. Anne's Church. "Rachelle would have ensured the stained-glass windows were accurate."

"Maybe she wanted to do something different." But she knew Jonathan was right. Her mom loved that church, always had. Mom had wanted to renew her vows there but changed her mind when Alanna refused to come. Remorse cloaked Alanna at her selfishness. She should have swallowed her anger and forced herself to return for one ceremony. She could have taken the ferry back as soon as the celebration ended. Instead, she'd claimed a case wouldn't let her escape. She'd let her pride and fear hold her back.

Now that seemed ridiculous. After all, how many locals had hounded her the few days she'd been back?

"You with me?" Jonathan's voice jerked her from her thoughts.

"You're still wrong."

"Nope, and I'll find a way to prove it."

She turned from the painting and felt pulled into his gaze. His eyes reflected his high intelligence. If she wasn't careful, he would identify what was wrong with the painting. "What?"

"You know I'm tenacious."

With everything but chasing her. How many mistaken relationships could she have avoided if he'd asked her to come back? "Most of the time."

His eyebrow arched. "Really. Then I'll show you how much it's woven in the fabric of who I am."

"Why waste your time on something so insignificant?"

"It's not if I suggest a client buy a painting from your mother only to learn he didn't get what he paid for."

She tore her gaze from his and pivoted so her body angled toward the painting and away from him. Heat flushed her cheeks, but she prayed he didn't notice. If he did, he'd know immediately that the possibility bothered her, too.

"What about Jacklyn?"

He looked at her like she'd gone crazy. "What?"

"Don't you have a child with her?"

Color flushed up his neck. "Seriously? You think that?"

The shrill ring of the phone pierced the space between them like a wonderful warning. She hurried toward the desk, her stomach twisting at his expression. "I've got to get that."

Jonathan didn't move. His stillness reminded her of an alert Doberman. Poised and ready to pounce but studying the surroundings first. Exactly what she didn't need.

She had to call Mom and find out what was going on with those paintings.

The phone rang as she picked it up. "The Painted Stone."

"Hello. This is Patience. Is this Alanna?"

Alanna's heart sank at the sound of her mom's best friend. She shouldn't be surprised that Mrs. Matthews would eventually call.

"A little birdie told me you'd returned." The voice held the warmth of someone welcoming the prodigal home.

Alanna rubbed at a knot of tension at her temple. "Arrived a few days ago."

"And you haven't called?" The woman clucked her tongue. "My dear child, I promised your mother I would keep an eye on you. Can't do that if you never come by."

Alanna couldn't think of the last time she'd been called a child. She'd slipped that title off at least fifteen years earlier.

"Are you there?"

"Yes, ma'am." She sighed. "I've been busy keeping everything going."

"For a successful attorney like you? I doubt the studio is the least challenge."

Jonathan cleared his throat, and Alanna glanced his way. He pointed to his watch then the door. "I'll be back."

"All right." They'd have to finish their conversation. But postponing it until after she talked to Mom provided a needed reprieve. She had to figure out what was going on. Shouldn't be too difficult for someone who pieced together complex disputes.

"Alanna Stone." Mrs. Matthews's tone was tinged with welcome.

She rubbed her temple harder. "I'll stop by soon. It's tricky with the studio's hours."

"Your mother always managed."

Alanna didn't even attempt to hide her sigh. "I'm not Mom."

"That is true." The old woman chuckled. "Your mother's life would have been easier these last years if you'd been more like her in your teens."

The bell jangled, and Alanna turned back around. She smiled as she watched Mr. Tomkin walk in, a padfolio tucked under his arm. Just the distraction she needed.

"Well, thank you for calling. I've got to assist a customer."

Alanna hung up without waiting for Mrs. Matthews's good-bye. She'd learned in fourth-grade Sunday school that little short of perfection satisfied the woman. She already knew she wasn't perfect.

"Mr. Tomkin. What can I do for you?" Anything he needed couldn't be harder than dealing with Mrs. Matthews and Jonathan.

Chapter 12

The man ignored the art as he approached the counter. He had the intent focus of a man on a mission from which he would not be distracted. By the set of his chin, she wasn't certain she'd like whatever had brought him to the studio. Maybe she should have stayed on the phone.

"Alanna, we need someone talented like you to set up shop in this town. You'll notice there aren't any attorneys."

She took a step back and sank onto the stool her mother used. "We've never needed them when Mackinaw City and St. Ignace have attorneys."

"Not true. We need someone who's involved here."

The thought of practicing law on the island made her skin itch. She fought not to scratch her arms as she stared at him. "I already work in Grand Rapids."

"For someone else. Here you could work for yourself."

"No thanks."

He stared a moment as if formulating his next argument then shrugged. "Think about it. I'm here because I need your help on a foundation matter. Your dad was instrumental as a founding member. Now he's gone, and you can fill his shoes." He set his padfolio on the counter and pulled out a paper. "Here's the agenda for the next meeting. As you'll see, we have many important items to discuss and vote on."

The bell jingled, but Alanna focused on Gerald. "I'll see what I can do."

"Alanna Stone." She turned with a start. Brendan Tomkin? What was he doing here, with the same baby face and nose-in-the-air look he'd had in high school? "I heard you were back."

He'd changed since high school, bulked up and thickened from the scrawny high schooler. He approached his dad with a strut. "Ready to grab a bite?"

Gerald glanced at his watch and frowned. "I was in the middle of an important conversation."

"Come on, Pops. I'm hungry. Alanna will still be here when we're done."

Alanna bit back a sharp comment but forced her lips to curve. "We can talk after the meeting."

"I suppose. It really is urgent." He turned to his son. "Where are your manners?"

Brendan rolled his eyes before he plastered on a crooked smile. "Like to join us, Alanna?"

"I really can't. Have to stay here."

Brendan made a motion toward her. "See?"

Gerald mouthed, "Sorry." Alanna shrugged. It looked like at the core Brendan hadn't changed since high school. "How are you doing, Brendan?"

"Fine. Selling insurance like crazy on the mainland. Why?"

"I just thought with the anniversary of Grady's death you might be. . .melancholy." Boy, that sounded stupid, and the look he gave her reinforced that.

"Why would that matter?"

"You were friends. Always looked like good friends."

"Not really. The island didn't give me too many options. Our school didn't need two guys jockeying for the girls. He just thought he was in my league. Besides, he was too pompous for my taste. He thought he was better than the rest of us. Too bad he couldn't swim better." Brendan grabbed his dad's arm and tugged him toward the door. "Catch ya later, Alanna."

Not if she could help it. If her class had contained more than eight students, she never would have spent any time with Brendan as a teen. His attitude hadn't changed, and even then it made her want to listen to fingernails on a chalkboard rather than his self-important monologues.

Alanna watched the two round the sidewalk a moment then tried to remember what she'd been doing when Mr. Tomkin showed up. From the brief moment with Brendan, it seemed clear he'd inherited his father's pushy personality. She shook off the moment, shoved the paperwork to the side, and picked up the phone. Maybe she'd catch Mom between doctors' appointments and visiting Dad. She dialed the number and left a quick message at the beep.

"Mom, call me on my cell as soon as you get this. I need to ask you some questions about the studio."

She set the phone back on the hook. She'd never thought of practicing law on Mackinac Island. But then she'd never considered going to law school until the police interviewed Trevor after Grady's death. Dad had found an attorney, but the man hadn't impressed her. She'd determined to treat her clients differently. With respect and full information about what was happening in their matters. Could she find the kind of cases she loved up here? Complex litigation like the murder trial she'd just braved. Cases that required a creative approach to pull the jury and judge into the story.

While the cases drained her, she loved the puzzle of putting together a compelling defense. But the last murder trial had really zapped her energy. The thought of diving into another case that would consume every hour and spare thought exhausted her. Should she consider the slower approach of small-town practice?

Who was she kidding? The last thing she wanted to do was stay here. She shouldn't entertain the idea.

Alanna rolled the mouse back and forth, waking the computer from sleep mode. First, she placed an ad in the *Grand Rapids Press*. It would run online immediately and in the paper after Memorial Day, and she prayed the right person would read and apply. Then she opened a spreadsheet that listed paintings, artists, and if an item had sold. Maybe she could figure out who her parents bought art from. If she could determine that, she could see if a painting had been mislabeled.

Mom used to fill the studio with her own pieces; then, as she built a following that spread across the region thanks to the island's faithful visitors, she slowly added other artists. Usually they were friends from the art community or they had a resonating style. Either way, the studio acquired a more eclectic feel. Maybe with managing others' art, Mom had less time to create her own.

The bell on the front door jangled as a group of tourists entered. Alanna stood and approached the group of middle-aged couples.

"Is there anything I can help you find?"

A woman with bouncing copper curls turned to her with a grin. "A souvenir. I need something that will help me remember this remarkable place."

"It is that." Alanna made a mental note to find smaller pieces to display. Anything less pricey than the big canvasses currently in the showroom. Shouldn't Mom have done that a long time ago? Like the art professor suggested, a rack of postcards and assorted note cards based on Mom's paintings would be a simple improvement. "I'll check the back, but perhaps you'll find something in one of the pieces here. Is there a certain place that is especially meaningful?"

"The Grand Hotel. I'd love a scene that makes me think of *Somewhere in Time*."

Alanna hid a smile as the woman gushed about the old movie filmed at the landmark hotel starring Christopher Reeve and Jane Seymour. Surely any of the paintings would satisfy that criteria.

She slipped into the back and rummaged through a stack of smaller canvasses. These didn't have frames and looked unfinished compared to the ones hanging on the walls in the main room. She pulled several of the smaller pieces to the side and inspected them to make sure someone had stretched the canvas tight. She could display several immediately at a lower price point many of the island's tourists could afford. By leaving the framing to the purchaser, they could perfectly match the frame to their décor.

Muffled voices carried to her as she carried the art to the showroom.

"These really are nice pieces." A gentleman in khakis and a polo shirt stood in front of a large watercolor. Alanna bit off a frown when she saw it wasn't one of Mom's pieces. "The artist has a nice eye."

"Only the best at the Painted Stone." Alanna arranged the small canvasses on the countertop. "Here are a few pieces that might interest you as well."

The woman with the curly hair hurried to the counter. "Oh, these are perfect. How much?"

"Two hundred and fifty dollars each." She hoped her mom hadn't agreed to pay the artists more.

Another woman, this one about ten years younger than the others, walked over. "Why aren't they framed?"

Time to test her theory. "To allow you to frame a bit of the island in a way that fits your style."

"Hmmm." The woman tapped a lacquered fingernail against her lip and studied the paintings. "Interesting idea, but I prefer those I don't have to work on."

"Don't worry about her." The redhead leaned across the counter and made a show of lowering her voice. "She likes to think she's an interior designer. We just call her the know-it-all."

The man next to her snorted while Alanna bit her lip to keep from smiling. "What brings you to Mackinac?"

"A niece's wedding, which corresponds to our thirtieth anniversary. I keep telling Ted he's getting twice the bang for his dollars. A wedding trip and a second honeymoon."

Her husband bumped against her side and grinned at her. "That's my Alice—always thinking, even if you aren't always kind."

Confusion furrowed the redhead's brow before a flash of something like indignation replaced it. "Leanna is a know-it-all. She knows it, too, don't you, darling?" Alice put a hand on her hip and a pout on her lips.

"Sure enough. Mark likes me with a bit of contrariness."

"See?"

Her husband leaned down and kissed Alice's pout off. "Find anything you want?"

"I've already got it." She grinned at him with a look that came only after years of marriage.

"You do?" He waggled his eyebrows at her, and Alice laughed.

"Yep, but if you'd like to make me really happy, there's a little painting over here I'd love to take home."

Alanna tried not to let her longing for a love like that mar the moment as Alice led Ted to a medium-sized painting of the porch at the Grand with a beautiful gold frame. The red geraniums that lined the porch provided a pop of color against the white rockers and yellow awnings. Alanna closed her eyes to block the view of the lovebirds considering the painting. She was ridiculous, really. She didn't know what that couple had been through or endured, only that they seemed to reap the reward now.

Would she ever have the same? A lifetime of love to come home to?

The image seemed improbable even as she longed for it. A partner-track attorney at even a medium-sized firm had to give too much time to her job to have an outside life. The partners had only allowed her this time off after realizing she'd fried her last brain cell in the murder trial. It wasn't the fact her family needed her, but the idea she could embarrass the firm as easily as she'd brought it positive media. Though she didn't think working at an art studio qualified as a vacation.

The low ding from the computer let her know she had e-mail waiting. As Ted tugged the painting from the wall, she winced. Maybe the e-mail would be from the perfect person who had found the online listing already. This person could sweep onto the island, take over the studio, and allow her to return to Grand Rapids.

"This is the one." Ted slammed the painting down on the

counter, scattering canvasses.

"Be careful, you big lug. I don't want it damaged before we leave the store."

Ted winked at Alanna before he turned to Alice. "Of course not, though then we wouldn't have to haul this monstrosity back."

"Whatcha calling a monstrosity? You'll look at that every day in our dining room."

"That's what I'm afraid of."

If a twinkle hadn't lit his eyes, Alanna might have created a reason he couldn't buy that particular piece. Instead, she gladly swiped his credit card and then swaddled the painting in bubble wrap. "I added an extra layer to protect it from bumping."

Leanna tapped a bubble until it popped. "It'd take another layer to get it through the weekend. You have no idea how rough and tumble these two are."

Her husband walked up and slipped an arm around her shoulders. "You want one?"

"Of these?" She ran a finger around the room. "Not on your life. They aren't our style."

As the couples exited with Ted lugging the painting against his chest, good-natured bickering followed them.

Another ding reminded her to check e-mail. If she didn't get some résumés in pronto, she'd need to place more than one old-fashioned newspaper ad. While part of her wondered if anyone still read the paper, she had to try something, because she couldn't stay on the island indefinitely. Not if she wanted to keep her real job at the firm.

After a few clicks, her in-box filled the screen. One looked like a promising prospect for the job. Then she opened the résumé and changed her mind. If a person couldn't spell basic words, she didn't want to trust that person with her parents' livelihood. Guess she'd keep praying and looking.

As she scrolled down the list of e-mail, she didn't see anything worth answering until she reached an e-mail from her brother. Maybe he had an update on Dad's condition. She opened the e-mail.

A groan slipped out as she scanned it.

Chapter 13

Weight pressed against Jonathan throughout the afternoon. He raced around downtown finalizing the details for the wedding rehearsal and ceremony. The events would run flawlessly, but he couldn't focus on them. Instead, the image of Alanna's blond hair serving as a frame that partly hid her face kept cropping up. He'd drive it from his mind, only to have her image reappear.

He hadn't been this distracted—well, ever.

He strived to be the consummate professional, completely devoted to his work. Then she returned. And his brain didn't comply with his instructions anymore. The more he told himself to focus and get the job done, the more his thoughts strayed. And that didn't mention the chaos she brought to his personal life.

When he finally returned to his office, he sank into his chair. He swiveled away from the computer and rubbed his face. He didn't need the distraction. Not now. Not from her.

His cell phone vibrated against his hip. "Jonathan Covington."

"Hear anything from the artist?" Edward Morris's unmistakable voice telegraphed he had other things on his mind.

"I've talked to her daughter. I should know something soon." Like whether Rachelle still painted. Had her arthritis flared up, causing painting to be too painful?

"All right. There isn't much time. I'm willing to pay for an original."

"I'll feel her out before connecting you. Mrs. Stone is

a very good artist."

"You're hesitating."

"Only because her husband has health issues that might require her focus."

"That I understand."

Jonathan nodded. Edward could understand those pressures. "How is Bonnie?"

"Holding up. I think our plans for the anniversary celebration have given her something to focus on. A date to live for."

"I'll do all I can to make it everything she dreams."

A moment of silence, and then Edward sighed. "I'm counting on it."

After he hung up, Jonathan stared out his office window. This was an important event. It was smaller than many he organized, but if he made it memorable for Bonnie Morris, all his effort and time would be worthwhile. Her fight with cancer reminded him too much of his mother's. He stopped to pray for Bonnie.

Tugging the Lyster wedding file in front of him, he double-checked the myriad details involved in the intimate event. Based on the guest list, he could expect new clients from this wedding. If there was one thing he'd learned in event planning, it was that each event generated future leads.

After confirming the setup for the rehearsal dinner, Jonathan pulled out the Standeford file. This couple had differing views on how their wedding should play out, with the groom refusing to bow to the bride. Did he really want to tackle the job of bringing harmony to the event? After a moment of prayer, he dove back into his notes. Ideas began to flow on how to incorporate a movie theme along with the more formal tone the groom and his mother wanted.

He pulled up his planning software and plugged in details. An hour later, he had the outlines of a proposal. He'd expand it later, but for now he needed to check in with Theresa Lyster. Her phone rang to voice mail, and he started a message when she buzzed him.

"Jonathan Covington, if I weren't getting married in a few days, I'd kiss you."

He laughed at her giddy words. "Analise and Nicole did a great job?"

"Phenomenal. I may have to move here just to have them keep me relaxed. What a wonderful idea!"

"You're welcome."

He heard a rustling, then Theresa whispered, "You should take Jaclyn to dinner and add it to Daddy's bill."

Jonathan laughed. "That's not how I do business, but tell Jaclyn I'll meet her at Man O' War at seven."

Theresa repeated his words. "Thanks again for everything."

"My pleasure." He hung up, grinning. If only it were so easy to keep everyone satisfied.

He turned back to his computer and printed the Standeford proposal. Then he spent a few minutes fleshing out thoughts for the Wenzes' anniversary celebration before shoving his files in his bag. After dinner with Jaclyn, he'd work from home.

As he dodged foot traffic on the way to Man O' War, Jonathan whistled a Michael Bublé tune—one of Jaclyn's favorites. When he walked through the restaurant's door, he scanned the dining room for Jaclyn. Often she arrived first to claim a great table for them, but he didn't spot her.

He approached the hostess.

"How many?" The gal spoke with a slight accent, one he couldn't place, but she blended with the numerous international students who found summer employment on the island.

"Two."

"Yes, sir." Another sign she wasn't a native, or she'd know his name. "It'll be fifteen to twenty minutes."

He gave her his name and accepted a pager. Guess he had a few minutes to wander, though she warned him the pager had a limited range.

He strolled Main Street and watched for Jaclyn. Her tight red curls were the kind that made a man want to tease them with his fingers. Though she'd sent every signal she wouldn't mind, their relationship tended toward friendly but inched toward romance. Her son accepted him with enthusiasm on picnics and bike rides. That had felt like enough.

Before Alanna returned.

He wasn't sure how that impacted Jaclyn.

Jaclyn bounced into him. "Hey there, handsome."

"Jaclyn."

She lifted her cheek for a kiss. He obliged, wondering why their customary greeting felt odd. He couldn't let Alanna get to him. It wasn't fair to Jaclyn or him.

He forced his attention to the beautiful woman in front of him as Jaclyn chattered about her day. When the pager vibrated, he pointed her to the door.

"Sorry I didn't get here earlier." She tossed her curls. "It's a big weekend at the Grand. Everybody wants special treatment. The phone didn't stop ringing all day."

"Thanks for squeezing in Theresa."

"Anything for you, Jonathan. You know that."

406

The way she said it with stars in her eyes made him feel small. She gave every indication she'd fallen deep—despite his efforts to proceed cautiously. Where her adoration used to make him feel bigger, stronger, tonight it made him question what kind of man he was. He shouldn't vacillate. A real man committed for the long haul. One glance at Jaclyn showed she thought he had. Leave it to him to lead a great gal along while his heart remained secretly entrenched with another.

The hostess led them to a table under the big plate-glass window. Jonathan pulled out the chair for Jaclyn and then angled his away from the window.

"I've filled the air. Your turn. How was your day?" Jaclyn plopped her elbows on the table and then her chin on her hands as she studied him.

"After you helped me with a nervous bride, I worked on her special day and planned another."

"I'll never understand how you find so many concepts."

"Lots of magazine subscriptions."

"Are you serious?"

He straightened the silverware. "That and files. My mom and dad kept everything. That gives me lots to work from."

"They're talking about you at the Grand." Pride showed in her eyes.

That was great news. Prospects from the hotel could fill his calendar.

She frowned, the expression uncommon. "You don't seem excited."

"You didn't see my smile?" He grinned widely. "That's really good news. Tell them thanks."

"You can do it next time you come to see me." She batted her eyelashes.

"Sure." He leaned back and glanced around the restaurant. Where was their server? A young man in a white shirt and black pants caught his eye and threaded tables toward them.

"What can I get y'all to drink?" A southern accent tinged his words as he slid a basket of warm sourdough rolls between them.

After taking their drink orders, he disappeared, and Jonathan found himself looking at Jaclyn. Tightness etched around her eyes.

"Was there somewhere else you needed to be tonight?"

Jonathan shook his head. He adjusted his stance in the chair, leaned toward her, and grabbed a piece of bread from the basket. He tore it into small pieces as he studied her. "Guess I'm distracted."

"You think?"

"Tell me more about your day." The meal flowed quickly with the server sliding salads in front of them, soon followed by sandwiches. They waived off dessert and stood to leave.

Jaclyn waited in front of him, a question in her eyes.

Regret pierced him. "Sorry about tonight."

"At least you paid." While he could tell she meant it as a joke, there was truth to her statement. He hadn't given her the attention she deserved, but he'd paid.

"Promise next time I'll be a better companion."

"All right. I'll give you another chance. Join me for a picnic at Arch Rock on Memorial Day."

"I have a wedding."

"The day before then."

He could squeeze in time then. "I thought it was one of your busiest days."

"Nothing I can't have someone else cover for a couple hours." Her expression wavered as she swayed from side to side, her skirt swirling around her knees in a slow dance. "Please? We miss you."

"All right." The image of her son with eyes the same color as hers confronted him. It had been awhile since he'd seen Dylan. "We'll do something Sunday afternoon."

Jaclyn rolled her eyes, but the smile had returned. "See you then."

She turned to head up the street toward the Grand Hotel. His gaze followed her until it slammed into Alanna's. All of a sudden he felt as if she'd caught him doing something he shouldn't. That was ridiculous. He needed to get her out of his head.

Make that his heart.

He spun on his heel without acknowledging her.

Right now he needed to put distance between them. As quickly as possible. Not an easy feat on the small island with their cottages next door to each other. He stopped when he realized he couldn't get home this way. He had to pass her if he wanted to sleep in his bed. Muttering under his breath that he was a fool, he reversed direction and headed toward her. He'd cut up the street as soon as he could, but he had to get his bike or it would be a long walk home. A long one that provided too much time to berate his foolish, rebellious heart.

Chapter 14

Alanna's thoughts swirled as she strolled Main Street. She should head home, should have hours earlier. Mom's e-mail had informed her Daddy had taken a turn for the worse, and Alanna had to stay longer. Mom simply couldn't return to the island without Dad. Each time she'd tried to reach Mom, voice mail was all she heard. Now her thoughts strayed to that awful graduation party while she wandered the streets.

Without Grady's death, she would have skipped law school. All the years of study she would have invested in something else. Something closer to home. Returning left her wondering whether she had wasted so much time for nothing. She certainly didn't feel fulfilled. The rush of winning a case wore off much too fast.

Someone bumped into her, and she pulled her attention back to the busy sidewalk. "Brendan?"

"Lookie here. It's Miss Alanna. Imagine bumping into you twice in one day."

"How are you? I'm kind of surprised you're still here. All that talk of leaving."

"I'm on the mainland. Just came back for the party weekend." His breath smelled of alcohol as he grinned. He'd had as much to drink as any of the kids at the graduation party. A leer creased his face, one Alanna hoped came from the alcohol. "It'd be great to catch up, but I'm off to see a girl. A pretty one. One you know."

"Who?"

Brendan ignored her as he moved down the street, looking far steadier than she expected. A mumble reached her. "Enjoy the surprise."

Must be the alcohol talking. Certainly made no sense, but in her short interactions with him, Brendan didn't shine in that area. She wondered how he managed to sell any insurance with that surly personality.

She'd forgotten how crazy the island became on long weekends like Memorial Day. Guess people started the weekend on Thursday. The hum and pulse of activity used to excite her. Now. . .she didn't know what she thought. A little quiet sounded good.

She glanced up and spied Jonathan on the sidewalk a hundred feet or so in front of her, standing very close to a cute twentysomething. Jaclyn?

Electricity fairly crackled in the space between them. As she watched, Alanna remembered the times Jonathan had eyes only for her. She'd left so much behind all because of that tragic graduation party. Why had everyone been so quick to blame Trevor—and by extension her—when most of the island's teens had turned out for the celebration-turned-tragedy?

Her phone vibrated against her hip, but she couldn't pull her gaze from the two. Not as she saw what had been her future play out in front of her.

She turned on her heel and stepped away. Any appetite she'd had disappeared in the vision before her. Who was she kidding? She'd dated other men, one even seriously, since leaving. Jonathan had to do the same.

She'd read too many fairy tales. Too many stories of Prince Charming waiting for the perfect woman. Even hunting for her. Jonathan had certainly never bothered to do that.

One call, that's all she needed then. She brushed moisture from her cheek as she rushed up the sidewalk toward the white clapboard library and narrow beach behind it. The sun had lowered in the sky, and she told herself she'd watch it set behind the lighthouse.

She stumbled when she hit the rough pebbles of the beach, nothing like the sand beaches near the oceans or even at the Dunes in Indiana. She slowed her pace, extending her arms as if walking a tightrope. That's what her life had become. Drained from the trial and media assault, she'd driven to the island, braced against the thought of what waited. Now she could add the pain of Jonathan's nearness to her concerns about the paintings.

What had happened to the simple time in the studio her mother had promised? In and out in a few weeks, a couple of months at most, with no problems. Instead, everywhere she turned she encountered a challenge. She thought she'd prepared for the season, but now she wanted to run as fast as she could, abandoning the island and all it held.

A cool breeze blew off Lake Huron, sending a shiver down her arms and back. She hugged her middle and hunkered down on the beach. Small whitecaps teased the shoreline a few feet away. The last few years had felt quiet, almost docile outside of courtroom tussles. Now she wondered if it only felt that way because she stuffed all her real emotions so far beneath the surface she hadn't recognized them.

Anger over her brother's treatment? Ignored.

Fear over returning to Mackinac? Shoved to the side.

Questions about how her family could remain? Oblivious.

For someone who was known for her strength, she'd lived a deluded life. Sheltered in her Grand Rapids condo, working for a hard-driving firm, she could pretend she had everything she needed. After all, she had a handful of girlfriends and the occasional relationship.

Now it all seemed as shallow as the water lapping the shore. She didn't have a single person she could call to share her concerns. Even her roommate would wonder at the sudden attempt at intimacy. Conversations moving from "It's your turn to clean the kitchen" to "I think my mother is committing art fraud" didn't happen every day.

She pulled her knees up and wrapped her arms around them. She glanced at the sky. Watched as God painted stripes of vibrant color across the clouds. A rich salmon chased magenta, turquoise, and violet. She needed to get up, start moving. If she didn't, she'd have to find her way home in the dark. She could do it, but with the way her thoughts wandered, it wouldn't be a good idea.

Her gaze traveled the length of the vista. Sometimes it was hard to believe the God who created such beauty on a cosmic scale cared about the details of her life, but she prayed He did.

If He didn't, she was lost.

Memorial Day weekend started with ferry loads of tourists. The population on the island exploded with those who needed a dose of relaxation. Alanna spent Friday ringing up orders and answering questions. By the time she biked home, she could hardly move. Her body was used to sitting all day, not the up and down of running a retail shop followed by an uphill bike ride.

All she wanted was to sit down on the dock with a good book until the light got too dim to read. She turned the bike into her drive then slipped off it to park it in the shed. The key dangled in her hand, useless as the shed's door slid open with ease.

Hadn't she locked it that morning? She must have, since it was part of her routine. She might have left the big city behind, but she hadn't abandoned her habits. Even from this remote location, it begged trouble to leave the door unlocked.

She stared into the shadow-encrusted interior. Should she go ahead and push the bike in or run for help?

Don't overreact. She'd feel ridiculous if she ran next door only to find nothing wrong. But if she didn't and something was wrong in that dark space. . .

She shook off the thought. "This is ridiculous."

Her words filled the silence but didn't settle the creepy crawlies on her back. A whine that sounded like a cat's screech came from inside.

Alanna dropped the bike and backed away from the shed. She spun on her heel and hurried toward the house. The broken pansies lining the paving stones that connected the house and shed almost stopped her. What had happened? Someone or something had trampled the flowers and unlocked the shed.

After fumbling to unlock the back door, she rushed into the kitchen and called Jonathan.

"Alanna?"

"Do you have a flashlight?"

"Flashlight?"

"Yes." She nodded then felt like a fool. "Something's wrong in my shed." He yawned, and Alanna wished she hadn't called. "Never mind."

"I'm coming. Give me a few minutes."

Alanna hung up and filled the teakettle. It had started to hum a shrill tune when Jonathan walked in the kitchen. He wore khaki shorts that had more holes than fabric and an oversized Michigan State sweatshirt. His hair looked rumpled and his face tired.

"Did I wake you?"

"Don't worry about it. I thought I'd get ahead of the weekend. Won't sleep much between now and the wedding." He hurried to the stove and picked up the kettle. After setting it on a cold burner, Jonathan turned back to her, his green eyes probing. "What's wrong?"

Biting her lower lip, Alanna grabbed a couple of mugs from the cabinet. "The shed was unlocked when I got home."

"Happens."

"I always lock up."

"Always? Even here?"

She nodded. "I've seen the worst in people. And tonight it's confirmed. The plants along the path are broken like someone stepped all over them. And the shed. . ."

"There had to be more than it being unlocked." He studied her like he knew she wouldn't be that kind of woman. The one who panicked at every sound or event.

"It's too dark to see what's in there."

Jonathan hefted the flashlight and flicked it on. She squinted against its light. "Bright enough to penetrate any dark corner and hefty enough to knock out any lurkers." His tone was light, yet he didn't laugh at her concerns. "I'll go check, and you can wait here."

"No way. I want to see."

He shrugged and headed out the door. Alanna flipped on the back-porch light then hurried to catch up. The crickets had started their evening music, filling the night with a sweet melody. Against that backdrop, her earlier fear seemed blown out of proportion. Then a shrieking wail filled the night. She hurried forward and collided with Jonathan. He let out an *uhf* as the flashlight fell from his hand, clattered to the ground, then blinked out.

Jonathan's arms slipped around her. "Steady there."

She stilled, a flood of electricity zipping through her. A longing to stay right where she was warred against the need for space—lots of it. Jonathan dropped his hold and stooped to collect the flashlight. He thwumped it against his thigh, and it sputtered to life.

"That's better."

She nodded, even though she disagreed. She'd felt safe while he'd shielded her. Now she felt foolish and alone.

Jonathan hurried to the shed and stepped inside, and she watched the light play across the entrance.

"Lanna, stay back." His words pulled her forward even as his command pressed her back.

"What did you find?"

"Nothing I want you to see. Go back inside." She hesitated, and he must have seen. "Go."

"No, this is my home right now. I need to know what's going on." She tried to look around him as he stepped from side to side, anticipating her moves. "Let me see."

"You don't want this in your mind."

She hesitated another moment then pushed around him. A trap of some sort had been slid into a back corner. In its clutches writhed a young rabbit, weakly trying to escape. "Who would do something like this?"

"I don't know. Please go inside."

Alanna glanced at the rabbit once more then spun on her heel and hurried back to the kitchen. She rummaged through the cupboard for tea bags with shaking hands. Her dad never set traps. He might complain about the rabbits and other animals that chomped at his plants, but he'd never use something like that. So how had it ended up in the shed? Someone must have purposefully placed it there. Why?

Did she want to know even if she could find out?

She shuddered and prayed for peace while waiting for Jonathan to rejoin her. Heaviness weighed his face as he came inside. She handed him a mug of tea.

"Thanks." He took a sip without looking in the cup and then spewed his mouthful across the table. He swiped a hand across his mouth. "What is this?"

"Mint tea."

Jonathan set the mug on the table. "No thanks." Concern shadowed his eyes as he looked at her. "I've got a call in to the police. Not sure when they'll get here. I don't like this, Lanna."

"Me neither."

He slipped around the table and sat next to her. As he placed an arm around her shoulders, she sank into his side. For the first time in a long time, she let someone else be strong for her.

Would he prove worthy of that trust?

As she felt him wrap his other arm around her, she prayed he would.

Chapter 15

Saturday passed in a flood of tourists and long hours, made even longer by the late police visit the prior night. When the chief had finally left, Alanna got the distinct impression he didn't like her.

"You sure there wasn't a trap in the shed."

Alanna had nodded. "Daddy never trapped or hunted."

"Hmmm. It didn't just crawl in that shed." He studied her as if searching for more.

"I've never seen it before."

"I'll take it back with me." He looked at the trap with the enthusiasm of a condemned man. "Means a trip off the island in the morning." He heaved a sigh. "All for something that will have your daddy's prints on it."

Alanna had wanted to argue, but fatigue won. Now Saturday passed in a collage of images, none distinct, yet all tied together. The image of tourists morphed into customers that melded with the paintings. When her stomach growled a rousing chorus, she locked up and headed for Main Street. The island would have to endure a closed studio long enough for her to find food.

Fifteen minutes later, she waited in line at the deli. A flock of tourists made slow decisions in front of her. She'd have to remember to call ahead. After waiting awhile, Alanna spun and collided with the person behind her.

"I am so sorry." Heat flashed up her cheeks as she took in the perfectly groomed woman. Short black hair stood in gelled spikes that gave the woman a funky edge when combined with her artsy earrings and large necklace.

"Alanna Stone. Some things never change. Still head in the clouds."

Alanna took a step back and tried to smile. "Ginger?"

Ginger Hoffmeister studied her as if waiting for another breakdown. "When I heard you were back, I couldn't believe it. After all this time? Are things that bad for your dad?"

"It's still touch and go." She cocked her head as she studied Ginger. "You've changed your look."

"My daughter dared me to be different. The things a mom will do to make her child happy. I think I let her talk me into something a bit edgier than I should have." Ginger brushed the hair at the nape of her neck. "Auburn to black. Shoulder length to spikes. What do you think? Should I refuse the next time Kaitlyn talks me into mother-daughter bonding?"

Alanna considered her old friend another minute. "I like it. Reminds me of the girl who wanted a dragon tattoo in high school."

"Yeah, I guess. I'm glad my parents threatened the convent over that one. Can you imagine a tail wrapped around my neck?" Ginger mock shuddered.

"Probably wouldn't have liked it long."

Ginger quirked an eyebrow. "You never did anything like that? Even in college?"

"No. Remember I couldn't even get my ears pierced? I'm such a chicken."

"I'll never forget how green you turned simply walking by that store in Cheboygan."

"So how are you?"

"Single and one kid." Ginger's eyes softened with the

pride of a mama. "Kaitlyn is my life. We live in St. Ignace, but I'm here most days for work. Will your dad be okay?"

"We don't know yet. Day by day." The line moved forward. Alanna placed a quick order then turned her attention back to Ginger. "Where do you work?"

"The police department. I heard you had some excitement last night."

Alanna grimaced. "I'm sure the chief is telling all kinds of stories."

"Don't worry. He's investigating."

"Who knows if he can find anything." A thought struck her. Could Ginger help Alanna review Grady's file? "How hard is it to get access to old police files?"

"For a case?"

"Yes."

Lines appeared around Ginger's eyes as she studied Alanna. "Why would you want that?"

"No particular reason."

Ginger thought a moment. "The chief doesn't hand out files willy-nilly."

"Aren't there freedom of information requirements?"

"Sure, but do you want to wait that long?"

"No. I just wanted to review Grady's file."

Ginger tapped a perfectly manicured finger against her lips. "Tell you what—I'll see what I can scrounge up. Not making any promises though. But it'll have to wait until after the weekend. The fudgies will keep me hopping in dispatch."

"Okay." Alanna grabbed her sack. "Thank you."

"What do you think you'll find?"

"Maybe nothing, but I want to read it." Alanna slipped from the store and hurried back to the studio. If Ginger came through with the file, that would be easier than explaining her reasons for seeing the file to the police chief.

Sunday morning Alanna hurried to reach the island's community church in time for the service. She'd lingered in bed too long worrying about who'd attend that morning and if any of them had heard about the chief coming to the cottage. Add her eleven-year absence, and it could be an awkward morning filled with people who remembered the old her. After fifteen minutes imagining how they'd treat her, she decided Jonathan was right. She needed to move past Grady's death and her assumption that people blamed her, too. She hadn't accepted his challenge and jumped in the water. Neither had she pushed him in and forced him to swim in the bitter water. The thoughts propelled her down the road away from her home.

Half a block from the church, she slowed to a stop and closed her eyes. This morning wasn't about her. It was about stepping back and spending time worshipping her Creator and Lord. *Father, help me pull my focus from me. Forgive me for being so selfish that I can't pull my gaze up. I long to worship You wholeheartedly.*

A whisper floated through the trees, a breeze that kissed her cheek. In that moment, her concerns disappeared, and she walked into the small sanctuary with a smile on her face. Her low-heeled sandals clicked against the oak plank flooring. Sunlight filtered through stained-glass windows lining the pews, the mix of soft colors lending an Impressionist light to her white skirt. She settled on a pew in the middle as the pianist played the opening notes to a hymn. Alanna leaned back and let the music wash over, peace floating through her.

More people filtered in before the pastor took his place at the front and led the small congregation in a few songs. Alanna kept her eyes closed to avoid the distraction of whoever might stand near her. When the sermon started, she opened her Bible and journal, taking notes on the pastor's comments about finding freedom in the Lord.

Freedom was certainly something she needed. Freedom from the painful hold of the past. Freedom from the quandary of her mother's paintings. Freedom from her fears about what others thought of her.

Most important, the freedom to be the woman God had created her to be.

As the congregation stood for the benediction, Alanna glanced back. In an instant, her peace evaporated as she glimpsed Piper Cadieux. Piper's hair was longer and lighter than when she'd watched Grady with the adoring eyes of a girl who thought her older brother could do no wrong.

Alanna turned forward, a heavy cloak of dread flowing over her. Piper tied her directly to the past. The girl's middle-school crush on Trevor had led to her spending every spare moment at the Stones until Grady's death. Alanna would never forget the pained accusations in the girl's eyes after that.

How would Piper respond now?

The service ended, and Alanna sank onto her seat. Maybe if she stayed put until the sanctuary cleared she could avoid Piper. Only cowards acted that way, but she didn't want a confrontation. Not in church.

This was ridiculous. What was the worst that could happen? Piper turned her back on Alanna? After all this time, that shouldn't matter.

Alanna stood and stepped into the walkway. "Piper."

The petite young woman stood in front of her, shoulders back and feet apart. "Alanna. I assumed you'd never slink back."

"Guess everyone did." Alanna swallowed and clasped her hands in front of her. "How are you?"

"Fine. Running Mom and Dad's gift shop while they squeeze in a last vacation. Then I'll take over the B&B when they return. We're shorthanded."

What could she say to that? "I'm having trouble finding a clerk for the studio."

"Tight labor market this year. We'll manage even if I have to run both places. Hard to imagine this little girl can do all that?" A glint matched her words.

Alanna nodded. "Guess I pictured you as you were when I left."

The sanctuary emptied, and they started toward the door. "Want to grab lunch?"

Piper's words surprised Alanna. Maybe Piper remained the friendly person she'd been when not shadowed by a shocking death. Maybe an agenda lurked beneath her words. Either way, Alanna couldn't walk away.

"I think I'd like that."

Piper led the way down the street to one of the island's many restaurants, only the sound of horses' hooves clomping against the road filling the space between them. Alanna tried to think of something to say, but everything felt forced like she wanted to try too hard.

As the hostess seated them at a table, Piper picked the seat across from Alanna. "Are you settled?"

"As much as I can be when I'll only be here a bit."

"Not staying?"

"No, just helping Mom and Dad."

Piper nodded. "You always had such a great relationship. So much better than the happy little home I had."

"It wasn't perfect."

"From all I saw, it looked that way. I loved spending time at your home. Your mom always treated me so well." Sadness lingered in Piper's eyes. "After Grady died, it just got worse. Only this time it was quiet. Like Mom and Dad retreated into their pain."

"It must have been awful."

Piper shrugged. "Proof life doesn't happen like we expect."

The waitress took their orders, and Piper talked about former classmates. As she rattled on, Alanna imagined the yearbook sitting on the table, Piper telling what each person had done since she graduated. When the waitress returned with salads for the girls, Piper took a breath. "That's everybody. I talk. . .a lot. . .when I'm nervous."

"Nervous? Why?"

"It's been a long time since I've seen you. Why didn't you come back earlier?"

"Guess I worried about what everyone would say."

"And now?"

"It isn't what I imagined. It's almost like that day has disappeared from our history. I'm surprised nobody talks about Grady."

Piper nodded. "It's like they've forgotten."

"Or moved on."

"When he died, everything changed."

Alanna nodded. "In unexpected ways. Coming back makes it like it just happened."

"Maybe. The island is frozen in time to me. To the week Grady died." Piper rolled her napkin into a tight roll.

Alanna reached toward her then pulled back. "I'm so sorry he died."

"That makes two of us. I dream, and he's still here. Sometimes the college basketball star he imagined. Other times he's stocking shelves at some big store. Then I wake up."

"Do you blame anyone?" Alanna studied Piper as she asked the question, looking for any sign that contradicted the young woman's strong words.

"No. Grady didn't have a lot of common sense. He'd take any dare, no matter how foolish. Anybody who grew up here knows swimming to the lighthouse that early in the season is a recipe for disaster." Piper sighed, and then her hazel gaze locked on Alanna's. "I've grieved. Do you think you still question because you ran?"

"Not with the way people blamed Trevor for the race. If I'd heard one more time he's the one who should have died since he took Grady on. . ."

Piper nodded. "A lot of people said that, didn't they? I'm glad two boys didn't die."

Alanna paused, something Piper said catching her attention. "Two?"

"Yes." She tilted her chin and stared at Alanna. "You know. You were there."

Alanna shook her head. "There were more than two people in the water. At least Brendan went in, too."

"No." Piper pushed against the table. "I'd remember."

"You weren't there. Not then. There were at least three, and at one point four, in the water." Alanna couldn't be wrong. More than Grady and Trevor jumped in the water. If she'd been wrong all this time, it changed everything.

That's why she'd left.

Why she'd abandoned her life on the island, her friends, her families. People had targeted Trevor, and she couldn't watch. Not when others joined in the race.

Chapter 16

After lunch Alanna hurried to the studio. If she'd hoped for her swirling thoughts to calm when surrounded by her mother's art, reality disappointed her.

Instead of peace, the longer she looked at the paintings, the more the belief her mom couldn't have painted them confronted her. One more piece of the truth she'd built that threatened to crumble at a touch. If she probed too hard, she didn't know what she'd find.

Life was supposed to be something she controlled. That's why she'd left. But as each day passed, God stripped another layer of the protective veneer she'd applied so carefully. Every illusion she'd created that coming to the island was risky but could be a break disappeared with the idea she had been wrong.

Wrong.

The word stuck in her throat.

Tourists flowed in and out of the shop, but it wasn't enough to still her roller-coaster thoughts. Each time she convinced herself Piper had it wrong, a wave of doubt assaulted her.

At five she had to escape. She turned off the lights and locked the front door.

"Where are you going?"

She stilled at Jonathan's voice as her pulse picked up. "I thought you had a picnic. And rehearsal dinner."

"I do and did. The bride had the rehearsal early. Wanted it in the same light as tomorrow's wedding. And I forgot something important. Dylan needs a kite with the wind like this." He held up a narrow package.

"Oh." She fumbled the keys to hide. He couldn't know she'd hoped he'd changed his mind and wanted to spend the evening with her. She couldn't lean on Jonathan. Not when she planned to leave and he had no plans to move. Not when he had Jaclyn and Dylan.

"Are you okay?"

She couldn't face him and his concern. He'd seen too much weakness already. She nodded, eyes on her keys. "Have a great time."

Jonathan stood a moment longer then nodded. As he stepped away, she glanced up. He didn't look back as he hurried toward Fort Mackinac. Why did she want him to so much? She grabbed her bike and pushed through the traffic until she could break free and pedal the rest of the way home.

The balance of the long weekend passed in a flood of tourists and avoidance. She didn't see Jonathan but didn't expect to between his picnic and wedding. Instead, she spent any moments not at the studio alone. After her experience with Piper, she couldn't stomach trying to find people to ask what they remembered about the accident. Not yet. Besides, all the visitors kept residents busy as they made the island memorable. In the tight economy, everyone needed the tourists to come, stay, and return again and again.

She pasted on a smile when at the studio and tried to settle into a book when home. By Monday night, she tired of moping. Patience Matthews had told her to check in, so she would. Alanna shuffled through the junk drawer for Mom's address book. After sifting through discarded keys, enough pens to equip Congress, and a stack of miscellaneous appliance guides, she finally found the thin spiral-bound book. Slipping to the *M*s, she found Patience's number.

"Mrs. Matthews?"

"Yes?"

"This is Alanna Stone."

"Have plans for tonight?"

Alanna looked at the frozen pizza she'd pulled out. "Not really."

"Good. We're getting ready to grill a few burgers and brats. Come on over."

"Can I bring anything?"

"Just yourself."

Alanna brushed her teeth then grabbed a gallon of lemonade and hopped on her bike. After zigzagging the island on roads most people would never discover, Alanna worked her way along Mackinac to the Matthews's cabin. A dilapidated hotel stood next to it, looking like the perfect setting for a horror movie or ghost. She bumped across the grass to the porch. After leaning her bike against the rail, she climbed the two stairs. She and Trevor had spent many summer days playing along the beach in front of the house with the Matthews kids. Now they'd left, and the rocky beach held a few kids who tripped into the water then screamed and ran out. Alanna shook her head. Crazy kids. The lake wouldn't be warm for at least a month. Even then, *warm* was a relative term.

The screen door bounced against the wall. "Alanna Stone."

Alanna turned to see Patience approaching her, arms wide open for a hug. She slid into the older woman's arms and sighed. She felt safe, protected.

"It's about time you got over here."

"I've only been on Mackinac a week."

"That's an eternity, and you know it. How many days did you spend over here growing up? It's practically your other home." Patience pulled back and studied Alanna. "You carry the burdens of the world still."

"Something like that."

"Well, burgers are coming off the grill, so first we eat."

Alanna followed Patience around the house to the backyard where a patio table waited adorned with a bucket of early flowers, platter of corn on the cob, and stacks of buns and condiments. The aroma of cooking meat colliding with early lilacs embraced Alanna. She inhaled and felt her muscles relax.

Earl Matthews pivoted from the grill. "Hey, girl. Still like them medium well?"

"Yes, sir. No mooing please."

He grinned and pulled the last burger off. After a prayer, they settled down and ate. When they finished, Earl scooped up the plates. "I'll leave you to catch up."

"I didn't mean to chase you away."

Patience made a brushing motion. "Don't worry. He has some DVD he wants to watch. One of those macho adventure movies." Patience grabbed the lemonade and refilled their cups. "So tell me what's worrying you."

"Have you seen Mom painting?"

"Lately? No, she's been gone." Patience looked at her with lines between her eyes.

"That's not. . ." Alanna tried again. "Has she done much painting around the island? You know, hauling all her paints and things around like she used to."

"Some, but she also said she didn't need to see it anymore since she's painted so much. I think her arthritis has bothered her, too. Must make holding a paintbrush challenging."

"Didn't she worry about capturing the light?" Mom had prided herself on following in the Impressionist line of chasing the light and capturing the ways it played.

"I'm no artist. That falls to your mom and brother."

"Right." Alanna took a sip of her lemonade, the tartness puckering her lips even as it cooled her throat. "Does anyone talk about. . ."

"That day?"

Heat climbed Alanna's throat. "Yes."

"Only occasionally. Days like the anniversary. Guess you missed that, huh?" When Alanna nodded, stomach tightening at the thought, Patience slid her chair closer. "You could have stayed. Everyone else did." She sighed. "You aren't the only one that day impacted. We all hurt. You can't have a tight-knit community like this without a death—especially tragic—impacting everyone. We've moved on. Even the Cadieuxs understand it was an accident. Exactly what happens when young men go crazy. They haven't figured out yet that life isn't guaranteed. The stunts I've seen." She shook her head. "Unfortunately, that one didn't end well."

The truth echoed through Patience's words. Running hadn't solved anything. Instead, all the emotions of that day exploded inside with each new turn or person confronted.

As she rode home, she prayed. She needed to find the truth, whether or not it was what she remembered.

It was time to let the truth set her free.

Alanna spent Tuesday morning evaluating how many paintings she'd sold during the weekend. If sales continued at this steady pace, the Painted Stone needed more large art.

Alanna hated the idea her mother would ship more paintings while Alanna continued to believe they were frauds. The only alternative was bare walls, and that wouldn't pay her father's medical bills.

Several times she had picked up the phone to call, only to be interrupted by customers. This morning she sat in the shop with her e-mail application open trying to form the words for an e-mail. Maybe that would make the tough questions easier to ask. At least then she wouldn't have to hear the hurt in Mom's voice when she took it as an accusation.

Mom, business has picked up. People have bought several paintings since I arrived. Which leads me to a question. . .

Alanna stared at the words. They would only make Mom defensive. She rubbed her temples as she considered how to rephrase the note.

The phone rang, and Alanna snatched it up. "The Painted Stone Studio."

"This is Gerald Tomkin."

She sighed and pushed back the thought that she should have let his call go to voice mail. "Good morning."

"Now that the holiday weekend is behind us, I hope you've had a chance to consider joining the foundation board."

The pounding in her temples intensified. "I'm honored.

But I'm an attorney. Wouldn't a CPA be more helpful?"

"You understand the island and its history. You'll understand what we're trying to do with the foundation better than some outsider who might have the right piece of paper. After all, you can't get into law school without brain power."

She bit back the urge to correct that fallacy. "I really don't plan to be here long."

"Mackinac will work its magic. I'm betting you stay." His cajoling wore down her defenses. It wasn't like she couldn't continue via e-mail and teleconferencing after she left. If she wanted.

"You're persistent."

"Part of my charm."

This sounded more like the man she remembered from school, convinced he was always right. . .and usually correct in that assumption. "All right. I'm happy to do what I can while I'm here." As for the rest, she'd wait and see how the meetings went.

"That's all I ask. See you tonight at seven thirty."

"What?"

He hung up before answering.

After the long weekend, the last thing she wanted was to spend the evening sitting at a table with people she barely knew and discuss business she didn't care about. No, she'd imagined a night with quiet music, a bit of candlelight, and a heaping bubble bath—lilac scented to match the flowers emerging across the island.

A ding from her computer pulled her attention from the burgeoning pity party. "Let this be good news." She crossed her fingers and moved the mouse to click on the envelope.

An e-mail from Trevor popped up, subject line reading *Ready for more?*

Increased ability to tell people no? Sure.

Added chances for true love? Certainly.

More peace and hope in her life? Absolutely.

But as she opened the e-mail, Alanna knew Trevor didn't mean any of those.

Hey, sis. Mom mentioned this weekend the studio might be low on paintings. Especially if you've sold more. You have, haven't you? I'll get some up there ASAP. I've got three or four medium-sized canvasses ready to ship as it is. And with a bit of nose to the grindstone this week could have another three ready to go. TTYS. Trevor.

She read and reread the words, a heavy sensation cloaking her.

The words confirmed in black and white Jonathan's accusations and her fears. What it didn't do was explain why. Dread shrouded her at the thought. Could she fix this?

Alanna looked out the window, wondering when Mom stopped and Trevor started painting. No wonder something felt different. He would have the feel for Mackinac, but his perspective would differ from Mom's. That would also explain the lack of geraniums. A guy wouldn't notice that detail. No matter how much he trained himself to copy her style, he wouldn't achieve perfection.

Jonathan walked by, and Alanna swiveled on her heel, hand to her face, and ducked beneath the counter. Maybe he hadn't seen her. The last thing she could handle at this moment was talking to him. He'd see right through her when he asked how she was. He always could.

After the three-day weekend, she didn't have the reserves

to pretend this latest twist didn't upset her. The rest of her family might not follow Christ, but she did—one good thing that came from leaving the island and heading south for college. She'd looked for friendship wherever she could find it, even in campus ministries. She hadn't expected to find Christ at the same time. How could she reconcile what they were doing? Was it even possible? Her gut told her it wasn't, which meant she'd have to confront them and figure out how to get them to understand why it mattered.

Alanna waited another moment. Surely Jonathan had continued on his way. After all, he'd had a busy weekend, too, with that wedding.

For years she'd imagined she'd marry long before her thirtieth birthday. Now she just avoided weddings. That was easier than seeing how close she'd inched to the date without even a boyfriend.

Boyfriend.

She puffed hair off her forehead with a breath. What a ridiculous word after a certain age. Namely anytime after college. Really, couldn't someone come up with anything better?

And who said thirty made her an old maid? She needed to get her nose out of a book and into the real world. A world where women married later and later. She deflated. It might work for them, but she'd imagined life with someone to share it with before adding a couple of kids to their union. In fact, that someone had been the man on the other side of the window for too long. But like it or not, he was taken—it was time to slay that vision permanently.

Maybe then she could move on and find her Prince Charming.

And maybe one day he would stop looking like Jonathan Covington each time she pictured him on his white horse.

Alanna's calf muscles tightened, and she groaned. Hiding here all day wouldn't work.

She inched her way up until she could see over the top of the counter. Her gaze locked with Jonathan's, where he stood looking in the window. Heat flooded her cheeks, and she sank back down.

Could things get worse?

Chapter 17

A hint of warmth touched the day as Jonathan headed down Market Street. The clock said it was time for lunch, and his stomach agreed. He ignored the fact he could have reached restaurants faster if he'd taken Main.

His path had nothing to do with passing the Painted Stone.

Yeah right. He shook his head but didn't alter course. If he happened to glance in that large window as he passed, it didn't mean anything.

Other than the fact he had a divided heart. He'd spent part of Sunday evening with Jaclyn and Dylan, and when his thoughts hadn't strayed to Alanna, he'd enjoyed it. But his mind wandered more as the picnic wore on.

He sidestepped a bike and frowned at the kid riding it. The sidewalks weren't the place for those. At least the island had emptied at the close of the long weekend. He had a couple of weeks until his next event, giving him plenty of time to plan and dream up business. If he could maintain focus. . .a big "if" right now.

Maybe he should find a replacement for Alanna and usher her to the ferry and off his island home. His peace had abandoned him the morning she showed up at the cottage. He didn't like being poised for any sound from her side of the tree line. Took all the relaxation out of being home. In fact, he might as well move down to a Main Street apartment.

He slowed at the studio, hands in his pockets, and looked

inside. A blur of motion by the counter caught his eye. He glanced around but didn't notice anyone in the Painted Stone. Maybe he should make sure Alanna was okay.

"Jonathan. Just the man I wanted to find."

"Hello, Gerald. Headed to lunch?"

The man patted his trim stomach. "In a bit. First, I need a favor."

Jonathan eyed him. What would it be this time? "If I can."

"Escort Alanna Stone to tonight's meeting." He eyed Jonathan like an eagle spies its prey. He must have found what he was looking for in Jonathan's expression. "I knew you wouldn't mind."

"There's a meeting tonight?" Jonathan scrambled for any plausible excuse to get out of going. Alanna wouldn't agree to anything Gerald asked. After all, she'd spent hours during the summers bemoaning what an awful teacher and principal he was.

"Got to finalize some plans for the lilac festival if we hope to raise any money. If we want to use your plan for the swing festival, we'll try out the process during the lilac festival."

Sounded like another way to get free services. Too bad he didn't have an out since he sat on the board. "I'll see what I can do."

"I knew you would. See you tonight."

Jonathan bit back the impulse to say, "Yes, sir," and turned back to the window. As he did, Alanna's blond head peeked above the counter. Had she hidden there this whole time?

He bit back a smirk. She must feel something, even if he merely annoyed her. It gave him a place to start.

He set his chin at a cocky angle and sauntered into the studio. All he missed was the fedora to pull off the Humphrey

Bogart air she'd always loved in those old black-and-white movies.

As the bell jingled, she stood and brushed the front of her shirt. Now that he looked more closely, she seemed to have adopted the style of one of those classic actresses. Boatneck T-shirt and pedal pushers, or whatever they called those short pants.

"Jonathan, you can't tell me you came here this often when my parents ran the studio." She crossed her arms, and a soft swipe of color lit her cheeks from the inside.

"Gerald asked me to escort you to tonight's foundation meeting."

"You don't need to do that." The color leeched from her cheeks.

"It's no problem." He leaned an elbow on the counter and invaded her personal space.

"Really, I'll be there without someone playing babysitter."

"Doesn't matter. I always keep my promises." He stood. He hadn't meant the jab that accompanied the words, yet by her stiffening, she'd caught it all the same. "I'll come at seven."

"But the studio is open until then."

"Not tonight." He shrugged as he moved toward the door. "You know how it is. Gerald snaps his fingers and gets what he wants."

Jonathan didn't have to look back as he left to feel the heat of her gaze.

After a full afternoon plotting with the manager at a local B&B that couldn't afford its own event planner, he scrubbed his face and then swiped his teeth with a toothbrush. The effort wasn't for Alanna. He needed to look his best if he wanted the foundation to hire him. And as he looked at his calendar, he needed the business to fill out his late summer. Otherwise it had the makings of a slim year. Unless he started working out of his cabin, he didn't have places left to cut back. Like it or not, Alanna had to come with him to the foundation. He couldn't afford annoying Gerald Tomkin.

He hurried down the stairs and onto the street. He needed to get to the studio before she left. Knowing her, she'd try to escape before he arrived.

The studio's lights flashed off as he approached. He waited in front, and a moment later Alanna opened the door and turned to lock it. She spun around then jumped back with a squeak.

"Jonathan!" She pressed a hand over her heart then reached out and smacked him. "Are you trying to scare me?"

He rubbed his chest and frowned. "No."

She sighed, and a bit of the stiffness eased from her shoulders. "Well you did. I really don't need you to baby-sit me."

He offered his arm. "I won't bite."

Alanna eyed his arm then decided it would be okay for the short walk. She filled the space with small talk as they walked to the foundation building. A few bikes lined the rack in front.

"How many people serve on the board?" Alanna licked her lips as she examined the bikes.

"Eight. The tried-and-true island lovers."

"So they'll all know me."

He heard the unsaid "and my history" and wanted to throttle her. "Someday you have to shed that, Alanna."

"Sure. As soon as men like Gerald Tomkin don't look at

me with knowing in their eyes. You have no idea what that's like. I've decided to find the truth so I can put that day behind me. It's time."

"More than time."

"I've heard you each time you've said that." She removed her hand from his arm and studied the building. "Might as well get this over with. Guess I have 'fool' stamped on my forehead."

"What?"

"There's no other reason I'd do this." She marched up the stairs, her flat slippers echoing against the wood.

"What about your heart to help anytime you can? You always jumped in to causes."

"I guess that hasn't changed." She said it with an eye roll, but he was glad. That was the part of her he'd first fallen in love with. Well, after her long legs and beautiful smile.

The moment she stepped through the door, Alanna knew she should leave. This wasn't where she wanted to be. Not now. Not with Jonathan next to her. They'd look like a couple to all the people who'd known her as a teen. But some things couldn't begin again, and she couldn't erase the past.

Instead of a reception area, there was a thin desk with a laptop and phone. In front of it sat two folding chairs. A short hallway fed off that room, and a light shone from a doorway.

"It's this way."

"I know." She brushed past Jonathan, only mildly regretting taking out her anxiety on him. He might not deserve it at the moment, but give him a few minutes, and he'd say or do something that would make her forget he could still be sweet.

As she entered the hall, the soft murmur of voices filtered toward her. She closed her eyes and sucked in a breath. *Help me do this, Lord.*

Steps approached the doorway, and a moment later Gerald Tomkin stepped in front of her. "There you are. I was about to call the cavalry."

"No worries. Jonathan ensured I got here."

"Even though she didn't need me." Jonathan stuck out his hand, and Mr. Tomkin gave it a quick pump.

"Come in, come in." He clapped his hands together as soon as they were in the room, and the conversations around the table ceased. "You remember Alanna Stone. She's agreed to fill her dad's spot on the board until he returns."

A few folks had the courtesy to wear pasted-on smiles, but Alanna sensed they wanted her here even less than she wanted to join them. She studied Mr. Tomkin's profile. Why would he insist?

She glanced around the table and smiled when she reached Mr. Hoffmeister. "I didn't know you were on the board."

"From time to time." He patted the vacant chair next to him. "I do my part."

Alanna squeezed around the oak table and slid into the chair. "Thanks."

"You need to come back by the shop."

"Maybe now that the weekend's over. Bet you sold lots of fudge."

"Enough." He pointed his chin at Mr. Tomkin standing at the head of the table. "He'll keep us here all night if we aren't vigilant."

"Sounds fun."

The older man snorted then shook his head. "You always did have a sharp way with words."

If he only knew. That's one thing that made her effective in the courtroom, but not so much in the studio.

The meeting started, and Alanna held back her surprise when Jonathan didn't sit at the table. Instead, he leaned against the wall, a position that looked more uncomfortable as the meeting droned on and he stifled a yawn. Alanna shifted against the seat, frowning as the faux leather squeaked. She felt like a kid again, trapped in another of Mr. Tomkin's unending classes. It didn't look like he intended to have any more mercy on her now than he did then.

A yawn stretched her mouth, and she snagged a glance at her watch. Nine o'clock? No wonder it felt like she'd sat there forever and a day. She slumped back against the headrest.

"Are we boring you, Alanna?" Mr. Tomkin's pointed words jerked her upright.

"No, sir."

"Good. Is there any other business?" He looked around the room, but everybody shook their heads until he reached Bette Standeford. "Yes?"

"I thought we planned to discuss Mr. Covington's proposal."

"That's at the next meeting."

Jonathan straightened at his words, and a frown tugged his face down. "If we wait, I won't have enough time to get everything implemented."

"Tonight we have to focus on the lilac festival. We've got to raise some money, or there won't be anything left to give."

Mr. Hoffmeister leaned close to Alanna, the rich scent of chocolate making her stomach rumble. "That I don't understand."

"What?"

"I thought there was extra in the account before he took over." Hoffmeister rubbed his eyes. "I've never much liked numbers. But Gerald's comments have me rethinking the books."

Mr. Tomkin cleared his throat. "Anything you'd like to share, Tony?"

Mr. Hoffmeister skewered Mr. Tomkin with a glare before waving his hand. "Not at the moment."

"We'll wait with bated breath."

"I bet you will," Mr. Hoffmeister muttered under his breath then glanced at Alanna. "Sorry about that. We can't seem to have a civil conversation anymore thanks to his stupid house plans. The island has clear requirements for houses. . .but he's above it all." He stopped as if catching himself. "Well, come visit me."

Alanna nodded, keeping her eyes trained on her old teacher. "Not tonight."

"As soon as you can. There are things we should discuss." He stood and edged toward the door. "See you at the next meeting. These old bones have to get home if I'm going to work tomorrow. If you need me, you know where to find me."

The others took that as their opportunity to escape, too. In a few minutes, the room had emptied, but Alanna remained. Where before she thought the meeting would never end, now she wondered what game Mr. Tomkin was up to and why he'd insisted she attend.

Chapter 18

T here's something I don't understand."

Mr. Tomkin didn't turn from where he stood at the whiteboard working the eraser back and forth across the smooth surface. Alanna waited a moment. Why ignore her?

"You don't need me." She glanced around the now-empty boardroom. "The brightest people who live here serve on the board. I don't add anything."

"You're wrong." He turned toward her and propped his hands on the table. A furrow lined the top of his nose. "Something strange is going on, and we need someone who can dig."

"Why me? I've been gone years. You're the local stalwart."

"True." Something glinted in his expression as he leaned closer. "It has drawbacks. I've made my share of enemies. People who think I created the problems. You're an outsider, just what we need."

She could see that. The man seemed pricklier under the surface than when she'd known him. "I really don't have time. . .and won't be here long."

"Sure you do. What do you have to do after the studio closes. . .unless you're spending all your time with Covington?" She bristled as his tone scraped over her. He crossed his arms and stared her down. "Even then this doesn't require much. Just the skills lawyers have. Here." He walked to a stack of books. "I just need you to review these."

Alanna looked down at her stenographer's notebook. As he'd talked, she'd doodled a series of interlocking circles. That summed up life on Mackinac. The island was small enough the people and events that tried to remain separate ended up bound together, like the ripples a stone makes in the water circling ever outward.

He must have noticed her distraction. He sighed. "It's late now. I'll stop by tomorrow with these."

"All right." She'd like to stop him, but he'd aroused her curiosity. She wanted to know what those books contained.

A stiff wind blew off the lake as she exited the building. Twilight had melted into darkness, and she wished she'd grabbed her bike rather than walking. Now she'd have to swing by the studio before working her way home. She glanced around, half expecting Jonathan to be waiting near the streetlight, but he wasn't. She shook away the disappointment. He hadn't promised he'd wait. She'd hoped though.

She stuck to Main Street where there would be more people and the streetlights cast wide circles of light. Soon the sound of music slipped from the restaurants, and a man stumbled from the first one she passed.

"Hey, gorgeous. Just who I was looking for." He tripped into her path, and she stepped onto the street to avoid him. One of the taxis pulled to a quick stop behind her, and she raised a hand in apology as she continued on her way. She kept her steps quick and her eyes locked in front of her as she stepped back on the sidewalk. Many of the stores were dark, and she wished for a bit more traffic as she heard the man bumbling behind her. His movements didn't sound co-ordinated enough to be a threat, but she kept her eyes peeled for a police officer on bicycle.

Even though she'd decided to discourage Jonathan, right about now she'd love to have him beside her. His strong presence and broad shoulders would deter many from bothering her.

Now she felt exposed. Vulnerable. Alone.

A shiver skittered up her spine, and she picked up her pace. Light poured from several more restaurants, but still no sign of an officer. As she passed I'm Not Sharing Fudge Shop, she glanced in. Mr. Hoffmeister sat on his stool talking to someone on the phone. She waved, but he didn't notice.

Alanna picked up her pace and crossed the street. She glanced over her shoulder and saw the drunk slouched beneath a lightpost. While his posture said inebriated, his gaze had locked on her. She tossed her hair and scurried around the corner out of his line of sight. Once she reached her bike, she could leave him far behind and hurry home. Did he have anything to do with what happened in her storage shed? She shook the thought free.

All she wanted was the sanctuary inside her childhood home.

Jonathan let the night embrace him as he sat on the rocking chair. His heavy fleece parka kept him warm in the cool air as long as he buried his hands in its pockets. The house next door looked empty from what he could tell through the trees. Should he have waited?

Maybe he'd misinterpreted her signals that she wanted him to leave her alone.

It rankled, but he'd honor it. Didn't mean he had to relax before she made it home. He'd feel ridiculous if she'd slipped in and was tucked in her bed sound asleep while he played night watchman. He could think of a few choice things to call himself, including fool.

He rubbed his neck where the breeze snuck under his collar. Kind of like how Alanna had slipped under his guard. Amazing how one could spend eleven years actively forgetting someone, only to have the walls tumble down the moment she reappeared.

The cicadas sang their lullaby, loud and in tune. The faint scent of pine slipped around him as the trees rustled. He glanced at the Indiglo symbols on his watch. He'd give her fifteen more minutes then call to make sure he hadn't missed her.

The evening had wasted his time, plain and simple. He couldn't identify Gerald's game, but it annoyed him. He'd joined the foundation board before Gerald became president. Ever since he could make better use of his time at home. Then to have Gerald delay any decision on his proposal. . .Jonathan had to force his anger back. He wouldn't jump too many more times for the man.

In fact, if he invested more time in working with the island's many bed-and-breakfasts, he'd land plenty of new projects. And it wouldn't mean the silly games the older man threw around in some twisted power play. Come on, this was a small town on a small island. There were much bigger things to invest his time in than a tug-of-war over who had the last say.

Something crunched on the road. He stood and took a step to the edge of the porch. Was that Alanna?

He toyed with acting nonchalant and ignoring the sound, but he needed to know she was okay. Gerald had something on her, but Jonathan didn't think she knew it yet.

He rubbed his hands over his head. Time to get a

haircut. But that would mean stopping by the Grand and seeing Jaclyn. Right now he didn't want the complication. He bit back a yawn. When had she become a complication in his life?

He didn't want to answer, so he walked down the path to the road. His steps crunched through the debris of fallen leaves and branches. He wouldn't sneak up on whoever worked their way up the road. It was too dark to see much, except what the small light on the approaching bike illuminated. The bike turned onto the drive to the Stone home.

Slowly he released a breath. At least now he knew she was home. He glanced at his watch again and frowned. Alanna shouldn't be this late. What could he do? She didn't want him to be her protector.

"Jonathan?" The word carried like a whisper over the stillness.

The song of peepers filled the quiet. In the morning, he should get down to the pond, see what changes had occurred as spring reached the island. Sounds crunched his direction, and he waited.

A soft sigh filtered toward him, and Alanna leaned against the split-wood fence lining the road.

"Long night?"

"Long week." Her shoulders were pushed forward as if by unseen forces. "I never should have come back."

Not this old argument. He'd tired of it. "Really? We all face the past."

"But I'm learning things. Things that change what I've always thought." She scrubbed her face with her hands. "I'm not making sense. That's part of the problem. Nothing adds up."

Jonathan considered the faint outline of her profile. Her shoulders slumped in a defeated slant. He stepped closer as he thought about how to respond. "Have you talked to your mom?"

"No." She snorted. "Reaching her right now is like calling the president. No one's answering when the number's mine." She pulled straight. "Can I ask you a question?"

He nodded then realized she might not be watching. "Sure."

"What would you do if you caught your family in a lie? One that doesn't necessarily hurt anybody, but it's still a lie?"

"Depends."

She didn't respond at first, but he held his tongue. How much did she want to know what he thought?

"That's the great wisdom you have to offer?"

He turned toward her and brushed his fingers along her jaw, noting the way she shivered. "Alanna, there's a lot about my family I would change. Some days we get along, other days we can hardly stand each other. But we're family. So I put up with some things. Most of what we do impacts nobody else. If my sister did something that hurt others, then I'd have to say something. Or if she hurt herself, I'd speak up. It's part of being family."

"But it's not hurting anyone else." Her words didn't have the fierceness that came with conviction. "And I can't anticipate the consequences."

"What do you mean, consequences?"

"I'm not sure." She sighed and pulled back from his touch. His fingers felt chilled by her absence. "But that's my problem."

"You're an attorney. A good one. You can figure out the

consequences. But I think you already know what you need to do."

"It doesn't mean I like it."

He chuckled at the fight in her tone. "True. But aren't families worth fighting for?"

She pushed from the fence and took a step toward home. "Thanks."

"That's what friends are for."

"Yeah, friends." She brushed hair from her face as she paused a few steps away. "I've meant to ask, did you ever catch Grandpappy?"

Her question surprised him. Grandpappy? "You remember that old fish?"

"The one that always got away?" A smile colored her words. "Of course. I take it you never caught him?"

"I didn't have my good-luck charm."

"I haven't been that for a long time." She leaned forward and kissed his cheek. "Good night, Jonathan."

Jonathan stood there, rooted by the sensation of her quick kiss as she melted into the shadows. How much closeness could he handle?

The sound of her bike moving up to the house followed by the click of her door echoed in the stillness. He leaned against the fence as waves of memories crashed over him. The times they'd sat on the small dock "fishing" as an excuse to spend time together. He'd use worms while she pretended to fish with marshmallows. They'd sit shoulder to shoulder, ready to reel in the fish that lived in the pond, the descendants of the fish he and his grandpa had initially stocked the pond with.

At the time, he'd thought they'd spend the rest of their

lives shoulder to shoulder, taking on the world.

Another dynamic duo. Poised to change the world.

Then life happened. The world changed.

And so did they.

Chapter 19

Alanna leaned against the door. What had she been thinking? Kissing Jonathan, even if on the cheek?

She covered her face with her hands and sank to the floor. She felt drained, exhausted. Yet her mind whirled. If she didn't get some rest, the next day would be a nightmare. But all she could think of was her ridiculous question. Grandpappy? The island had muddled her brain. Why else would she ask about a fish? A fish?

That sealed it. If Jonathan hadn't already decided he was better off without her, she'd left no doubts. Who would want to be with a woman who focused on a fish that had probably died years ago when her family overflowed with liars? Especially when she wasn't sure she wanted to confront them and bring the truth to light.

Her mind hurt from the implications. At some point her mom had started selling her brother's art as hers. She must add her signature to the corner after the paintings arrived. Alanna didn't know whether she should hope Trevor knew about it or if she wanted him to be oblivious to the fact the paintings weren't sold as his. But she couldn't imagine her mom doing something like that.

Alanna pulled her knees up and lowered her forehead to rest on top of them. Cold seeped through the floor into her seat, but she didn't move.

Her parents had dragged them to church growing up, but the extent of any faith seemed to end at the church doors. And many cold winter mornings, it had been easier to stay home than trek via snowmobile. It wasn't until she started college and searched for answers to the mess of her life that she found a personal relationship with God.

In the years since, she hadn't probed the depths of her parents' faith. In the short pockets of time she had with them, it hadn't seemed important. Now. . .

Now she wished she'd pushed.

Because as things stood, she couldn't imagine how to start the conversation. *So, Mom, how long have you defrauded the world?* That couldn't end well.

God, give me wisdom.

A way to turn the problem around existed. She just needed to think creatively. That's how she handled clients' legal problems. Look at the situation from every possible angle. Examine it until she could finally find one that minimized the potential problems. The one that put them in the best possible position.

That's what she'd do. Pretend her family was her client. For the moment, she'd ignore the fact that if she truly represented them, she'd have to choose, since a conflict existed between her mom and brother. That complicated the matter too much.

A yawn stretched her mouth to the point her jaw popped. Tomorrow she'd research the legal issues. Now she'd sleep.

The next morning when the shop stood quiet, Alanna turned on the computer and prepared to dive into the legal issues. Each time Alanna opened the search engine, her fingers froze, poised over the keys. If she started searching, she'd confirm the problem. She clicked over to LexisNexis and entered a search string. Hundreds of cases pulled up. This could take forever. She glanced around the studio. Guess it was a good thing the shop remained empty.

Alanna pulled up the first case and scanned the facts. Not relevant. She'd worked her way through the first twenty when the door opened.

Police Chief Ryan stopped just inside the door. "Miss Stone."

"Hello, Chief." She swallowed and tried to smile. "Do you know anything?"

"The trap was wiped clean. Without something there, we don't have much to investigate."

"Nobody else have an unpleasant surprise like this?"

"No, ma'am."

Alanna nodded. "Thank you for letting me know."

"Easy enough to do. Wish I had better news." He slipped back out the door before Alanna could say anything else.

She turned back to the cases and read a few more before the door opened again.

"Good morning, sweetheart."

Alanna's head jerked up at her mother's voice. "Mom?"

"Yes, ma'am. In the flesh." Rachelle Stone looked like a radiant rose with her strawberry-blond hair piled in a loose chignon and an evergreen trench coat laced tight around her waist. Only the dark circles under her violet eyes gave any indication of her trials.

"What are you doing here? Why aren't you with Dad?"

"Trevor's with him." A cloud sailed across Mom's face before she painted on another smile. "There's nothing I can do for him, and we're boring each other. The space will do us good. Besides, Trevor said you needed more art. Guess he's tracked sales."

"You can do that?"

"I can't. But he can. He's much savvier about technology." Her mother waved a hand in the air then pulled off her gloves. "The Internet still baffles me."

Alanna pulled in a deep breath. Was this God's answer to her prayers? Sending her mom? "I'm glad you're here."

"I certainly hope so." Mom loosened the floral scarf from around her neck. "I am your mother, and this is my home."

"Yes." Alanna bit her lip. "I have some things I need to talk about."

The door opened again, and Mom spun on the heel of her pointed boot. "Ah, good." She stepped toward the employee of the ferry service. "I trust you were gentle with the paintings?"

"Always am, Mrs. Stone."

"That's why I like you."

Alanna rolled her eyes as her mother practically tweaked the grown man's cheek, and he blushed. When had Mom developed this larger-than-life personality?

The man stacked the boxes against the wall, leaning each carefully next to the others. Alanna couldn't wait to explore the contents even as she dreaded discussing them with her mom. What if Mom hauled them in back and added signatures?

Alanna closed the window on the computer. No need explaining her search to Mom. A few minutes later, Mom pressed a bill into the man's hand, and he tipped his hat as he headed out with a whistle. Mom studied the stack of boxes.

"I really should have asked him to haul these to the back. Shortsighted of me." She brushed a hand across her brow, and Alanna saw a flash of worry. "It's amazing how quickly one loses the routine."

Alanna slipped around the counter and hurried to Mom. She hugged her, concerned about how pronounced her shoulder blades felt. "I'm sorry about everything with Dad. How is he?"

"Good as can be expected. That's what the doctors like to say. 'But it's going to be a long recovery.'" She bracketed the words then slumped. "The doctors are saying months. We'll miss the whole season."

"The whole season?"

"Yes, couldn't do it without your help."

Alanna swallowed hard as Mom sank deeper into her hug. "I can't stay that long. I'll be lucky to last another week, maybe two, before the partners demand my return."

"We need you here."

"I have a job."

"We're your family." Mom pushed away and studied Alanna. "You've hidden long enough. I wouldn't be surprised if one good that comes from this is you giving up your ridiculous phobia of Mackinac."

"Mom. Maybe Trevor could come. Take care of the studio when I need to leave."

"You know he can't do that." Mom planted her hands on her hips and jutted her chin out. "He can't until everything's cleared up. You, on the other hand, have acted like a child long enough. He had to endure two years of people looking at him like he should have died rather than Grady. You left for college. You weren't involved in the stunt like he was."

"It's not that simple. Besides, I don't think anyone else still thinks about it like we do. Maybe we're fixated."

"Don't muddy the water, young lady. Your experience is not your brother's."

The door opened, and Alanna looked up, hoping for some relief from the intense conversation. Her heart sank as Mr. Tomkin entered.

"Rachelle."

Her mother spun around and stiffened. "Gerald."

"I heard you were back." Alanna didn't like the way he studied her mother.

"I see the grapevine still works."

"You haven't been gone that long."

Alanna leaned forward as her mother muttered, "Not long enough."

"Is there anything we can do for you?" Alanna took a step and slid between the two. The vibes between them were odd. Uncomfortable. She searched her memory for any reason but came up empty.

Mr. Tomkin smiled at her in a manner that looked more like a grimace. "I said I'd come by last night." He tapped the briefcase pinched under his arm. "These are the ledgers."

"Gerald, Alanna's not back to give you legal advice."

"You're the only one she can help?" There was something about the way he said it that worried Alanna. Like he knew about the paintings. "How's your arthritis, Rachelle?"

Alanna pointed at the briefcase. "I can't promise anything, but I'll look."

He strode to the counter, and Alanna joined him.

"I'll carry these back." Mom fluttered a hand at the stack of paintings, a pointed look shooting from Alanna to the paintings and back.

"This won't take long," Alanna emphasized.

Gerald opened the case and spread the papers across the counter then wiped his hands down his shirt. "These spreadsheets tell the story."

The numbers swam in orderly rows across the pages. Alanna stared at them as her eyes glazed over. If she'd wanted to study spreadsheets for hours, she would have taken the CPA exam.

"Don't you see?"

"I see lots of numbers." She moved a hand across the pages. "I need context."

"A few months ago, we held elections, and I became president of the foundation." He held up his hands. "Look, I didn't want the position, but it's a small island. There aren't many people to volunteer for jobs like this."

That made sense.

"First thing, I sat down with the books. I've had to balance budgets at the school for years. If the books aren't good, you're in trouble before you even start. Besides, I needed to know if we had anything to give away. The foundation's still new—about five years old. Enthusiasm's high, but people's dreams are often bigger than their pocketbooks."

"So what did you find?"

"That's the thing. Something's fishy. See here." He picked up a spreadsheet and pointed to a couple of columns. "From what I can see, there's an account here that doesn't match any the board approved. The policy is that after the board approves a grant, the bookkeeper opens an account. Then each time a check is issued, it's entered here." He pointed at another line. "I've identified six accounts totaling about twenty-five thousand dollars that I don't think are valid. I had my bookkeeper look at things, and she can't figure out why those accounts are there."

"Then what do you think I'll find?"

"Not sure, but you're smart and you aren't involved. I

need proof that something is wrong before I say anything. Hoffmeister was the president before me, and with the bad feelings between us, I must have solid proof before I say a word." He pulled the pages into a stack and slid them into the folder. "Here you go. Technically, there's still money in the accounts. But I'm nervous about making disbursements until I have a better sense of where that twenty-five thousand went and whether we'll get it back. That's the big reason I keep postponing action on Jonathan's proposal. He's got good ideas. But. . .if we don't have the money, we can't add anything."

Mom came back and grabbed another box. "No need to dramatize everything, Gerald."

"We've got a problem here."

"Maybe, but you're just asking Alanna to confirm suspicions. She can do it if she wants. You always said she was the smartest student you ever had." She dragged the box a few feet down the hall.

Alanna wished she were as certain as Mom. The thought of spending her evenings poring over pages of numbers sounded as much fun as having her wisdom teeth yanked. "I'm not a forensic accountant."

"Who said anything about CSI?" Gerald picked up the folder and shoved it into her stomach. "Just take it. You'll find a way." His gaze followed her mom until she disappeared down the hall.

This really wasn't as complex as any of her cases. She could spend a few evenings on it. "All right. I'll see what I can do." Alanna stared at the papers she really didn't want to accept. Guess she knew how she'd spend her free time for a while.

Chapter 20

The day had evolved from one call to a dozen e-mails to a large crisis. By the time five o'clock arrived, Jonathan couldn't wait to lock the door and escape. Tonight he'd pick up a few things at the deli then head home and sit on the dock. Maybe he'd catch Grandpappy this time.

A smile crooked the corner of his mouth at the thought. All the times he'd fished, he'd stopped looking for that old catfish years ago. Guess every fisherman had to have the one that always got away.

But Alanna remembered.

If she dredged up that memory, there must be more—important things—she recalled.

When he reached the cabin, he shoved the grocery items in the fridge and strolled to the dock. He collected his fishing gear from the small shed and plopped down on the edge. The shadows from the trees edged along it, playing a cold game of peekaboo with him. Maybe he should wait for a day when he could fish before dusk shadowed the dock.

Still, he sat there a minute.

Had Alanna figured out what was wrong with the paintings? What would he do if she did? He only had guesses. But based on her intensity, he had a feeling she'd uncovered the fraud.

Now the question was what she would do about it. He was just glad he wasn't in her place. He only had to delay Mr. Morris. She'd been thrust into the family business, tasked to keep it running, and faced with the unknown. All while wrestling the past—alone.

He marveled that Alanna hadn't married yet. Surely through law school and her career she'd met men who shared her goals and ambition. Maybe her experience with love mirrored his. Disappointment that couldn't be overcome. Close but never a fit. He enjoyed Jaclyn, but it wasn't love. He shifted on the dock and fed bait on the hook. Thrust the pole to the side and swung it forward, watching the line spool out.

The dock shook, and he stilled.

A minute later Alanna settled next to him. "Mom's here."

"What brought her back?"

"Other than spending time with her daughter?" Alanna bumped his shoulder with hers. He stilled at her playfulness, wondering if it was forced. She sighed, a sound that seemed to come from her toes. "She brought paintings."

Oh. He chewed his lower lip. "That's good, right? Means you sold some."

"I guess." She ran a hand through her bobbed hair. "I'm not sure what to do with them. How to address the paintings with her."

"Family can be tough."

"You have no idea." Alanna turned her gaze from the water to him. "Why did you move here? You could go anywhere."

I waited for you. But he couldn't say that. . .not without scaring her off or sounding like a fool. Instead, he shrugged. "I always liked it. When an opportunity came to buy the event-planning business from Mom and Dad, it made sense. I'd done a bit of that for a small Christian university and was ready for a new challenge."

"Has it lived up to your expectations?"

He tugged the line and watched the bobber dance. "Yeah. It's hard work, but most days I enjoy it. There's something special about bringing someone's vision to life. Speaking of, I need to talk to your mom about that commissioned painting."

Alanna stood and brushed her khakis off. "I don't know."

"She'd appreciate the extra money."

"What if she's not painting?" Alanna sealed her lips and grimaced. Did she want to reclaim the words that hovered in the silence?

"You figured it out?"

She nodded. The sound of birds rustling in the trees drifted around them as he studied her locked jaw. After a minute, she shuddered then looked at him. "But what am I supposed to do with that? I have no idea when it started. I don't know what to do with the paintings she brought today. I can't be a party to lying. . .but how do I fix it?" A tear slipped down her cheek. "I'm not even sure they'll realize it's wrong. And if I don't handle this right, Mom could land in serious trouble."

Jonathan considered his words. Did she want to be heard, or did she want his opinion? "Have you talked to her?"

"Mr. Tomkin arrived with his set of trouble before I broached the topic."

"Start with her. See what she says before you get too worked up."

She swiped at the tear and gave a watery smile. "Too late for that."

"What does it hurt?"

"You're right." Alanna swallowed. "Guess God gave me

the perfect opportunity. We'll be face-to-face rather than over the phone or e-mail. He seems to be loading my plate pretty full."

"Deal with your mom first. She's a great lady. I can't imagine it's anything so horrible you can't work it out."

"I hope so. I'll let you get back to catching Grandpappy." She started toward land then turned. "What are you doing for supper?"

"What bachelors do. Making a sandwich or something easy."

"Come over. Mom's making pasta, and she'll make enough for a small army. Say in an hour?"

"As long as you won't use me as an excuse not to talk."

"Are you kidding? You'll be our buffer." She smiled then turned and hurried toward her home.

Jonathan watched her a minute. She might be upset, but she was still the most beautiful woman he knew. And she'd found a strong faith.

An hour later he wandered around the fence separating their yards, holding an island guidebook. He hadn't been sure what to bring, and none of his grandma's flowers bloomed yet, though he'd seen some around the island. Another couple of days and the lilacs would color the world with beautiful fragrance but for now provided nothing for his hostesses. He couldn't wait to see Alanna's face at his offering.

He slipped around the back of the house. Mrs. Stone had told him to use the back door after he showed up one too many times at the front. Mrs. Stone opened the door before he knocked.

"Jonathan. We've missed you. You taking good care of my girl?" A mischievous light glinted in her eyes.

"Trying."

She laughed. "That I understand. She's an independent one."

"Mom, I'm right here."

"I'm not saying anything I haven't told you." Rachelle turned back to him. "I'm glad you came. One of Alanna's better ideas."

"Mom. . ."

Jonathan chuckled at Alanna's exasperated tone. In some ways, the clock rolled back to before Grady died. These two always picked at each other in this good-natured manner. At the time, he'd assumed that's what teenage girls and their moms did. Now he decided it must be moms and daughters. He leaned down and kissed Rachelle's cheek. "Thanks for letting me invade."

"I haven't been gone long enough to forget those crazy meals you called real food."

"What can I say? Cooking's not my thing."

"That's an understatement." Rachelle ushered him into the cozy kitchen. "Make yourself at home. We'll be ready to eat in a bit."

Alanna turned from her station near the sink where she shredded lettuce into a large bowl. "What do you have?"

Jonathan patted the cover of the book after he placed it on the granite island. "Just a guidebook."

Alanna stepped closer, her nose wrinkling as she read the title. "A guidebook to Mackinac? Don't you think I know everything there is to know? I grew up here."

"Sure. But aren't people notorious for missing the things in their own backyards? Thought you might enjoy flipping through it."

"In all my spare time?"

"Exactly." He matched her grin. Alanna finished the salad while he stood and filled glasses with filtered water from the fridge. Wonderful, tangy aromas filled the room, tomato tinged with Italian seasoning and garlic. Rachelle shoved a pan of garlic bread in the oven and then dumped a pile of pasta in a colander in the sink. "Anything else I can do?"

"Sit down and get out of the way, young man." Rachelle winked at him as she turned back to the oven and checked the toast. "So tell me what's happened while I've been gone."

"Did Alanna tell you about what happened here?"

"No."

Jonathan explained about the shed. "I'm not sure if the police learned anything."

"Alanna, you need to move down to the apartment when I leave. We can't have you out here alone. I've never heard of anything like this happening."

Alanna glared at him. "It's not anything to get upset about, Mom. I talked to the police chief when he stopped by. It looks like a one-time event with nothing for them to follow." She tossed carrots and cheese into the salad with a little more force than necessary and then added a few cherry tomatoes on top. She set it on the table and then sank onto the stool catty-corner from him. Circles darkened the skin beneath her eyes, highlighting the worry that crowded out the joy he'd seen earlier.

After another minute, Rachelle turned from the stove. "We're ready."

She carried a bowl filled with bow-tie pasta and marinara sauce to the small, round table. After placing it in the center, she took a seat in front of a bank of windows overlooking the pond.

Jonathan loved being in this kitchen, embraced by this family. When his parents' marriage had fallen apart, he'd known he could count on the Stones to love deeply. Now he wanted to be there for them, though he'd leave the instant Alanna asked. The idea she even wanted him there for the conversation surprised him. Miss Independent might not be so sure of herself after all.

Mrs. Stone started passing the bowls of food. "Forgot the salad dressing. Still like ranch, Jonathan?"

"You haven't been gone that long, ma'am."

She smiled at his mirrored words and popped to her feet to retrieve a bottle from the fridge before handing it to him. He poured a generous amount on top of the lettuce.

Alanna snickered. "Like some salad with that dressing?"

"You know it."

"You always have buried the good stuff."

"Only way to eat it." Man, he loved the banter. But he hated how it reinforced the silence that waited at his cabin. Most days it didn't bother him, but now that Alanna had returned, the echoes seemed highlighted.

Easy conversation filled the spaces, but Jonathan could sense Alanna's hesitation. He glanced at her, and her eyes held a slightly panicked edge as she met his gaze. He nudged her under the table, and she took a deep breath.

"Mom, I need to ask you something."

Rachelle looked at her. "Of course."

Stillness cloaked the room until Alanna shifted on her chair.

Rachelle placed her napkin on the table and put her hand on Alanna's. "What's going on, honey? You've always been able to talk to me. Is this about you and Jonathan?"

Alanna's eyes widened. "I wish it were that easy."

Jonathan sat back and crossed his arms. "Hey."

"You know what I mean." Alanna frowned at him and then turned to her mom. "I don't know where to start."

"The beginning is usually the best place. As long as you aren't pregnant, this should be simple."

Chapter 21

"Pregnant?" Heat flashed up Alanna's cheeks as she buried her face in her hands. Leave it to her mother to go to such a ridiculous place. "Mother!"

Jonathan snickered and coughed across the table. She glared at him, longing for nothing more than an opportunity to smack him upside the head. . .after she shook her mother. He cleared his throat and pressed his napkin against his face. "Sorry."

"Sure you are." She turned back to her mom. "Seriously? Pregnant?"

"Well, you are almost thirty. You wouldn't be the first woman to give up on finding the right man. Just tell me it wasn't that last boyfriend of yours. What was his name? Scott?"

"Spencer, Mom." Alanna rolled her eyes. All of a sudden, bringing up the forgeries didn't seem quite so daunting. "This isn't about me. And I'm not pregnant."

"Then what's it about? Good gravy, you acted like it had something to do with a death."

She sucked in a breath and squared her shoulders. Now or never. "Mom, those paintings you brought to the studio today. Did you paint them?"

Her mom's gaze darted from Alanna to Jonathan and back again. "What?"

Jonathan leaned forward, but Alanna stopped him with a stare. "Don't even. . ."

He smirked but put his hands up. "This is all you, Alanna.

In fact, I'll leave if you like."

"No you don't." She pinned his foot under the table and turned back to Mom. "We have to talk about the studio."

"So talk." Confusion flashed across Mom's face and colored her violet eyes. "But why would you question who painted them?"

"Because the paintings aren't right." Alanna's tongue refused to cooperate further.

"I didn't notice anything today. In fact, I like how you pulled out some of the unframed pieces. Setting them at lower price points was a good idea. Makes them more accessible."

"The problem is"—Jonathan interrupted, and Alanna didn't know whether to hug or slug him—"we're not sure who painted some of them." As her mother began to sputter, he held up his hand. "That's a problem, because I'm sending potential clients your way, but they want to buy one of your paintings. Not one with your signature."

As Jonathan explained, Alanna couldn't help wondering if he'd figured it out, how many others had. The damage-control potential numbed her.

Mom looked between the two of them then laughed, a high, shrill noise. "You can't be serious." She paused then frowned. "You are. I can't believe my own daughter and a man who's practically a son would insinuate such things."

"Then tell me they're yours. That you painted each stroke and didn't add your name at the end." Alanna refused to back down even as a bright red flushed her mother's face. "Tell me the canvasses you brought today weren't painted by Trevor."

"Of course I did." Mom tipped her nose in the air as she studied them. "What else would I do?"

Alanna swallowed her disappointment. Her mother had

just lied. Without blinking. "Then why did Trevor e-mail asking if I was ready for more of his paintings?"

"We. . .your father and I. . .have discussed for years adding some of his paintings. Maybe Trevor thought he could push you into doing it." Mom rolled her shoulders. "I'm sure that's all. Why would I stop painting? I've always loved it."

"I don't know. Maybe arthritis has made it difficult. Patience mentioned it's flared up. Jonathan, too. And he has clients who want to commission one of your pieces. Trevor's good, but he's not you. Anyone who knows your work can tell. Jonathan figured it out. There could be others."

Her mother turned to Jonathan, ice in her eyes. "Explain what you mean when you say the paintings aren't mine."

"They don't have your passion, your vibrant use of color. The emotion is missing from them."

"Pshaw. That doesn't mean anything."

"But it does when your signature element is missing." He leaned closer to Mom. "Rachelle, Trevor doesn't place the warbler in each painting. I had to look a long time before I identified that. Yours always have the warbler tucked in a tree near the front."

Alanna stared at him, amused he'd found a marker she hadn't. "They also don't have your usual nod to the Grand Hotel."

"My what?"

"The red geraniums." Alanna shrugged. "And I've never seen a winter scene. You love color too much."

"Maybe I decided to try something new."

Jonathan shook his head. "I don't think so."

Alanna watched the exchange, noting the softness in Jonathan's expression as he engaged Mom.

"Well, it's too bad I can't catch the last ferry. You've made me feel quite unwelcome in my own home." Rachelle pushed to her feet. "I'll leave the cleanup for you."

Alanna watched her mother stalk down the hallway. She groaned and covered her face with her hands.

"I'd say that went well."

"What?" Alanna parted her fingers and stared at him as if he'd gone crazy. "That went well? My mother is furious and ready to leave. That's a rousing success?"

"You don't need to yell."

"Oh, I feel like it." She looked at the ceiling. "That's not how it's supposed to go, God."

Jonathan looked around, a worried crinkle at the corner of his eyes.

"What?"

"Praying I don't get caught in the fire when lightning flashes."

"Har, har." Alanna tried to keep her voice strict but failed miserably. "What will I do?"

"Pray, and knowing you like I do, come up with a brilliant plan to fix everything."

Alanna shook her head. "I don't think enough time's passed. Besides, people made up their minds about us a long time ago."

"No." Jonathan took her hand, and shivers slipped up her arm. "You gave up on them. There's a difference."

Alanna lurched to her feet and pulled her hand free. "That's your theory."

"It's a good one. You'd admit it if you weren't so close to everything."

She grabbed dishes and carried them to the sink where

she turned on the water and plugged the drain. She ran her fingers through the spray, testing the temperature before she added soap. If only she could dunk this situation in warm, soapy water and fix it. Too bad life didn't work that way.

She brushed hair out of her face then dropped the plates in the water. It sloshed onto her blouse, but she didn't care. She ran a dishrag over a plate, rinsed it, and placed it in the drain. The silence pressed against her. Wouldn't he say something? Or had his impression of her plummeted with the confirmation her mom and brother defrauded art collectors?

Jonathan was right. This problem could be solved. If a client came to her with a tangle like this, she'd work through it with them and reach some kind of resolution. When it involved her family, she quit? That didn't seem right. . .at all.

She spun on her heel, flinging suds around her. One landed on Jonathan's cheek, and he didn't crack a smile or make a joke out of it.

"You're right."

"Me?" He placed a hand on his chest. "You're admitting I'm right?"

"Don't get all carried away. . .but we'll fix this."

"All right."

"You're going to plan an amazing event where we will unveil my brother as an artist. It'll be a big homecoming. By the time it's over, everyone will want one of his paintings and consider it an honor to have one of those with Mom's John Hancock."

"Now wait a minute. I'm not sure I can do that."

"Sure you can." She grinned at him. "It's the least you can do."

"Fine. What's your role?"

"I'll clear his name."

Jonathan left shortly after her bold statement, and the next morning Alanna woke up to the sound of the door slamming. She groaned and rolled over. Her mother had stayed locked in her room the rest of the night, and Alanna didn't have the energy to smooth things over. Mom would find her when she was ready.

At the sound of something scraping through the gravel, Alanna threw back the covers and hurried to her window. The sight startled her.

Her mother yanked her suitcase through the gravel, making tracks down the path to the road. A taxi waited at the edge to collect her. Maybe she would have to track Mom down to make things right. Especially if the woman abandoned the island before seven o'clock.

Alanna pulled on the sweatshirt she'd tossed across the chair. She slid down the hallway and hurried down the stairs. Yanking open the front door, she stopped as the cold air slapped her in the face. She wrapped her arms around her stomach and shivered. "Mom?"

Her mother's back stiffened even more.

Fine. She'd follow the stubborn woman to the cab. The gravel poked through her socks, making her dance on tiptoes down the space between them. "Come on, Mom."

"I have to go." Her jaw was squared in the hard line it took when anger flooded her.

"Don't leave like this."

Mom huffed then turned on her heel, thrusting the suitcase between them. "Alanna, you're doing a nice job with the studio. But do not pretend you have any idea what we've experienced the last few years as we kept everything going."

"Then tell me those paintings are yours." Alanna thrust her hands on her hips.

"I don't need to justify anything to you."

"If they're yours, say so. If not, we have a problem. That's fraud, Mom."

"In whose opinion? Yours? You lost the right to say anything when you left and never came back." Mom's words rose from her whisper before she dragged the volume down.

The words punched through Alanna, stealing her breath. She tried to gather her thoughts, but they fled with the animosity flashing in her mother's eyes.

Mom snorted. "That's what I thought. You left and got your fancy degree that makes you think you know better than the rest of us. Well, wake up. You can think whatever you like. I've done nothing you can censor." She thrust back her shoulders and flipped around. She pasted a smile on her face as she handed her suitcase to the driver. "Thank you, George."

The cab pulled away and was soon nothing more than the steady clop of the horses' hooves. Alanna watched until the wagon disappeared from view over a hill. She rubbed her hands over her arms, trying to dissolve the chill that settled over her with her mother's words.

Was she wrong? Did it really matter that her brother painted the artwork rather than her mother? The angry words cycled around her mind, counter to the soft smell of lilacs carried on the breeze. She stood there, paralyzed until the soft crunch of shoes on gravel interrupted the song of the morning birds.

The musky scent alerted her to Jonathan's presence. "Good morning."

She nodded, unsure she could force any words past the rock sitting in her throat.

"So, Rachelle left."

"Yep."

"Guess she didn't like our questions."

Alanna chuckled. It was that or cry. "That's Mom for you. Passive-aggressive is alive and well."

"Don't see anything passive about walking out like that." Jonathan slid around until he stepped closer and their shoulders nearly touched. "I'm sorry."

At his simple words, the lump in her throat locked into place. How long had it been since someone said such simple and direct words to her? Her emotions collided in a pool of conflict. Part of her wanted to collapse into the strength he offered. Another part resisted the thought of allowing her weakness to show.

Chapter 22

While their shoulders might barely touch, Jonathan felt the moment Alanna distanced herself from him. One moment she leaned into the comfort he offered. The next he might as well move to Antarctica for the lack of openness on her face. He sighed and stepped away.

"If you need anything, you know how to find me." He waited a minute, giving her a chance to call him back. In the face of her continued silence, he started back to his cabin but paused to look at her again.

"Thanks." The whispered word reached him as Alanna stared at the trees gathered across the road. Her jaw clenched a moment then released.

Jonathan ran his hands over his head as he hurried home. Alanna didn't make anything easy. He'd volunteered to help, so rather than moon over her, he should start fleshing out the event she wanted.

He didn't like the idea of her waltzing around the island asking questions. She'd been gone a long time. Old wounds had scabbed over. She was bound to irritate others if she refused to leave the past alone. Until she asked for his help though, there wasn't much he could do.

Now that she knew about the paintings, she'd add that to the questions burning through her. If she was determined to clear her brother, she'd bulldog residents about the graduation party. Asking the questions no one wanted to answer. And she didn't have a clue. Well, maybe she did now that her mom had left without a word.

It would benefit everyone to unbury the event people ignored. The wound festered below the surface, and now Alanna would change that.

Jonathan entered his cabin and sped through getting ready. A protein bar served as breakfast as he biked downtown. Maybe he couldn't ask the questions for her, but he could poke around the edges. If he didn't, she'd only make things worse.

Alanna fumed through her morning routine. Between her mother leaving like a spoiled teenager and Jonathan, she felt wrung out before she'd been awake an hour.

The simple solution? Leave.

Head back to her job at the firm. Her apartment in Grand Rapids. Her roommate and cat.

She couldn't do it though. It wasn't in her to slide back into that world before she resolved the questions and problems she'd uncovered. She didn't walk away from a fight. She was a litigator after all. But those battles hadn't revolved around her family.

The coffee perked in the pot while she stared out the window across the pond.

God, what do I do?

He was truth. Would He lead her to truth? She wasn't sure how to begin, other than investigate Grady's death. That would be tricky. Everyone seemed to have placed the event firmly in the past. But if she could clear Trevor, he could put his name on the paintings, and her parents could properly display and sell the work. Then only the people who'd already bought the wrongly signed art would need some type of restitution. For now they could wait.

Alanna poured coffee into a traveling mug and doctored it with flavored syrup and milk. Her thoughts gave her a headache, the kind that could pound a drum beat the rest of the day if she didn't tackle it now. She rubbed her temples in an effort to loosen its hold before she opened the studio.

She had to find an employee. Then she could investigate to her heart's content and eventually leave.

When she reached the Painted Stone, Alanna made short work of the opening duties. As soon as she flipped the sign to OPEN, she settled on the stool at the counter. While the computer booted up, she made a short list of people to talk to. . .people who lived on the island all those years ago and who might have memories about what happened.

Then she opened her e-mail. As the messages poured in, she glanced through them for résumés. She sorted through the few, disappointed only a couple lived close enough to interview. Guess she'd need to advertise in closer newspapers if she wanted to find someone quickly rather than spend the season on Mackinac. The partners would love that.

The bells announced a new arrival. She glanced up and smiled when Ginger entered. The woman had a firm set to her posture. A small smile pasted on her face almost looked as if it belonged.

"Good morning, Alanna."

"Hi, Ginger. What can I do for you?"

"I've got what you wanted." Ginger placed a thin file on the counter.

Alanna pivoted it toward her so she could read the label.

CADIEUX, GRADY. His case file. She'd almost forgotten about asking for it. "Thank you."

"I hope you enjoy the reading." Ginger's lips tightened. "Some things are better left in the past."

"Some," Alanna agreed. "But not this."

Ginger blinked quickly. "Another example of life not being fair."

Alanna studied her. Why did she care so much about someone who had died so long ago? Had they still been dating when he died? She tried to remember.

Ginger swiped at her eyes then squared her shoulders. "The past is over, right?"

"Is it?"

"Not when my baby never knew her daddy." Ginger spun on her heel and hurried from the studio as her words hovered.

Her baby? Grady's? How come she hadn't heard that? She might have left Mackinac, but Mom had done a good job the first few years of keeping her up-to-date on the lives of her friends. Then she resigned herself to the reality Alanna wouldn't return.

Ginger's daughter was Grady's. Would her search hurt the girl? Bringing to the surface questions Ginger wouldn't want to answer?

A couple wandered in, both looking vaguely familiar, but Alanna couldn't place them. A common occurrence after eleven years away. "Can I help you find anything?"

"Looking for inspiration." The tall woman smiled, but it didn't reach her eyes.

"Enjoy." Alanna watched the two a minute then turned back to the file Ginger had thrown at her, thoughts spinning.

She scanned the file but didn't see anything she hadn't expected. Still, she'd needed to look. Next she'd dig up news articles from Grady's death. See what she could learn there.

The door banged open, the bell jangling an angry song. Alanna looked up and straightened when Mr. Hoffmeister marched in. He nodded to the couple but didn't slow as he approached Alanna.

"Good morning." The lines drawn deep in his face didn't match the words. He wiped his hands on his formerly white apron, smudges of rich chocolate fudge coloring it. The cloud of chocolate following him made Alanna's mouth water.

"Mr. Hoffmeister. You just missed Ginger."

"I know. She's why I'm here." The lines around his eyes tightened, and Alanna could almost feel his pain.

"Are you all right?"

"Fine."

She eyed him, unconvinced. "What are you doing away from the fudge?"

"Needed to clear the air a bit." His words bit between them.

Alanna leaned back, wishing the stool had a backrest and slanting a quick glance at the couple. They seemed focused on the paintings, but the woman had pivoted slightly toward them. Great. "Okay."

"I know you've been away awhile. So you might have forgotten a few things. Like how those who live here take care of their own. Well, we do."

"Yes, sir. I remember." The violation of that code had kept her away.

"We don't like people poking around in matters best left alone. You have to be careful, or you'll get hurt." He placed his palms on the counter as if to steady himself. "Leave the past where it belongs."

"I will if I can, but I need to see if I can uncover what happened. Free Trevor to return."

"There's no 'maybe' about it." He slammed a hand on the counter, and she jumped. What happened to the sweet man she'd always known? "Alanna, I've always liked you and your family. But if you dig into the past too deeply, it will only harm your parents. They still live here. . .try to make a living here. I know you don't mean to jeopardize that. Please stop asking your questions."

What did he mean? She'd barely asked any. Her glance landed on the folder. Did this have something to do with Ginger? "I promise to be careful."

"I don't want to see my daughter or granddaughter hurt. And be careful about Tomkin."

Alanna let that soak in as he studied her intently. She resisted the need to squirm. "I've known him a long time."

"But not the last eleven years. He's changed. Devious." Odd how his words mirrored the ones Mr. Tomkin said of him. Finally, he nodded. "Someone will get hurt if you don't leave the past alone. I've said what I needed."

Alanna's jaw dropped as he spun and marched out of the studio as abruptly as he'd appeared. What had happened to the man who wanted to talk to her? Share secrets from the past with her?

She hurried to the windows and watched him hustle down the sidewalk. Where his posture had always been board straight, he now walked like a man burdened. He'd shoved his hands in the pockets of his navy Dockers and hunched his shoulders. Without much breeze, he didn't fight the elements. No, it looked like he fought a war within himself. A battle she wanted to glimpse. Especially if that shed light on her brother's mess.

The rest of the morning passed with a few people glancing in the windows, but no one ventured inside the store. Once she'd freshly dusted each piece, Alanna sat back down at the computer. She pulled up an article on Grady's death. As she read it, the details leaped into her mind in fresh color.

It had been a quiet spring day. The kind that still had a chill that bit through clothes whenever the wind kicked in off the lake. That didn't stop the high school seniors from heading to the narrow beach the moment Mr. Tomkin dismissed them. Within an hour, a towering bonfire burned, kicking heat around as the flames danced higher and higher, as if straining to touch the sky.

Her classmates had paired off, but Alanna remained alone. If Jonathan had lived on the island, she wouldn't have sat on a log by herself. Grady brought a cooler with him, and when she opened it, longneck bottles waited in a bed of ice. She closed the lid, refusing to join in that part of the celebration. As the alcohol flowed, each person's plans for the future spiraled into crazier and crazier areas. According to them, she'd attended high school with a future president, cancer-eradicating doctor, and next NFL pro-bowl quarterback.

The laughter rolled around the fire after Grady made that claim. She still lay awake some nights wondering if they had all backed off, would Grady have stopped there? Instead, the juniors and sophomores had arrived—Trevor with them. Grady scanned the group and launched to his full height.

"Who wants to race?" He puffed out his chest and flexed his arms. "I can beat any of you to the round lighthouse."

"Don't do it, Grady." Alanna wrapped her arms around her

and shivered. "It's too cold to do anything in the water."

"Yeah, at least wait until summer to prove you're a man." Alanna had cringed as Brendan Tomkin egged Grady on. Didn't he know that's all it would take to make Grady follow his insane plan? One glance at his face reinforced that Brendan knew exactly what he was doing.

From that moment, the afternoon spiraled along its deadly path.

First Grady then Trevor had entered the water. She tried to pull Trevor back, but he wore his goofy grin. "It's no big deal, sis."

Nobody had seen what was coming.

The door opened, and the bell jarred Alanna from the past.

Jonathan's cell phone rang, and with a glance at the caller display, he reached for it then pulled back. What did he have to tell Edward Morris? Not what the man needed to hear. No, he'd let voice mail get the call then track down Rachelle Stone. He couldn't wait any longer to let Edward know whether he could order a painting. She'd need time to create the perfect painting to honor Edward and Bonnie's marriage. And he needed confirmation Rachelle would paint it. Trevor might be a capable artist, but without his name on it, Jonathan wouldn't connect him to Mr. Morris.

As soon as his phone beeped to indicate he had voice mail, he scrolled through his contacts until he found Rachelle's cell number. He entered it then waited for an answer.

It rang several times, and he wondered if he'd joined her

do-not-talk-to list.

"Hello?" The voice sounded bone weary, unlike the usual pep that filled her words.

"Rachelle? This is Jonathan."

"Yes?"

"A client would like to commission a painting."

"Jonathan, stop."

"He likes your work. This fits with commissions you've painted before."

"Used to. My time isn't my own now."

"Wouldn't the income help?"

She sighed, and he heard her burdens. "You have no idea. I know Alanna is trying, but the studio must make more." She was silent, and he waited. "Trevor could do something."

"Not good enough. This is to honor a client's wife who's fighting cancer. It has to be you or not at all." He pushed back in his chair, gut tightening. Maybe she'd just say no again, and that would be the end. It felt like he'd crossed a line with his pushing. Perhaps she couldn't paint now. Maybe creative types needed more than physical energy to work their magic.

A rustling sound like she'd placed her hand over the phone scratched his ear. Then muffled voices bantered for a moment.

"Jonathan, I'll see what I can do."

"Can he contact you at this number?"

"He can try. It all depends on how Don feels."

"Of course." He couldn't ask her to sacrifice her husband's needs for a client. "You'll hear from him soon." He cleared his throat. "You didn't need to leave this morning."

"I did." An alarm sounded in the background. "I've got to go. Take care of my girl, Jonathan."

"Yes, ma'am." The call disconnected before he was certain she'd heard. Didn't matter. She knew he'd do anything for Alanna.

His e-mail dinged, and he opened the message. Edward. He smiled ruefully. The man knew how to get what he wanted. Jonathan composed a quick message and hit SEND. Then he turned back to his plans for another wedding, this one a fifties theme. He wondered if the bridesmaids would wear poodle skirts. That would create unforgettable images for the photographer and make a fun reception. In fact, he knew the performer to call, an Upper Peninsula singer who specialized in the sounds of the fifties and sixties.

He sketched out some thoughts and then sent an e-mail to the bride and her mother. With any luck, the women would sign off on his ideas and he could get the performer signed for the event.

His phone rang and didn't stop the rest of the afternoon. When he finally reached a break, he stood then stretched. He wandered to the window and looked down on the foot traffic. There weren't many people around. Guess the tourists weren't in the mood for a chilly last day of May on the island. It would pick up; it always did.

Until then he knew the business owners would pray for the day the mainland folks flooded the island. Much as he loved the peace and tranquillity, without the chaos of non-locals, the island remained a shell of itself.

Something clomped against the stairs. He glanced at his watch. Company now?

Chapter 23

As soon as the clock reached six, Alanna bolted. Tomorrow she'd interview potential employees by phone, but for now she needed to clear her head. Forget about everything.

A trip around the island might clear her mind. At least that's what she hoped as she mounted her bike. At the end of the street, she stopped at the library. Biking around the island could wait, but the search for answers couldn't. She wandered the aisles of the small building until she found the slim section of yearbooks. She flipped through the one from her senior year. So many photos showed a small group of tightly knit teens. When there were only a couple handfuls of students in a class, you got to know each other well.

Alanna stopped flipping when she reached Trevor's picture. He looked so young and full of boyish excitement. He'd been all of a sophomore with the future waiting. A few pages more and she stared into Grady's cocky face. He looked like he ruled the world rather than the small kingdom of the Mackinac Island school. Even her photo conveyed someone with big dreams.

What happened to those? Somehow her vision of her future died along with Grady. She'd fled the island rather than return after college. She'd wanted to make a difference; now she invested herself in a job she was good at but didn't love.

Someone cleared her throat, and Alanna glanced up with a start. An elderly woman with gray hair cut in short layers around her face studied Alanna.

"Sorry, ma'am, but it's time to close." She cocked her head.

"Of course." Alanna closed the yearbook. "I'll get out of here now."

"Don't I know you?"

Alanna shrugged as she pulled the book close like a shield. "Maybe, but it's been years since I've been in the library."

"Hmmm. I could swear you're the image of Rachelle Stone."

"I've heard that before."

"Alanna?" The woman grinned. "Well, it's time you came back, kid. You probably don't remember me. Tricia McCormick. Went to college with your mom and followed her here."

"That's right." Alanna carried the yearbook to the copier and started copying the pages showing the classes. "Sorry I didn't recognize you."

"It's been years." Tricia's look traveled to the bookshelf. "Reminiscing or searching?"

"A bit of both." Alanna returned the yearbook back to its slot.

"Your mom said you could never let it go." The woman sighed. "It was a sad day, but the rest of us moved on. Time for you to do the same."

"I can't."

"Still stubborn I see. I don't know what you'll find here, but feel free to come back as often as you need."

Alanna nodded then hurried to her bike and away from the woman's gaze. Tricia McCormick knew the old her as well as anyone on the island. Well enough to know she bulldogged questions. And this was one she couldn't walk away from.

Should she continue around the island?

The shadows had lengthened while she read inside. Maybe she'd find Mr. Hoffmeister. See if he was still angry. It seemed so out of character for him to make accusations like he had. Especially when she hadn't really started digging. After all, how would he know about her conversation with her mom? And what did that have to do with him? It wasn't as if she'd done much yet to look into Grady's death. Her presence alone couldn't be enough to get him out of sorts. Could it? Had Ginger run to him after she dropped off the file? That seemed unlikely but possible.

She eased her bike to a stop in front of I'm Not Sharing. The lights warmed the windows and inside of the shop. It looked empty, but she got off anyway. As long as the lights were on, the shop was open.

The door opened easily as she pushed it, the bell announcing her entrance. As soon as she entered, the familiar fudge-laced air flooded around her. She waited inside the door on the mahogany-stained, plank floor. The display cases stood with shelves almost bare of fudge. Looked like the morning would be early and busy or the store wouldn't have fudge to sell.

Muffled voices whispered from the back area, but Alanna couldn't see anyone. She waited a minute, taking in the shop. Whoever worked tonight had worked hard to get things ready for closing.

A couple of empty marble tables sat in the prep area. Counters stood clean and ready for new batches of fudge to be worked and cut into yummy slabs. She waited a few minutes to give the conversation in the back a minute to wrap up, but still no one came out to check on who had entered.

Had they missed the bells when the door opened? Must be an intense conversation.

Guess she'd use the little bell resting on top of the glass case on the counter next to the old-fashioned cash register. None of those fancy computers for I'm Not Sharing employees. They still made change the old-fashioned way, one dime at a time.

Alanna hit the bell, the tinny sound not reaching far. She waited a moment then knocked it again, harder this time. "Hello?"

It sounded like a door in the back slammed, and she ran her hands over the smooth, walnut counter. Clearing her throat, she tried again. "Hello? Mr. Hoffmeister?"

Maybe someone else worked tonight.

"Coming." He huffed around the corner, sounding out of breath, then skidded to a stop when he spotted her. "Alanna Stone. You're the last person I expected tonight."

"I know. I was headed home, but decided I needed to check on you."

"Why?"

"This morning was. . .surreal. Have I done anything to offend you?"

He pulled his glasses down and rubbed his eyes. "Just a long few weeks."

That didn't explain why he'd come and publicly scolded her. He must have seen her skepticism.

"I probably got carried away. Between your questions and that monstrosity Tomkin wants to build"—he shuddered at the words—"I'm distracted. But you need to let everything drop between Grady and Trevor. That's done and over."

"Trevor still walks under a cloud of suspicion. Can you

say you don't blame him for the accident?"

"Each of you played some part in it."

Alanna winced as his words slammed into her, the edge hard and on target. "Still. . ."

"It's unsolvable, so stop. Find an employee for the shop and go home."

"This is my home." She paused at the word, shocked she'd said it and even more surprised that she meant it.

"Hasn't been for eleven years. A few weeks won't make that much difference. Go back to your job, friends, and new life. Leave us alone."

Alanna stepped back, unsure what to do next. "Why warn me about Tomkin?"

"No reason."

"Not buying it. You don't make accusations unless you have something to back it up."

"Let's not talk about this now. Come back tomorrow. It's been a long day, and I'm ready to head home."

He looked exhausted, strung out, with crow's feet etched into the corners of his eyes. "Just one minute."

"Fine." He looked at the counter then raised worried eyes to hers. "Didn't you ever find it odd the amount of thrashing out there?"

"Out where?"

"In the water. Think about who was there. And what happened. It wasn't an accident. Roughhousing's one thing. This wasn't."

"Then why didn't you say anything?"

"What makes you think I didn't?"

A clang erupted from the back. Mr. Hoffmeister jerked as if he'd been prodded. "Think you want some fudge?"

What had smelled so good when she stepped in now turned her stomach, but as she looked at Mr. Hoffmeister, she nodded. "A slice of the mint chocolate please."

The older man grabbed a piece of wax paper from the box and then reached into the display case, his hand shaking as he claimed a slice.

"Not that one." Alanna couldn't remember him ever reaching for the wrong kind. Peanut-butter fudge didn't look anything like the mint. "Mint please."

"That's right. Old brain is fuddled at the moment." He chuckled weakly as he grabbed the right kind. He pulled out a bag but seemed to take extra time before he handed it over. He ran her debit card through the machine that looked oddly out of place next to the giant cash register. His movements jerked abnormally as he slid the receipt to her. "Have a good evening."

"You, too, Mr. Hoffmeister." Alanna left the store then turned to watch him from the window. He shuffled across the floor as if he carried the weight of a hundred problems then locked the door and flipped the sign. She waved, and he lifted a hand.

The street was quiet as she shoved off and pedaled home. The white bag glowed like a flag in her bike's basket, waving a surrender to all who passed her. When she got home, she opened the bag. A small piece of paper, like it had been torn from the cash-register tape, fluttered to the table. Mr. Hoffmeister's scrawl had her squinting as she tried to decipher it.

Alanna, come by my house tomorrow night. I'll ex-
plain then. If I don't answer, you'll find the key by the

German shepherd. She guards the house for me.

She stared at the slip. When had he found time to write it? She'd been there the whole time. And why not just tell her when she was in the shop? Why all the secrecy?

The questions bothered her as she tried to go to sleep and woke her during the night.

The next morning Alanna got a late start after her restless sleep. She slipped a headband on to hold back damp hair as she hurried to the studio. She slowed when she approached I'm Not Sharing. Police crime-scene tape fluttered around the outside. Dread sank like a weight through her at the image. What happened after she left? A few of the island police officers stood around the perimeter of the tape, their expressions hard and unwelcoming.

She eased to a stop.

"Keep moving, miss." A uniformed officer still wearing his bike helmet gestured her on.

"What happened?"

"Can't say." He waved his arm. "Please keep moving."

She eased back into the bike traffic. After she opened the Painted Stone, she'd call the island grapevine to find out what happened. Until then she had a couple of job interviews to conduct. At the pace her investigation wasn't moving, she needed to leave the island as soon as possible. In fact, yesterday sounded better all the time.

With a last glance at the yellow tape flapping across the

shop's door, Alanna finished biking to work, her thoughts shadowed by the unknown. She focused on the interviews, which passed smoothly enough, with only one of the candidates showing enough interest to invite for an in-person interview. It helped that the college student lived in St. Ignace during the summer. After arranging the interview for the following morning, Alanna helped several people who wandered into the store. She sold paintings with mixed emotions.

She vowed to unravel the twisted mire around the art as soon as humanly possible. She munched a sandwich at the counter, counting down until she could take a legitimate lunch break again. Peanut butter and jelly had never been her favorite sandwich, and right now she'd give anything for a pot roast sandwich at the Yankee Rebel. She tried to imagine the nutty aroma of her sandwich was the meaty one the Yankee Rebel served instead, but her imagination couldn't quite make the transition.

She finished the sandwich then placed a want ad in another paper. Eventually one would work. It had to.

Early that afternoon she looked up from the web page she'd opened. Jonathan stormed into the studio, a frown creasing the bridge of his nose.

"Jonathan, what's wrong?"

"Didn't you hear?"

She shook her head. "Hear what?"

"Mr. Hoffmeister was murdered last night."

The blood drained from her face, and she felt an accompanying dizziness. "The tape. . ."

"The state police detective and crime scene unit have been at I'm Not Sharing since one of the employees discovered him this morning." Jonathan leaned against the counter. "I can't imagine who would kill him."

Alanna sagged against the wall. A weight plunged her stomach to her toes while spots danced in her vision. "He seemed all right." Just distracted. Her thoughts spiraled as she considered what could have happened.

"He seemed all right?"

"Last night. I stopped to get some fudge on the way home." Jonathan didn't need to know what they discussed. Or about Mr. H.'s odd actions when he came to the studio. "That poor man."

Jonathan nodded. "I can't imagine anyone killing him. It must have been a botched robbery. The island's been so quiet, I can't imagine whoever did this got away with much money."

"I hope you're right." The idea that a murderer could be a neighbor chilled her.

"How did he seem when you saw him?"

"Okay. Distracted." What more could she say? She hadn't been Mr. Hoffmeister's closest friend, but she'd always liked the man. He'd been like the uncle you loved to be annoyed at. Soft and gushy sometimes and mildly odd the rest. She hadn't spent enough time with him since returning though. Whatever he might have known about Grady's death had died with him.

Alanna tried to rein in her thoughts, but they returned to what he might have known.

"I hope the police close this soon." Jonathan rubbed his face as if trying to wipe away his grief. "I always liked him. Nobody deserves to die like that."

"How. . .how was he killed?"

"I don't know. Nobody knew at lunch." His face clouded as if listening again.

"I got here and forgot. I assumed it was a robbery." She shivered as a deep chill settled over her and the words of his note waved through her mind. He'd known. Somehow he'd known. "How horrible."

Jonathan nodded. After a minute, he pushed back from the counter. "Be careful. We don't know who did this."

"You, too."

"Promise you'll wait for me to ride home. Your parents won't want you out alone."

Alanna considered protesting but realized he was right. The thought that someone would murder anyone. . .on Mackinac? It didn't compute. She couldn't think of a time someone had been killed. Maybe the island had changed in ways too terrible to contemplate.

The rest of the afternoon evaporated as Alanna searched the online news services for information. As she scanned for anything, she wondered if she should give the note to the police. The lack of details had her nerves bunched. Was it important? As she considered its cryptic message, she decided to wait until she had time to collect what she knew in an organized manner for the police. As the stream of customers continued, she knew she'd have to wait until she reached the sanctuary of her home.

The shadows had started to lengthen by the time Jonathan returned. She hurried out to meet him, locking the door behind her. The cleaning and prep for tomorrow would wait. Right now she wanted to feel safe within the four walls of her house.

The silent ride up the hills felt rushed. Like they both fled to a place of peace, but Jonathan wouldn't do that. Usually she wouldn't either. What if she'd been the last person other than the killer to see Mr. Hoffmeister alive? After she got home, she'd write down everything she could remember from his rush into the studio to their short conversation and his halting actions at the shop. Then she'd talk to the police. If only she'd caught a glimpse of whoever had been there when she'd arrived.

Her sigh must have reached Jonathan as he pumped up the hill in front of her.

He turned in his seat and glanced at her. "You okay?"

She swallowed. How to answer that? She hadn't been great friends with Mr. Hoffmeister, yet she felt his death.

They reached her driveway and turned down it. Once she parked her bike, he followed her to the door and then walked through the house with her.

"This is silly." A giggle ended the sentence, one she'd love to swallow back. "It's not like whoever did this would come here. Mr. Hoffmeister lived on the opposite side of the island."

Jonathan continued his search, opening the pantry door. "Better safe. . ."

Alanna didn't say anything else until he'd looked in each of the upstairs rooms. "Would you like to stay for supper?"

"The last time I did that, your mom left."

"Tonight will be different." As she studied his serious eyes, she wished she could form the words. *Please stay. Don't leave me alone.* Instead, she prayed he could read it in her gaze. What happened to the independent woman from Grand Rapids?

Murders normally didn't affect her.

Usually she didn't know the victim.

Chapter 24

Alanna moved around the kitchen, her movements stilted and jerky. She must look like Mr. Hoffmeister had the night before—a tad off. Jonathan sat at the island, awkward and out of place like he didn't know how to help and wondered if he should stay. She needed him here. While her mind knew whoever killed Mr. Hoffmeister had no reason to venture this far into the island, she couldn't relax and feel safe.

She opened the refrigerator, scrambling for what to offer as a meal. "Sandwiches okay? It's not glamorous. . ."

"I'm a bachelor." Jonathan cut off her excuses. "Any meal I don't prepare is a good one."

She grabbed meat and cheese. Jonathan stood and selected glasses from the cabinet. "What would you like?"

Alanna pulled back from the fridge, her hands filled with ranch dressing and other condiments she set on the counter next to the ham and swiss. "Water's fine."

He turned on the faucet and watched the water fill first one glass and then the other. The silence felt awkward yet necessary. Jonathan seemed lost in his thoughts, and she didn't rush to fill the dead air as she sliced a tomato and some lettuce before arranging them in salad bowls. She didn't blame him. Something like this didn't happen on Mackinac.

She bet if she asked the police chief, the man would affirm her gut that no one had been murdered since before she was born. Still, in the age of the Internet, the outside world intruded on Mackinac. In a minute, she had sandwiches prepared and a simple salad for each of them.

"Mind if I grab some chips from the pantry? Your mom always keeps a stash."

"No, but that's Dad's stash." He'd always had a weakness for chips, especially Cheetos. The more fake cheese colored his fingers, the better.

Jonathan pulled back the door and tugged a tube of Pringles from the bottom shelf. "These work?"

"Sure."

They sat at the table, and Jonathan said a quick grace.

"I talked to Rachelle yesterday."

Her gaze collided with Jonathan's. "And?"

"I asked her about commissioning a piece."

"I bet that went well."

He shrugged and shoved another Pringle in his mouth. "Not as bad as I expected. She didn't say yes, but she didn't say no either. I insisted she had to paint, not Trevor, since that's what the client wants."

"She admitted the paintings aren't hers?"

"Not in so many words, but I connected her with the Morrises. We'll see what happens."

Much would be resolved if Mom started painting again. Then Alanna wouldn't have to worry about what to do with new paintings. Mom probably wouldn't deliver any again.

As she took the last bite of her sandwich, someone knocked. She looked at Jonathan, and he shrugged.

"Expecting anyone?"

"No." Who would it be? People hadn't exactly lined up since she'd returned.

Jonathan followed her to the door and peeked out the window before she opened the door.

Police Chief Ryan stood there with a man in a bedraggled suit that identified him as an underpaid detective. They were here? With a murder to investigate? She straightened and quirked an eyebrow. "Can I help you?"

"Alanna, this is Detective Brian Bull from the state police. Do you have a few minutes?"

Jonathan started to push past her, but she shook her head. He frowned but planted himself at her side. "What's this about?"

"Don't get worked up, Covington. This doesn't concern you."

By the way Jonathan's chin hardened, the chief's words were the wrong ones.

Alanna sucked in a breath. There weren't any attorneys to call on the island, so she'd handle this on her own for the moment. Shouldn't be too hard, even if the old saw stated only a fool had himself for an attorney.

"Alanna." Chief Ryan frowned at her, his bushy gray eyebrows meeting in the middle of his face. "Shouldn't take long, assuming you don't have anything to hide."

"I'd like to know the subject matter." She studied him as carefully as he did her, not missing the challenge in his expression.

"Hoffmeister."

Jonathan gaped at the police chief. "You think Alanna knows something?"

"Pretty certain." The police chief studied Alanna coldly. Yet the detective was the one who worried Alanna. He had a slouched appearance, but his eyes moved constantly, taking in everything. What did the man expect to find here of all places?

Alanna sighed as she caught Jonathan's shocked expression. Maybe she should have emphasized her visit. No, she didn't know it would add anything to the investigation, and her plan to contact the police in the morning was sound. He'd have to understand when she explained later.

"I'll answer your questions here on the porch, but first I need to grab something." Alanna slipped inside and grabbed the folder she'd slid Mr. Hoffmeister's note into last night. She also grabbed a pad of paper and pen before returning to the porch and sitting on the nearest white rocking chair. She placed the items in her lap and folded her hands across them. In a moment, her knuckles turned white from her laced fingers, and she tried to relax. She needed to remember all the advice she'd ever given clients when preparing for interviews or depositions. It had seemed easy then. Now she could barely pull the first word into her mind.

Jonathan stood in the doorway, the stiffness in his posture telegraphing he would stick close until she asked him to leave. Right now, that was the last thing she planned. She needed someone with her. A witness who could vouch for her in case things didn't go well.

Detective Bull pulled a slim notepad from his inside breast pocket and flipped it open. He poised a pen over the paper. "When was the last time you saw Mr. Hoffmeister?"

"Yesterday." No reason to hide that piece of information.

He jotted a note. "Where did you see him?"

"First at the studio. Later at the shop."

Jonathan frowned at her. She ignored him. Her focus had to stay locked on the police chief and detective. She only hoped she could remember everything after they left. It seemed like her vision narrowed with gray areas on the outskirts. She wanted to shake it off, but would that look somehow guilty? She should have paid more attention in her criminal law continuing education classes.

"When you say, 'the studio,' where is that?"

"The Painted Stone, the studio my parents own."

"Are they in town?"

"No, my father has a health issue, which is why I'm here." She bit her lower lip to stop elaborating. Stick to the question asked. How many times had she instructed clients that way? But she'd also tell them never to talk to police without an attorney present.

Detective Bull studied her, and she relaxed her posture. He glanced at Chief Ryan, who nodded. "How long have you been on Mackinac?"

"Since the week before Memorial Day."

"Have you spent much time with Mr. Hoffmeister?"

"We've talked a couple times."

"Prior to yesterday?"

"Yes." A trickle of sweat slid down her shoulder blade.

"What were those conversations about?"

Why wasn't he asking her more about yesterday? "Different things. An accident from eleven years ago."

"The one where the teenager died?" the detective asked.

Chief Ryan shook his head. "I warned you to leave it alone."

At his words, Alanna wished she had her digital recorder out and on. He wouldn't have inserted himself like that with a recorder capturing every word.

Detective Bull frowned at the chief then turned back at Alanna. "Why did you see Mr. Hoffmeister yesterday?"

"He came to the studio to tell me to quit looking into

that death. It was unusual for him, especially since I haven't done much other than talk to him once. He'd been pretty open then."

"And last night?"

"I stopped by the fudge shop to see if he was all right."

"Why wouldn't he be?"

"I don't know. He seemed out of character at the studio. I needed to know he was okay."

Chief Ryan snorted. "Meaning you needed to harass him and the librarian last night."

He knew she'd stopped at the library? She turned toward him. "I flipped through an old yearbook. Nothing more. I need to piece together what happened. Since Mr. Hoffmeister lived near the accident location, he suggested he knew something."

Jonathan placed a restraining hand on her arm. Alanna sucked in a breath and vowed not to say another word to the chief. Let him egg her on all he wanted; he wouldn't get another word from her. Not now.

The chief crossed his arms and stared at her. Fine. She'd ignore him. She had bigger concerns with the detective leaning against the porch railing. Her eye was drawn to the peeling paint that had started to flake from the railing. Her dad always kept the house meticulously maintained. How many summers had he made Trevor and her scrape and paint? What had distracted him from the appearance of perfection?

"And last night?"

"I stopped at the shop on my way home. When I entered, nobody was out front. I waited a minute then heard voices in the back. After a minute, I rang the bell, a door closed, and

Mr. Hoffmeister came out. He seemed agitated, but I bought a slice of fudge and left."

"Did you see anyone around?"

"No. When I left, I didn't see anyone." *Stick to the question, Alanna.* Jonathan removed his hand and stepped back, and she felt cold and alone in his distance. She shivered and rubbed her hands along her arms. "When I got home and opened my bag of fudge, this fell out." She slid the note from the folder and handed it over.

The detective pulled on a glove and then accepted it. He took a moment to read it before handing it to Chief Ryan. "Why wouldn't he just come out and say he needed to talk to you?"

"I don't know. Maybe he was afraid of the man in the back."

"I thought you said he'd left?"

Had she? Alanna couldn't remember and understood why someone could get rattled in the middle of questioning. "Do you need anything else right now?"

The detective studied her, seeming to test whether he could press her. Whatever he saw in her posture turned him to his notes, difficult to see now in the shadows created by the sinking sun. "Not at the moment." He pinned her with his gaze. "However, I recommend you don't leave the island. Certainly not without letting the chief know first."

"Excuse me?" Indignation flared in her chest at his order.

"Right now you're the last person who saw Mr. Hoffmeister. That either makes you his murderer or a material witness. We'll be in touch."

The two men nodded then faded off the porch and into the shadows. A headache pounded at one temple. Alanna tried to regulate her breathing and force her muscles to relax. She might have sat in numerous interviews, but she'd never been the interviewee. She prayed she didn't repeat the honor.

"Are you going to tell me what that was about?"

Jonathan's voice snapped her head around. "Sorry?"

"You had an exciting day yesterday."

"I had no idea how exciting until you told me about Mr. Hoffmeister." She sighed.

"Alanna, they think you did it."

"No, I wouldn't still be here if they could prove that."

"There's a step between believing and proving."

She shivered again and pushed out of the chair. "I'm going inside." She left it open about whether he'd follow her. Maybe Jonathan didn't want to stay. She wouldn't blame him. It wasn't every day the police interviewed her.

"It's not that simple." Jonathan joined her in the kitchen.

Alanna opened the freezer and pulled out some chocolate-chip cookie dough chunks. After turning on the oven, she plopped the pieces on a cookie tray. Chocolate-chip cookies and milk wouldn't solve everything, but they made a good start on comfort food. It wasn't like she could call her mom for commiseration. She rubbed her temple then slid the pan in the oven.

"Alanna, sit down and explain what happened." Jonathan pulled out a chair, led her to it, and eased her down.

"Somehow the police knew I was at the shop last night." How? It hit her. "The debit card. They must have checked the transactions. Makes sense."

"You don't have anything to hide?" Hope edged his words.

"No. In fact, I planned to sit down tonight and write out what I remembered and call Chief Ryan in the morning.

Once you told me he was dead, I knew they needed the note. I couldn't break away or organize my thoughts at work, or I'd have called him earlier. I wish Mr. Hoffmeister hadn't locked the door after I left."

Jonathan frowned at her. "Why?"

"Then someone else could have been the last person to see him alive."

Chapter 25

When he got home, Jonathan looked for something to distract him. Instead, he stalked the edges of the small cabin as questions chased him. How could one person get in so much trouble so quickly? He could tick off the problems: Alanna's investigation into Grady's death coupled with the odd things around her house and now becoming a person of interest in Mr. Hoffmeister's death. He didn't like any of them, including the fact there were no suspects involving the break-in at her shed. Could it have been a warning to back off that she'd missed?

That girl knew how to return to town and wreak havoc.

He'd never believe she had anything to do with Mr. Hoffmeister. Someone had. Someone who might still be on the island or left on the last ferry.

Mr. Hoffmeister didn't seem like the kind with enemies. Even his dispute with Gerald only led to silence or heated arguments. Never fists.

Jonathan moved across the backyard and sat on the dock. For once the thought of finding that elusive bird or catching an elusive fish didn't hold his thoughts.

Not since Alanna arrived.

Alanna.

How could he help her? He doubted she'd call her parents. That left her alone since Trevor wouldn't be much help. The kid had enough problems, and he was too selfish to notice others. Jonathan sighed. That wasn't completely fair.

His phone rang, and he tugged it from his pocket. Jaclyn. "Hey."

"What's wrong?"

"Nothing."

"Sorry." He could almost see her forehead wrinkle. "I know you too well."

"Just got back from Alanna's. Long day with what happened to Mr. Hoffmeister."

"You were with Alanna?" Her voice rose to a hysterical pitch.

Jonathan rubbed his jaw. What did he say now? He could understand she wouldn't be thrilled at the news, but Alanna had needed him. He heaved a sigh. "Yeah."

"I knew her being so close to you would be a problem."

"We're just friends."

"Sure you are." She huffed. "Friends with quite the past."

"What did you need?"

"Just wanted to talk to you. Never mind." She clicked off, and Jonathan knew she was upset. He'd have to do something about that. Tomorrow.

A breeze rippled small waves that were barely visible on the surface of the pond. He could almost hear God whispering in it. He needed to release Alanna and the whole mess to the Master. He gritted his teeth. He wanted to fix it. Make a plan like an event. Steps 1 through 144. Step by step, execution by execution, he'd manage her out of the mess.

Too bad that wouldn't work.

If anyone could figure it out, Alanna would. She was the attorney, after all. She'd know what she needed to do. He was kidding himself to think he could do something she couldn't.

Except she hadn't been on the island for years. He had.

Surely he knew the players better than she did. He couldn't imagine Rachelle keeping her up-to-date on all the gossip from here. Alanna had made it clear when she left that she was done with the island and its residents.

He let his mind wander over the people Hoffmeister spent time with.

Tomkin. Mrs. Washington. Who did he talk with over coffee in the winter? The list wasn't very long.

How could a man have spent a lifetime on the same small patch of earth and not have many friends? Everyone on the island knew him. . .but that was different than someone who would kill him.

If something was taken, then the murder might make sense. Hoffmeister had simply been in the wrong place. It sounded cliché, but nothing else made sense. Not for the man he knew.

He let his thoughts wander as the leaves rustled overhead. The soft scent of lilacs mixed with something sweet like vanilla alerted him to Alanna's presence. She settled down next to him until their shoulders touched.

"Hi." The word was so quiet, he had to lean closer.

They stared across the dark pond, nature providing the only backdrop and music. He lost track of time until he felt her shiver.

"Come here." He tugged her closer and put his arm around her shoulder. "Crazy night."

"Yeah."

"Wanna talk about it?"

"Not really. I'd rather think about something else." She brushed a strand of hair from her face. "I've gone over yesterday a dozen times. I can't think of anything to tell the police that can point them to who killed Mr. Hoffmeister." Another shiver shook her. "I wish I knew who was in the back of the shop. Maybe they didn't leave. Maybe he left the back door unlocked, and the person came back. That's all I have. A bunch of maybes while the police want facts."

"Then we'll give them facts."

"How?"

"Tell me what you remember about the voice. Could you identify the speaker?"

"No, it was too muffled. Probably a man, but I'm not certain. See how helpful that is?"

This didn't look good. She hadn't said anything that would direct the police to someone else. "Anyone loitering when you left?"

She sighed and studied her hands. "No. It was a pretty dead night. See why I didn't rush to the police? I don't know anything. There has to be something. I didn't do it."

He held up his hands to protect himself from the vehemence in her words. "Hey, I'm in your corner."

"I know." Alanna rubbed her temple again. "This is so frustrating. How do I tell them anything that will prove I'm innocent? I don't even have an alibi. No one saw me come home or spend the evening alone."

He grimaced. "Sorry I didn't stop by."

"Who knew that would matter?"

A seemingly simple decision—come to the island but keep people at arm's length—might now turn her into a prime murder suspect. Anyone who knew her would know she couldn't do something like that—ever. Yet Alanna had done nothing to endear herself to the community and rebuild friendships. As a result, she'd been alone last night, knowing if she'd invited Jonathan over—while it would have relieved her loneliness—it might further ignite the strong attraction between them.

It had been late, and she'd thought the better decision was to remain alone.

Now she wished she had a roommate, a talking parrot, a video system. . .anything that could vouch for her.

"You still with me?" Jonathan's voice tugged her from the quagmire of thoughts.

She looked at him, pulled into the concern she saw etched on his face. He'd always had a face that would make a movie star proud. Part Brad Pitt and part Ethan Hawk. "I'm sorry."

"So what do we do to change this up?"

There was only one thing. Stir up the hornet's nest and see what flew out. "Guess we dig deeper."

"Into what?"

"I want to know what was happening at I'm Not Sharing. Mr. Hoffmeister wasn't alone."

"The police won't like that."

"I don't appreciate being their number one suspect." Alanna stood. "Let's go inside." She stood and walked to the house and grabbed a pad of paper and pen. "I'm going to keep poking at Grady's death. It's unlikely they're connected. . . but Mr. Hoffmeister was ready to tell me something." She started listing the names of the kids at the bonfire. "I should have done this the moment I got back. With the help of my friend Google, I'll track down my classmates and see what they remember. Maybe Grady's death wasn't an accident."

Jonathan grabbed her hand, and the pen stilled. "You understand what you're saying?"

Alanna nodded around the sudden boulder sitting in her throat. "It might have been murder."

"Why would teenagers do something like that?"

"Maybe it was an accident that got covered up, and now they can't afford to have the facts changed."

Jonathan's eyebrows arched. "That's a stretch. How does Hoffmeister tie in?"

"I don't know yet." That was the problem. She only had suspicions. The kind that got people killed? "I'm checking anyway. There weren't that many people. How long can it take?"

"What about your mom and Trevor?"

"You still have a party to plan." She pointed a finger at his chest. "You have to make it the event of the season. Hold it during the lilac festival."

"Impossible! That's a week away."

"I thought you liked doing the impossible for your clients."

He rubbed his square jaw, a flash of competition in his eyes. "Sure, but they have to give me time."

With her sweetest smile, she leaned across the island toward him. Only a breath separated them, and she felt the tug to lean closer. She licked her lips and tried to break the connection. "If you're as good as you say, a week or two is plenty."

His laughter startled her. "Darling, I'll take your challenge, but that also means you have a deadline. You can't unveil your brother as the artist without clearing the air."

"I know." One more reason to wrap everything up. As if avoiding jail wasn't enough.

Jonathan sobered, seeming to accept she was serious about investigating. That's what attorneys do. Track down facts. And she'd check in to Mr. Tomkin's accusations. Maybe they tied into Mr. Hoffmeister's woes. All of a sudden she felt exhausted.

"So what's next?"

Alanna smiled. "How good are you with numbers?"

The next morning, Jonathan's mind swam with the image of rows of numbers. He'd thought when he passed his accounting class in college he wouldn't have to audit someone else's books again. After a few hours trying to decipher the foundation's books and comparing them to the various grants, he agreed with Mr. Tomkin. There were more accounts than grants. The problem was figuring out why. Was there a mistake with the bookkeeping or with the minutes? He hadn't been on the foundation long enough to know if something had been missed. Mr. Hoffmeister could have helped since he served as president two of the four years prior to Tomkin assuming the role.

Alanna had pretended to review the books as she sat next to him. If he inhaled, he could still smell her faint lilac perfume. Each time he'd looked up, she'd ducked as if he'd caught her in the middle of watching him.

It wasn't right to enjoy every moment with Alanna the way he did without addressing his relationship with Jaclyn. It wasn't fair to either woman.

Was what sparked between him and Alanna real? Or

would it evaporate the moment she could leave Mackinac?

He didn't want to experience the desolation that blanketed him when she left and never looked back. It didn't matter that they jumped back to their teenage dynamics. What mattered was whether they could build a lifetime together. Anything less didn't interest him.

All morning he worked through plans for clients. When those events had up-to-date checklists, he turned to his conversation with Alanna last night.

She hadn't murdered Hoffmeister. Period.

No matter how much she'd changed in the eleven years she'd been gone, she couldn't do something like that. Especially to someone she gave every indication of liking. That left one option. He had to help her clear up what happened.

Too bad he didn't know how to start.

Jonathan closed his eyes and leaned back in his chair, praying for wisdom. While Alanna might believe Grady's death was connected to Hoffmeister's murder, Jonathan would start with the more pressing issue: proving her innocence.

Hoffmeister had kept to himself this season. Strange for a man who usually stood in the middle of every gathering sharing jokes and swapping stories. Jonathan couldn't count the number of times Hoffmeister had introduced him to one more woman, this one guaranteed to be the love of his life. The twinkle in his brown eyes had made each exchange memorable. He'd had nothing but disdain in his eyes when Jonathan introduced him to Jaclyn—she hadn't measured up. Instead, Hoffmeister had let him know she wasn't the one.

Hoffmeister had complained about Tomkin each time

Jonathan ran into him that spring. Real trouble brewed between the two. So he'd start with a trip to Hoffmeister's house. See what the man had grumbled about. Alanna could go with him.

Maybe if she stood on the site and saw the past from a different perspective, she'd remember something. Now to figure out how to package the idea in a way she couldn't refuse.

Chapter 26

The cordless phone clicked into the handset even though Alanna wanted to throw it across the room. The college gal came in for her interview. Any hopes Alanna had that she'd work out evaporated when she looked around the studio.

"I really don't know anything about art. Guess this isn't for me."

"Do you want to talk about the responsibilities?"

"I guess."

Half an hour later, she mentioned that her father had told her she didn't have to work over the summer after all. If she was going to spend time on Mackinac, she'd come as a tourist not an employee. After the gal left, Alanna sank onto the stool. At this rate, she would spend the summer on Mackinac.

Considering that the police wouldn't let her leave, she couldn't return to Grand Rapids anytime soon. But the idea of taking even one day off a week sounded as exotic as tea with the queen of England at Buckingham Palace.

Alanna dropped her forehead to her arms. She needed help, but where to get it? All the locals would have jobs. And she didn't have the time to find an international student like so many hotels relied on to fill the summer season employment gap. Honestly, she didn't want the headaches of helping someone find housing, even with the upstairs apartment. She didn't have time to get it ready for a resident. Time to call someone in the know.

The phone rang a couple of times before Patience picked up. "Hello?"

"Patience, this is Alanna. I need help."

"At the studio? I wondered when you'd ask."

"What?"

The woman snorted. "Who do you think gave your mom time off? Your dad hasn't worked for a while."

Why didn't Mom say anything? Alanna had no idea his health had deteriorated until he'd landed in the hospital. "Was I that out of touch?"

"*Protected* is how I'd frame it. Want me to come tomorrow? I could work after services."

"That would be great. Any ideas who might like a job?"

"I'll talk to a few people. See what I can stir up."

"Thank you." Alanna hung up. It wasn't a permanent solution, but having one day to herself sounded like a kiss from heaven. The uninterrupted time to find answers could be a gift.

When she walked out, something barreled into her. "Oof."

She glanced up and saw she'd stepped into the path of a towheaded little boy.

Jaclyn hurried up, an apology coloring her cheeks. "Dylan, get back here." She grabbed his hand and tugged the toddler closer. "I'm so sorry." She wiped her free hand on her skirt then stuck it out toward Alanna. "Nice to see you again."

Sure it was. Alanna took a breath to end that train of thought. "Dylan is a cute little guy."

"I like him. He just runs faster than I do sometimes." She eyed her strappy, three-inch-heel sandals. "I forgot to pack different shoes. I've teetered from the Grand and am ready to get out of these things."

Alanna would take them off—then she looked at the road. Horses were quieter than cars but provided a waste product unknown to vehicles.

Jaclyn seemed to read Alanna's mind as she grinned. "Not the safest place to go barefoot." Dylan tugged on her hand. "Where are you headed?"

"Home. I decided to lock up a few minutes early." Start that day off now.

"Mind if we walk with you? We're headed to the fort. Jonathan's meeting us." The slightest glint reflected in her eyes, and it wasn't the sun shining off Jaclyn's cute glasses. Just when Alanna had begun to like her.

"That's fine." Alanna swallowed as the trio started down the sidewalk, Dylan tearing ahead. "Is he okay?"

"As long as I can see him."

Alanna nodded and glanced at her companion out of the corner of her eye. So this was the woman Jonathan spent time with. Jaclyn had a sparkle that would attract men even if her curves in all the right places didn't. No wonder Jonathan liked her. It shouldn't bother her, since Alanna was an independent woman, one who didn't need or want a man. Not even Jonathan. She almost choked on the thought.

"How long will you stay?"

"I'm not sure. I have to find someone for the studio before I think of leaving."

"Maybe I can help."

Sure she could. Anything to remove competition. Alanna blanched. Where had this attitude come from? Jaclyn was welcome to Jonathan. If she said it often enough, surely she'd come to mean it. Right?

It was a theory.

She pasted on a smile, feeling the strain. "I could use help. My leads have disappeared. The firm partners will call soon, and I'm stuck here. They won't like that at all."

"I'll check around. Send people your way."

"Thanks." Whatever the motivation, she needed employees. If she could find some soon, she could focus on clearing her name. She didn't even want to think what the partners would say when she had to tell them about the murder investigation. She hadn't found time to open a web browser, let alone start tracking down her classmates during the day. There'd been enough customers to keep her busy. She'd start the search tonight.

They reached the green space in front of the fort. The rows of stairs running up the steep hill exhausted Alanna each time she saw them. It didn't matter how fit she was, her calves burned each time she climbed those steps.

Dylan squealed and ran toward someone. "Jonathan!" Then his words blurred together as Jonathan knelt down to his level. In an instant, Alanna pictured him interacting with a daughter. Hers. He'd be an amazing dad, and his kids would be blessed.

"I'll call with possibilities." Jaclyn nodded toward Dylan and Jonathan. "I'd better catch up with them. Nice to see you."

"Bye." Alanna stood a moment watching the interaction between Jonathan and Jaclyn. Jonathan's response to Jaclyn seemed less enthusiastic than his intense interaction with Dylan. Instead, he smiled, gave the pretty woman a half-hearted hug, then turned back to Dylan. Could Dylan be the reason he stayed?

The insight surprised Alanna, and then she felt guilty

for watching. If Jonathan wanted to be with Jaclyn, he was a grown man and could do what he liked.

See, it was easier to say this time.

It did get easier to lie to herself.

Jonathan focused his attention on Dylan and Jaclyn, not on the beauty watching from a distance. He didn't know whether to be annoyed or flattered at her attention. Then she left without even a small wave, and he wanted to punch something.

He never should have violated his one-date policy. It was easier to avoid the thought of lifelong relationships if one never allowed things to advance past one or two dates.

Jaclyn sidled up to him and tried to grab his hand, but he slid free. "Hey, isn't Hoffmeister's home near the Grand Hotel's property?"

She shook her head a bit and looked at him with a blank look. "Hoffmeister?"

"The old guy who was murdered."

"Oh. I don't know. I suppose he lived close. Jonathan, I work in the spa. Schedule appointments. I don't know all the hotel's neighbors. You know how big the property is, right? And then there's the golf course."

"Right."

"Why the interest?"

"Curiosity."

Dylan joined them by grabbing one of each of their hands and running then swinging as he hung between them. Jaclyn tugged him to a stop then looked at Jonathan. "Just curious? Really? You expect me to believe that?"

"It's not every day a murder happens here."

"Or every day that a long-lost love returns." She stared him down. "I'm not saying this again, Jonathan. You have to choose, because you can't have both of us. It's her"— she gestured to where Alanna had stood—"or me. One or the other. Make up your mind, and let me know." She swiped at her eyes in a short, angry chop. "Come on, Dylan. We're going home."

Dylan looked over his shoulder at Jonathan, confusion twisting his face as his mom tugged him down the sidewalk.

Jonathan took the long way home. He needed every step to pray and sort through Jaclyn's challenge. Part of him wanted to push them both away. Reestablish his independence and live life without the risks and entanglements that getting close to a woman involved.

Who did he love: Jaclyn or Dylan?

It was a question he didn't want to chase to an answer. The implications bothered him. It wasn't right to maintain a relationship with Jaclyn for Dylan's sake. At the same time, he couldn't imagine facing Dylan if he did end any hope of a future with Jaclyn. Spending time with her hadn't seemed like a bad idea when dinner with her served as an attractive alternative to another long evening alone.

Still, it wasn't fair to Jaclyn if Dylan held them together.

He turned up the path to his cabin but detoured to the shed and his fishing gear. He carried his pole and tackle box to the dock. The small circles on the surface indicated fish. Maybe a couple would try his bait rather than a tasty fly. And maybe insight would hop in his mind while he waited. A guy could hope.

Jonathan settled on the edge and baited the hook. He cast to the side and watched the bobber dip up and down in the placid pond. The *chuck-chucking* call of the gray jay pulled his attention to the trees. After a minute, he spotted the white face and gray feathers of the bird. Soon an answering call echoed back. Jonathan reached for the binoculars tucked in the box. Since nothing seemed to be happening with the fish, he'd scan the trees and see if the Kirtland's warbler hid in the trees along with the gray jays.

At the sound of steps on the dock, Jonathan swung around, the binoculars catching the midsection of someone. He lowered the device. Alanna stood a few feet away, an uncertainness in the slump of her shoulders and question in her eyes.

"May I join you?"

The fishing pole bobbed, so Jonathan dropped the glasses and tugged the pole up. She took his silence as an invitation and moved to sit next to him. Jonathan swallowed as he set the hook, her lilac perfume weaving around him.

"I'm sorry about tonight."

He turned to look at her, noting the sadness around her eyes. "What do you mean?"

"I don't mean to cause trouble for you with Jaclyn." Wistfulness softened her words.

The pole jumped, and Jonathan tugged again. He didn't want to let whatever fought on the other end get away.

"I don't do relationships well, Jonathan. I haven't since. . ."

He could fill in the thought. "Since you left." Me. "Funny, I don't do relationships either."

She pulled her knees up and wrapped her arms around

them. "Guess we're a mess."

"Yeah." He gave a final tug and pulled up nothing. The hook dangled naked.

"Guess he got away again."

"Who?"

"Grandpappy." She stood and disappeared down the dock.

As he watched the dusk wrap around her, Grandpappy wasn't the only one who slipped away.

Chapter 27

Sunday after church, Alanna returned home, grateful that Patience Matthews had been willing to work. As she settled at the small kitchen table with her laptop, Alanna knew she needed the break. Not just from the store, but to have time to investigate. The view of the pond and her mother's gardens tried to woo her from her task of tracking down classmates. Instead, she lit a lavender candle and forced herself to focus on finding those on her list. Time passed and the distraction grew as her searches didn't lead anywhere productive. She stared at the names she'd copied from her yearbook, slowly crossing off each one as she located former classmates.

With each mark, her hope that she'd learn something spiraled. Only a handful still lived on the island. She'd already run into Ginger and Piper and knew she'd bump into the other couple eventually. Still she wrote down phone numbers. A phone call might be easier than a face-to-face interview.

When she checked the last name, she pulled the cordless in front of her and started dialing. The first several numbers had jumped to voice mail, and she dutifully left messages. If her classmates listened, she had no doubt they'd find the calls odd. After all, she hadn't contacted any in eleven years. After reaching voicemail again, she marked that she'd left a message next to a name then stood to stretch. *Guide me, Father.*

She would find the truth. She'd become tenacious to a fault for clients. Now that she could be the one landing in jail, she had even more reason to stick to this until she un-raveled the tangled problem.

A knock at the door pulled her to the front room. She opened the door, uncertain whether to smile or close the door when she saw Jonathan on the other side. She hadn't come here to break up his relationship. But she couldn't deny the way her heart leapt when she saw him.

He stood a few feet back, his stance wide and hands behind him. He looked ready to tackle a day of hiking in his navy T-shirt and khaki cargo shorts. A grin tweaked only one side of his mouth, not the full-out glad-to-see-her smile she'd received even a day ago.

"What do you need, Jonathan?"

"Wondered if you had time for a field trip?"

"A field trip? This is my first day off, and I've got a list of calls to make." Though she'd really wrapped those up.

"Since it's your first day, let me take you on a tour."

She studied him, uncertain what he was up to but knowing the unknown with him was more appealing than another round of messages. "I grew up here. I don't think I need a tour."

"You do today."

Alanna crossed her arms and leaned against the door frame.

"I want to ride out to Hoffmeister's house. He was having that property dispute."

"I know that."

"Let's poke around. See if we can find anything up there that might shed some light on things. At the same time, you can see the perspective he had for the accident."

A breeze ruffled her hair as if teasing her to go play.

Maybe she could combine a bit of fun with investigating. She could maintain a professional distance with Jonathan. She did it all the time in Grand Rapids, though none of the men she worked with were her first love.

"Come on."

"Let me lock up." She grabbed her keys and cell phone then closed and locked the door. When she started toward the shed and her bike, Jonathan stopped her.

"I've got it covered."

"Covered?"

"Come on."

She hesitated then followed him toward the road. Only then did she notice the tandem bike leaning against the fence. "Jonathan. . ."

"I'll ride in front, and this way you won't confront a scene unexpectedly again. If you still freeze, I can get you home."

She didn't know whether to be touched or furious. "I'm not that weak."

He held his hands up. "I never said you were." He straddled the bike and steadied it. "Climb on."

It seemed romantic and intimate, being that close and letting him control where they went. Still, she found herself climbing behind him and grasping the handlebars. It had been years since she'd ridden a tandem bike. She blocked the image of the romantic sunset picnic they'd shared from her mind. One stray thought that direction and she'd never recover. All the dreams she'd harbored for them would rush over her. She swallowed and closed her eyes, forcing herself to stay.

"It'll take a few minutes to find our balance." She wanted to correct him. Every time she was near him, her careful equilibrium abandoned her faster than a racehorse leaving the starting gate. He pushed off, and she gripped the handlebars. "Here we go."

The bike teetered on the verge of calamity as they bumped across the path. Alanna tried to focus on the trail but decided it was better if she looked at anything except where they were headed. Nobody wanted a backseat driver, especially on a tandem bike. But when she pinned her gaze on what was in front of her, she stared at the expanse of his shoulders. Now she didn't know where to look.

Finally, Jonathan steered them off the trail to a smoother path. Her teeth quit jarring, and she glanced around.

"Where does this path go?"

He glanced over his shoulder then turned back to the path. "I forgot it's new since you left. It's kind of a back pass as it skirts the golf course and then reaches that collection of homes where Hoffmeister lives."

"Lived."

Jonathan nodded. "It saves time from going through town to the paved street and then around the island on Lake Shore."

Only the sound of the tires against the path broke the background music of tree branches fanning and birds singing. Alanna glanced around, trying to spot some of the songbirds, surprised Jonathan didn't. "I thought you were a birder."

"I am. There's not much I haven't seen along this path though. There are only so many places to go without swimming."

Alanna laughed at the image that generated. Jonathan in full birding gear, vest stuffed with a guide in every pocket and a hat and binoculars, flailing his way to the mainland.

"So what are we hearing?"

Did she really want to know? Alanna had never expressed an interest before. Instead, she'd called it odd the summer he started getting interested. Maybe she needed the distraction right now. He could humor her.

"The *beecher-beecher-beecher* comes from a Connecticut warbler. I wouldn't normally expect to hear one here. Guess the undergrowth is dense enough." He listened a moment. "The abrupt clicking comes from a black-backed woodpecker. He must not like the company." A small brown bird flew from one tree to another. "There goes the boreal chickadee."

"Where do you like to go birding?"

"The backyard. With the pond and all the trees, I really don't have to wander far to see a variety. To see any great number though, I do have to get to the mainland. Either side works, depending on my mood and how far I want to roam." As a fork in the road neared, he slowed. "I haven't gotten away for a while." He pointed down one path. "After this turn, you'll see the golf course. Watch for flying golf balls. Some of the visitors think they're better golfers than they are."

"Tell me about this neighborhood. Mr. Hoffmeister's house sat by itself. . ."

He could hear her unspoken *back then*. A lot had changed. "He broke up his piece and subdivided it. Sold the lots and made a nice penny. You'll see the homes are pretty standard.

Small cottages with a Victorian flair. He sold the lot next to his house last."

"How many houses?"

"Five or six. Not too many. And most of them are occupied by weekenders. They come for a week or two at a time and rent the homes the rest of the time."

"Keep the tourists coming."

Jonathan nodded as they rounded a corner and the gated entrance to the Wawashkamo Golf Course came into view.

"Jonathan, why didn't we take Leslie Road? Why the roundabout?"

"It's your day off." Guess he should have known she'd question his path once she understood where they were.

"I think the thick trees will protect us from any misdirected golf balls." Alanna seemed to turn behind him. "You sure you should be in front?"

He pushed harder against the pedals, propelling the tandem bike across the crushed gravel. "Yep."

Quiet fell as they pedaled the rest of the way to Straits Trail. Here's where Alanna needed him. She'd keep going on Stonecliffe, never connecting to Morton Trail. That trail hadn't led much of anywhere when she lived here. Now the group of homes strung between the two.

The bike bounced across the trail. A mountain bike would have been better suited but not as much fun as having Alanna immediately behind him. He turned slightly and flicked a thumb in the other direction. "Here's the start of the homes." Alanna glanced around, and he turned back to the front. "Mr. Hoffmeister's home is up here a bit."

"He had such a great location. Secluded. Great view of Lake Huron. Relatively close to town. I wonder why he sold land."

"I heard the fudge shop had money problems. Needed the cash infusion." Could those cash-flow problems have pushed him to skim money from the foundation? He didn't seem like the type to do anything like that. He'd always seemed like an honorable man when Jonathan interacted with him.

"Hmm. I'm surprised he didn't find another way. He always valued his privacy."

"Maybe he did. Do you think he could have created the fake accounts?"

Silence followed his question. "I don't know." Alanna sighed, her breath tickling his neck. "I hate to think about him that way."

"Still, there are only a handful of people who would have access to create those accounts."

"Guess we need to figure out who else could have done it. Those accounts were created during his presidency, so it's not Tomkin."

"Could be anyone on the board."

"How easy would it be for someone on the board to do it?"

Jonathan thought a moment. "Outside the bookkeeper? It wouldn't be easy at all."

"Who was the bookkeeper then?"

"I'm not sure. I've only been on the board since Gerald came on. Here we are." Jonathan stopped the bike in front of the small Victorian cottage. On the surface it looked well maintained, but when he looked closer, Jonathan saw peeling paint and a lack of landscaping. Mr. Hoffmeister had let the details go.

Alanna slid off the bike, and the weight shifted, bumping the bike against his calves. She walked toward the side yard and around to the front. "We came here once for a barbecue. It had been a hard winter. Lots of snow and bitter cold. Even more than usual." She turned and studied the house. "Everybody was so glad to see the snow melt, and Mr. Hoffmeister invited the church over for a spring celebration. He loved the impromptu baseball game and the wild game of tag."

"He didn't do that anymore."

She glanced around and swept the area with a hand. "He couldn't after letting these other homes in. No space for baseballs to go wild."

Jonathan scanned the area, trying to imagine what it had looked like before. The homes were tucked in the trees, and he couldn't imagine a clearing large enough for baseball. "So where do we start?"

"Well. . ." Alanna frowned.

"What?"

"I don't see any crime-scene tape."

"Why would you? He was murdered in town, not down here."

"True, but if I led the investigation, I'd want people to stay back." She climbed the two stairs to the porch. She glanced around then hurried toward the front door. "That's odd."

"What?"

"Mr. Hoffmeister always had a life-size German shepherd statue right beside the door. Said since he was allergic, it was the closest he could come to a guard dog. I never thought he needed one out here by himself. He mentioned it in his note, so it should still be here." She stopped and brushed the floor. "There's still a mark where the dog sat."

Jonathan glanced around. "No dog."

"No dog." Alanna tugged at a floorboard, scooped something out, and stood.

"What are you doing?"

"Getting us into the house."

Chapter 28

It didn't feel right, but she knew where the key was. And Mr. Hoffmeister had invited her to explore his home with the note he gave her. No, it didn't say anything about going inside his home if he were murdered, but in light of what happened, he seemed to know something was wrong. Maybe he'd left some indication in his home.

Alanna stood on the small porch, the spare key in her hand. Sometimes she wished people weren't so stuck to their habits. If the key had disappeared, then she'd leave right then. Instead, the tiny key felt like it weighed a million pounds. Go in? Stay out?

With a key, it wasn't really breaking in—she hoped.

But if she stayed outside, she'd never find answers that waited on the other side of the door. With a murderer on the loose, she had to try. The Mackinac Island police weren't any more equipped to investigate a murder than she. The difference was they thought she was a prime suspect.

She didn't kill Mr. Hoffmeister. Now she had to prove it. She glanced at the man standing next to her, arms crossed. He'd brought her here, but would he go along with searching the house?

"So?" Jonathan studied her, his chin tilted toward the house. "Are we going in or waiting for someone to call the police?"

Alanna glanced around the houses that appeared empty. It only took one nosy neighbor to compound her problems with the police. "In we go." She slotted the key into the lock and listened for the click. The door swung open with a soft groan.

"Now what?"

Alanna let her eyes adjust to the dim light. "Let's start with a quick survey of the rooms. That shouldn't take long." The front room stood pretty empty. A dilapidated couch pushed against one wall while a row of leaning bookcases lined another. She ran a finger along the spines. "He took such pride in his collection. And this room used to have nice furniture. I wonder what happened."

Jonathan shrugged and then shoved his hands in his pockets. "Not sure. I didn't know him very well. Just friendly greetings when we bumped into each other. Maybe he had to help Ginger out when she got pregnant. She was pretty young when she became a mom."

Nothing stuck out in the quick survey of the living area, so Alanna walked to the kitchen. "Did you know Mr. Hoffmeister was something of a gourmet cook?" Jonathan shook his head. "He favored vegetarian dishes, but I liked sampling them. Usually had hints of spices my mom never touched. Made for a new experience even if I did keep a glass of water close."

"Did your family spend a lot of time here?"

"Maybe once a season. We all worked hard but liked to play when we peeled away the time." Alanna opened drawers, finding only silverware and the expected hodgepodge drawer filled with junk. At this rate, she'd never find anything valuable.

Jonathan opened a couple of cupboards but didn't seem to find anything interesting either. "Upstairs?"

"I guess." Alanna had never been upstairs. Mr. Hoffmeister

had treated it as off-limits, an easy request to comply with when a wide-open expanse around the house and the hike down to the beach awaited. As soon as she got upstairs, Alanna entered the bedroom that overlooked the beach. She pulled back the curtains.

"See anything?"

She shook her head. "Why did I think this view or perspective would make a difference? I was so much closer on the beach."

"Maybe Hoffmeister saw something. Or maybe you wanted to believe this would add key data."

"Maybe." Alanna's shoulders slumped forward under the challenge of finding answers. She shifted to try a different angle. "I just want to find the truth. Even if it's not what I want, the truth is the key to bringing Trevor home. His paintings are too good not to sell with his name."

Jonathan stood next to her, his shoulder brushing hers. He stared out the window, shifting his head slightly as he scanned. "Where exactly was the party?"

Alanna scanned over the trees, trying to find the crop of rocks where they had built the bonfire. Had the trees grown that much? She couldn't find the rocks but pointed toward the left. "It should be down there."

"Should be?" The skepticism in his words pierced her.

"Things have changed." Even as she said the words, she heard her defensiveness. She couldn't help wondering what else had changed that she hadn't noticed. Alanna leaned against the windowsill, breaking contact with Jonathan. "What now?"

"We keep looking. Mr. Hoffmeister had something for you. We should at least check all the rooms. Maybe we'll find it." Jonathan moved to the small closet and opened the door. "I don't see anything in here."

"Why would he leave it in a closet? Unless he worried someone else would come?"

"Whoever killed him would have come up here next if there was something to find."

It made sense. But it didn't answer the question what that item could be. As they moved into the other bedroom, Alanna tried to imagine what it might be.

From the way Alanna's nose screwed up, she was deep in thought. He gave her some space to formulate her thoughts while he surveyed this last room. So far nothing had jumped out at him—other than the fact that Alanna wasn't finding anything from the view of the accident site or the elusive item Mr. Hoffmeister mentioned.

Had she imagined it?

He brushed the question aside. He didn't want to think Alanna had fabricated the situation. Yet nothing added up.

He watched her, hoping something would exonerate her and remove the cloud of suspicion. The bedroom was a clean widower's pad. If anyone came in to search the house after Hoffmeister's death, they'd been extremely careful to leave no trace of their presence. The house didn't look anything like the trashed houses he saw in movies. Instead, if anyone had come in, they'd done a thorough job of keeping their presence and identity hidden.

Alanna moved like one in a trance. Her steps faltered

as she entered his bedroom. He couldn't discern what had caught her attention, since the room looked like a typical man's room. Plain bedspread in a deep navy with a couple of pillows tossed on top. A dresser with a cluttered surface. Closet door cracked.

"Why's the door open?" Alanna's whisper almost didn't reach him.

"What?"

"All the other doors have been firmly closed. Yet this one is open."

He studied it then turned to her. "I wouldn't call it open." Still, he could see her point. "Maybe it's different because this was his room."

She shook her head, her eyes wide. The door barged open, slapping the wall. A man barreled from it, gun drawn, but instead of shooting, he shoved into Alanna, knocking her to the ground. Clad in jeans, a hunting jacket, and stocking cap, the man rushed toward the stairs. Jonathan pushed after him, jumping over Alanna. She groaned but seemed okay. The man, however, would disappear if Jonathan couldn't catch him.

"Stay here," Jonathan yelled over his shoulder as he rushed after the man. The front door was flung open when he reached the main room. He raced toward it then stopped. What if the man had done that to get him to chase into the yard, leaving Alanna by herself? Then the invader could circle back upstairs and hurt her. He glanced around the room and stepped back to glance behind the couch. No one lurked there or in the kitchen, so he raced out the door and launched off the porch.

Jonathan froze, listening for any sound as he scanned the

area. The bright hunting jacket disappeared into a copse of trees. Jonathan took off in that direction. The thrashing of breaking branches and leaves underfoot pulled him forward. He had to catch the man. Find out why he'd been in the house. The man left a trail as wide as an elephant, not slowing as he ran pell-mell through the trees. Jonathan huffed as he pushed to gain ground.

He pumped his arms. Willed his legs to move. For all the biking and walking the island required, he should be in good enough shape to catch the intruder. Instead, the distance spread between them.

Jonathan dug deep and pushed on with a spurt of energy. He had to catch this guy.

He tugged his cell phone from his pocket. No bars. Argh! He shoved it back in his pocket and sucked in a breath. The man stumbled, and Jonathan gained a few feet. There was something familiar about the way the man moved. Racing, Jonathan couldn't identify him from behind. The man crossed a trail, and Jonathan skidded to a stop as a group on bicycles pedaled past. By the time the straggler cleared, the man had disappeared.

Jonathan raced across the trail but couldn't see the man anywhere. Even with the bright hunting jacket, he'd disappeared. Jonathan hurried forward anyway. He had to try.

A bright blob of color caught his eye, and he sped toward it. He let out a groan when he got closer and saw the runner had hung the jacket from a branch.

He leaned over, hands on his knees, and gulped air. How could he explain this to Alanna?

Alanna rubbed her shoulder, massaging the spot that collided with the floor. It throbbed, but she ignored the pain. She hurried downstairs. She couldn't leave Jonathan to catch the intruder alone. Yet when she made it to the porch, Jonathan and the brightly clothed stranger had disappeared.

A headache started to pound as she wandered back into the house. She'd barely settled on the saggy couch when the door banged open.

"Jonathan?"

"No, but I'd like to know what you're doing here."

She turned and froze. Detective Bull didn't look any happier to see her there than he sounded. His brows were drawn together, his stance wide like he was ready for a fight. She slowly raised her hands. "Does it help that I was getting ready to call?"

"Good thing a neighbor took care of that, complaining about a lot of activity in a dead man's house."

"I had a key. And you saw the note. He wanted me to see something."

"So you took it upon yourself to come? Without checking?"

She nodded, knowing how foolish and ridiculous it sounded. And looked.

"I don't know whether to haul you immediately to jail or laugh. You're an attorney."

"Maybe, but I'm also your prime suspect." Alanna stood, refusing to let him intimidate her with his size. She thrust her hands on her hips and stepped closer. "I can't rely on you to check things like this. Not when I might go to jail."

"Am I interrupting anything?" A bedraggled Jonathan stood in the doorway, fire in his eyes.

"Just hauling this gal off to jail. You bring your girlfriend up here on that tandem bike?"

Alanna started to sputter. "We're not. . ." But she couldn't deny she wanted to be. Especially as she watched the fire in Jonathan's eyes. He looked ready to attack the detective in an effort to protect her. How she longed for that security he offered. But what about Jaclyn and Dylan? She sank back to the saggy couch. This was too complicated.

Detective Bull looked at Jonathan, eyeing the coat he carried. "Why don't you tell me what that's about?"

"After you call down to Ryan and let him know that a guy in jeans and a stocking cap is running into town. He'll be sweaty and out of breath. He was hiding in an upstairs closet when we got here. Knocked Alanna to the ground and kept running. Thought I had him, but he hung this on a tree to distract me."

Detective Bull quirked an eyebrow. "Guess it worked."

"Yeah," Jonathan growled. He looked like he regretted every moment of their time up here. This probably wasn't the time to remind him he'd gotten the tandem bike. If he hadn't come, she'd have done this alone eventually, just not today. "Do you want this thing?"

The detective nodded. "I'll have the techs look it over. I doubt it has any connection to the murder, but it's worth evaluating." He crossed his arms across his wide chest. "Let's get back to what the two of you are doing here."

Chapter 29

The bald truth was there was no good reason.

Jonathan had a crazy idea, acted without thinking, and Alanna almost got killed. Now she sat on the couch probably headed straight to jail, do not pass go, do not collect two hundred dollars.

And it was his fault.

She'd been perfectly content working through her lists and phone calls. His teasing got her on the bike and up here. It was still a good idea but would have been better if he'd cleared it with the police first.

"You can blame me."

Detective Bull studied him, skepticism tightening his already tense posture. "Really?"

"Alanna was at home working when I came up with the tandem bike. I steered us here."

Alanna looked up and started to sputter. "I would have made the trip eventually. And since that other guy was here, better now than later. At least he didn't get away with anything."

"That we know of." Jonathan shrugged. "He could have stuffed something in the jacket."

"But we have that."

Detective Bull glanced through the pockets. "Nothing clearly important."

Alanna sighed. "That would be too easy."

"Tell me everything that happened from the moment you hit this property." Bull pulled a chair over from the kitchen and took out a pen and notebook. Alanna and Jonathan tag-teamed the telling. When they were done, Bull studied Alanna. "Is there anything you aren't telling me?"

"No." She spread her hands in front of her. "That's it. We didn't see anything worth noting until that man opened the closet."

"All right." He closed his notebook and stood. "Then let's finish searching."

Jonathan couldn't believe his ears. "What?"

"I don't trust you two not to come back, so I'm staying right here while you satisfy yourselves that there's no secret code."

Alanna nodded. "I haven't seen any records from I'm Not Sharing. He was also on a couple boards, but there's no office. He had to keep those somewhere."

"Some were at his shop, but not enough to run the business. Let's start where Mystery Man waited." Bull let them precede him up the stairs. Alanna looked back as she scurried up. He had an appraising look on his face as he watched her. While it bothered her to be under his scrutiny, maybe he didn't think she'd committed a crime when she entered the house.

Now to find whatever Mr. Hoffmeister had left.

Mr. Tomkin seemed intent to point a finger at Mr. Hoffmeister, who had pointed the finger right back. They used to be good friends. Maybe it was one more thing her mind had altered with the distance and time.

As she reentered the bedroom, Alanna took in the details. Somewhere Mr. Hoffmeister had kept records. If he was like her clients, finding those documents could be key. Especially if Gerald Tomkin's allegations were valid. She turned to

Detective Bull. "Have you examined Mr. Hoffmeister's finances?"

He shook his head with a barely audible snort. "I can't comment on an ongoing investigation, especially one where you're the suspect."

"It never hurts to ask."

"Why do you want to know?"

"Just curious." She couldn't tell him about Tomkin's allegations. Not without more to back them up.

"Humph."

Alanna opened the closet doors and started pushing against the back wall. "Financials make short work of determining if something was wrong with his money."

Jonathan knelt by the floor and pulled up the bed skirt. "Bingo."

"What?" Detective Bull tucked his notebook in his inside jacket pocket and took a quick step in his direction.

"What guy puts one of these on his bed?" Jonathan thumped the piece of cloth with disgust. "There are file boxes under here. Maybe these have the missing office documents." Jonathan tugged the first box free.

"Maybe." Detective Bull pulled a pair of gloves from a pocket and slipped them on. "Let me."

Jonathan stepped out of the way while Alanna edged closer. She held her breath as Detective Bull eased the lid off the first box. When a stack of ledgers and array of files appeared, the man remained unflappable while Alanna wanted to grab the box and start uncovering the secrets hidden inside.

"Could be promising." Bull tapped the lid back on. "I'll take this back to the office."

Alanna bit back a sharp word—or two—at the thought

of whatever the box contained disappearing off the island.

"Sure we can't glance at it here?" Jonathan spread his hands and grinned. "We've gone to a lot of trouble to find that box."

"You can drag out the other boxes. Here's a pair of gloves."

Jonathan slipped them on and knelt down again. "There's only one more."

Alanna frowned. Could two boxes be sufficient to contain all the records? Especially since the detective suggested there weren't many at the shop?

"Feel free to check for yourself." Jonathan tugged up the skirt and made a sweeping motion. "Maybe my x-ray vision missed something."

Alanna made a face at his sarcasm. "Trust me, businesses have lots of paper. No matter how small, I usually spend days wading through paper looking for one important fact."

As Jonathan watched, he knew Lanna wasn't thinking straight. She kept focusing on what she expected to see. Mr. Hoffmeister was a nice guy, but he wasn't the world's most effective businessman. If he were, he'd have a string of fudge shops like the others. Instead, he'd had one that did a good business but hadn't differentiated from all the other fudge on the island. It wouldn't surprise Jonathan if the two meager boxes contained everything.

If she'd decided the paperwork would save her and eventually Trevor, she'd misplaced her faith. "We've got more places to poke. Maybe we'll find something there."

Detective Bull again let them precede him. That action annoyed Jonathan. Why didn't the man get in front and investigate? He was the detective after all.

"So how long you been with the state police?"

Bull did one of those annoying shoulder slouches that communicated he didn't care enough to really comment.

"Five years? Ten?"

"Enough."

"Like the St. Ignace office?"

Bull shrugged again. "It's fine."

"Until January?" Jonathan entered the other bedroom and checked under the bed, behind the dresser, and in the closet. Nothing.

"Snow's not bad."

"If you've got four-wheel drive and a snowmobile."

"Don't forget the cross-country skis."

Alanna studied him, a question in her eyes. He ignored it as he avoided looking at the detective. Something just wasn't right.

Jonathan stood and looked out the window. Where was the detective's bike? "How do you plan to get those boxes down to the dock?"

Alanna must have caught the warning, because she slid toward the hallway as Bull stepped to the closet. The man made a perfunctory search.

"Not too worried about it."

"Didn't think so. Still, it makes me wonder what you're doing here. Alone. Wouldn't you bring someone with you?" Jonathan stepped closer to the man, trying to block his view of Alanna as she slipped into the hallway.

"Not enough manpower." Sounded plausible, but after

the way the chief shadowed him earlier, Jonathan wasn't sure.

All he knew was he had a clear signal from his gut that he didn't like the situation. He might not make a living as a detective, but something smelled. As he tried to evaluate the situation, he knew he couldn't let anything happen to Alanna. If the situation was off, he needed to do everything possible to keep her safe. She meant too much to him to pretend otherwise.

"Where'd Ms. Stone go?" The detective stepped into his space, puffing up as if to make himself look bigger.

Jonathan made a show of looking around. "She's right here."

"Nope. Out of the way."

The thought of going toe-to-toe with a second person wore Jonathan out. Still, he squared himself in front of Bull. He'd pull energy from deep resources to give Alanna time to slip away.

Bull growled. "Move now."

When Jonathan remained in place, the man shoved him against the door frame. Jonathan fought for his balance then stuck a foot out. He hoped that didn't count as assaulting an officer as Bull slammed into a wall.

"Bad choice, Covington."

As a commotion erupted downstairs, Jonathan took his place in the doorway. "It's nothing personal."

"You can tell that to the judge."

"We'll see." Fortunately, he knew a good attorney.

Alanna rushed back up the stairs. She'd had her cell phone out, dialing 911, when she'd reached the porch and heard the distinctive crunch of horses' hooves against the trail. A small taxi had pulled up, and Police Chief Ryan climbed out followed by another man in police uniform.

"Chief Ryan." Alanna closed her phone. "How did you know to come?"

"Research."

Yes, the man used an economy of words, but that one word struck Alanna as exceptionally sparse. "Jonathan and Detective Bull are upstairs."

The young officer shook his head. "He's a maverick."

The two uniformed men moved in front of her. As the screen door eased shut, Chief Ryan looked back at her. "Stay here, Ms. Stone."

While his words sounded good, no way she'd stay in place and let whatever happened take place without helping Jonathan. She slipped off her shoes and then eased the door open. Her feet didn't make any noise as she crept through the lower rooms to the stairs.

"Bull, what are you doing? I thought we agreed to do this together." Chief Ryan's voice left no doubt he expected an immediate answer.

"Chief, I got a tip and followed it. That's what we do in the state police."

Alanna slipped around the corner and placed her foot on a stair. It protested as if an entire marching band wanted to pass by. Chief Ryan turned with a frown. "I told you to stay put."

"Yes, sir." He hadn't been around before she left, so he wouldn't know she'd struggle to obey that instruction, but Jonathan's snort made it clear he did.

"Someone want to fill me in?" Chief Ryan looked from one to the other. "We got a call but didn't find the suspect that launched from here."

"We've got his jacket over here, but that's it." Bull shrugged. "There's no indication why he was here or how long. All we know is he didn't take anything visible with him." He tapped the boxes. "Do you have transportation?"

"Outside."

"Good, then these boxes and I can hitchhike along."

Chief Ryan turned to Jonathan. "You and Miss Stone need a ride, or do you plan to use that tandem bike?"

"We'll bike down."

"Okay, so long as you come straight to the station."

"Yes, sir."

Chief Ryan looked at Alanna.

"We'll be there." She had too many questions she wanted him to answer.

Two hours later, she sat in the police chief's overloaded office, feeling like she'd never get an answer since the only talking she got to do was answering his questions.

"Explain again why you thought it was a good idea to invade a murdered man's home." Chief Ryan sat on the corner of his industrial desk and knocked the top with his knuckles as he studied Alanna intently.

"We had the key." The words sounded weak, but she still believed that allowed her actions.

"But Mr. Hoffmeister hadn't given it to you, correct?"

"Yes." She rubbed at the pounding in her temples.

"I'm not charging you with breaking and entering right now, since Detective Bull vouches you didn't take anything. But if you pull a stunt like that again, I will ask the prosecutor to bring every charge against you that has a 20 percent chance of sticking. You leave the investigating to us, or it will be interfering with a police investigation."

She opened her mouth to respond then shut it. She'd only make matters worse.

Jonathan tugged at her hand. "Let's head home."

"All right." She stood then paused. "You still haven't said whether you have ideas on who the intruder was."

"The other one?" She winced at the words. "Maybe the murderer's looking for something. If that's the case, you were lucky. Don't count on being so fortunate next time."

Alanna followed Jonathan to the door but turned when Chief Ryan cleared his throat.

"Miss Stone, I've checked with friends in Grand Rapids. They say you're quite the tenacious investigator." He crossed his arms and leaned back. "Let me give you some advice. Stop. Anything you do could actually muddy things up rather than clear you. What if the crucial fact hides in one of those boxes? What if those boxes had gotten destroyed? What if you'd gone through them without Detective Bull? You could have removed anything you didn't like. Destroyed evidence. Or created the impression that could have happened. They would have sat there a long time undisturbed if you hadn't taken it upon yourselves to investigate."

"With all due respect, Chief, don't forget about the guy we chased away." Jonathan stared at him. "He was in that room and could have found them as easily as I did."

"Chances of finding him are slim to none. Officers are

watching for him, but you know he's ditched the coat, cap, and anything else that IDs him."

And with that, Alanna was no closer to finding the real murderer or clearing Trevor.

Chapter 30

Jonathan had to get Alanna out of the City Hall building before she exploded. He could almost watch her mind process what they'd learned and piece it together with what she already knew.

The chief studied Alanna with a hard look. "Stay out of the investigation. I know it's a challenge for you to leave things to the police. But we have it under control. You getting in the way doesn't help your case."

Alanna opened her mouth, but Jonathan raced to answer. "Thank you for your help, Chief. We'll head out now." He grabbed Alanna's hand and pulled her from the room and out of the police offices.

"What are you doing?"

"Saving you from doing or saying something that will get you in trouble."

Alanna shielded her eyes as they stepped into the sunlight.

"Let's get this bike turned back in and head home. Then we'll grab dinner, fish on the dock."

"You want to let it drop?"

"We've done enough getting in the way, don't you think?"

She shook her head, and his hope of keeping her distracted from the murder and mess evaporated. "There's too much. . . . Somehow this ties together. Grady's death. The property. Mr. Hoffmeister's murder. Even the foundation books."

Jonathan disagreed. "There's no reason to connect

Grady's death and Mr. Hoffmeister. Eleven years is too long." He sighed, wishing he'd never suggested the bike ride. He'd thought it would be a quick trip and a romantic time pedaling around the island. Now he'd leave sorting everything out to the police.

Alanna sank onto a bench. Her shoulders slumped, and she looked wrung out. Worry lines crossed the bridge of her nose and forehead as she studied her hands. She seemed oblivious to the flowers and other details that would normally bring her pleasure. She didn't even seem curious to know how the Painted Stone was doing without her in its slot across the street from City Hall.

"Come on, let's head back."

She startled, as if he'd pulled her from deep thoughts. "What am I going to do, Jonathan?"

"We'll forget about this for a little while. Let the police do their job."

"What if it's so tangled they can't find the real murderer? What if I'm easier to focus on?"

"Then we'll show them you didn't do it."

"Without an alibi?" Her voice rose, and then she stopped. She glanced around then seemed to gather herself. "You're right. I can't do anything right now. It's Sunday evening." Her stomach grumbled. "Guess I am hungry."

"Let's get something to eat and go from there." He led her to one of the island's restaurants, but the meal was quiet. Alanna couldn't seem to rouse from wherever she'd disappeared. Her fears seemed to envelop her as she pushed the food around her plate.

Jonathan scooped food in his mouth as fast as was polite. Maybe she needed to get back to the house. Maybe in her home she'd find sanctuary and lose the clouds building on her face.

"Jonathan." The young voice pulled Jonathan's head up. Jonathan smiled at the grinning body torpedoing down the aisle toward him. Then he caught the resignation on Alanna's face. Before he could say anything, try to explain, the torpedo flung himself into Jonathan's arms.

Dylan.

Alanna turned toward the adorable boy. She might not like the way Jaclyn had claimed Jonathan, but she had to admit Dylan was the image of the little boy she'd love to have someday. The blond curls made her want to pull him into her lap for a squeeze.

"Where's your mommy?"

He grinned up at Jonathan, his tiny teeth barely filling his mouth. "She's outside talking." He climbed in Jonathan's lap, and a look swept Jonathan, a mixture of love and distance.

Jonathan wasn't hers. He belonged to Jaclyn and Dylan. Alanna swallowed against the pain and launched to her feet.

"Where are you going?" Confusion laced his words.

"I need to get home, and I know you need to spend time with this cute little guy." She forced a smile. "Thanks for your help and being a friend, Jonathan." She ducked her head and hurried from the restaurant, brushing past Jaclyn talking on her cell.

She could check on the studio, but honestly, after

everything that had transpired, she didn't care if it still stood. Patience had closed, and Alanna could check sales in the morning. What she needed right now was solitude. Her life seemed to erupt more each day, losing the carefully defined shape and parameters she'd crafted around it.

It would take a long time to walk home, but the fresh air and solitude would help her sort through the latest developments.

One, her heart fully belonged to Jonathan. After everything that had happened today, and the way it had trembled when she thought he was in danger, she couldn't deny the truth. Her heart remained fully committed to Jonathan. Pressure squeezed her chest as she turned up the hill next to Fort Mackinac. Her steps slowed as she tried to catch a deep breath. Instead, it felt like the sobs would explode from her, and she couldn't let that happen. Not here.

Two, the murder investigation remained outside her grasp. Anytime she tried to do anything about it, she only mucked up the situation. She should thank God she wouldn't spend the night in the tiny Mackinac jail.

Three, she couldn't walk away from the mysteries surrounding Grady's death and the paintings. She might know Trevor had painted many of the landscapes, but she couldn't help him if she didn't understand what happened to Grady. And this was too central to her life to leave alone. She had to find the truth. For Trevor and for herself. After eleven years, she longed to walk away from the mess and somehow find peace.

Four, the day's events had reinforced that she couldn't orchestrate things on her own. In fact, when she tried, disasters happened. She needed to turn the tangled web of problems over to God. So much easier said than accomplished.

After a long hike, she finally reached the sanctuary of her parents' home. She slipped through the house, grabbing a glass of iced tea, then hurried to the back porch. As the shadows cast by the trees teased across the yard, she felt drawn to the dock. She sat at the end, letting her feet dangle off the edge, toes skimming the top of the water.

She closed her eyes and let the quiet sounds of cicadas and bullfrogs bounce around her, punctuated by the occasional bird-song. She tried to grab hold of the moment, clearing her mind of everything that happened. Maybe if she refocused, her subconscious would untangle the mess of facts and inferences.

Alanna tipped her chin up, fighting the tears that pushed against her eyelids.

She wanted Jonathan back.

And she couldn't have him.

All the ways he'd cared for her slipped through her mind. In the last two weeks, he'd continued to treat her with respect. He'd treated her like a treasure, standing beside her when she confronted her mother and pushing her to acknowledge the truth.

He'd stood beside her even as he challenged her to break free from the past. He stood separated from other men she knew in the way he put her first.

Yet he belonged to another.

She could only imagine what it would be like to be the focus of his love and attention. The tears escaped as she admitted she'd walked away from him when she abandoned Mackinac. Would life have separated them anyway? She'd never know.

All she knew for sure was he wasn't hers. She pulled her knees to her chest and lowered her head to the top.

What now, God?

Could she walk away from Jonathan and Mackinac?

As she considered the idea, she knew it wasn't possible. She still had to fight for Trevor so she could end the lies her family lived. And she had to untangle the allegations between Mr. Tomkin and Mr. Hoffmeister.

Then she'd leave.

Jaclyn hadn't smiled when she entered the restaurant and found Dylan on his lap. Still, Jonathan didn't apologize. It wasn't his fault the boy adored him. Frankly, it felt good to have the little man chattering on his lap, filling him in on a disjointed account of his day.

"Then I caught a frog." He spread his hands. "He was this big."

"Impressive."

"I know! Hi, Mommy."

Jaclyn smiled at her boy, but it didn't reach her eyes. "Hey, Dylan. Are you bothering Jonathan?"

"You know he's not a bother."

"I don't know anything right now." Dark circles undergirded her eyes. Had he caused her lack of sleep? "Dylan, we need to go home."

Dylan stuck out his lip and wrapped his arms around Jonathan's neck. Jonathan swallowed but slowly extricated himself from Dylan's grip. "You've got to obey your mom, Dylan."

"I want to stay with you." The lip extended even farther.

"Not today." Jonathan glanced at Jaclyn. "You okay?"

"Always am." Her jaw firmed, and she studied him. "We'll be okay regardless of what you decide. Don't take too long. I won't wait forever." She tugged Dylan free. "Time to go, bud. We'll go walk around the fort again."

Jonathan watched them leave. Earlier this afternoon he'd been absolutely certain that Alanna was the one he wanted. Then Dylan came back.

He couldn't fall in love with a two-year-old. There had to be a connection, a love for Jaclyn, or it wouldn't work. Loving one without the other wasn't fair to Jaclyn. He had to tell her. But as Jaclyn walked outside, Dylan looking behind, he didn't know how to change things.

Somehow he had to find an honorable way to let Jaclyn know where his heart lay. And then he had to tell Alanna.

He might as well walk by the office and grab a file before heading home. As he walked by I'm Not Sharing, the fudge shop remained cloaked in darkness. Someday it would reopen, but right now it was a shell. Mr. Hoffmeister had been the lifeblood of the store, especially after Ginger had decided to stop working there. Jonathan wondered if he had any succession plan or if the business would eventually peter out and close.

Too bad he didn't want a fudge shop.

Jonathan raced upstairs, grabbed the file, and headed back down. When he passed the foundation, Gerald strode out.

"Covington."

"Hello, Gerald."

"Heard there was excitement up at the Hoffmeister place."

"You could say that."

"Now that he's gone, I'll get to build my house without all his noise. It's amazing how much he gummed everything up."

Jonathan picked up his pace, and Tomkin kept up. "It was his property."

"Not after he sold it to me. If he didn't want it changed, he shouldn't have subdivided. His rigid thoughts constricted any creativity." Gerald shrugged. "At least now I can do what I want within those silly Victorian restrictions. Can't say I'm fond of people telling me what to do. Any thoughts on the festival?"

"Been working on a couple other projects, but I'll have something to you soon."

"Good." Gerald slapped him on the back. "See you later."

"One question."

Gerald paused with a slight frown. "Yes."

"Have the police talked to you about Hoffmeister?"

"Of course. Especially with our dispute. Glad I had a solid alibi. After they confirmed it, they said I'm clear."

"That's good news."

"Yes." Gerald cleared his throat. "We may not have been the best of friends these last couple years, but we'd known each other a long time. There was a reason I bought that lot close to him. Thought it would be nice to be closer to a friend. Wish I'd known what a bad decision that would turn out to be. Well, see you later." He nodded at Jonathan and then strode down the sidewalk.

Jonathan watched a moment then continued toward home. Sad how a dispute over a house had effectively ended a time-tested friendship. By the time he reached his section of the woods, dusk had fallen and he was glad he hadn't waited longer.

As soon as he entered his cottage, he headed for the sink. The glass of water tasted great as it slid down his throat. Something caught his attention outside on the dock. He pressed his face against the window trying to see through the darkening sky.

The shape was too big to be a small animal or bird, and it wasn't moving.

Jonathan threw the plastic glass in the sink, where it bounced as he hurried toward the dock.

Chapter 31

The shape didn't move. With only a few steps to go, the shape turned into a person, and he slowed down. Alanna?

His pulse spiked, from racing or concern he didn't know. Still he stopped. If she were asleep, he didn't want to surprise her, but if she was in trouble, he couldn't wait to see if she'd move on her own.

"Alanna?" He slid down next to her.

Her cheek lay slack against her arm, and peace cloaked her face maybe for the first time since she returned to the island. Her chest rose on a breath, and he backed off. He could imagine the flush of color she'd hide in the darkness if she woke up to his hovering.

He sank back against the base of the dock and watched her. What would have chased her outside to fall asleep?

No one had returned to her house since they'd found the rabbit in the trap. That appeared to be a one-time, dead-end event unless she'd found something today. If she had, he doubted she'd stay in the open.

Prayers lifted as he watched. He prayed for wisdom to know how to proceed. Creativity to satisfy his clients. Clear direction to know his heart. Alanna longed for the truth to illuminate her past. He wanted the truth to display his future. The present felt fine, but he wanted more. He longed to feel the way he did when Alanna stared at him with the eyes that said he could do anything. There hadn't been many people in his life that made him feel invincible like that.

As her form shifted deeper into the shadows, he knew that's what he wanted. To become the man who could protect those dear to him. The man who could bring the smile back to her face and coax it out frequently. Ideas formed as he watched and waited. He tried to remember the details as his mind filled with ways to sort through the art problems.

He might not be an investigator, but he knew events. That night ideas for an event unlike anything Mackinac Island had seen played through his mind. He tweaked the guest list here, added art there, and by the time Alanna began to stir, Jonathan had the outlines in place. Now he just needed his phone, e-mail, and computer.

Alanna groaned. She pushed up, her head hanging, then slowly glanced around. "Jonathan?"

"Sleepyhead."

She snorted, an unladylike sound he loved. "Help me up. I've fallen asleep in places I didn't know I could."

He eased her up, and she sagged against him. She felt so right next to him. How could he convince her he wanted to come alongside her and support her the rest of her life?

His earlier plea for direction seemed answered in a crystal-clear moment. His heart hadn't played tricks on him. It knew exactly what it wanted: the woman next to him rather than the one across the island.

Their shoulders brushed, and Alanna fought to clear her mind. Jonathan had that effect on her, and she wished she could wash it away. Join the chorus line in *South Pacific* and wash this man right out of her hair. He had a perfectly lovely young woman already with an adorable son who worshipped Jonathan. Alanna had to get out of the way. And the only way to do that was to leave.

She was right back where she'd started. Somehow she had to clear her brother so he could take his place at the Painted Stone. He's the one who should sit there day in and day out. He could paint in the back or even in the showroom, live in the empty apartment if he wanted independence. Then sell the art he'd created. Lies replaced by transparency.

Trevor didn't have a career waiting on the mainland. Still, the thought of her law practice and her apartment didn't bring Alanna joy. She wasn't sure she wanted to leave. But she had to. Staying would hurt too much.

"Where'd you go?"

"Home." She felt her lips curve, a soft, resigned acknowledgment. It would hurt too much to stay on Mackinac—after rediscovering Jonathan only to find him taken. She needed to refocus, take control, and get back home where she belonged.

"Sure you're all right?" If the light were better, Alanna knew she'd see a row of questions in his eyes, followed by the little stutter-step he made whenever he couldn't stay put.

"Just help me get inside. I've still got a lot to do tonight."

Ten minutes later, she sat at the dining room table, the foundation's ledgers strewn around her. "The answer is in those boxes from Hoffmeister's house."

"Why do you say that?" Jonathan sat across the table, arms crossed on his chest as he watched her.

"If something funny started happening while he was the president, it might have taken him awhile to notice. But he would have eventually. I bet he'd take it on himself to find the answer because he would feel responsible. Happened on his watch kind of thing. On an island this small, you have to keep things close to make sure the word doesn't spread."

"Let me make a call." Jonathan stepped to the other room, and she heard a muffled conversation as she continued to stare at the pages. When Jonathan returned, he handed her a piece of paper. "Okay, here's the list of people who served on the board during Hoffmeister's tenure. And Gerald said Brendan was the bookkeeper with assistance from the foundation's secretary."

"Really." Alanna rubbed her cheeks. "He hated math. Why would anyone trust him with books?"

"Not liking a subject isn't the same as being bad at it."

"True. But Brendan always sat next to Grady in math class so he could copy answers. Grady was headed to Purdue on an engineering scholarship. He might have loved basketball, but his real ticket away was his brain. Brendan. . .not so much."

Jonathan shrugged. "Just relaying what I was told."

"Someone had to help him. Or if he was pretty much allowed to do what he wanted, it would explain how everything got messed up, if not where the money went." Alanna tapped the pencil against her teeth. "Guess I need to find him and ask him about that."

"Do you want me to handle that?"

Alanna laughed as she chucked her pencil at him. "You're the numbers guy."

"Only marginally more than you." He tapped a cover. "I'd be happy to probe though."

"Thanks. I'll touch base with Laura at the foundation. See if she remembers anything." Alanna glanced at her watch.

"I'll try her now." After digging up the woman's number, Alanna waited while the phone rang and Laura answered. "Hi, Laura. This is Alanna Stone. Do you have a couple minutes?"

"Sure. Just reading a novel before bed."

"I promise this will be quick. Was Brendan the bookkeeper for the foundation a couple years ago?"

"Sure. He only stopped when his dad became president."

That was odd. What happened to fathers giving their sons more work? "Did he handle the job well?"

"As well as could be expected. I'd glance at the books every once in a while, but he didn't need me. Why all the questions?"

"Just thinking about something Gerald said. Thanks for your time."

Jonathan had cleared the table and stood when she ended. "Anything?"

"Nothing other than the fact she didn't provide oversight. If he'd wanted to, Brendan could do just about anything to the books."

"Still doesn't explain why he would if he did."

"True." Alanna stood. "Thanks for your help."

"Happy to do it. I'll let you know if I learn anything from Brendan."

"Don't you love the drama I've dragged you into?"

"Absolutely. My life has been a lot more interesting since you returned." He leaned toward her, and she couldn't have backed away if she'd wanted. All her grand ideas evaporated in a moment. There'd never been another man for her. Not in all this time.

If only he cared for her. Something deeper, more real

than the tension they generated without effort. She wanted someone who knew her heart, her fears, her qualms—and loved her anyway. Who chose her in spite of the hang-ups and baggage she brought to the party.

His gaze traveled from her eyes, slid down her nose, and then landed on her lips. She clung to the table, grateful for the hard barrier keeping them apart, because she knew if he slipped around the table, she wouldn't be able to push him away. She didn't want to, not anymore.

She closed her eyes, brought Jaclyn's image to mind, and then pasted on a smile.

She had to get Trevor up here now.

Tomorrow wouldn't be soon enough.

Yesterday would have been better.

But it was time for her to escape.

One moment he could practically read Alanna's thoughts. The next she might as well have shipped to the Amazon. The woman could disappear without moving, and the reality left him desperate.

He couldn't convince her he loved her if she constantly pushed him away. Left.

This time he wouldn't let her leave. He'd follow her to the jungle to prove he loved her.

Alanna tapped the ledger. His gaze bounced toward it, and he started.

"You'll call Brendan?"

He cracked a smile. "Already promised."

"You won't forget?" Alanna ran her fingers through her hair, leaving it all disorganized. "Do you think Gerald could be behind Mr. Hoffmeister's death?"

"He said the police have already cleared him."

"You didn't think you should mention that?"

"Guess I forgot. You'll unravel everything. From Grady's death to the books to Mr. Hoffmeister's murder. You and I both know it all ties together."

"The last time we tried to do something, some guy blows me over. So much for Mackinac Island being a place that slows down."

"I bet you're not bored."

His words seemed to shock her. She stared at him then laughed. And kept laughing. To the point he wondered if the hysteria would stop. Tears streamed down her cheeks, and he sat watching. This was when he needed that guide, the one that explained why women behaved in such bizarre ways. The one his dad never handed down.

"Alanna. . ."

She held up a hand then left. A minute later he heard clunking in the kitchen, and soon she returned with glasses of water. "Here you go."

"Thanks." He studied her as he took a sip. "You all right?"

"Sure." Sadness swept over her face only to be brushed aside as she sat, and he followed suit. "I'll be back in Grand Rapids in no time. The partners expect a call tomorrow. I'll get Patience to fill in until Mom returns. Then it's back to the grindstone."

"You can't leave the island."

She looked at him then waved. "The police won't mind."

"Really? And if they don't, you're running away? Again?"

He wanted to recapture the words as soon as they escaped.

"Yes. Yes I am. That's what I do, after all. When the going gets tough, Alanna Stone is ready to leave." She guzzled the rest of her water. "Besides, you have Jaclyn and Dylan. You don't need me around, distracting you from your work and love."

"What are you talking about?"

"Don't worry. Your event will be lovely." She lurched to her feet. "If you'll excuse me, I'm going to bed." She clutched the ledgers as she moved toward the stairs. "Good night."

She swept away, leaving him in the dining room.

Jonathan gathered the glasses and put them in the kitchen sink. After turning out the lights, he locked the door behind him and hurried to his cabin. Once in the living room, he fired up his laptop. Time to flesh out the plan that had dropped in his mind. Alanna could wade through those ledgers again if she wanted, but there was nothing there other than evidence of embezzling. He had more productive trails to follow.

As soon as his e-mail loaded, he clicked through the messages, sorting them by event and client. Edward Morris's question about the gift for Bonnie gave him pause. Rachelle hadn't called him back. Now was the perfect time to push her for an answer. And while they were talking, he'd see if he couldn't extract a few more answers at the same time.

Alanna might not get the full truth from her mom, but that didn't mean he couldn't.

Chapter 32

The alarm blared for what felt like hours before Alanna bopped it off. One glance at the time told her the hours hadn't been so long after all.

She rubbed her eyes. It felt like a truck had hit her overnight—impossible considering she was on the island, but she wouldn't be surprised to reach the bathroom mirror and find tire tracks across her face. Somewhere she had to find some energy. Time was running out. When she talked to the managing partner that morning, he'd want specifics she couldn't give.

Alanna got ready as quickly as possible then headed toward the Painted Stone. She didn't have any guarantees Patience Matthews would accept the job, so she'd have to craft the best package possible. Maybe commission, maybe hourly. She only prayed Patience would agree this sounded like the perfect way to spend the summer. If not. . .well, she'd have to cooperate.

When she arrived at the studio and turned on the computer, a résumé sat in her e-mail. As Alanna scanned it, she decided this woman with her art degree might fit well at a studio. She fired an e-mail back, setting up a time for a phone interview. Maybe she wouldn't need Patience after all.

The morning flew as Alanna prepped new pieces for the walls and fiddled with a display of small prints. By the time the phone rang, the Painted Stone had already welcomed several groups of tourists. Alanna stepped down the hallway with the phone and tried to shield it from the noise while keeping an eye on the art.

"Ms. Stone. Ready to leave that little island and come back to the real world?" The managing partner seemed in a good mood, but Alanna stayed on guard.

"Yes, sir. I should be ready in two or three weeks."

A whistle made Alanna pull the phone away from her ear. "That's a long time. We've already given you two."

"I asked for at least a month. After that trial, I need the time."

"Doesn't sound like a vacation from what I've heard. Bennett told us he bought art from you. Odd considering you cleaned him out in court. Now you cleaned his billfold, too."

Alanna leaned against the wall and covered her eyes. "Small world."

"Well, two weeks. That's it. A day more, and you'll need to find a new firm. We have clients waiting for you who can't wait forever. The courts have deadlines."

Alanna hung up and tried to imagine everything she loved about her job. Her stomach knotted at the thought of marching back into the office. Handling more crazy clients and their insane demands. Then walking those into court. Never knowing exactly what would happen next. Having a script that could be abandoned in an instant. She tried to conjure up her bedroom at the apartment. The peace that usually swept her at the thought of the gray room with lavender accents didn't appear.

Then the image of practicing here, with the quiet pace of the island, flowed into her mind. Maybe she could work with Jonathan. He enjoyed event planning. She could, too. She certainly had the organizational skills to make it successful.

Reality grabbed her runaway thoughts. She couldn't stay

here. Definitely not work with Jonathan.

But she didn't want to go home.

Jonathan stared out the window as he waited for Trevor to answer the phone before he called Brendan. He'd heard Alanna's version of events. Now it was time to get Trevor's. Somewhere in the middle he'd find the truth. At least that's what he counted on.

He'd start by clearing the date for the event. Couldn't have the shindig without the guest of honor. Overnight his vision for the event had continued to emerge. It would be easy to craft another show. What the Painted Stone needed was a launch or introduction on a large scale. Something that drew folks to the island, causing them to hop on a ferry and venture across the lake for a couple of hours. That would take something compelling. Something out of the ordinary that made people talk before and after the event.

Food was a given.

Music.

But there needed to be something. . .more. Something unexpected. Something fresh and unique.

"Hello?" The groggy voice had Jonathan conjuring up the image of an artist who stayed up too late with the party scene.

"Trevor Stone. Good morning."

"Morning?" There was a pause as if the phone was pulled away.

"Do I know you?"

Jonathan chuckled. "You probably don't remember me. I'm Jonathan Covington."

"Sure. Dude on the dock with my sister every summer. She there now?"

"Something like that. Hey, we've got a project for you." Jonathan filled him in on the art. "Alanna figured out pretty quickly your mom wasn't painting."

"Hasn't for five years." A pause, maybe a yawn, before the young man continued. "Alanna's had her head buried in the city."

"Is there a reason your mom stopped?"

"Arthritis. She can't hold the paintbrush like she used to, but they still need the income."

"Alanna's determined to get your name on your paintings."

"Don Quixote."

The image of Alanna on a horse jousting windmills settled in front of Jonathan. It fit. Too well. "You have no idea."

"So what's this got to do with me?"

"We're going to have a launch party for you. Bring you into the light."

"You haven't told Mom." His voice was flat, like he'd already disengaged from the conversation.

"Not yet. We need to make sure the date works for you." The door banged open, and Jonathan turned toward it. Alanna stepped into his office, her cheeks flooded with color and a slightly wild look about her eyes. She marched up to him and started gesturing like a mad woman. "Can you hang on one second?"

He covered the mouthpiece and queried Alanna. "What?"

"You've got to help me. Now."

He looked from the phone to her. "Can it wait a few minutes?"

Her eyes turned red, and she collapsed in a chair. "I'm trapped."

"Trevor, I'll call you back."

"Whatever."

Jonathan hung up the phone, never taking his gaze off Alanna's frantic features. "Fill me in."

"The partners just threatened my job."

"Okay."

"I have to be back in two weeks or find a new job."

"We'll get you back."

Tears cascaded down her cheeks.

"Alanna, what's wrong?"

"What if I don't want to go back but I can't stay?"

"What?"

"What if I'm trapped either way? Staying or leaving?" Her shoulders shuddered, and she turned away from him. "We have two weeks to wrap it up, and then I'm gone."

"Is that what you want?"

She seemed to find something within her, because she straightened and pushed to her feet. "It doesn't matter. I knew I shouldn't have come back. Now I just have to leave. Again."

He almost didn't hear the last word. Then he wondered if he just wished it. Maybe he'd imagined everything restarting between them. He shouldn't assume she felt anything for him. But as he studied her, he couldn't discount everything that had happened. It wasn't a mistake she'd come back to Mackinac. It wasn't a mistake they'd rediscovered each other.

He wouldn't let her walk away. Not this time.

"I was on the phone with Trevor."

She spun around. "Why?"

"Because you asked me to organize his launch party. I talk to the person to capture their personality. You should have told me he still has no drive."

"What?"

"Sounded like he was still in bed, and it's after eleven."

"Not everybody's as accomplished as you are."

Her sarcasm made him snort. "I'll remember that next time I need a shot of encouragement." He shoved his hands in his back pockets. It was either that or pull her to him for a good, long kiss. Maybe then she'd stop fighting him long enough to hear what he said. He studied her, the war of fire and ice in her eyes. Maybe self-control wasn't all it was cracked up to be. Maybe they both needed to lose their hold and see what happened when they let go.

That couldn't be easy for an attorney to do. The thought scared the spit from his mouth.

"Jonathan, I think we'd better leave it all alone."

"Not happening." He stepped closer, and she edged back. "You came back against your will because your family needed you. They still do. And so does Mr. Hoffmeister. Who'll fight to the truth if you don't?"

"Police Chief Ryan. That's his job."

"And when the case goes cold? And there's another Grady kind of case? When the island decides you were involved even if it's never proven?"

"That won't happen."

"Like it didn't for Trevor?" He knew it was low, but he had to get her attention.

She stepped away, back landing against the wall with a smack as her mouth opened and shut like a fish desperate for air. "You don't mean that."

Jonathan didn't say anything, letting his gaze speak for him. The truth had to be confronted. "Come on, Alanna. Let's see this through to the end."

"Two weeks. That's all the time we have." She spun and pulled the door open. "I have to get back home."

Her feet pounded down the stairs with finality. He started after her but stopped when his phone blared to life. With a sigh, he opened it. "Jonathan Covington."

"That artist is a genius."

"Edward?"

"Of course. Her work is perfect. Bonnie will love it. Promise she'll have a piece ready."

"You know artists. . . ."

"No time for temperament. Bonnie's treatment isn't going well. The doctor isn't making any promises, so this party has to be perfect from start to finish." Edward cleared his throat. "Perfection, Jonathan."

"Yes, sir." He didn't know how, but he'd have a Rachelle Stone original painting for Bonnie Morris if he had to watch her paint each and every stroke. Mrs. Stone needed the work and encouragement as much as Mrs. Morris needed the breath of light and life. "I'm glad you like her."

"It's perfect. Bonnie finished the invitation list last night. I'll send it in an hour. We may need extra rooms, but guests can overflow in Mackinaw City if needed. Family are the key folks for the island." A phone buzzed in the background. "Got to get that. Keep me posted."

"Will do."

Jonathan moved to his desk and made a few notes before calling Brendan. The need to have a perfect event increased with each conversation. He didn't see a love as rich and deep as the Morrises often. Instead, most people seemed to manage only a cheap counterfeit. Someday he'd have to ask Edward the secret.

At this point, his love life was enough of a morass he needed to get out of relationships. Maybe after he'd squared things with Jaclyn, he could relaunch things with Alanna. If her frame of mind when she left gave any indication, he'd have a challenge convincing her to stay. She seemed intent on going back to Grand Rapids. Maybe he just hadn't made his case yet.

A guy could hope.

Chapter 33

The grill fired up with a sputter as Alanna twisted the knob. The chicken breast looked well marinated, and she longed for a quick bite before tackling the mysteries surrounding her. Jonathan had left a couple of messages for Brendan. Alanna doubted he'd return the calls. He seemed as self-centered as ever.

Could the mess with the foundation books be the crux of the broken relationship between Mr. Hoffmeister and Mr. Tomkin? It had to be more than house plans. Surely that wouldn't destroy a decades-long friendship.

If the problem generated on Hoffmeister's watch but while Tomkin's son was bookkeeper, it would certainly make finding a resolution tricky. Could that be the real reason Mr. Tomkin had asked her to look into the problem? He knew the source but didn't know how to confront his son? Without talking to Brendan, she had no idea what would motivate him to steal from the foundation.

Maybe Detective Bull had looked through Hoffmeister's books by now. Alanna placed the chicken on the grill then found his card and dialed the number.

"Detective Bull."

"Hi, this is Alanna Stone."

"How can I help you?" His tone was ultraformal.

"Have you looked through Mr. Hoffmeister's books yet?"

"Why?"

"I wondered if you could confirm that they were copies of the Mackinac Island Foundation's financial records."

"Why?"

"Because someone has embezzled from the foundation, and I think Mr. Hoffmeister was looking into it. It happened when he was president, and I think he felt a need to figure out who did it and why."

"That's a lot of theorizing. Any facts?"

"The embezzlement is evident in the foundation books. I don't know why someone's been doing it. But I think Mr. Tomkin's son, Brendan, at least knew about it since he was the bookkeeper at the time."

"Isn't his father president of the foundation now?"

"Yes. And I think it's interesting that Mr. Tomkin hired a new bookkeeper when he took over."

"Thanks for the information."

"Are you going to do anything with it?"

"I'll follow up on it." After the usual good nights, he hung up.

Maybe it was a wasted call, but at least he could work on it now if he chose. Bet he'd have a little more luck getting Brendan to cooperate.

The door slammed open at Jonathan's cabin. As it bounced off the hinges, a little body propelled out and flew down the dock. Alanna watched, mouth agape.

"Dylan, get back here." Jaclyn's voice sounded panicked as Dylan's little legs kept pumping. Alanna wiped her hands on a dish towel, keeping her gaze locked on the boy. "Dylan!"

The little body flew off the edge of the dock, and Alanna

tore after him as Jaclyn screamed and Jonathan hurried out his door. Alanna kicked off her shoes and jumped after Dylan. The boy thrashed and sputtered, tears and pond water streaming down his face.

"Mommy!" Hiccups choked off his words before he sank under.

Alanna grabbed him and held his head above water. "I've got you."

Jaclyn reached for Dylan as Jonathan hefted him onto the dock. Alanna treaded water a moment before gathering her energy to pull onto the dock. She coughed and rolled to her side as she watched Jaclyn clutch Dylan to her.

"Don't ever do that again, Dylan! You scared Mommy."

"Jonathan doesn't love me."

A stricken look crossed Jonathan's face at the boy's whine. "Jaclyn. . ."

She turned from Jonathan and struggled to her feet with the dripping boy. "What did you expect? He's two years old. You're the only father he's known." Jaclyn swiped at tears then moved down the dock.

Smoke poured from Alanna's grill. There went dinner. She pushed to her feet and pulled limp hair from her eyes. She started to slip past Jonathan, who stood frozen. Now wasn't the time to ask him what resolution he'd reached with Jaclyn. Yet the anguish on his face made it hard to walk away and leave him in his pain. She continued to the house and pulled the chicken off the grill.

Jonathan followed her, sank into a chair on her patio, then launched back to his feet. "I need to make sure she gets Dylan home okay."

He hurried away. Any appetite she'd had disappeared

with her dry clothes. A shiver whispered through her as she sat on the steps. Fish circles blipped across the pond, forming little punctuations on the evening.

Utter stillness settled over her like a suffocating blanket as she remained on the patio. Her mind worked over the details. A twist in time had placed Mr. Tomkin next to Mr. Hoffmeister. The two didn't get along, but Mr. Tomkin had a solid alibi. Still, there had to be more to the story. More that involved the embezzling Mr. Tomkin had figured out. She needed to visit him. Give him a chance to explain.

Alanna went inside, changed, and then called Patience. The woman agreed to come in and work the following afternoon. The books still sat on the dining room table. Alanna ran a hand over the cover. She'd let Detective Bull talk to Brendan. She'd focus on Brendan's dad.

People didn't go from Friday night buddies to enemies without cause. Could it have anything to do with Grady's death? Add in Brendan and the skirmish over Mr. Tomkin's house plans, and many seeds for conflict grew. She had to believe Mr. Tomkin wouldn't have bought the plot next to Mr. Hoffmeister if the rift had already existed.

She almost picked up the phone to call Jonathan and see what he thought of her approach. She shook her head. She would update him after she talked to Mr. Tomkin. He had too much to do at work, especially if he wanted to plan something for Trevor. She needed to do her part and clear her brother—and herself.

Her thoughts turned back to the graduation party. Trevor and Grady had been the first in the water but weren't the only ones stupid enough to dive into the frigid lake. She still remembered how Trevor had trembled, his skin bluish as he stumbled back onto the rocky beach. He'd mumbled something as he fell against her.

"Something happened, Alanna. Something bad." He shivered as he collapsed to the ground. Before she could clarify, a paramedic pushed her aside and went to work on Trevor.

"Stupid kid. He could have died like the other one."

Alanna had stared then glanced down the beach where a couple of paramedics pounded frantically on Grady's chest. The compressions didn't seem to work as they kept pumping. Then the life-flight helicopter landed.

Two or three more teen boys huddled in a group. Brendan Tomkin had been in the group along with Randy Raeder and Chuck Matthews. Despite witnessing the event, nobody ever talked about it.

That's what bothered Alanna. To this day, a cloak of silence dominated Grady's death. It was as if everyone had gathered together and decided to leave it alone. What was past was history. Yet they'd all decided Trevor must have done something. Was it because he'd required the paramedics? Last time she checked, that didn't make one guilty. Yet she'd never brought the issue back up with Trevor. He'd seemed traumatized, and Mom had spent the summer keeping him close, relieved to have her baby, unlike Grady's mother.

She picked up the phone. Waited for Trevor to pick up.

"You think I'll come to some event."

"Hello to you, too, Trevor."

"Alanna, I can't do that." Her brother's voice shook. "I swore I'd never go back."

"Because of Grady."

"Of course."

"What if I find out what happened? Once and for

all. Then you wouldn't have to wonder what people were thinking."

"I can't do that, sis."

"Sure you can." Alanna tapped the counter. "I just need to hear what happened from your perspective."

"I was stupid. I let the older guys talk me into a race. I've never felt so cold. I really should move to Florida or Arizona 'cause every winter when the cold slaps me in the face, I feel like I'm back in the water."

"Who else raced?"

Trevor swallowed. "Grady, Chuck, and Brendan. May have been another kid or two. But those were the ones I tried to keep up with. Chuck rammed into me when I turned around to come back. When I got oriented, that's when I saw Grady. I tried to help him, Alanna, I really did." His voice shuddered. "I always wonder if I'd said no to that stupid race, would Grady have been okay, or would he have still jumped in?"

The next afternoon, as soon as Patience arrived, Alanna headed to the foundation. Laura sat at the front desk filing a nail. "Is Mr. Tomkin in?"

"Nope. He hightailed it out of here for lunch and hasn't been back." Laura leaned forward on her desk. "If you ask me, the man isn't himself."

"Really? Any reason?"

"Not that I can tell." The woman checked her fingers then tapped them on the desk. "Guess it doesn't matter. But if you need him, I'd call his cell. He's probably up at his land. He spends all his time there. Communing with the property or some such nonsense. If you ask me, he should build already. At this rate, he'll die before he builds."

"Thanks. I'll give him a call." As she left, her phone vibrated in her pocket. Pulling it out, she clicked it on. "Hello?"

"Hey, Alanna." Jonathan sounded excited. "Are you at the studio?"

"Nope. Running around. Having Patience is a great help."

"Patience. Yeah, always your strong suit."

"Hey." She must look like an idiot standing in the street wearing a huge smile at Jonathan's teasing.

"Just calling it like I see it." He paused, and his voice sobered. "How are you doing?"

"Okay. Headed out to talk to Tomkin if I can find him."

"Want company?"

"You've already spent too much time helping me plan a brilliant event for the Morrises. I'll be okay."

"Okay, I'll try Brendan again." He paused a moment. "Meet me on the dock tonight. We can try to catch Grandpappy."

She laughed. "Still think you can catch him?"

"If you're with me."

Warmth flooded her. "Thanks. See you tonight."

Next she called Tomkin on his cell. "I wondered if I could come see you."

"Any problems?"

"Just a couple questions."

"Ask away."

She frowned. It would be better if she could watch his response as he answered. "I promise I won't take much of your time. Patience is at the studio, so I'm free to come to you."

"All right. I'm up at my property."

A minute later, she hopped on her bike and started biking up the hills toward the Grand Hotel and then behind it toward Tomkin's plot of land.

When she arrived, Mr. Tomkin stood facing the lake, even though she could barely make him out through the trees as they swayed in the wind. Alanna turned up the collar of her jacket then shoved her hands deep in her pockets as she approached. She couldn't help glancing around to see if anyone in a ski mask hid in the trees. It was ridiculous, but the events of her last trip still lingered.

"Mr. Tomkin?"

He didn't turn, fixed on something only he could see.

Alanna eased toward him. "Are you okay, sir?"

"Fine and dandy. Why wouldn't I be?"

"Your friend is dead."

"That's not the worst part." He turned toward her, a haunted expression twisting his features into a shadowed mask. His shoulders hunched forward, and he looked every one of his sixtysome years, bowed by events. "Don't you see?" His voice shook. "I started studying the land. Figuring out where to get the best views of the lake." He turned a bit as if seeing the view for the first time again. "And it hit me."

Alanna studied him, a wariness churning through her. Something wasn't right, but she couldn't tell what yet.

"Don't you see?" He pinned her with a stare. "Brendan lied." His Adam's apple bobbed. "He lied."

"What do you mean?"

"He couldn't have been where he said when Grady died. He knew things he couldn't know if he'd been on the shore.

He said he only went in to help Grady to shore. I believed him. And no one ever questioned." He shook his head. "I didn't. Maybe I should have, but I didn't."

Alanna tried to picture the scene. Brendan had been in the water. Why lie about that? Especially since plenty had to see him in wet clothes. "What did Brendan say?"

"He insisted Grady and Trevor raced toward the lighthouse but got knocked around by the waves from a passing boat."

"There wasn't a boat." She was almost certain. She'd remember a detail like that. "But there were more boys in the water. At least five that I remember."

"Could you see from where you were on the beach?"

She closed her eyes and pictured the beach panorama. The large cropping of rocks still clustered around in a loose interpretation of Stonehenge. But the lighthouse was around the bend of the island. That was one reason she'd thought the boys were crazy to attempt the race in the frigid water. Only a fool or a teenage boy intent on proving something would launch a dare like that. Trevor had fallen into the easily led category. Grady had been out to prove something. And Brendan? As she looked at the scene, she realized he'd stared at Grady with an intensity that smoldered when his gaze slid to Ginger Hoffmeister. The look between Grady and Brendan had been layered with meaning.

"I see you're making the connections." Mr. Tomkin's shoulders slumped, and he stared across the expanse at Lake Huron lapping the shore. "I don't know why I never considered that before I came up here, determined to build a house that would shame everyone else. Then I couldn't imagine looking at that scene every day. And Hoffmeister wouldn't let me back out of the contract."

"You wanted out?" No one had mentioned that.

"I couldn't stare at this scene day after day. Yet I'm still drawn here. Blasted contract."

"You had to honor it."

"Sure. But a lifetime of friendship should have made a difference." He shrugged. "I was wrong about a lot of things."

"Did you tell Mr. Hoffmeister why you wanted out?"

"No...but I think he figured it out. He got real quiet and uncomfortable around me."

"I think that could have more to do with the foundation embezzling."

"You figured that out, too?" He sighed. "I knew you would bulldog just like you used to with trig problems. I hate to think that Brendan would do something like that. But I couldn't let him continue with the books until I could prove who did it."

"Maybe someone else did it. I can't figure out his motive. Yes, he took money, but why?"

"There's a lot about my son I don't understand. I tried to give him the best of everything. Maybe all I did was create a monster who believes he's entitled to do whatever he wants."

"What are you going to do?" She could tell the police chief, but it would sound stronger coming from Mr. Tomkin. He'd need to tell the man why he thought Brendan was involved in Grady's death and the embezzling. While it didn't help her with Mr. Hoffmeister's murder, it would certainly help clear Trevor's name and go a long way toward bringing him into his own on Mackinac.

"Guess I'll find Chief Ryan. Fill him in. I don't suppose the statute of limitations has expired?"

"Ten years for murder for a juvenile."

"Then he'll be okay." The stiffness evaporated from his shoulders, and he stumbled.

"More than likely." Alanna didn't have the heart to point out that if the court treated him like an adult, then there was no statute of limitations. But if they treated him like the seventeen-year-old kid he was, then Grady's death had occurred too long ago. If it was an accident, then Brendan should have admitted what happened back then. Still, the truth now was better than an ongoing feast of lies. "Maybe you can talk Brendan into telling Chief Ryan everything."

"I don't know. It's been a long time to risk opening that back up to scrutiny."

Alanna stepped toward Tomkin, intensity pounding through her. "Brendan owes Trevor the truth. He deserved it eleven long years ago, and if you don't make your son do the right thing, so help me, I will make sure he doesn't have a choice. Do not tempt me."

"I don't know."

"You have until the studio show. If Brendan doesn't tell the truth before that, I'll make sure it's announced there in a way that nobody will forget." She studied him and then felt the wave of frustration begin to recede. "Good-bye, Mr. Tomkin."

When she left, Mr. Tomkin still stood staring across the lake toward Mackinaw City. The burden of lies and fear held him in place. She prayed he could convince Brendan to come clean. The town needed the truth to be revealed. Eleven years of secrets and shadows had layered to the point she wondered how to fully clear them away.

She hurried to Jonathan's office, eager to share her news,

but took her time climbing the stairs, trying to quiet her breathing. The sound of voices in hushed conversation made her pause with her hand on the knob.

Chapter 34

No matter how he switched his perspective, Jonathan couldn't see the connection between Mr. Hoffmeister and Grady Cadieux.

Both lived on the island.

Both died.

There had to be more than those two facts connecting them. Until then, he felt stymied to clear Trevor. And without that, no matter how wonderful the event, Trevor would still paint under a cloud with the other island residents.

Guess he needed to ask Tomkin a few questions. The man knew everything about the island and the people who lived here. Maybe he could fill in pieces for Jonathan. First, he'd try Brendan again. The guy must not have his phone with him, because every time he dialed, the call went straight to voice mail. Jonathan left another message.

He dialed the foundation next, and the phone rang to the point Jonathan expected more voice mail then someone picked up. "Hello?"

"Hi, Laura. Is Gerald there?"

"Nope."

Jonathan frowned when nothing more was said. "Any way to reach him?"

"I'm sure he's on his cell somewhere. Probably back up on his land staring at the lake. He likes doing that. Boy, he's popular today."

"Okay. Well, let him know Jonathan Covington called."

Her lazy voice waited a beat. "Any reason?"

"Had a question for him about Hoffmeister. And something from a while ago."

"Grady?" The surprise couldn't be hidden.

"Yep. Thanks, Laura." Jonathan hung up. Someone needed to talk to the woman about a professional phone presence. Trevor had given him a date, so the plans for that event were started. He might as well nail down the catering details while he waited for Brendan and Gerald to return his calls. Then he needed to finalize the details for the Morrises' dinner. The night had all the hallmarks of turning unforgettable. That was exactly what he wanted to accomplish for the special couple.

Time flew as he worked through details and firmed up instructions. His door pounded open, and he glanced up.

Brendan Tomkin stood over Jonathan, a grimace pasted on his mouth. "You couldn't keep your nose out of the past."

What was the guy talking about? He didn't know why Jonathan had asked him to call. "You didn't need to come by. A call would have worked."

"No. This is better face-to-face. See, everything was going fine until you and Alanna started poking around."

"Poking where?"

"The past. You'll regret that, Covington." Brendan slipped a gun from his pocket and held it pointed at Jonathan's gut. "Amazing how everything can be fine for years. Then you and Alanna start poking around. Then Ginger decides she needs more money. Can you believe she left me alone for almost two years? Two good years after all her harassing me for more money. I finally tell her I can't pay any more, and she agrees. Then her kid needs braces. . .at ten. . .and she decides I should pay for them." He snorted as if he expected Jonathan to understand.

"So what did you do?" Jonathan studied the gun. Too bad he knew nothing about weapons, preferring a pair of binoculars or rod and pole. Brendan held it steady, with too much competence for Jonathan. It looked like he enjoyed holding it. Knew how to make it work.

"The only thing a fine, upstanding citizen can do. Tell her daddy to get her back in line. It's not like I can sneak money like I did last time. My dad's not as sloppy as hers is. My old man wouldn't even let me play at bookkeeper like Hoffmeister did."

Jonathan scrambled to make the connections. Brendan embezzled money to pay off Ginger, who was blackmailing him? But blackmailing him why? That important piece of information eluded Jonathan.

Brendan took a step closer, but a movement caught Jonathan's attention. He glanced toward the door out the corner of his eye. A shadow moved across the frosted glass. He pulled his attention back to Brendan, not wanting the man to realize someone waited.

His cell phone sat in the top drawer of his desk. So far he hadn't had an opportunity to slip it out or try anything with the computer. Brendan stood vigilant, eyes locked on Jonathan and his movements. He had to try before something happened to him or the person on the other side of the door

"So what did you tell her father?"

"The typical. Get your girl to leave me alone. Had him good and intimidated until your girlfriend interrupted our little powwow." He snarled. "Then things spun out of control."

So he killed Hoffmeister. Too bad Jonathan hadn't had

his phone recording that little confession. He raised his voice as he kept his gaze locked on Brendan. "What now?"

Brendan frowned and inched closer to the desk. The gun felt like it sat mere inches from Jonathan's nose. "I'm tired of talking. You need a lesson in keeping your mouth shut."

"Did it work for Ginger's father?"

"What?"

"The lesson?"

Brendan's lips twisted into a sardonic mask. "Yeah. He won't be talking again."

"Mr. Hoffmeister."

"Who else?"

Jonathan felt a tightening in his middle as if everything coiled in preparation for one stand. He wouldn't go down without a fight. If Brendan had killed Mr. Hoffmeister, nothing would stop him from killing again. If anything happened, he wanted Alanna to know he'd done his best to spread the truth. He balled his fists and pushed from the chair. Brendan stepped back and smiled without a drip of mirth.

"I wouldn't come any closer if I were you. See, I have the gun. You. . .don't."

"I'm okay with that." He whistled a moment, enjoying the flummoxed look that crossed Brendan's face. "How much did you pay Ginger?"

"Doesn't matter. She won't get another dime. I made sure of that."

"Was it close to twenty-five thousand? The amount that disappeared from the foundation's books?"

Confusion flashed across Brendan's face. "How do you know?"

"Your dad sent us on a fishing expedition. Didn't expect

to catch you when we started, but it didn't take long to figure out you had the access and opportunity. What I haven't figured out is why. What did she have against you anyway?" Just keep him talking. That's all he could do with that gun pointed squarely at his gut.

"Said her kid was Grady's. And if she couldn't have a daddy, I could pay the equivalent of child support since I killed her child's daddy. Crazy woman thinks I killed Grady. Can't prove it, but I can't disprove it either. Everyone knows we weren't best friends."

"Why not turn you in if she thought you killed him?"

"Can't pay from jail. She decided this was better. And it worked until I decided I was done paying. If she wants more, she has to find a new sugar daddy. This bank is closed."

The door blew open, and Brendan spun toward it. Jonathan felt a sinking sensation when Alanna stepped into the room—alone. "What are you doing?" His voice trembled, and he couldn't hide it. Didn't she know to go for help rather than come alone? At least the cops would have weapons. She must have left all her common sense at home.

"Brendan Tomkin." She didn't seem surprised to see him. "I just had the most enlightening conversation with your daddy. He's got it all figured out."

"Doesn't matter." A band of sweat appeared on his forehead.

"I don't know. The truth has a way of clearing old misunderstandings."

Brendan's posture stiffened. Jonathan watched with growing concern. How could he get Alanna out of here before the man decided she was a better target? From her steady gaze, Jonathan had the uneasy sensation she wouldn't leave. Not easily. She might make this her last stand. If only he knew what Gerald had told her. Maybe something in that would move Brendan.

"Why didn't you say anything then, when it mattered?" Alanna took another step toward Brendan, and Jonathan shifted. He had to get between them.

Brendan spun toward him. "Stay where you are." The Beretta pivoted back and forth between Alanna and Jonathan. A faint tremble shook the chunky barrel. "Nothing was supposed to happen."

"But it did." Alanna's voice held steady.

"Trevor could have changed the story but didn't."

"True. And something I'll talk to him about. But you were the upperclassman. He was a sophomore. You should have manned up."

"I planned to, but then Grady died. I was headed to college on a scholarship. Trevor still had two years of high school. I was an adult. They weren't going to do anything to Trevor."

"Other than leave him under a cloud of suspicion." Alanna crossed her arms and looked down her nose at Brendan. "And you were this big hero." She shook her head. "You had us all fooled. Somehow you got people to forget you were in the water."

"I just revised details. Instead of swimming, I dove in to save Grady. Too bad it didn't work. I thought if people forgot, I'd be clean. Funny, I never felt clean." He studied the subcompact a moment then raised it toward her head. "Guess now I never will."

Jonathan stepped away from the desk. "What do you think will happen if you kill us? You disappear and no one figures it out?"

He shrugged. "It's worked so far." He waved the gun back at Jonathan. Now to keep it focused there. "Get behind that desk."

"I don't like you threatening a woman. Your dispute's with me."

"Funny how it's people I like who keep getting hurt. And the one person I want to hurt is off-limits." He shook his head. "I'll take care of her, too. Before she gets braces out of me." He studied Jonathan. "It's nothing personal."

Alanna caught Jonathan's gaze and tried to communicate something. Too bad they hadn't spent more time staring into each other's eyes on the dock, around the island, and in the fudge shops over ice cream. Maybe then he could interpret her message. Instead, he couldn't decipher what she wanted as she started making small, chopping motions with her chin. His eyes followed the direction of the motion. The window? He made a slight shrug. Hopefully she caught he didn't understand.

She rolled her eyes. He'd missed that annoying, but oh-so-Alanna action.

Brendan twisted slightly as if looking for something. Maybe he wouldn't find it. Jonathan prayed he wouldn't, since he had the distinct impression time slipped away. At some point, Brendan would run out of patience.

Grady's death might have happened, but Brendan could have avoided Mr. Hoffmeister's. Maybe he didn't care anymore. After so many deaths, did another couple even register?

Jonathan didn't want to find out.

Enough waiting to see what happened. He edged another step past the desk. Brendan spun toward him. "Get back."

Jonathan shook his head. "Nope."

"I've got the gun."

"You don't want to use it." Jonathan raised his hands in front of him.

Brendan lifted his arm, and the gun steadied. "Quite a gamble." He eyed Jonathan with a hard glint. Then he pivoted to Alanna and cocked the hammer. "Want to test your theory?"

"Nope." He held up three fingers, and Alanna closed her eyes slowly. He lowered one finger, and Brendan turned toward him. He dropped his hand and tapped his side once, twice. Alanna collapsed, and Jonathan launched at Brendan. The man hit the floor.

Jonathan landed on top of him. Felt the barrel jam his side. Twisted.

He had to move. Now. Before the gun exploded.

Alanna screamed.

"Call. Help." Jonathan bit the words out.

Brendan jammed the gun deeper. "You should have left this alone."

Jonathan made a desperate twist. A flame of fire blazed across him as his world exploded.

Jonathan groaned, ears ringing as he slumped to the side.

Alanna.

He had to help her. Couldn't protect her if the blackness won. He fought the heaviness. It pressed harder.

Chapter 35

*T*he monster shot Jonathan.

The thought pounded her even as her ears rang and she braced for him to shoot her. She should move but felt frozen in place, shock warring with impotence.

Clutching her cell phone wouldn't shield her from a bullet.

Yet as Brendan lunged to his feet, Alanna stared at him, the blood splatter across his shirt choking off her oxygen. Jonathan's blood.

Her gaze strayed to where he lay still, so pale on the floor. Then bounced back to Brendan. This man wasn't anything like the kid she remembered from school. The arrogant yet insecure kid had disappeared. In his place stood a monster. A monster with a gun.

The cold steel drew her attention. She had to get out. Now.

She fidgeted with the phone as she backed toward the door.

If she left, would Brendan follow her?

She couldn't help Jonathan if she waited. The touch screen made it impossible to dial 911 without looking.

"Nowhere to run, Alanna. Not this time." Brendan's face twisted into a mask. "You should have stayed away. Left everything alone. She wouldn't have come back if you hadn't got her thinking."

Alanna reached behind her and connected with the doorknob. Just twist it and fly. Fast as she could. Down the stairs. Without tripping. That's all. Praying that someone in the real-estate office below had called the police.

"Everybody forgot Grady. Not hard to do with a loser like him."

"Loser? Really? He had big plans."

"Never would have done anything with them."

"Like you did?" Alanna twisted the knob, freezing when it squeaked.

"I've had good jobs. Made good money when I wasn't paying her off. Then I got the great idea to help myself to some money. Seemed like the perfect way to have her dad pay her off."

She had to make it across the street. Someone would be at the police station. It wasn't even a block. Her gaze tripped down to Jonathan. The red had spread across his shoulder. She couldn't let him die without trying. This time she wouldn't stand on the side watching. This time she would act.

"You know what it's like? You get a wad of cash only to have some sniveling woman come along and take it. Over. And over. And over. Each time I'd get so mad. But I'd give her the money like a fool. Well, I'm done. Thanks to you. It ends here."

"Why would you pay, Brendan? What did you do that gave her that power?"

"Somehow she saw Grady and me wrestling."

"Trevor never said anything."

"Course not. The fool kid actually believed it was a race. The competition really was for Ginger. To think I thought that girl was someone I wanted. She deceived us all—and I'd decided Grady couldn't have her anymore."

Alanna nodded. She'd seen the hate in his eyes, just hadn't understood the reason. "Wrestling isn't murder."

"It is if you hold your opponent underwater. Then I hauled him back to shore. Trevor even thought he'd help. Just made it easier to question what he'd done."

Alanna choked back her anger at his callous words. Instead, she sipped in a breath. Now or never.

She spun open the door and ducked as she raced out. Hobbled over like a turtle, she hurried down the stairs.

A roar braced the air.

Can't stop.

She fought the urge to turn around. The thumping above gave every indication Brendan was on his way. She had to get out of the stairway before he entered or there'd be nothing to stop the bullet he'd fire from that awful gun.

Her foot caught, and she stumbled.

She yanked against the handrail and kept moving as her ankle throbbed. Where were the people from the real-estate office? She had to move. Finally, she reached the bottom step and crashed against the door as she felt a bullet whiz past.

She ducked and slammed outside.

The light blinded her, but she kept her feet pumping. She had to get lost in the crowd. But no one seemed nearby. She raced past the darkened real-estate office below Jonathan's and across the street, sidestepping a horse-drawn taxi.

The door opened again. She glanced over her shoulder long enough to confirm Brendan followed. Gulping in oxygen, she poured on speed as she darted around a couple kids on her way up Market to the police station. It felt like she slogged through a quagmire that sucked her down. She hurried past the normally serene scene. Tourists on bikes and

horses stood in front of the bright buildings lined with beautiful flower boxes oblivious to the scene she'd just left. Finally,
the two-story structure came into view. Now to get up the
steps and inside before Brendan broke across the street and
reached her.

A few more feet.

She scrambled toward the steps. Slipped on a step.
Crashed to her knees. Scurried back up and threw open the
door.

"Help!" She tried to scream the word, but it barely
scratched out. "Gun. He's got a gun."

The lady behind the counter jerked to attention. Ginger's
eyes widened. "Gun? Here?"

"He's right behind me." Alanna searched for someplace
to hide. "You've got to move."

Ginger grabbed the phone and punched a couple buttons. "Chief, Alanna Stone claims someone's after her with
a gun."

"Not anyone. Brendan Tomkin."

Ginger's face drained of color so fast that Alanna wondered if she'd faint. "I've got to hide."

"Yeah. He's not happy with you."

"Then why lead him here?" Ginger's gaze darted, and she
pushed from the seat.

"I focused on surviving. He's already shot Jonathan." A
tremble coursed through her. Jonathan needed help. She
tapped in 911 on her phone. "Need the ambulance." She slid
behind the counter as she relayed the information. The island's nod to modern transportation was the ambulance. No
horse-drawn vehicle when lives were at stake. She'd never
been more grateful.

Chief Ryan stuck his head around the corner. "What did you do now, Alanna?"

"Please hurry. Jonathan was bleeding when I escaped." She kept the phone pressed to her ear as she turned to the chief. His hand rested on his gun, but she wished he had it out and ready. Where was Brendan? "Brendan Tomkin shot Jonathan. Threatened me." She gulped air.

"Where is he?"

"Right behind me." Maybe he wasn't dumb enough to follow her into the police station with a gun and fresh gun powder residue on his hands. Would they even test for that here? "Maybe he's headed to a ferry."

"Stay put." The chief edged down the hallway. "I'll slip out back. See if I spot him."

"Don't you need someone with you?"

"Not a civilian."

Before Alanna could beg, he disappeared. She turned to Ginger. "Braces?"

A blank expression covered the woman's face.

"There are better ways to get even than making him pay for your kid's braces."

"If you had kids, you'd understand how expensive those pieces of metal are."

"Seriously? Brendan shot Jonathan. Because you demanded more money." Alanna wanted to shake her. Might as well go for the jugular. "What about your dad?"

Ginger's expression remained blank. "What about him?"

"What if Brendan killed him because of you?"

"Then he'll go to jail for a long time." Ginger glanced away. "Maybe you killed him."

Alanna snorted. "Sure you believe that."

"The police looked at you. I heard it all."

"They had to, but your dad was alive when I left." Alanna did not want to have this conversation now. Not when every fiber of her heart wanted to make sure Jonathan was still alive. She felt woozy around the edges as his red-stained shirt filled her mind. Static filtered from her phone. Sliding to the floor, Alanna pulled the cell back to her ear.

"You there, Ms. Stone?"

"Yes, yes I am." Her breath caught as if she wore a corset.

"The ambulance is at the office. They'll transport him to the Mackinac Island Medical Center."

"Is he okay?" Was there any way that facility could handle a gunshot wound?

"We'll know soon. He's got to stabilize before he's transported to the hospital in the Upper Peninsula."

"So he'll be here for a bit? Until he's stabilized?" Her throat closed as the paramedic relayed the information. Nothing sounded good. "Thank you."

Alanna stood. Waiting here wouldn't work. She had to get to Jonathan. See for herself the doctors could save him.

Ginger skidded back. "What are you doing?"

"I can't sit here." Jonathan needed her. And she needed him.

"You can't leave. The chief doesn't have Brendan."

"That we know of." Alanna brushed past Ginger and around the corner. She tried to stay aware of whether Brendan might wait, but she wanted Jonathan. She eased open the door and saw a clear hallway. She hurried to the outside door. Taking a deep breath, she opened the door and poked her head out. No Brendan.

She slipped into the flow of foot traffic down Market up the few buildings to the clinic.

Shouts caught her attention. She slid behind a bench, hoping it would provide some protection.

"Brendan, stop right there." Chief Ryan thundered across the street. Brendan Tomkin kept running, gun held in his hand but pointed down. The officer swore and took off after him.

Alanna watched a moment. Brendan ran down an alley. If she remembered, that one dead-ended at the lake. Right next to the ferry. A taxi clopped through with a bell ringing. Good thing she didn't need that one. She'd gladly leave Brendan to the police. For now she had to get to the clinic.

After running the distance to the medical center, Alanna rushed to the receptionist. "Can you tell me where Jonathan Covington is?"

The woman studied her with a professional detachment. "Are you a family member?"

"No, a good friend."

"I'm sorry, I can't help you."

Alanna leaned on the counter. "Could you tell me if he's alive? Please?"

The woman shook her head, gray curls swaying. "I'm sorry, but I can't. You're welcome to wait in the lobby."

Alanna didn't want to wait. If she couldn't see him, was there anyone who could? He didn't have family on the island. By the time she could track someone down, surely they'd transport him elsewhere. A clinic this size couldn't provide too much in the way of trauma care.

Pacing, Alanna edged closer to the door that led to the ER beds. He had to be in one of those. As soon as the receptionist turned to the side to work on her computer while answering a phone question, Alanna eased through the doors. The serenity ended abruptly as a nurse bustled past her, arms loaded with IV bags.

"Push more fluids." A woman's voice held the calm command of one who knew what needed to happen.

A young man in a paramedic jacket stood against a wall, watching the action. The way his eyes darted, he didn't miss a thing happening behind the curtain. He pushed off the wall and headed her direction. "You are?"

"Alanna Stone. I placed the 911 call."

"You shouldn't be back here."

"I have to see Jonathan."

"You'll get in the way. Look, the best thing you can do is let the doc and nurses work their magic. Once they do, we'll transport him to the ferry and across to St. Ignace where another ambulance will meet us." He gently turned her and steered her back toward the lobby. "What's your number?"

Alanna rattled it off.

"I'll call when we leave. Now go wait by the docks."

"Which ferry will you use?"

"Whichever is slated to leave next. Getting him to a trauma hospital is our number one objective." He gave her a slight push. "Let us take care of him."

She was through the door, and when she turned around, the paramedic had already returned to his post. Alanna pulled out her cell, checked the volume, then sank onto a chair in the waiting room. Guess she'd have to pray.

Her thoughts refused to form coherent streams of prayers. Instead, it felt like she groaned as she begged God to spare Jonathan.

She couldn't lose him. Not like this.

Chapter 36

The next hours passed in a blur. Waiting for the ambulance. Hurrying to purchase a ticket on the Star Line. Praying the ferry wouldn't leave without her, while also praying it wouldn't delay. Begging the ambulance driver for a ride. She could figure out how to get back to Mackinac later. For now she wanted to make sure hers was the first face Jonathan saw.

She'd sat in the waiting room outside surgery alone. Her phone in her hand, she couldn't think of anyone to call. Certainly not anyone who could reach her while it mattered. Mom and Dad were in Grand Rapids, and she wasn't sure where Trevor lived. Her few friends lived in Grand Rapids, too, and she didn't know how to reach Jonathan's family. She didn't even know who to call to find out. She might have called Mr. Hoffmeister, and Mr. Tomkin had enough to deal with, though he and Jonathan didn't seem that close.

Then she thought of Jaclyn. Surely she would want to know. And if not, she might know how to reach his parents.

What was her last name?

Reeder? No, Raeder.

Alanna dialed 411 then paused. Wasn't there anyone else she could try? The thought that Jaclyn might come, and Jonathan might want her, pierced Alanna.

Could she handle the reality Jonathan might not choose her? What her future would look like without him? A dismal reflection of the past?

She breathed deeply then hit CALL. Her wants didn't matter as much as getting Jonathan's family here. A minute later, the automated system connected her to Jaclyn's phone. As it rang, Alanna prayed for wisdom and peace.

"Hello?" Jaclyn's voice sounded strained.

"Jaclyn? This is Alanna Stone."

Silence lengthened. "What do you want?"

"Jonathan's been shot. I don't know how to reach his family. Do you have a number?"

"What happened?" Jaclyn's voice rose. Alanna filled her in then asked for the number again. "I might have it."

"Thank you." Alanna waited as papers rustled.

"Try this." Jaclyn listed a string of numbers. "Is he okay?"

"I don't know. They haven't let me see him since I'm not family."

"Yet."

"What?"

"Never mind." The girl cleared her throat. "Tell him we'll pray for him. Hope everything goes well."

"You won't come up?"

"Not unless he asks for me. I don't want Dylan in that kind of environment. Too much like when his father died."

She didn't know as much about Jaclyn as she'd surmised. "Thanks for the number."

A minute later, she dialed the number Jaclyn had given her and left a voice mail asking for a return call. Then she stood and walked to the window. It looked over the parking lot, gray and metallic, but all she saw was Jonathan at his dock. He shouldn't be trapped in here. Instead, he should be outside bird watching or fishing. And if not that, then planning the most wonderful events for his clients.

Would he do any of that again?

Or had he sacrificed himself so she could escape?

Darkness weighted him. Tugged him back. Cloaked him.

Jonathan tried to swim against its midnight pull but sagged against the heaviness.

He wanted to open his eyes but couldn't. A knife of pain sliced through his torso. The darkness offered relief. Maybe he should succumb. Give up. Let the darkness win.

A cool hand touched his forehead. It felt good, like when his mother used to care for him.

"You may stay five minutes. Then he'll need to rest." The words sounded distant. Remote.

Why five minutes? Why rest? Would that relieve the searing pain?

Jonathan fought to crack his eyelids. The brightness blinded him, and they fell shut.

A soft hand touched his. Held it lightly. "Jonathan, you made it through surgery. The doctor says you'll be okay. Really sore but okay. Your mom and dad are on the way."

Silence settled as Alanna stroked his hand.

"I'm so glad you didn't die. There's been too much death, and I need you, Jonathan. So much. Get better."

Something soft brushed his hand. Hair? Then he felt soft skin and dampness. Her cheek? A tear? He forced his eyes to open, and as they focused, he saw Alanna leaning against his hand. He licked his lips. So dry. So very dry. Tried to speak but croaked.

She sat up, studied him with large eyes. "Jonathan?"

He croaked again.

She pressed the nurse call button then jumped up and ran to the door. "He's awake. He's awake!"

A moment later, a woman in scrubs entered the room. He tried to focus on her, but the more he tried, the less defined she was until he faded back to blackness.

Alanna left Jonathan's side only when the nurse insisted. She wanted the rights of a wife to stay next to her man. To watch each time he inhaled. To assure herself he still lived.

Instead, she waited in the lobby for the occasional gift of a few minutes to watch his chest rise and fall. Other than those moments of awareness, Jonathan lay under a blanket of unconsciousness. The kind that held him tight in its grasp.

The day melted into night, and still she waited, unwilling to leave long enough to find a car. Nor willing to go back to the island and be separated from him by so many miles. Guess she'd sleep on the uncomfortable and overly firm couch, catnapping as best she could while she waited for his parents to arrive. They should be here anytime from their homes in Naubinway, Michigan. Until then she'd stay. Surely her motives had everything to do with helping them and nothing to do with her own need to see him five minutes every hour.

Her stomach growled, but she ignored it. The doors to the wing jolted open, and she glanced toward them. Patience and Earl Matthews strode through followed by Jaclyn without her small shadow.

Alanna swallowed. "What are you doing here?"

Patience reached her and pulled her into a motherly embrace. "We're here to make sure you take care of yourself. And give you a ride back when you need one."

Alanna let herself sink into Patience's arms. "How did you know?"

"Jaclyn, of course. Once you called her, it didn't take too much time before she found me. We had to get organized, but here we are now. Earl keeps a car in St. Ignace, and we can head back or get a hotel room here. Either works for us."

"Jaclyn came with you?"

"Someone had to make sure she got here. She wanted to see Jonathan."

Alanna had hoped she'd stay away. She'd wanted the other day to truly mark the end of Jonathan's relationship with Jaclyn. Maybe she'd deluded herself. Maybe she and Jonathan were destined for nothing more than a friendship filled with enough attraction to drive any girl to distraction.

The kind of friendship she'd have to abandon again as soon as he was okay.

Staying and watching him with someone else would hurt too much. Especially now that she'd admitted she cared deeply for him.

"I'm glad she's here then. Jonathan's parents should arrive anytime, too." Alanna tried to smile as she managed not to choke on the words. Someday she might believe herself. For now she'd try to welcome Jaclyn and support her friend as he chose the other woman. Being single wasn't so bad. She'd done it a long time. Now that she'd remembered what could exist, she couldn't imagine settling for someone less than Jonathan. Her eyes clouded at the thought. She'd learn to be content.

She had to since the alternative seemed terrible.

Patience eyed her with skepticism. "You're just going to settle back?"

"What else can I do?"

"Fight for the man. He's had several weeks to watch you side by side. At least make him choose. Don't give up."

"Then why bring her here?"

A slow smile spread across Patience's cheeks. "Because you need to decide if you're fighting. If you're not, Jonathan needs someone. She's the other contender."

That sounded crass. Jonathan wasn't a prize to fight over, yet in a way that's how it felt.

"Miss Stone?"

Alanna looked up at the nurse who'd walked into the waiting area. "Yes?"

"Would you like five minutes?"

"Thank you." Alanna shot to her feet before anyone else could say anything and followed the nurse back to Jonathan's room. "Has there been any change?"

"No, but we don't expect him to be too alert yet. He endured some major surgery on his shoulder." The nurse glanced at her, calm exuding from her steady gaze. "He'll recover barring any complications. Just talk to him. Often that pulls people from their haze."

Alanna nodded then pushed into the room. It remained antiseptic and harsh. Her shoes squeaked against the linoleum, and she collapsed in the chair next to the sterile hospital bed. All the soft wall colors and paintings couldn't change the fact he lay in a bed, IV tubes extending from his hands, and monitors strapped across him. The Jonathan she knew overflowed with vitality. This person formed a shell of that man.

She touched his fingers, trying to avoid the IV. "Hey, Jonathan. They've let me back in."

No response, not even a twitch from his fingers.

Alanna sighed and stroked his knuckles. "Jaclyn's here. Patience and Earl brought her so she could be here. Maybe I should have let her come in this time, but I'm selfish. I wanted this time with you. Depending on what happens when you wake up, I might not have more time like this." Her voice hitched, and she forced herself to go on. "I love you, Jonathan. I know you won't remember this, but I had to tell you. I won't watch if you choose Jaclyn, but I won't get in your way. I don't have that right after all this time." She looked away, blinking back the tears flooding her vision. "Coming back wasn't easy, but it reminded me how much you mean to me. I'll always wonder what would have happened if I'd stayed. . .but I didn't."

She paused. Could she go on? Did it matter? He wouldn't remember anything she said, but she'd know.

Glancing up, she startled. His green eyes locked on hers. Maybe he'd remember everything she'd said after all.

She swallowed, unsure whether she wanted to retract the words or risk the outcome. The only way to know what the future held was to pray he'd heard and would say something, anything, in response.

The nurse knocked on the door, and Alanna saw his parents. Time to leave, but his gaze held her hostage. She liked it. Oh, how she liked it. What if he chose Jaclyn? She prayed that wouldn't happen. That, instead, he'd hold her for life.

Chapter 37

Jonathan tried to focus on the beautiful woman sitting in front of him. Alanna's soothing voice reached him deep in the blackness. He'd fought his way to the surface, heard her words. They resonated through him.

She loved him.

He'd wanted to say the words first. Now he could feel her pulling away. Attempting to hide. He couldn't let her, not with her tendency to run. If she left, chances were she'd never return. She'd leave for good.

Did she mean what she'd said?

How could he convince her the love wasn't one-sided? He wanted to sit and meet her on even footing, but the slightest tightening of his core sent waves of fire through his shoulder. He groaned, and she bolted upright.

"Don't move, Jonathan. Do you need the nurse?"

He wanted to shake his head but didn't dare move. Instead, he licked his lips. His mouth felt squeegeed clean of any moisture.

"Here." Alanna grabbed a mug of water from his bedside table and held it to his mouth, pointing the straw toward him. "Take a sip."

He tested the action. Then swallowed as the cool liquid hit his throat. Heaven. He tested his voice. "Alanna."

The word sounded like a croak, weak and worn.

"Hey." A soft look settled over her face, reminding him so much of the girl he'd known all those summers ago. The one he'd fallen in love with. Planned to spend his life with. "Your parents are here. I should go."

"You're here."

"Of course."

"Brendan?"

"Chief Ryan chased him last I saw. I'll let the police get him."

"This time?"

"Yeah, this time." She chuckled softly then set down the mug. "Brendan should go away for a long time."

Jonathan frowned, trying to remember all that had happened. "He murdered?"

"Yes. It looks like he murdered Mr. Hoffmeister. Everything started with Grady's death. Then Ginger Hoffmeister blackmailed him off and on all these years. He started embezzling, and both his dad and Hoffmeister knew. Then I came back and started pushing to clear Trevor. If I hadn't, she might not have blackmailed Brendan again. With her position at the police station, she knew exactly what was going on with the investigation and used that knowledge to hound Brendan."

"Why kill Hoffmeister?"

"I don't think he meant to. He just wanted to get Ginger to stop. Thought her dad would stop her. But he killed Mr. Hoffmeister."

"What now?"

"Miss Stone." The nurse stepped into the room then smiled as her gaze landed on Jonathan. "Mr. Covington, your parents are eager to see you. Miss Stone, time to leave so they can come in."

Jonathan wanted to protest, but the nurse's no-nonsense air made him doubt he'd be successful.

"We need to check your dressing and see how your wound looks."

Alanna stood. "Should I send Jaclyn in next time?"

"No." Jonathan watched her reaction as her eyes widened and a pink climbed her neck. "I just want you."

Hope blazed to life in her eyes. He would spend the rest of his days convincing her how very much she was the one he wanted. That was a task he'd gladly add to his planner and check off multiple times a day.

He didn't want to see Jaclyn?

Did that mean he'd made his decision?

She wanted to believe, but at the same time she needed to use caution. For all she knew the medication could affect Jonathan's decisions.

"Rest if you can, Jonathan. I'll send your folks in." She backed from the room and hurried to the waiting room.

Patience glanced up from a Colleen Coble novel as his parents moved into the ICU. "How is he?"

"Awake." The word tasted wonderful on her tongue. "He'll be okay."

Earl turned from the baseball game on the TV and chuckled. "Of course he will. It'll take more than a bullet to the shoulder to keep him down."

"Did he ask about me?" Jaclyn stood with her back to the window, a guarded expression protecting her.

"I asked if he wanted to see you at the next opportunity." How to say this in a way that protected them both in the event Jonathan changed his mind? "We'll have to let the nurse tell us what he wants next time."

Patience glanced at her watch. "It's already after ten. How much longer do you plan to stay? We've probably missed the last ferry."

Alanna shrugged. "I'll spend the night here."

"Don't you think you should get a good night's sleep?"

"I don't want to miss a chance to see him."

Patience nodded. "I understand. But his parents are here, and you'll do him more good rested. Someone's got to be with Dylan, too."

"He's okay tonight." Jaclyn chewed her lower lip as she studied Alanna. "I'll need to get back in the morning."

Earl turned back to his game, the faint sound of the announcers and crowd noise making a soft backdrop in the quiet room. Alanna watched Jaclyn from the corner of her eye. Would it be kinder to leave and give Jaclyn a chance to see Jonathan? Or would he expect her to stay and wonder where she went? Patience thought she should leave. Maybe the older woman was right.

Everything in Alanna wanted to stay. But something told her to leave. Give Jaclyn her chance.

Alanna sank onto the couch next to Patience. "Do you think we could find a hotel room?"

"Already have a reservation just down the road. We can leave the number with the nurse so they can let us know if anything changes with Jonathan. He'll still be sleepy after surgery. You probably won't get to see him much before morning anyway."

Alanna chewed her lower lip as she considered Jaclyn. "All right. Jaclyn, do you want to stay?"

A flash of hope slid across the woman's face. "Yes."

"Then we'll be back in the morning. Tell Jonathan I'll return."

Hopefully he'd still want to see her. If a few hours' absence changed the direction of his feelings, he wasn't hers anyway. Better find out now rather than later after she'd dared to hope.

The next morning, Earl dropped her off at the door. "You sure you don't want us to stay?"

"No. I'll get a ride to the ferry when it's time."

"All right. Tell Jaclyn to call by ten if she'd like a ride back."

"Thanks, Earl." Alanna slipped into the hospital, feeling good after a decent night's rest and a shower. Her clothes might be the same, but she felt clean. Her stomach fluttered as the elevator carried her to the trauma floor. How would Jonathan look this morning?

The doors opened, and the antiseptic smell slapped her in the face. Her stomach clenched in rebellion, and she swallowed to keep the bile down.

The nurse at the station looked up, a question in her expression. "Can I help you?"

"I'm here to see Jonathan Covington."

"Are you on his list?"

"I was last night."

The woman punched a few buttons on the keyboard then studied the screen. "Hmm, what did you say your name was?"

"Alanna Stone."

More punching ensued, and then the nurse turned to her. "I don't see you in his record."

"Could you buzz his room?"

"I'll walk down there. If he's sleeping, I don't want to wake him." Another nurse approached. "Would you sit here while I check a patient?"

The nurse nodded and slid in front of the bank of monitors. Alanna paced in front of the nurses' station as she waited. Finally, the first nurse returned.

"I'm sorry, but the patient is asleep. Someone else is with him and says he doesn't want to be disturbed."

Alanna nodded, her heart falling. She reached into her bag and pulled out a notebook. "Can I leave a note for him?"

"Sure."

She scribbled a quick page then folded it and gave it to the nurse. "Thank you."

A moment later, she stood in the waiting room. Should she stay? Leave? Would the note even reach Jonathan?

By early afternoon, Jonathan had tired of Jaclyn's presence. She talked almost nonstop with his mother, and he missed the quiet. Anytime he asked where Alanna was, Jaclyn made some excuse for her. At one point, the nurse brought in a note, but Jaclyn took it before Jonathan could read it. The glimpse he caught made him think Alanna had written it, but Jaclyn tucked it in her purse before he could do anything.

Being tied down with all these wires and IV lines, not to mention the never-ending burning in his shoulder, was enough to drive him crazy. He wanted his small cabin and some privacy. The ability to tell people to leave sounded wonderful. Especially when Jaclyn had somehow convinced the nurses he wanted her there—all the time.

"Where's Dylan?"

She looked away from the TV where she'd clicked through channels endlessly. Didn't she get nothing was on daytime TV, no matter how many times you surfed? Nothing still equaled nothing.

"He's with a friend."

Jonathan couldn't imagine whom she'd left the boy with overnight. He was the only one who'd ever kept him other than the day care. "And your job?"

"Someone's covering the shift."

"Hmm."

A doctor entered the room. "Let's check how you're doing today, Mr. Covington."

"Do you mind?" Jonathan glanced at Jaclyn, and color tinged her cheeks. She slid from the room.

As the doctor rewrapped his bandages, Jonathan held his breath. The pain punched him but had lost a bit of its edge. "Any chance you could keep her from coming back?"

The doctor studied him. "If that's what you want, absolutely."

"The gal I want here isn't. I'll recover faster without Jaclyn hovering."

A knowing grin crossed the doctor's face before he wiped it off. "Glad to get you some peace and quiet."

"When will I get to go home?"

"Do you have anyone to take care of you?"

"My parents or a friend."

The doctor eyed him. "Assuming you stay infection free, maybe in a couple days we can transport you home. I can confer with the doctor at the island's medical center. Make

617

sure she feels comfortable continuing your care."

"Thanks."

As soon as the doctor left, Jonathan pulled out his cell and started dialing. He wanted out of this prison the moment it was possible. Anything was better than one extra day lying here.

He had too many events to wrap up and a woman's heart to win.

Chapter 38

Rachelle Stone should arrive any minute. Jonathan had been surprised she agreed to pick him up, but he couldn't thank her enough for freeing him from the prison of his hospital room. His parents had planned to get him settled at home when his uncle had a stroke. They'd left only when he'd insisted his uncle needed more help than he did. All he wanted was his cabin and being left alone. He'd considered calling Alanna but decided not to. He didn't want to see her again until he was at home in real clothes. The nurses and physical therapists delighted in torturing him. He tried to mask the pain. Reality remained that his shoulder felt like someone routinely speared him.

Now after three days inside the four walls of this room, he wanted his cabin. At least there he could sit on his deck, fire up his computer for a few minutes, and make sure the details of the Morrises' event still held together.

And now that Brendan had been arrested for involuntary man-slaughter, murder, and attempted murder, he could throw his efforts into finalizing Trevor's official debut at the studio.

Rachelle sailed into the room, a Kentucky Derby-worthy hat resting on her sophisticated bob. He smiled at the image of Alanna looking like her in twenty years.

Now to convince Alanna he meant forever.

That was the next item on his agenda. Two successful events and one heart won. Not necessarily in that order.

"You don't look too much worse for wear."

"You haven't seen my stitches."

Rachelle held up a hand. "That's all right. I appreciate the way you protected Alanna. More than you know. But I don't need to see the evidence of your bravery."

Jonathan wished he had some dark corner to hide as heat flooded his face. Maybe he could blame the closed air in the room.

"So where are your things?"

"Don't have any. It didn't cross my mind before Mom and Dad had to leave."

"Why didn't you say anything?" She sighed with a motherly expression. "I'll get you some clothes." After writing down his sizes, she left.

Jonathan barely had time to wonder if Alanna would be glad to see her before Rachelle returned with a bag of undergarments, button-up shirts, and jeans.

"I figured you wouldn't want anything that pulled over your head."

"Thanks." Ten minutes later, he'd changed and finished checking out.

The drive to St. Ignace and the ferry passed in silence, only the strains of some classical symphony filling the car. Then Rachelle followed him onto the ferry.

"Pushing things a bit." There was no question in her statement.

"I'll be good as soon as I'm home."

"Sure you will."

Silence settled again as the ferry pulled away from the dock and picked up speed. The lake spray threatened to soak him as the ferry worked across the water. As soon as they reached the dock on Mackinac Island, Rachelle edged him to a bench and forced him down. "I'll find a taxi. No way you're walking or biking home."

The island felt the same—abuzz with summer activity, even as he saw it tinged with tragedy. No one had mentioned Ginger yet. Would she pay for her part in the crime spree?

Rachelle came back and dragged him to the taxi. Then she got him settled in his cabin. "I'll go check on Alanna. Send her here."

"You don't need to do that."

She gave him a knowing smile. "I'm not the Stone you want babysitting you. Besides, I need to work at the studio. I have a painting to finish for your client."

"So you took the commission? Is your arthritis allowing you to paint?"

"The doctor has me on a medicine that's helping. I figured after the ways I let you and Alanna down, the least I could do was help him." She fiddled with her purse strap. "I have a few things to do for this party you've planned for Trevor, too." She turned to the door then back. "Thank you for all you're doing for him. It'll be nice to see his name on his paintings."

Before he could say anything, she disappeared through the door. It was a start. The woman might not admit what she'd done by putting her name on Trevor's paintings was wrong. But she could start fresh now with the painting for Bonnie.

He couldn't wait to see what she created. Somehow he knew she would craft the perfect image.

Now he just needed to do the same for Lanna.

It was past time for that.

Alanna dusted the canvases. She couldn't see a speck of dust, not surprising since she'd circled the studio at least twice a day since Jonathan was shot. Her body refused to sit still, and she had nothing left to investigate. The only details to wrap up related to Trevor's debut. She didn't know enough about what was left to do without consulting Jonathan, and she couldn't do that while he remained in the hospital.

Everything seemed squared away. Trevor would move up for the balance of the summer with Patience helping him. Mom had indicated she could slip up here a couple of times a month now that Dad seemed on the mend.

They didn't need her. She needed to decide if she could handle a return to her old life in Grand Rapids. The thought sapped her energy; yet if nothing changed with Jonathan, she had no reason to stay. She didn't want to leave, but she couldn't remain, not like this.

The feathers tickled another canvas, and she finished.

Now what? The studio sparkled. Everything was ready for next Saturday's event.

The bell sounded, and Alanna turned. "Mom? What are you doing here?"

"Just deposited Jonathan at his cabin."

The words struck her like a blow. Jonathan hadn't called her, but had asked her mom for help? Ouch. "Are you staying long?"

"Through Trevor's party. Your aunt Mary is staying with your father. She'll bring him up for the party if he's well enough. So I'm here to paint and send you to the house.

Jonathan didn't want me babysitting him. I have a feeling you're much more what he had in mind."

"Or Jaclyn."

"Who?" Mom wrinkled her nose. "That woman? I don't think so. Go gather your things and scoot. The day's still young. And I have lots of painting to do." Mom made a shooing motion with her hands, and Alanna obeyed.

Jonathan was at his cabin. That must be good.

She hurried home but stalled when she saw a bike outside his door. Who could that be?

A woman stepped out of the cabin. "I'll be back tomorrow. But all looks good for now. Don't push too hard, and get some help. You may be home, but if you're not careful, we'll have to transport you right back to the hospital."

"Thanks." Jonathan's voice reached her, though she couldn't see him.

The woman hopped on the bike and pedaled past Alanna without a wave. She'd have to ask Jonathan, but right now she just wanted to see him. Alanna biked to Jonathan's door and dismounted. After leaning the bike against the wall, she knocked and entered. "Jonathan?"

He lay on the couch, a pillow shoved beneath his head and another at his side. "Lanna."

"Are you okay?"

"I will be. Glad to be home. Your mom sent you?"

"She thought you'd rather have me."

He grinned, which only emphasized the purple bruises under his eyes. "She's pretty insightful."

His laptop beeped, and she frowned at him. "What are you doing?"

"Shooting out a few e-mails about Trevor's event and the Morrises' party."

623

"Aren't you supposed to rest?"

"Sure, but this is resting. Anyway, if I didn't do it, I'd lay here and worry. That wouldn't help me heal." He patted the couch next to him. "Come here."

She edged toward him but decided the couch was too narrow for two. Especially when one had a wound. She grabbed the kitchen chair and set it next to him. "What can I do?"

"Tell me why you didn't come see me again at the hospital."

She looked away. Would he understand? "I wasn't sure where things stood, so I came back to the island. I knew I'd see you. But I had to figure us out."

"Did you?" He studied her, his intensity almost knocking her from the chair. "Did you figure us out?"

"Not really." She sucked in a breath and studied her hands. "That's not true." She risked looking in his eyes again. "Jonathan, I can't imagine my life without you."

"That's what I remembered."

"What?" Did he somehow remember what she'd said? She'd die of embarrassment.

"I heard words I've wanted to tell you." He reached up to stroke her cheek, and she leaned closer, tugged by the electricity of his touch. "I love you, Alanna. I've loved you since all those times out there on that dock. I loved you when you disappeared, but this time I won't let you leave. Not without a promise to come back. Again. And again. And again."

"Jonathan."

He pressed a finger against her mouth, stilling further words. "Alanna, I've told Jaclyn several times we aren't going anywhere. I'm sorry she keeps getting in the way, but since you came back, I've realized she's not the woman for me. Not when the only woman I've really loved is sitting in front of me."

Alanna swallowed hard. It felt like a golf ball had lodged in her throat. He'd just said the words she longed to hear. They felt like a balm to her heart and soothed her questions.

"What about Dylan?"

A frown crept across Jonathan's handsome features. "I'll miss him. But I couldn't stay with Jaclyn just for him. It's not fair to either of them." He took her hand and tugged her close. "Tell me you feel the same way."

She braced against the couch, trying not to jar him as he tugged her closer still. She felt his breath against her cheek, closed her eyes, and inhaled.

In that moment, she could imagine a future with him. A future that involved the island and building a life together. Moisture flooded her eyes at the realization that she could give up everything in Grand Rapids without a second thought. Nothing there mattered—not in the light of his love.

"Say something. . . You're making me nervous."

She swiped at her eyes and then laughed, a watery sound. "I love you, too, Jonathan. Always have."

His face lit from the inside, and he grinned. "Come here, Lanna."

His lips settled on hers in the perfect kiss.

Chapter 39

The next Saturday morning, Alanna woke early, started running, and didn't stop even as people gathered at the Painted Stone. Excitement thrummed through her, though it was lined with an edge of tension. Would people respond to Trevor? Would all the pain be worth the end result?

Jonathan had insisted on coming, but she'd made Mom promise not to collect him until the last possible moment. His shoulder didn't seem to bother him much. Still she worried even though he deserved to see the fruits of his labor.

She touched her lips, still warm from the kiss they'd shared last night. In the days since Jonathan returned to Mackinac, their relationship had accelerated from a reborn friendship to dreams of what the future held. Tomorrow she could bask in that. Today she would celebrate Trevor and his art.

The studio looked amazing. She'd accented his largest paintings with spotlights and cards explaining the setting and story behind each painting. Jonathan had postcards made of Trevor's best work and grouped them in packets for the guests who attended. She'd spent two nights at his cabin wrapping the packets in raffia. Now that she'd collected them in baskets, the overall effect made the time worth it.

One of Jonathan's contacts had made the hors d'oeuvres. A long banquet table stood on each side of the room, sheathed in creamy white tablecloths and loaded with tiers of finger foods. Quiche, cocktail shrimp, and things she couldn't name filled one table, while the other had all kinds of sweets. She couldn't wait to try a pint-sized fruit tart, popping one in her mouth as she walked past.

A crystal punch bowl sat on a round table in one corner, rows of punch cups surrounding the bowl. The peach liquid looked great and smelled even better.

Everything looked ready. She just needed the guest of honor.

Trevor had assured her he'd arrive at least an hour early. Alanna glanced at her watch again. If he walked through the door that instant, he'd only arrive ten minutes early. She pulled out her phone and dialed his number. It went straight to voice mail. It would take all her restraint not to throttle him the moment she saw him.

She fought the urge to chew her fingernails for the first time since middle school.

Patience sailed toward her, an elegant dress sheathing her body. "Where's your mom?"

"Collecting Jonathan."

"And Trevor?" Patience looked around. "I haven't missed him, have I?"

"No. My brother is delinquent."

Patience clucked. "He can't control everything."

"He can be on time." Alanna glanced toward the door as another group entered. Jonathan brought up the rear. He looked so good in khakis and a button-down shirt, his left arm resting in a sling. She didn't fight the smile as he worked toward her.

"Quite a crowd you've got here, young lady."

She nodded. "Someone amazing organized this event."

Patience chuckled. "You two act like you're back in school. I'll leave you to make eyes at each other."

Jonathan grinned then leaned down to brush her lips with a kiss. She leaned gently into him, thanking God for bringing them together. Even the frustrating moments didn't seem so daunting with Jonathan next to her.

Reluctantly, Alanna stepped back. "I've got a chair tucked behind the counter for you."

"Putting me to work?"

"Of course." She grinned up at him then sobered. "Thank you, Jonathan. This could be an amazing event—especially if Trevor graces us with his presence."

"He will." Mom slid an arm around Alanna's shoulder. "He called an hour ago to say he was on his way but running late." Mom straightened the pink silk scarf at her throat. "You kids have done quite a job. Thank you."

Alanna cleared her throat, trying to push words around the sudden lump. "You're welcome."

"And if you ever try something as stupid as chasing down a murderer again, I may kill you myself. The gray hairs I have thanks to you."

Alanna rolled her eyes then caught Jonathan's gaze. His snicker pulled an answering one from her. She raised her hand as if on the stand. "I swear I will never do anything like that again. Once was more than enough."

"I would certainly hope so." Mom turned to Jonathan. "Jonathan?"

"I can't promise I'll never do it. If anything similar happens, I won't back down."

It was Mom's turn to roll her eyes. And she wondered why Alanna did it. "Well, I'm going to check on my painting then mingle with all these people you've drawn. Maybe even sell some art."

Alanna smiled as another group came in. Even if Trevor bailed, she could sell his art. Only the island's long-term residents cared, and now they knew the truth. Truth had come at a cost, and she prayed Trevor would accept his freedom and steward it.

An arm slipped around her waist, and she startled and spun around. "Trevor Stone!"

"Hey, sis. So all of this is for little ole me?"

"Yes, though I'm ready to strangle you. Where have you been?"

"Getting Dad." Trevor pointed toward the hall where a wheelchair sat. "It took longer to check him out of the rehabilitation hospital than I planned."

"Dad." The word whispered from her.

"Go tell him hi." Trevor glanced around the room. "Guess I'd better say hello to everyone."

"Yep. And sell lots of paintings. We need to sell another three or four this month."

He saluted. "Yes, ma'am."

Alanna watched Trevor as he moved around the room, stopping to say a word to each group. He could make this work. He seemed to have found a natural ease as he talked to everybody.

Jonathan nodded toward the hall. "I know your dad is eager to make sure you're okay."

Alanna eased down the hallway then knelt beside the wheelchair. "Hi, Daddy."

"Lanna." A slow grin spread across his face. "You're okay."

"Yes, sir. God kept me safe through everything."

"You shouldn't tempt Him."

"I didn't mean to. Things kind of spiraled."

"How's Jonathan?" The change in topic caught her, but one look into her daddy's eyes confirmed he wanted the honest answer.

"Good, I think." She sighed. "I'm not sure I can go back to Grand Rapids. The thought of separating kills me."

"Long distance can work."

"But I don't want it to. Not sure I can live here though."

"You'll figure it out." His assurance settled over her, and she breathed it in. "Get me into the studio. I want to see Trevor's moment."

"He's doing well, Daddy."

"Of course. He's a Stone, isn't he?"

Soon the regulars greeted her father like a returning hero. In some ways he was, even as his road to full recovery still had many steps.

Servers in their white shirts and black pants flowed seamlessly among the guests, refilling the hors d'oeuvres and punch. Alanna ended up sitting next to Jonathan at the cash register ringing up sales while Jonathan handed out postcards. Her family members took care of welcoming one and all.

Hours later the last guest left, and she studied Jonathan. He'd held up well, but she didn't want to push him too much. "Ready to head home?"

"Sure." He watched the waitstaff tear down the tables. "We did it."

"Yes we did." Satisfaction filled her. "Thank you."

He took her hand, rubbing his thumb over her knuckles. "You're welcome. Now on to the other event that matters."

Two weeks later, the Morrises' guests started arriving by ferry and settling into their rooms at a couple of bed-and-breakfasts. Jonathan felt almost completely recovered, and it was a good thing. He'd already made numerous trips between the sites to make sure everything was ready for the guests.

Nothing would mar this event. Not if he had anything to do with it.

Bonnie looked thin but serene as Edward pushed her wheelchair up the hill toward the fort. Edward grunted and pushed harder. "Why did I pick this location? Remind me."

Jonathan laughed. "Because Bonnie loved the view. Next time let the taxi bring you around the backside of Fort Mackinac. It's easier from there."

"Next time."

A large tent sat in the open field to the side of the fort. Rows of tables and chairs filled the tent, and he'd arranged for a multitude of games to be brought from the fort for the younger guests to play. Already he could see some playing with the wooden hoops and sticks and others with the horseshoes.

The aroma of barbecue filtered from the pit the caterer had installed. The spicy scent made Jonathan's stomach rumble in anticipation. He couldn't wait to have a couple of sandwiches once everyone had been served.

This was exactly the type of event Edward had ordered. And based on the delighted grins on his and his wife's faces, they planned to make wonderful memories with their family and friends as they celebrated a lifetime of love.

Maybe it really was possible to have a love of a lifetime. One laced with both joy and pain. One only had to look at the Morrises to believe it just might happen.

Edward whistled. "Lookie there."

Jonathan turned to follow his gaze. His heart stuttered in his chest as Alanna approached. She looked amazing in a flowing sundress that revealed narrow ankles and athletic calves. The sweater knotted around her shoulders was the only nod to the bite in the breeze on an end-of-June day on the island. The bright flowers on the gauzy material were perfect against the blue sky. He couldn't tear his gaze from her as she approached.

She took Bonnie's hand. "Thanks so much for inviting me."

Bonnie smiled. "Delighted to have you. The more the merrier in my opinion."

"That's my girl." Edward frowned though his voice was filled with affection. "She always said the only good party is one overflowing with friends and acquaintances."

"It's a great way to live." Alanna turned to Jonathan. "I'm sure you're busy. . . ."

Bonnie made a shooing motion. "Not at the moment. Edward will call if we need anything. Enjoy all your hard work."

Jonathan met Edward's gaze. They paid him too much to have him disappear as the events got under way. Edward shrugged and patted his pocket. "I'll call."

"Yes, sir."

Alanna slipped her hand into his, and they strolled toward the fort. When they reached a bench, he tugged her down. It felt so right to have her hand nestled in his, like an empty piece of him had found its home.

Children ran in wild circles while adults worked through the food line. Edward and Bonnie waited at the head of the line, welcoming everyone as if they stood in a receiving line at the wedding. The legacy of their lifetime together was clear from the simple touches and unspoken communication to the number of people who had come to the island to celebrate them.

That's what he wanted. A life well lived in forty years. One lived with the woman on the bench next to him.

"What are you thinking?"

Her quiet words pulled him to her. Did he dare say? He took in her smooth skin, direct gaze, and the slight upturn of her lips. He'd never been more certain of anything in his life.

He might be certain, but when he opened his mouth, nothing escaped. It was like a block existed between his thoughts and his vocal cords.

"Must be serious." She teased.

"Alanna, I want to spend the rest of my life with you." The words came out in a rush, blurted from a full heart.

"Jonathan. . ." Caution replaced the teasing light.

"Listen. . . When you returned this summer, everything that existed between us erupted to life. I know it took a few weeks for me to sort through everything with Jaclyn, but I've never loved anyone like I love you, Alanna. You make my days complete. You make me complete, a better person than I ever was without you. I love you, Alanna. For always." He stopped as she started biting her lower lip. Tears leaked from her eyes, and panic spiked through him. "Don't cry, Alanna.

This was supposed to make you happy."

"I am." The words were choked. Then a smile crested on her face, like the sun breaking through the clouds after the long Mackinac Island winter. "I love you, too, Jonathan."

Epilogue

Four weeks later

Alanna fidgeted in front of the mirror in her bedroom. The white gown was simple, its A-line design skimming her waist to balloon over her hips before it settled midcalf. She wore a hat rather than a veil. After everything they'd endured, she didn't want anything coming between her and Jonathan.

They'd waited eleven long years to find each other and rediscover their love. Now that they had, she'd insisted on a quick wedding. She was ready to begin life as Mrs. Jonathan Covington.

Mom bustled into the room, Patience Matthews entering behind her. Mom stilled and placed a hand on her chest. "Alanna, you look beautiful."

"Thanks, Mom." The rising tide of excitement crested over her. It wouldn't be much longer now. Soon. . .soon.

Patience extended the small bouquet she held. "I had quite the time finding lilacs but got them shipped in. Too bad you couldn't get married during the lilac festival. That would have made things simpler."

Alanna laughed, remembering how uncertain everything had been at the beginning of the season when the lilac festival had flooded the island with color. "These are perfect." The heady aroma of lilacs, a mix of white and lavender blooms, was better than any perfume she could wear.

Everything was perfect. Trevor had settled back into life on Mackinac. He'd even offered art lessons on various

Saturdays. So far the classes were small, but the idea seemed to catch on. By next summer, people would have to sign up in advance to get guidance from the great Trevor Stone. He'd started painting a couple days a week in front of the studio. It drew a crowd and pulled interested buyers into the store.

Dad was on the mend. He and Mom planned to move back to the island in time for the winter. Why they'd want to do that she wasn't sure, but he insisted nothing could happen the medical center on the island couldn't handle. Based on what she'd seen when Brendan shot Jonathan, he was right.

Her future wasn't quite so settled. She'd returned to Grand Rapids long enough to move her things to storage and reclaim Midnight. The cat seemed to enjoy sitting on the porch and stalking birds, but Alanna needed more than that. Maybe she'd open a small practice or work with Jonathan, but for now she continued to run the studio while she prayed about what God wanted her to do.

"Come on, Alanna. Dad's downstairs."

Alanna nodded. Her future plans could wait. Right now she wanted to become Mrs. Covington as quickly as possible.

She took one more glance in the mirror, excitement meeting her gaze.

Patience and Mom each grabbed an arm and eased her toward the door. She took a last glance around the room. Tonight she'd move into Jonathan's cabin next door. Even if it was small, that's where they decided to begin their lives together. It would be a great place to start their married life together. When they reached the downstairs, Dad sat in his wheelchair. Trevor stood behind him wearing a suit, ready to push Dad.

The pastor and Jonathan already stood outside on the

dock. A small group of close friends and family waited in chairs. In a twist, Jonathan had planned the event, pulling together the perfect ceremony from his web of contacts.

"Are you ready?" Dad smiled up at her.

"Yes. Yes I am."

"Good. It's time you married this man."

"Dad!"

He chuckled, but a serious look settled in his gaze. "I have no doubt he's the man for you. You'll have a good life, though nobody guarantees easy."

"Amen to that," Mom stage-whispered.

Patience chuckled then scooted around the group. "I'm off to claim my seat." She kissed Alanna. "Best wishes, dear."

"Thank you."

Mom kissed her cheek next. "I'll let that anxious groom of yours know it's almost time. Love you."

"Love you, too." Alanna loved the way God was rebuilding their relationship. He was so good to her.

Alanna sucked in a steadying breath as her daddy reached up. "Ready?"

"Yes, sir."

Trevor slowly pushed the wheelchair down the temporary path workers had installed. Alanna stalled when her gaze collided with Jonathan's. There might be rows of chairs between them, but at the arbor at the end of the dock, he was locked on her. She couldn't tear her gaze from his even if she wanted to.

In that moment, she thanked God for bringing her home. For showing her it was time to stop running from the truth, and for saving this man for her.

She had all she wanted and more for a lifetime of love.

Annalisa Daughety, a graduate of Freed-Hardeman University, writes contemporary fiction set in historic locations. *A Wedding to Remember in Charleston, South Carolina*, is her seventh novel. Annalisa lives in Arkansas with two spoiled dogs and is hard at work on her next book. She loves to connect with her readers through social media sites like Facebook and Twitter. More information about Annalisa can be found at her website, www.annalisadaughety.com.

Cara C. Putman lives in Indiana with her husband and four children. She's an attorney and a ministry leader and teacher at her church. She has loved reading and writing from a young age and now realizes it was all training for writing books. An honors graduate of the University of Nebraska and George Mason University School of Law, Cara loves bringing history to life. Learn more about Cara and her writing at caraputman.com and facebook.com/cara.putman.